# THE LADY
# WALKS
# ALONE

# THE LADY WALKS ALONE

## Chris Lions

Author of "A Secretary's Nightmare"

To order additional copies of this book, contact:
Xlibris Corporation
1-888-7-XLIBRIS
www.Xlibris.com
Orders@Xlibris.com
18062

# CHAPTER 1

Terrie was deep in thought as she sat staring out of the window of the airplane. "Here I go again—running, hiding, but most of all trusting the FBI The last time I trusted them—look at all the trouble I got into—running during the night, disrupting our lives, they didn't believe any thing I said to them"—-Terrie's thoughts were interrupted.

"Fasten your seat belt" Jack motioned to Terrie

Automatically Terrie shook her head yes and fastened her seat belt. "What was it Clem had said— 'I promise, I'll take care of you. I'll find a place that's peaceful and quiet' Terrie's thoughts continued "So here I sit next to Jack Stewart, a man from Clem's office and supposedly Clem's best friend. 'Next to me' she remembered Clem, saying 'Jack Stewart is one of the best operatives at the bureau.' The plane was landing and Terrie didn't even know where they were. She was taken on the plane, seated in first class and told to put the headset on. She truly was too frightened to ask any questions about what was going on—where they were going, what happened back in Atlanta was anybody's guess. The gunfire, my near miss, if it hadn't been for Clem having that car and grabbing me when he did and throwing me into the back seat— who knows if I'd be alive right now. I wonder if someone did die— wonder who those men were, they definitely were after me—were they, maybe Les's men—sure hope I get some answers soon". Terrie was thinking as she turned to Jack Stewart.

"May I take these off now?" Terrie asked pointing to the headset

"Oh sure I-I'm sorry" Jack stammered. He felt dumb, she could have taken them off, right after the pilot had finished his spiel, but he'd gotten busy with paper work and forgot to tell her. No harm done—she'd slept all the way even through the serving of food. 'Poor kid, she really was exhausted. Guess I would be too if I'd gone through what she's just gone through.'

"Welcome to San Francisco International Airport" Terrie heard the stewardess saying as she leaned over to Jack

"I'm sorry to be such a bother to you, Mr. Stewart," she bent over and whispered. "I'm sure that you'd rather be with your wife and family—you do have children, don't you—she said looking at him—rather than baby-sitting with me.

"I do have a wife and like Clem I lost my two children. That we will discuss later, if you'd like. For right now you are my wife" Jack whispered back to her. "We'll discuss personal things later, OK? Now just get ready to disembark"

Clem had talked a lot about Jack Stewart, so Terry wasn't surprised when Clem had put her on the plane with him. What was it Clem had told her—oh yes; Jack had been with the bureau since returning home from the war. During high school he had played most sports, but excelled in football. In fact, he was elected linebacker on the All-American High School team in his senior year. This was just one accomplishment in football, Clem had said. In his junior year as well as his senior year he was also all-academic. When he went to college everyone knew he would play football and probably turn pro after he graduated. He did play football and once again was elected All American his senior year. The important thing to Jack, according to Clem, were not his accomplishments in football, although they were great, he was getting his diploma and would be passing his bar exam. A lot like Chris, Clem had said. The war interrupted those dreams. When he returned home after the war he married his high school sweetheart, Nita and decided, instead of going back to school, to pass his bar exam, he would try for a position with the Federal Bureau of Investigation. He felt sure he'd get it due to his security rating he'd earned in the service. According to Clem, Jack said many times that this had been a decision that he never regretted.

The plane was stopping and the stewardess was just finishing her speech when Jack turned to Terrie—"Have you got everything Hon?" Jack said rather loudly. Laughing, he went on, "You do tend to loose or misplace things now and again—remember the key episode?"

At first Terrie was startled at the way Jack was talking, but then she remembered what was going on and reached up and kissed him on the cheek.

"Thanks Hon', you've always been thoughtful, and a big tease too." Terrie said smiling up at Jack "Yes, I have everything" she finished as she picked up her purse.

Jack and Terrie exited the airplane and found their way to the baggage area.

"I didn't realize how big this airport is when we came down the escalator," Terrie said as they were walking down their fourth aisle, looking for their rental car booth.

"All I hope" Jack said "Is that the last girl we asked knew what she was talking about when she said the car place was just down here a little—

Terrie interrupted Jack "There it is," she said as she almost ran towards the rental booth.

Jack looked at the rental agent. "I didn't think we'd ever find you. How come they put you way back here away from all of the other car rental companies?" he asked, sitting their luggage down and reaching for the rental papers.

"As I am sure," the agent behind the counter started "you noticed they are remodeling the terminal. So they have had to move all of us around, hopefully this will be my last move. I'm tired of trying to explain to people where I'm located. Just yesterday, for instance we were in the middle of the main concourse, then we were moved to A then to Concourse B and last night, err, rather tonight, they moved us down here. She went on sarcastically "this is for the benefit of people like you. Now how may I help you."?

"We are Mr. & Mrs. Jack Carrolle and we have a car reservation," Jack answered her.

"I will need your reservation number, driver's license and the length of your stay, please," the agent said looking at Jack.

Terrie noticed during this entire long-winded dissertation she never once moved, shifted her weight or changed her facial expression. 'She must really hate her job' Terrie thought.

"Oh, yes, I'm sorry, here it is." Jack said as he handed her the envelope that Nita had given him. "As far as length of stay I was under the impression that all of that had been answered when the reservations were made by my office." Jack said as he dug his driver's license out of his wallet.

"I'm sorry Mr. Carrolle. Everything does seem to be in order and yes, everything was taken care of when the order was made." The agent said as she handed him his driver's license and turned the paper around for him to sign. "If you will just sign on the bottom everything will be finished."

"Anything else you need" Jack asked as he put his license away and reached for the paper to fold and put away in his suit jacket.

"No sir, everything is in order," she said as she handed him his keys. "Please enjoy your stay her in California. You'll find your car in space 5 right outside this door on my left. That is if they haven't moved that too. I'm sorry for my sarcasm; it's just that I'm so tired from moving all of this that unfortunately you just bore the brunt of my unsettledness. Please forgive me and do have a great time in our area."

"Thank-you" Jack said as he took the keys I hope that they get this mess done soon so you don't have to move anymore."

Terrie and Jack picked up the suitcases and headed for the car.

'Boy,' Jack thought, '6 suitcases and her overnight case. What on earth did Clem and Nita pack for this girl? I've 2 suitcases and my briefcase. Guess a gal has to have lots of changes. Sure glad a man doesn't need that many clothes we'd never get them all in the car.'

"Boy was she windy or what. A little on the sarcastic side too." Terrie said as Jack unlocked the car door for her.

"Moved around as much as she's been moved and no one being able to find her I'm sure she's disgusted and maybe even a little bit lonesome, after all they've got her stuck way away from everybody. Didn't you notice, not even work men were near her."

"Guess you're right. I didn't think about her being lonely on top of everything else." Terrie said as she fastened her seatbelt.

"Would you like to stop and get something to eat? I'm sure you're starving by now. You slept through the meal the airline served. Can't say that you missed much tho', I didn't eat too much of it myself." Jack asked as he fastened his seat belt.

"Breakfast does sound awfully good. I guess the last meal or food I ate was lunch with your men from Atlanta, just before we went to the 'Mart" Terrie answered Jack "By the way, you threw me some kind of a curve there on the plane. Did I cover my surprise quickly enough?"

"Yes Terrie you were great. When we get to our apartment we can go over everything. Let's face it, we didn't exactly have the time before we left Atlanta." Jack said as he turned onto the freeway. It was close to 5 A.M. and traffic going south was extremely light. 'Thank heavens' Jack thought. I need time to figure out just how much I can tell her, but more important how I can win over her confidence so that she'll talk to me like she did Clem. We have to make sure her story jive with everything she's said and what we know, before we go to court.

Terrie sat quietly next to Jack looking out of the window and watching the scenery. She was thinking about the last few months—all that had happened—seeing Chris Ryan again after all of these years, what was it five-six years since he had come to the office to tell everyone goodbye when he left for college, his untimely death, 'was it connected to the information that I gave him' Terrie wondered and sighed, sad at what had happened to him. Clem told her about it on their way to the airport.

"Oh Jack, look at those beautiful trees in bloom. I wonder what kind they are? They look vaguely familiar." Terrie said

"I'm really not too sure, but they could be olive trees, since we are in Northern California and I hear that's where they grow." Jack said with some doubt in his voice.

"You could be right. I vaguely remember a tree, that belonged to a friend of mine, when I lived in Florida and it was an olive tree—that could be one" Terrie said a little excited thinking about Florida and some of the good times she'd had there.

"You truly are an amazing woman Terrie, just like Clem said" Jack looked at Terrie and remarked "Is there anything that you don't know something about in this world?"

"Oh, of course there are a lot of things, Jack. It's just that being an Executive Secretary for that company for so long and being in the flower business as long as I was—well, you learn a lot and I just happen to retain most of what I learn. In fact, I've been accused of having a memory like an elephant." Terrie said half heartedly, looking back out the window at the hillside of flowers that they were passing. 'He must think I'm some kind of a know-it-all, like a lot of people, but I'm not. What does he think got me into all of this mess after all—stupidity—not on your life. I kept my eyes open, ears open and mouth shut. Well, that is until Chris came, then I should have kept my mouth shut, maybe he'd still be alive today and I wouldn't be running again. Who knows, maybe Del wouldn't have left either—who knows?"

"Does this restaurant look okay to you" Jack asked as he pulled off the highway and into the parking lot.

"Sure, Jack. When you're hungry as I am any restaurant will just about do, providing they have good coffee. Besides, it's a little late for me to say no, isn't it?" Terrie laughed as Jack pulled into the parking place in front of the door.

"Well, I could back out and find someplace else to eat" Jack said crossly. He was tired and was in no mood to start any arguments, especially with someone he hardly knew.

"Oh, Jack, I was only teasing you. Besides it does look pretty clean outside. What have we got to loose? Let's go eat." Terrie said laughing and proceeded to get out of the car.

"Did you see some of the beautiful field of flowers that we've passed?" Terrie asked Jack as the hostess seated them.

"Would you like some coffee?" the hostess asked

"Yes please" Jack answered not waiting for Terrie to answer

"Thank-you your waitress's name is JoAnn and she'll be with you in a moment." The hostess replied. "Enjoy your breakfast

"Sorry Terrie I guess I should have let you tell her if you wanted coffee, but you did say 'if they have good coffee' so I just assumed that you drank it too. Yes, I did notice them and I suppose you can tell me what they were" Jack chided teasingly

"As a matter of fact, kind sir, I can." Terrie answered him. "They were both gerber daisies and I noticed a few marguerite daisies also. Weren't they just beautiful" Terrie said kind of dreamily remembering seeing them when she used to come out here for her wholesale flower business.

"They were beautiful, I was just wondering—do you still have friends or acquaintances out here?" Jack asked as he moved his hand to let the waitress set his coffee cup down.

"Thank you" he said smiling at the waitress

"Heavens no. That was back in the early 70's. I'm sure most of them are out of business or perhaps even dead. Why do you ask?" Terrie said as she too thanked the waitress.

"I was just wondering if maybe someone would recognize you out here, that's all" Jack replied

"Well you can quit you're worrying" Terrie's words were interrupted

"Hi, my name is JoAnn and I am your waitress. Are you ready to order or do you need a few more minutes?" she asked

"Order" both of them answered in unison and then started to laugh.

"It's good to see you laugh." Jack said to Terrie and thought to himself, she sure hasn't had much to laugh at lately. I wish I knew more about what really happened with her, what all she knows and why the 'mob' is trying to anielate her. Guess I'll learn that soon enough.

"One egg over easy, bacon and white toast, please and no potatoes." Terrie said to the waitress.

"Is that all you want? I thought you were hungry," Jack said to Terrie

"I am, but if I eat too much, then I won't be hungry when we get home. After all I did promise to fix waffles, that you've been hungry for, when we get home. Terrie said as she smiled and winked at Jack. 'Let's see if Jack can keep up with this conversation' Terrie thought. 'I can play double talk games too. I learned from the best.'

"You're right. I almost forgot about the waffles, but I also know you and I may not get those until dinner time, so if you don't mind I'll order a breakfast and worry about those later." Jack laughed as he gave the waitress his order.

"You're catching on pretty fast there, young lady" Jack said to Terrie as soon as the waitress left.

"Jack, seriously, I am getting tired of small talk. Can't we discuss some of what's been going on now?" Terrie said quietly to Jack across the table.

"I'm sorry Terrie, this just isn't the place. We'll have plenty of time to discuss everything after we get settled." Jack answered her

With that Terrie stared out of the window and watched the sun finish coming up. She lit a cigarette, blew smoke into the air, took a sip of her coffee then saw their breakfast coming.

"Might have known." Terrie said outloud

"Might have known what?" Jack asked

"Everytime I go to a restaurant to eat and light a cigarette, the food comes. I don't care if I wait 5 minutes or an hour before lighting up—if I want the food in a hurry then I light a cigarette and here it comes. See!" Terrie said as the waitress sat their food down in front of them.

"This pitcher is empty would you two like some more coffee?" the waitress asked as she picked up the pitcher.

"Yes, that would be nice." Jack answered as he started to cut his steak. 'Nothing like steak, eggs and potatoes to get one started in the morning.' Jack thought. 'If Nita or Clem, for that matter, could see me now. They both know I don't eat breakfast—at least not this early in the morning."

———

"That was just enough breakfast to tied me over to lunch. I'm really not a breakfast eater, but when I do eat it I order the samething. I never change. Well, once in awhile, but then I'm sorry because I don't figure I've had breakfast. Some stupid quirk in my make-up I guess." Terrie laughed. Some times when she was nervous she talked about nothing and this was one of those times. She knew they must be getting close to where they were going and she wasn't sure what to expect. How was Jack going to be—strictly professional, not try to put the make on her? Was she going to handle all of this all right or would she make a fool out of herself. Terrie's thoughts were interrupted

"Well, here we are in the large town of Sunnyvale. Now let's see if we can find the apartment building." Jack said

"What's the name of the apartment building, or does it have a name?" Terrie asked

"The Teddie Bear Motel and Apartments." Jack answered 'Terrific Jack had said to Nita when she'd told him the name. Sounds like some kind of 'Red-light' to me'. Nita laughed and said "Would I do that to the man I love." Jack was laughing and said, "Could be!" 'Well, the brochure that Nita gave him, sure did look nice, so there is hope, I think.' He thought.

"There it is, up ahead on the right" Terrie said "About a block and a half, I'd guess

"How on earth can you see two blocks ahead of us."

"That's easy. I just can't see up close." Terrie answered him.

"It looks a lot nicer than I thought it would" Jack said, "Nita showed me the brochure and I wasn't quite sure what exactly to expect. You know how brochure's can show things a lot nicer than they really are.

"It is pretty. Look at the Hibiscus and the Ivy around the front of the buildings" Terrie said This isn't the best place I've stayed in, but it sure isn't the worst either. Hopefully, the pool is heated. They do have one don't they?" I don't mind swimming in cold weather, as long as the water is heated. Could we be so lucky that they have an indoor pool." Terrie was babbling.

"Yes, they do have a pool, at least according to the brochure" Jack said as he pulled into the driveway. "I'll go in and register, or whatever, get the key and then we'll see what the inside looks like"

"Got the key and we're on the backside" Jack said as he got back into the car. "We're in number 107, ground level and supposedly we have a privacy fence that has a gate opening out to the pool."

"Oh, goodie" Terrie laughed "January, what on earth are we going to need a pool for—I'm no polar bear. Of course, if it's heated, then I'll swim cold or not.

"The clerk told me when I got the key, that the pool is heated to something like 80 degrees.

"That's great. I really do like to swim in the winter. Besides it helps me keep in shape."

"I hope they are as nice inside as they appear outside, with all of the flowers and trees." Terrie said as they got out of the car. "Shall we get our luggage?"

"No. Let's go check it out first. Not that we'll move or anything—it's just I'd like to see what were getting first." Jack said as he started for the front door and unlocked it. As he stepped through into the hallway a blast of hot air hit him in the face.

"Well, at least we know the heat works." Terrie said. "I hope that you really don't like an extra warm apartment." She said as she followed Jack down the short hall to the living room.

By the time they arrived in the living room Jack found the thermostat and turned it down to 72. He turned and looked at Terrie

"72 sound better to you than 90?"

"100 per cent." Terrie answered him as she went back down

the hall to the kitchen. "Want me to make a pot of coffee" Terrie asked Jack as he stood in the kitchen doorway watching her open and shut cabinets.

"That sounds great, but aren't you just a tad bit tired? Wouldn't you like to go lay down for awhile?" Jack asked as he crossed the floor and sat down at the table.

"Not really. At least not right now, maybe afterwhile I'll feel like lying down. Right now coffee sounds good. Whoever furnished this kitchen did it right down to coffee, sugar, milk, meat, the works." Terrie said turning towards Jack "Were you, rather Nita responsible for this?"

"No. The bureau arranged it through a couple of our operatives in San Francisco. Nita rented the place and then notified the bureau chief and he in turn got hold of the operatives out here. They came down and checked everything out and added whatever they thought we might need in the way of setting up housekeeping." Jack said as he looked in the cabinets for the coffee cups. "Do you take anything in your coffee? I don't remember what you did when we had breakfast."

"I like my coffee black." Terrie answered

Jack found the sugar and got two cups out of the cabinet and sat them next to the coffeepot. He went back to the table and sat down.

"Boy those two agents have thanks coming to them. They did a great job of providing everything. At least it seems as though everything is here, at least in the kitchen." Jack said looking around.

"Hey, have you checked out the patio and our 'fenced' in yard yet?" Terrie turned from the coffeepot and asked,

"No, I haven't. We'll check it out when the coffee has finished."

"Why don't you go on out and I'll come out when it gets done. It's so pretty this morning and it really isn't too cold so we can sit outside. I love doing that in the morning with coffee. I'm sure I can find a tray or something to put the cups on." Terrie said

"Okay" Jack said as he stood up and headed into the living room and out on to the patio.

"Terrie, come here quick." Jack yelled

"The coffee's not quite done."

"Forget the coffee. Just come out here now." Jack yelled back as he reread the card.

As Terrie approached the patio Jack had turned around to look at her and she could have sworn that he had tears in his eyes.

"What's so important that it couldn't wait until the coffee was done?" Terrie said looking around.

Jack said nothing he just handed Terrie the card and stepped to one side so she could see the flowers on the white wrought iron table.

Before reading the card Terrie saw the flowers and thought that it was a nice gesture from the operatives, Jack motioned to the card and she read it. Then she knew what and whom the flowers were from and why the tears in Jacks eyes. She burst out crying for the first time in a long time and couldn't stop. Jack helped Terrie sit down and went to find a washcloth. He hoped the agents had made sure they had some. He found a cloth, rinsed it in cold water and went back to Terrie. He took her face in his hands and gently wiped her face and eyes.

"Are you all right?" he asked

"Yeah, thank you. I don't know what happened to me. I saw the flowers and I thought how sweet your people were to leave flowers for us and I read the card." Terrie continued "Then I realized the significance of the flowers. The first time I met Clem—and the last time I saw Chris they brought me two pink roses. At the time I thought it was strange, but nice. Now I know. The pink rose there is for me from Clem. I'm sorry I cried just now, but it was so sweet of your wife to send them. I just wonder how she knew about the pink rose?" Terrie said staring at the flowers on the table.

"Wait a minute didn't you really read the card," Jack said as he reached down to the floor where Terrie had dropped it. "If you'd read it correctly you would have seen that it reads 'Good luck— All our love, Clem and Nita,' so as you just heard they are from both of them. That should answer your mystery of how she knew about the rose." Obviously Terrie didn't realize just how special she was to Clem. Jack and Nita had talked about Clem and how since they had known him, which was about 14 years now, that Terrie was the first lady he had shown the least inkling of being interested in since his wife and kids had died. At first they thought he just felt guilty about the bureau not listening to her the first time, but now they felt it was much more, than that. He had asked for their help in a plan of finding someplace where she could live for awhile without being found. Too many ways was he showing more than just a "client" responsibility. All he'd talked about since that kid Chris had been killed was Terrie and how the bureau and everybody had let her down and she was too nice to have that happen to her. Nita had told Jack that Clem was falling in love with Terrie, long before Clem had officially asked them for their help. Jack kept telling her that she was just a hopeless romantic. After all Nita had always hoped that Clem would find someone he could love after his wife died. "He has so much love to give to someone," Nita would say. "Maybe Nita was right after all. Well I guess we'll just have to wait and see." Jack thought.

"Now do you feel better about all this?" Jack asked as he gestured toward the flowers and champagne.

"Yes Jack much better. How'd about that cup of coffee now. I'll go in and get it." Terrie said as she stood up looking at the rose again.

"Sounds like a winner to me. How about taking the champagne in with you and put it into the refrigerator. That way it will be cold tonight, we might want to toast to something or other then." Jack said as he handed the bottle to Terrie and sat down at the table.

"You know, Terrie," Jack said as she came back to the patio. "Here let me set that down for you", he said as he took the tray and placed it next to the flowers. "As I was saying, here sit on the chaise and I'll pour the coffee. Anyway, Jack continued as he poured a cup for Terrie and handed it to her. "We all know that all of this is extremely hard on you. I mean Clem, Nita and myself. Well, I guess, what I'm trying to say is that Clem came to Nita and me about two weeks before he let you go to Atlanta and told us he needed a fool proof plan. If anything went wrong when you went up to there, in order to get you safely out of Atlanta and to a place where hopefully you wouldn't be found for awhile. So we all set out to come up plan B." Jack reached over and poured another cup of coffee for himself and offered Terrie some fresh, put in his two spoons of sugar and explained "It was Nita's idea. Rather all of this was. You and I would go someplace as man and wife until Clem, Nita and the bureau could rent, lease or buy a place where you could live without being found or afraid, at least until all of this mess was over with. Nita, who someday I hope you'll get to meet, is quite a gal; she made all the inquiries and found this place. She also made the airline reservations, tentatively, of course, rented this place and got our car too. Of course, most of the stuff she confirmed at the last minute. She and her Mom, when we found out, that you'd left for Atlanta and were in danger, went to your place and packed all of your clothes, along with your jewelry, make-up and anything else they thought you might want and/or need. She also suggested our names, Nita felt it best if we used our own first names, in your case, the name you've used for a few years, that you wouldn't feel too lost or scared. Guess she figured it would be like a security blanket. I'm not sure where she came up with the name Carrolle, but knowing her, it was probably some soap opera. Anyway, that's the scoop, simplified, on how you, we got here— welcome to sunny California, Mrs. Carrolle." Jack said as he tipped his coffee cup towards her.

Terrie had sat quietly listening to Jack and his explanation of what and how this had come about. At the same time she had thought back to when she'd been that secretary and everything leading up to today had started, about her children, her grandchildren—would she ever get to see any of them again? Would this damn nightmare ever end or would she be left to walk alone.

When Jack finished Terrie looked at him and again started to cry. Not hard this time just tears coming softly down her cheeks.

She'd never known anybody like these three people before. How very special they were. Maybe someday I'll get to meet Nita, I hope so, she must be a very special lady to lend her husband to a complete stranger, like this.

"More coffee" Terrie asked as she poured herself another cup.

"No, thanks. I've had enough. When you get through with your coffee what say we finish checking out the apartment and I'll go get the luggage." Jack said. He'd noticed that Terrie looked like she was a million miles away. Wonder what she was thinking about.

"We can do that right now. I don't need this cup." She said as she stood up. "In fact, if you'll carry the flowers, I'll carry the tray to the kitchen and we can get started."

Terrie reached for the tray and headed towards the door. 'Thank you Jack for changing the subject. I'm not ready for any heavy discussions.' She thought

It was really a nice apartment. It had two bedrooms, 2 baths, living room, and a nice size eat-in kitchen. The living room was nicely furnished with earth tone furniture. The carpeting was short shag in beige and the couch was a love seat tastefully done in a pattern of shades of browns, blues and a touch of green and ivory. The easy chair, that sat next to the couch, separated by an end table, was slightly too big for this room, but it was brown and one of those tilt back, just inches from the wall kind. The end tables and coffee table were rattan with glass tops. The living room also had a nice stereo, TV and VCR combination system. They had put silk flowers on the end tables and a nice low one on the coffee table. The flowers were done in the soft shades of blues, browns and ivory—very nicely done. Terrie thought as she looked at them. 'Perfect compliment to this room. Sure hope the rest of the place is this nice.'

"Well, shall we see what the bedrooms look like?" Jack said as he watched Terrie checking out the floral arrangements.

"Yes, I'm sorry, old habits are hard to break. I was just thinking how nicely done the arrangements were and how they compliment this room." Terrie said as she started for the hallway between the bedrooms.

Straight ahead of her was a bathroom, so she walked into there first. "This is a nice bathroom," She said as she looked at the yellow flowered shower curtain. "I'm not too sure why they would put that in here with the earth tones, but maybe someone felt it needed color."

"It is nice, but if we stay here too long that curtain is coming down." Jack laughed as he headed for the front bedroom.

It too was done in brown tones, 'Don't they have any other colors out here?' Jack thought as he looked at the bedspread and noticed the throw pillows with the mallards on them. "Guess this is supposed to be a man's bedroom, so I guess we may as well go and see what your room looks like." Jack said aloud as he walked towards the poolside bedroom.

Terrie tried to argue with him that she could sleep just as well in the first bedroom as she could in the poolside, but Jack wouldn't listen to her. For one thing, he said, it was too dangerous having her too close to the street and the front door. At least in the back bedroom, poolside, there was the fenced yard with a gate with a lock on the inside.

Terrie's room was gorgeous, very definitely a woman's room. The walls were done in light lavender and the accents were pink, white and dark lavender. The bathroom was also done in lavender, as was the dressing room that was between the bedroom and the bath.

"This settles it" Jack said as he stood in the dressing area. This is your room; if you're anything like my Nita you'll need all of this counter space to put out all of that female paraphernalia. Besides I don't think lavender does a thing for my complexion. Jack laughed and strode over to the bedroom door. "Is this satisfactory with you, my dear sweet maiden," he mocked

"Jack, with all of your silliness, you are a great guy to let me have this room. You're right lavender does nothing for your color. Did you notice if you have a waterbed? This one is and I won't give that up. I absolutely love them." Terrie laughed

"Yes, my fair Gwenevier, your Sir Lancelot has a water bed too. Does my fair maiden mind if I go out and get our luggage out of the car?" Jack waved as he headed towards the front door.

While Jack was attending to the suitcases, Terrie started cleaning up the kitchen, washing the cups and saucers and putting the sugar away.

"I put your suitcases in your bedroom and your make-up case on the vanity. I also unlocked all of them." Jack said as he walked into the kitchen and got a drink of water.

"Thanks Jack. Guess I best go unpack and see what all Nita and her Mom packed for me or I'll still be at it tomorrow morning."

"Hey, it's almost eleven o'clock. How's about going out for lunch when you get through unpacking?"

"We don't have to, we can stay here and eat, you're friends equipped the 'fridge with everything you could possibly want to eat, unless you want to go out, that is." Terrie said as she walked into the hallway hanging a blouse on a coat hanger. "By the way thank Nita for me for packing my iron. From the looks of some of these blouses I'm going to need it."

"We can eat in if you want to. I just thought maybe you'd like to go out and then come back and take a nap."

"I can fix lunch here and still do the nap thing, can't I"

"No problem. If that's what you want to do, then that's what we'll do. Eat, iron your blouses, rather you can iron while I do some more paper work, then you can take a nap."

Terry hung up the blouse on the doorknob and decided she'd totally unpack and see what all she would have to iron, before she put them in the closet. 'Oh, my gosh, they even packed my light blue dress.' Terrie thought as she pulled the dress out of the suitcase and started to hang it up 'Clem thought I looked especially pretty in this dress.' Shit, it would be great to get to talk to him. I hope he doesn't forget me and or what I look like. 'Stop it Terrie. You promised yourself that never, never another man in your life. So quit thinking about Clem in that way. It's just that I keep thinking how sweet he was when he found out Del had left me in the middle of all of this. Stop it I said' Terrie chastised herself. 'But really how can anyone turn their back on anyone that looks like an older Tom Selleck, besides I can't forget the rose' she thought as she hung up the dress and walked into the dressing room.

"Hey lady are you decent?"

"Sure Jack, come on in I'm in the dressing room putting stuff away."

"I forgot to tell you something, that I well—I think—you'll feel is important."

"What's that?" Terrie asked looking up from the floor where she was sitting putting stuff in the drawers.

"We have a dinner date tonight in San Francisco."

"Who with?"

"Yep, just like I figured, you need as much space as my Nita." Jack grinned down at Terrie sitting on the floor. "Does it make a difference? I mean who we're going out with."

"No, I trust you and I don't really care, I just hope Nita packed something respectable for me to wear that doesn't have to be pressed or washed. That's all. Have you any idea where we might be going to dinner?I mean fancy or a pub or just a walk on 'Fisherman's Wharf.' Now that's a great place to get sea food leisurely."

"Terrie" Jack said as he took hold of her shoulders and turned her away from the closet. "Don't worry about what you're going to wear, at least not right now. I'm sure you'll find something without any trouble and the people are the two agents that set up this apartment. Besides, if my memory serves me right, you don't have time to look for something to wear. We made a deal, that when you were finished unpacking we would have lunch and I notice you are through unpacking. Shall we go get something to eat?" Jack finished as he took Terrie's arm and steered her towards the bedroom door.

Laughing the two of them headed to the kitchen for Terrie to make them sandwiches.

"Jack" Terrie said as she got the cold cuts, cheese, tomatoes and onion out of the refrigerator. "Would you mind answering a couple of questions for me?"

"No, that is if I know the answers. Would you like for me to clean and slice the onion while I answer your questions?" he said as he reached into a drawer and pulled out a knife.

"Be my guest. I only really have one, I guess. You see all that has happened lately, well, I'm having trouble remembering things that Clem and I talked about when Chris brought him to Georgia— that is aside from Jay and all. What's his family, Clem that is, like?"

'Oh boy, I knew this was going to come sooner or later' Jack thought. In fact he and Clem had discussed how much he should tell her about Clem, really more how much he (Jack) could find out how much Terrie liked Clem.'

"Let's see. There really isn't a whole lot to tell about him. His wife and kids were killed in an accident some time back. He really doesn't talk about it much anymore. I guess if you were to ask him he'd talk about it, but Nita and I don't bring the subject up. Let me ask you a question.

"Shoot" Terrie said laughing "Not literally"

"How do you feel about Clem?" Jack asked 'rather blunt and to the point aren't you ole boy' Jack thought as he set the plate of onions on the table and reached for the plate of cheese and bread and set them on the table.

"I guess I put that rather badly. I was just curious, if you trusted him as an agent and/or a friend. I guess I'm, well, we, Nita and I are kind of hoping you like Clem a little more than just as an agent. That is if you get my drift." Jack finished blushing a little trying to figure out how to get his size 12 shoe out of his mouth.

"No apology necessary Jack. You have a right to know, I guess, to ask such a question."

"Not really" he interrupted

"Yes you do, after all Clem is your partner and best friend. You've told me so." Terrie went on as she put the finishing touches on the cold cut plates and set it on the table. "What would you like to drink? I can offer coke, tea, water and I also could make a fresh pot of coffee." She said as she stood staring into the refrigerator. "Coke is fine. I'll get the glasses." He said as he reached into the cabinet and pulled out two glasses and set them on the table. "Now" Terrie started as she filled the glasses with ice and handed Jack his coke. "Where were we—oh, yes, how do I feel about Clem. Well, it's like this, well, maybe it isn't. What I'm trying to say, or not say, is admit to myself, or anyone else, for that matter, exactly how I do feel about Clem. You see Jack, I made a promise to myself, the first time Del left me that I would never get involved with another man again. Del came back, we, for all practical purposes were a happily married couple, that is, so I thought and he left again. Then Clem was already in my life and when Del left me in Georgia, Clem was, at least, I wanted to believe, that he genuinely cared what happened to me. How I was taking Del's departure. The whole nine yards, that I thought—chee, I finally found someone who cares about me—not how much money I have or whether I kept a clean house, nothing but me, the person." Terrie rambled on while she and Jack sat down and started making sandwiches.

"I guess I really haven't answered your questions."

"I think I'm getting the picture. Let me tell you something." Jack started shit, I'm supposed to play it cool with this. I hope I'm not saying too much.' "Clem" Jack went on "really cares about you. and Nita and I believe that it's more than just the fact that the bureau did you an injustice. I don't want to mislead you or get your hopes up tho'."

"Like I said," Terrie went on in between bites of her sandwich "I made a promise not to get involved with anyone ever again, but I could sure be convinced to by him." 'Why do I have to babble so much. My heart is in my throat every time I think of him and I'm sitting here saying I don't know. What's wrong with me? What if he tells Clem and he really doesn't feel like they think he does about me? He really will believe I'm some kind of an idiot.'

Jack sat in silence and ate his sandwich while contemplating his reply.

"If you're through eating I'll clean the table off and put these things away." Not waiting for an answer Terrie started clearing off the table.

"Oops, guess I should have waited for your answer, shouldn't I" Terrie said as she realized Jack still had a piece of his sandwich on his plate.

"That's all right Terrie, I am finished. It's just—well, I was thinking, I guess Nita would accuse me of dreaming."

Now Jack was beginning to sound like he was rambling. ' What a dummy, he's as bad as I am. Come on spit the words out. Terrie thought as she finished cleaning off the table.

"What on earth are you trying to say?" 'I've been with him less than 24 hours and yet I know him well enough to know he's trying to tell me something without really coming out and telling me'

"Well?" She repeated

"I know. I'm beginning to sound like a babbling idiot. I was just wondering what it would be like for you and Clem to finally get together, without all this mess hanging over you. Kind of presumptuous of me, isn't it?"

Terrie turned back to the cold cuts and finished putting them in plastic bags. Resting her hands on the counter top to steady herself, all of a sudden she was weak in the knees, she looked at Jack. She kind of smiled seeing the look on Jack's face, he looked so pathetic. 'He truly is out of his league. He really looks like he put his foot in his mouth this time.'

"Jack will you quit worrying about Clem and me. If it's meant to be then it will be, if not, then it wasn't meant for us to any more than just good friends." Trying to ease Jack's mind. Her own was going 90 to nothing. 'How I wish Jack's dream would be true. Clem's the first thing I've seen that could really change my mind about men. Nix it Terrie, quit your dreaming and get down to the business at hand.' She admonished herself.

"Now the kitchen is clean, everything put away why don't we go sit in the living room for awhile and talk" Terrie asked Jack as she dried her hands. Looking at Jack she realized he was deep in thought. "You're quiet, what's wrong? Something I said or didn't say? Tell me and I'll try to set you straight."

"No, I was just thinking how two great people, like you and Clem, that have had shit all their lives, find each other and because of unfortunate circumstances don't feel like they can have or deserve each other. Such a pity. Yeah, let's go into the living room. Come to think of it wouldn't you rather go take a nap?" Jack said as he added ice and coke to his glass.

"A nap I can take after while." Terrie said following Jack into the living room. She motioned for him to sit in the tilt back chair, and took her shoes off and curled up on the couch. She leaned over and picked up her cigarettes and was about to light one when she looked at Jack. "Do you mind if I smoke in the apartment?"

"No. Smoke doesn't bother me. Nita smokes more than she'll admit to, so no go ahead light up." Jack watched Terrie and realized just how uneasy she was and her hands starting to shake. "Are you all right?" he asked

"I'm fine. It's just that I've been trying to quit and with everything that's happened lately—I know it's a cop out, but I'm really too nervous to quit." She said as she lit a cigarette, took a drag and leaned back against the couch and looked up at the ceiling. "You know Jack, we've bantered about the fact that I was Connie for the last few years and we should use it so I won't get any more confused than I already am. But I was thinking, if it is Les's men who are after me, don't you think they are more likely to 'chase' after Connie than Terrie? After all it's been a number of years since I really used Terrie and hopefully it will take them awhile to realize that maybe I'm not using Connie anymore and by that time—well—hopefully, it will be too late to do them any good."

"Maybe you're right. I guess we didn't stop and think that you'd be comfortable with that name back, since it had been so long. The only reason why we started using it was to try and confuse 'the enemy' Jack made the quotation marks with his fingers.

"Jack, if you all could just realize just how much I hated that name. It reminds me of all of this. Please can't we keep Terrie even out in public?" She asked in a pleading voice

"It's OK by me. If that's what you want, that's what it will be." Jack answered her looking at her and thinking 'she's got more guts than any of us gave her credit for'

"Tell me Jack—was anyone killed in the shooting in Atlanta yesterday? Is it, was it the mob? What on earth do they want of me? When will it ever end? What do you people expect of me?"

"Whoa, slow down lady. I thought you were going to have a coronary on me there for a minute. Are you all right?"

"Yes, I'm fine. There are just so many unanswered questions and I would really like to get back to a normal life, whatever that might be." Terrie said as she snuffed out her cigarette and lit another one.

"I don't want to criticize you, but that's the third one you've had in about ten minutes. You really are nervous. How about I answer, or at least try to answer your questions and then you go take a nice hot bath and a nap." Jack said as he put the chair into the upright position and stared at Terrie.

"Yes, that would be fine. I guess I am a little more tired than I thought." Terrie said as she put her cigarette out and finished her warm glass of coke.

"Well, let me see if I can remember your questions—not exactly in order, but here goes." Jack said as he folded his hands together and stared at his large knuckles. 'Mom told me not to crack my knuckles 'cause they'd grow big, and boy was she right' Jack thought as he contemplated his answers to her. 'Not going to be easy trying to put her mind at ease.'

"As far as anyone being killed in Atlanta, well, I'm not sure. I just had a few minutes with Clem before the airplane took off and all he said was that it looked kind of bad for a couple of our guys and maybe one or two of what we believed to be Les's boys.

They obviously want you for what they believe you know about them, their operations, the kingpins, whatever. My guess from years of experience, is that they believe you really know a lot and I believe they killed Chris because they believed you told him a lot of what you knew, or at least what they believe you knew. When will it end—when we get them to court 'hopefully we'll get them to court' Jack thought as he started to go on All we expect out of you is honesty and some piece of mind for you. And to answer a question you didn't ask, but thought about—I don't know how long we'll be here or where you're going from here. Clem is taking care of all of that. I do know we hope to have you moved into a more permanent type home by mid-April or May." Jack said as he offered more coke to Terrie and poured himself some. He leaned back in the chair and looked down at the bubbles coming up the side of the glass.

Terrie had been listening to everything Jack was saying. She knew he was being cautious with what he was saying, or not saying, whichever the case might be. She couldn't help but wonder what really had brought her here to this point in her life. What she had done to her family, friends, Chris, Clem—all she did was tell a story, not even the whole one, to a young man, attorney by trade, that wanted to know about his uncle as to the kind of a man he was. Now that young man was dead, others had been shot and possibly dead—and here she was in San Francisco never knowing when this would end and if she would ever have a normal life again. Would she always walk alone? Was telling Chris about Jay worth it? Terrie wondered.

"You go on and lay down. I'll take care of these glasses and straighten up the kitchen. If I lay down I'll be sure and get you up in plenty of time to get ready for tonight." Jack said as he got up, picked up the glasses and bottle of coke, that was sitting on the coffee table. May as well take the ashtray to the kitchen too, he thought as he juggled the bottle to pick up the ashtray.

# CHAPTER 2

Les poured himself a second cup of coffee, opened the drapes and stepped out onto the patio, through the open glass doors. He set his cup down on his new bamboo glass top table and walked across the patio to the jasmine hedge. This is the life new bamboo patio furniture and a bush that blooms just about year round. He had the previous owners of his houseplant the jasmine, not only for its beauty, but also for the sweet smell. He looked across the grounds towards the Caribbean. He could see crystal clear blue water coming in on the sandy shore. "I love this view—It's Les's thoughts were interrupted by the ringing of the telephone. He crossed the patio into the living room picking the phone up on the second ring.

"Hello" he snapped into the phone. How dare anybody disrupt his beautiful thoughts, besides who could possibly have this number? Curt was the only one who had it and he wasn't supposed to call for a couple more days.

"Well! Is anyone there?" Les snapped again into the telephone.

"Les, Les is that you," the man on the phone asked

"Who wants to know" Les answered

"It's Archie, Les"

"Where the hell are you, how'd you get my number and by the way how the hell are you? I heard you'd been injured pretty bad when Mark was killed. Then I heard that Curt ran into problems getting you off." Les screamed into the phone. Both angry because someone gave out his number and happy to hear from Archie his number one Sergeant.

"Calm down Les. Curt told me to call you and let you know what's happening up here. What with him trying to get ready for Kyle and them's trial he ain't got the time right now to fill you in. Besides, he figured you'd wantta be hearing from me to know that I'm OK and all."

"Yes, I'm glad that you called and I'm sorry I yelled at you. It's just that you caught me off guard 'cause no one's supposed to have this number, but Curt. Now fill me in on what really happened with you and Mark and how you're doing."

"Well, I'll hit the highlights about Atlanta. Mark and me grabbed Terrie according to plan, but when we got outside there was cops all over the place. Somebody grabbed Terrie and the cops opened fired. Mark got it in the chest and I don't know where else. Anyway he's dead as you know. Me, I was shot in the arm, leg, gut and a bad one in my shoulder. The shoulder will probably always give me some trouble according to the Docs, but otherwise the rest weren't too bad. Yeah, Curt had some trouble getting' me off, but I didn't have the gun and Curt said I was just walking beside them and was hit by accident or somethin' and since that Terrie dame couldn't testify they dropped the charges." Archie concluded.

"That's good to hear Arch. I'm sorry you got hit, but I'm glad you're back. What's the word from Curt on Morici?" Les asked

"He got Morici off like ya told him too. Somethin' about circumstantial evidence really cut down their supposed eyewitnesses I guess. That brings up another matter. Morici called me and wants to know where you are and if he can call you. He's wantin' to know if he's still on payroll or not since he'd screwed up with that kid."

"To answer Morici's question—Hell yes, he's still in. I've plans for him and I'm glad Curt got him off. I figured he would. No checks this time and nothing in writing. He'll be paid by cash. We don't need any slipups tracing him back to us, I mean. Now I want to know—has Doug kept in touch with anybody?"

"Yeah. I talked to him the other day. Guess he's not to busy right now. Seems he had a heckuva time trying to convince that Brown guy that he hadn't snitched and wasn't a double agent. Guess they're really not too sure as yet 'cause from what he says they're keeping a close touch on him. From what he said he's got more or less a menial type desk job now, just kinda researching stuff. Says that's so they can keep their eyes on him for awhile.

"Sounds good. Doug's a good man. I'd hate to lose him and his contacts, especially now. Call Lonnie and tell him there's to be a meeting at his place at 7 P.M. tonight and I'll be calling the boys at 8 P.M. sharp. That gives all the boys a chance to get there, have a drink and settle down before I call. Tell him to have that fancy speakerphone of his hooked up. Also get a hold of Morici, is he there in the Atlanta area? Tell him the scoop and take him to Lonnie's in Chattanooga with you. Have you got that straight Archie?"

"Sure Les, any—Archie realized he was talking into a dead phone. That was Les for you, say your piece and hang up. Archie crossed the room, poured a whiskey and went back to the phone.

"Funiak's Italian Cuisine." The girl announced

"Mr. Funiak please" Archie said as business sounding as he could.

"Just a moment sir"

"Pretty smooth using his Mom's maiden name. That way no one connects the restaurant or Lonnie with Les and 'the family' Archie thought as he waited for Lonnie to answer.

"Funiak here" Lonnie said when he picked up the receiver.

"Yeah Lonnie, it's me Archie. I talked to your brother and he wants that you have a meetin' of all the guys at your place at 7 tonight and he's callin' at 8 sharp. Said you—

"Oh yes, Mr. Archie, how are you" Lonnie interrupted "You want a party of 7 at 8 tonight. I'm sure we can accommodate you. Thank you for calling and I'll notify our reservationist at once to put your reservation down."

"What the shits the matter—" again Archie was talking into a dead line. Damn, we've been disconnected, he thought as he re-dialed the restaurant.

"Funiak's Ital—"

"Yeah" Archie interrupted "give me Funiak again."

"I'm sorry sir, but Mr. Funiak is in a meeting and told me not to disturb him again. May I have him call you?" the girl asked

"Naw, but you might tell him that Mr. Archie called again." Arch said as he slammed to phone. 'Stupid broad, I should've just told her to get me Funiak and no back talk, but if I did Les would probably get mad.'

"Federal Bureau of Investigation" the girl said into the phone.

"Mr. Doug Salem, please"

"Just a moment please and I'll ring his office for you."

"Investigation" some man said into the phone

"Mr. Doug Salem" Archie said

"He's away from his desk right now, may I help?"

"Naw, er yes, please have Mr. Salem call Mr. Archibald when he has the time. Just tell him I'm returning his call. Thank you." Archie said as he hung up. 'Sure hope he remembers that stupid code name.'

"Guess there's nothing for me to do, but just sit and wait for Doug to call me back and maybe Lonnie too, that is if he got my message." He walked over to refill his whiskey glass. 'Rather early in the day to start drinking isn't it. Yeah, but after all the BS I've gone through today, yesterday and forever, I deserve this drink. Maybe I better call Morici while I wait for everyone else to call back.' Before he could pick up the phone it rang.

"Hello"

"What the hell was so damn urgent? And what were you blabbering about earlier?" Lonnie snapped over the phone

Archie related everything Les had said on the phone earlier.

"OK Arch. I'll get right on it, by the way does that include Doug?"

"Yeah, but I already got a call into him."

"OK Arch. Sorry about awhile ago and all that mumbo-jumbo, but I was in a meeting with my staff and I couldn't let them know what was going on. Don't forget act like a customer. Let my boy park your car and when he's out of site go around the opposite end of the building and come through the back door. I'll have everything ready."

"Thanks Lonnie, see ya tonight."

Archie hadn't anymore than laid the phone down, when it rang again.

"Hello" he said into the receiver

"Yeah, Archie want'd you want:"

"Is everything OK. I mean can we talk?" Knowing that they taped most of the calls coming in and going out of the Bureau, especially on Doug's line, he thought he'd best ask.

"Yeah, I'm on the pay phone at the drug store"

"There's a meeting at Lonnie's tonight at 7. Les is callin' at 8 and he wants that you should be there. Can ya make it?"

"Sure. I'll be there. Lonnie's at 7. See ya" Doug said

"Come in the back door. Let the kid park you're car and when he's outta sight go around the other end of the building and to the back door. See ya tonight."

"Guess I best call Morici and see what he's up to, maybe he'll meet me for lunch."

"Hello"

"Morici is that you?"

"Yeah Archie who'd you think it'd be?"

"Ya didn't sound like yourself"

"How would you sound when someone called and got you out of a sound sleep?"

"Hell, Morici, it's the afternoon, what ya doin' sleepin'?'

"It's easy when you're an ex cop, not very well liked and you've been in the slammer. What'd ya want?"

"There's a meetin' tonight at Lonnie's place and Les says you gotta be there. But you and me, well, we gotta talk first. Can ya meet me at Charlie's Deli in about a half hour."

Morici looked at his watch. "It's 1 o'clock according to my watch. I'll be there by 1:30. If I'm not there exactly at that time order me a beer."

'Maybe this means I'm still in with the 'family'. Morici thought. He didn't know where Les was or why he hadn't called him. Maybe the answer would be coming from Archie. Maybe that's why he wants to talk first. He knew Les was sore with him for leaning so hard on the kid like he did. At least they got him off. How could he ever forget that night. He hadn't wanted to do what he did and he'd never forget it. If only the kid had just listened to me instead of trying to be big. Morici had been walking to the bathroom to wash his face, when he looked into the mirror he saw "that" night all over again.

*It had been a cold and drizzling rain when Chris walked out of the office building and headed for his car. It really had been almost too easy walking up behind him and sticking the gun in his back. Sure he knew that he was being watched, but that's part of a cops training—loosing tails. That made it really funny, they really thought they were hidden. Dumb feds. Whatta they know. Once inside of my car I knew enough to make Chris lay down on the front seat and of course he did, considering I had my gun pointed at him. The drive out to the gravel pit was really uneventful. The tails were still sitting there watching for Chris. How dumb were they, he walked out I walked in behind him and they didn't see a thing. Probably drinking too much coffee and reading the paper. Schmucks!! He really should have listened to me when we got out of the car. All I wanted to do was rough him up, scare him a bit and let him walk back to town. No-o-o instead I had to take care of him, drive him back to town, get into his car, prop him up and leave. No one would be the wiser, but I would always know I killed the kid, just as surely as if I had pulled the trigger. Why did he want to fight me for the gun!*

———

The air was icy cold and the smell of snow was in the air when Morici stepped outside of his apartment building. Pulling his coat collar up around his face he headed for Charlie's.

"Hi Arch, long time no see, how's tricks?" Morici asked as he caught up with Archie outside of the Deli.

"Let's go in and get something to eat and talk. It's too damn cold out here to do anything." Archie said as he reached for the door. "Shit" he continued as he went inside "I moved south to get outta this damn cold stuff."

Inside, the deli was decorated for Charlie's customers. Christmas was everywhere, with carols playing loud.

"Give me a ham on rye, mustard, pickle and a beer please Charlie." Archie said. He always had manners at Charlie's. He learned his lesson sometime ago when he was his normal rude self and Charlie made him wait an extra long time for his food. 'Charlie said something about he wasn't a dog. What ever that meant.'

"I'll take the same please Charlie, but add a piece of your delicious peanut butter pie to my order." Morici said smiling in anticipation that delicious pie.

"Ever tried the peanut butter pie Arch?"

"Naw, I'm not much of a pie or cake man myself."

They finished eating and Archie went over to the bar and ordered them another beer. When he sat back down he said, "Let's talk"

"OK Arch. What's happening and where do I stand with the 'family' and Les?"

"I talked to the boss and he said cash in advance from now on and no more checks. That's so you can't be traced back to us—comprenda?"

"Sure I do. I don't have a problem with that. I'm just happy to know I'm still with the 'family'. I'm sorry as hell about that kid and what happened. I didn't mean to do it. I really didn't want to it's just we wrestled for the gun and bam-o."

"Well, that's between you and the boss. There's a meeting tonight at Lonnie's place at 7 the boss is calling at 8. You and me are to go up together. You have any trouble with that?"

"Why would I?" Morici asked looking at Archie and wondering what the meeting was about. "What time did you say the meeting was?"

"The boss said we should be there at 7 'cause he's gonna call at 8 and he wants everyone settled down by the time he calls. I figured I'd pick you up about 4:30, so's we can be on time."

"It only takes about an hour and a half from here. It's not like we live in downtown Atlanta. Kennesaw is slightly north."

"I know that, it's just the boss is such a stickler that I want to make sure we're there early. That way I know we're on time."

"Well, if you'd look at your watch we've sat here eating and drinking almost 3 hours. It's almost 4 o'clock."

"Oh Shit. Do you have to go back to your apartment Morici?"

"Naw. We may as well have another beer and then leave from here."

"That sounds good to me." Archie said as he motioned to Charlie for another round.

———————

When they left the deli they talked about how cold it was and how they half expected it to snow sometime during the night. Most of the way to Chattanooga they were both quiet.

"Have you got any kind of an idea about this meeting?" Morici finally broke the silence and ask.

"Naw, the boss just said he'd call at 8. That's all I know."

"What the hell was that? It sounded like a gun shot inside the car." Morici yelled have afraid to move.

"Ah shit! It feels like a flat tire."

"Do you have a spare?" Morici said. He almost was afraid to ask. Archie's car wasn't the best in the world. It had a lot of miles on it for being only two years old and Archie wasn't one for getting tune-ups, oil changes, whatever. 'Let it fall apart and I'll get a new one.' Was his motto.

"Hell yes, Morici. What kind of a nut do you think I am? Everybody has to carry a spare for just such emergencies. Let's get it changed and get back on the road." Archie said as he carefully steered the car to the birm.

It was 8 o'clock on the button when they pulled up to Lonnie's place.

"Shit. We're late and the boss is gonna be pissed." Archie said as he handed the car keys to the parking lot attendant.

"It couldn't be helped Arch. We had a flat tire. I'm sure he'll understand."

"Yeah, sure, I hope so anyway." Archie replied half hoping they'd get inside before Les called. Tonight of all nights he didn't want Les mad. After all this was the first time, that he knew about, that anyone had heard from Les since the Atlanta job went sour.

"Where have you two been? Les has already called and he's talking to the guys right now and boy is he pissed at you for not being here. Come on in now." Lonnie said as he opened the back door and escorted the men to the meeting room. When they got inside the room Lonnie told Les that Morici and Archie finally made it.

"Where were you Archie? You know I believe in being on time."

"I know boss. I had a flat tire on the way up and we had to change it on the Interstate."

"Sounds like a pretty limp excuse to me."

"Honest boss, it's the truth. You know I wouldn't lie to you. Besides you can ask Morici, he's right here and he did most of the work."

"Hi Morici. It's nice to have you back. Now let's get down to business."

As Les started to tell the game plan Lonnie started to look around and watching the looks on the men's faces starting to change. From the scowls, looks of despair and disgust to smiles and grins. He could tell that finally everyone felt that the 'family' hadn't given up, that they were still going strong. Faith, hope and the family praise be they were still together.

The meeting started breaking up around 10 o'clock. The men left one or two at a time. Some went through the restaurant as customers and others went out the back door, so as not to draw attention to themselves or what had been going on in the backroom. By eleven o'clock everyone was gone with the exception of Archie, Morici and Lonnie. They were waiting for Les to call back. He had called Lonnie before the meeting and told him to tell Archie and Morici to expect the call after everyone left and that he wouldn't say anything about his calling back during the meeting.

"If the boss don't call soon we'll be leavin' too. He has my number if he wants to talk to me, like he told you he did then he can call me at home in three hours." Archie said "I don't like the looks of this weather and I want to head home." Archie hadn't finished talking when the telephone rang.

"Hello" Lonnie said into the speaker

"Are Archie and Morici still there Lonnie?"

"Yeah boss we're still here, but the weather's looking really bad outside and we'd like to get on the road."

"OK. Lonnie put the phone on the speaker and then you clear out. I want to yell at Morici and you don't need to hear it. If you know what I mean."

"Sure Les. The phone is already on the speaker. I'll be home later tonight if you need to talk to me."

"OK kid, I'll call you later. Take care."

Les listened for the door to open and shut. When he didn't hear it he questioned Archie.

"Is everyone gone?"

"Yes sir. Only me and Morici are here now boss." Archie leaned down and all but yelled into the speakerphone.

"Back away from the speaker Archie. You don't have to lean close or scream at it. Just talk natural and I can hear and understand you."

"OK boss" Archie replied trying hard not to lean into the speaker again. These new fangled gadgets, he thought.

"Morici"

"Yes Mr. R., I'm here," Morici answered. Since he'd brought on board, into the family, he had never called Les by anything, but Mr. R or Mr. Rudicio. Few people have respect for the boss anymore. They should have been brought up in my era. Respect or you got the ruler. Respect that's the key to everything.

"I just want to say, you are going to have to be more careful and follow orders more closely from now on. We can't always get you off."

"Hey, Mr. R. I'm really sorry about that. In all my years on the force I didn't draw my gun more than once or twice. Normally they'd listen to me. He just wouldn't listen and we wrestled and the gun—well it went off."

"Morici let's get something straight. No explanations are needed or expected. We're not the cops. You do your job and do it right and were fine. We let you off on this one, everyone makes one mistake, just don't screw up again. Understand."

"Yes sir. Mr. Rudicio. I understand, waste means waste and lean means lean. Yes sir. It won't happen again."

"Now—Terrie Cooper has disappeared again. I spoke with Doug and he's trying to find out where she's been hiding, but no leads yet. They're evidently keeping that pretty much under wraps. He did find out however, that our 'friend' Clem Brown left on vacation to go skiing. Doug seems to think that he's somewhere in Northern California or Colorado. That is not unusual because he normally goes skiing over the Christmas holidays; the unusual thing is it's normally 10 days, this time he's been gone for a little over a month. He also feels and I tend to agree that he's visiting Terrie somewhere out there."

"What can we do boss?" Archie asked. Remembering not to lean into the speaker

"Morici" Les said not bothering to answer Archie's question. "Have you followed what I've just been saying?"

"Yes sir and I've got an idea."

"I'm listening."

"How's about Archie and me going out west. Start in Colorado as skiers or tourists and look around and see what we can find out."

Archie was shaking his head NO so hard Morici thought it was going to fall off. He looked so silly it was all Morici could do not to laugh.

"Well, Morici I hadn't thought about Archie going, however, since it is mid January, you might be less conspicuous if you go that way. Arch, how does that sound to you?" Les asked, knowing full well Archie was going to scream. He hated cold weather.

"It's too damn cold. Boss, you know how I hate the cold. Please don't send me, send someone else."

"It's settled then. Go over to the office and I'll have Lonnie drive down and meet you there, tomorrow morning at 10 o'clock sharp with money, tickets, car reservations and anything else you two might need. You will report to Lonnie while you're gone or until you find Terrie. I'll call Lonnie after while and inform him what's going on and what he has to do. Should you feel you need to go all the way to the west coast, let Lonnie know so he can tell me and I may send someone from our west coast operations instead. Good-bye, good luck and don't forget to keep in touch with Lonnie."

Archie and Morici just stood in silence for a few minutes afraid to talk and yet wanting to talk, but not knowing exactly what to say to each other. Both were deep in thought about the next month or so. Thank heavens Archie liked Morici, at least Morici thought so. He knew that Archie was pissed because he had suggested his going with him. 'Oh well, he'll get over it. Besides, like Les said, two of us will be less conspicuous than me alone.'

Archie finally broke the silence.

"Come on Morici let's go into the bar, have a drink, and tell Lonnie goodnight, just like we was customers and head home. It sounds like we've a big day ahead of us. Sure hope the weather holds til we get home."

Morici not knowing of any comment to make followed silently behind Archie.

'Why are they still wanting Terrie? Surely they don't think

she'd talk, at least not after what I did to that kid.' Morici thought as they headed towards the front of the restaurant and into the bar.

Archie pulled up outside of Morici's apartment and laid on the horn. 'What's taking him so long' Archie was thinking as he honked again. 'He knew I'd be here at 9:30 this morning. That's going to give us just enough time to make it to the office by 10.' Archie sure didn't want to be late this morning. 'What if Les did call, he was going to be there. No more getting chewed out 'cause he was late' he thought as he laid on the horn again.'

"Mornin Archie. Are you ready to go skiing"

"Shit, you know I hate cold weather and yet you got me into this. Hell no, I'm not ready. Packed—yes—but ready I never will be." Archie answered him "Put your stuff in the back seat so we can head to the office. I'm not going to be late this time."

"Me, I'm kind of excited about this assignment. I haven't really skied since I was a youngster. Wonder if they give beginners lessons. I may need them." Morici said full of the anticipation of getting to go first class to Colorado.

"You really are crazy, do you know that Morici."

"Why 'cause I still love the cold and all that goes with it? You've forgotten I was a cop for a number of years in all kinds of weather and I really do love the snow. It's the heat I can't stand. I remember a few months back when I first went to Rutland lookin' for Terrie and how hot it was. I was sure hopin' I wouldn't be in Georgia another summer and of course I was. Part of one anyway. Hey, Arch tell me something" Morici went on without waiting for a reply. "Why does Les still want Terrie found and taken care of? I always considered myself to be a pretty good detective, but after taking the kid out I can't imagine her talking. Especially if she was just an innocent company employee like Les said."

"Come on Morici use your head man for christ sake. She'll talk more than ever to avenge that kid's death. I don't know much about her or what she knows, but if its bad enough for the boss to send you to Germany lookin' for her then its bad enough for you to keep your mouth shut and do as your told, that is if you wanta still have employment. Right?"

"Your right of course" Morici said "Just letting my police background curiosity interfere. Sorry about that. Wonder if Lonnie's here yet," he asked wanting to change the subject and wishing he'd learn to watch the questions.

"Yeah, there's his car." Archie said pointing to Lonnie's car as they pulled into the company's parking lot. "Yah know this is some kind of operation. The electronics, micro chips in the front and 'our' warehouse in the back and upstairs."

They found Lonnie waiting for them in the conference room.

"I've got your tickets, money and motel reservations. What else do you need?"

"Where do we start and what time do we leave here and do we rent or buy skis when we arrive?" Morici asked as he sat down across the table from Lonnie.

"Denver. Well more correctly your reservations are at a place called Pennsylvania Lodge. It's about forty miles west of Denver off I-70. All of your instructions are here in this envelope along with airline tickets, car and lodge confirmations. You can examine all of this on the plane, which leaves at noon, so I guess you best take off for the airport. As for the skis the answer is in the envelope and don't forget to keep in touch. Goodluck!

"Boy was that ever a fast shuffle," Morici said as they headed towards the car.

"Yes, but in case you haven't noticed Lonnie is Les's brother—don't waste your breath on small talk—business get it over with and shut up." Arch answered

When they got in the car and headed towards the airport Morici opened the envelope and took out their airline tickets.

"Leave—Noon Arv—1:05 PM Flt.687, a 727 stretch" Morici half read aloud.

"What the Hell are you muttering about over there?"

"Oh, sorry 'bout that Arch. I said we leave at noon on Delta's

Flight 687 and the plane is a 727 stretch. We arrive in Denver at 1:05 Denver time. Which means the plane won't sit down anywhere before it gets to Denver—in otherwords, it's a straight through flight.

"How come you know so much about flyin', I mean with you being a cop for so long and all."

"Well, besides flying when I was younger out to my sisters and all you've forgotten how much I did earlier this year and last chasin' half way round the world for this broad." Looking back at the tickets he reread them and continued "Hey we're even flyin' first class. I sure do like the 'family' everything goes first class all the way."

"Where'd he say we were staying?" Archie was finally getting excited about this trip. He'd never traveled like this before, first class and all that stuff. Archie had started out as a youngster with the 'family' and worked his way up to Sargent, but he still hadn't really traveled much before, especially first class. His jobs mostly involved cars like with Terrie—grab her, shove her in a car and go. What had gone wrong, he thought, Mark killed, me shot up—shoulder never will be the same. "What'd you say Morici"

"I said, you're gonna miss the airport turn off if you don't start trying to get over. This damn traffic, six lanes still ain't enough. It doesn't make any difference what time of day or night—it's always rotten driving."

With Morici's comment Archie checked the side mirror and crossed two lanes of traffic barely missing the front end of a Mercedes that had been coming up on his right.

"Watch where the Hell you're going" Archie yelled at the Mercedes

With the windows up on both cars he was sure the guy driving didn't hear what he said anymore than he heard what that man said. However, he did understand the mans hand gesture. The thought flitted through Arch's mind to run the Mercedes off the road, but realized he'd, they'd, be late to the airport, miss their flight and then Les would be pissed, so he kept his eyes on the road.

Boy, we're going to have to run to get our bags checked through." Morici said "Thank heavens Lonnie got our seat assignments for us. Park there on the left—long term, we're not sure just how long we'll be gone. Oh good here comes the shuttle. Quick get your stuff and lock the car. We'll grab the shuttle and then we don't have to run." Morici was saying as he grabbed his stuff off the back seat.

"Welcome to Delta. May I help you," the ticket agent asked

"Yes Ma'am" Morici said, "We need to check our bags for your flight 687 to Denver."

"Yes sir, they'll be loading from Gate 10 very shortly" the agent said "Thank you for flying Delta. Have a good flight," she said as she finished tagging their luggage and stapling their claim checks to the inside of their ticket pouches.

"Gate 10? How do we get there?" Morici asked

"Down this hall to your left and it will be halfway down on your right."

"Thanks" Morici said as he shoved Archie towards the hall.

# CHAPTER 3

"Terrie" Jack said as he tapped on her bedroom door. Terrie he repeated. Receiving no answer Jack slowly opened the door. As he got it far enough open to see the bed he realized Terrie wasn't in it. Jack started to go through the door—fear went through him. "Where the Hell is she?" As he took another step into the bedroom he could hear the water running and realized that she was in taking a shower. Quickly he closed the door and retreated to the kitchen to get a drink of water and compose himself.

He didn't want her to see how scared he was when he thought something had happened to her.

"Now that's what I call a good nap," Terrie said as she walked into the kitchen tying the sash to her robe. "I'm ready for almost anything now. Is there any coffee?"

"I just made a fresh pot, help yourself." Jack said looking at her with a silly grin on his face.

"You look like the cat that swallowed the canary. What are you grinning at?"

Terrie asked as she poured the coffee and set the cup down on the table.

"Well, you said you were almost ready for anything. Are you ready for a surprise?"

"What kind of a surprise?"

"Well, one I think you'll like. At least we all hope you will anyway." Jack said starting for his bedroom. "Wait just a minute and let me go get it. I hope you're not mad, upset, scared or angry with me because I set this dinner up for tonight?" Jack said as he strolled out of his bedroom carrying a coat hanger with a blue bag over it.

"No, of course, I'm not. How could I get upset with any of you for all that you've done for me? Besides I want to personally thank the two responsible for setting up this apartment. I am amazed, I don't know of anything they missed." Terrie said as she stared at the blue bag.

"Well, to be truthful with you, this really wasn't totally my idea. Clem thought it would be nice for a change. Maybe it would get your mind off what all has happened lately."

"Ta Dah!!!" Jack said as he pulled the sack off of the hanger to expose a new off white knit dress. "We hope you like it." He was to let her think that he, Nita AND Clem bought the dress, when in fact Clem not only picked it out, but paid for it out of his own pocket. He wouldn't let Nita or me pay a penny on it.

"Oh Jack!! It's beautiful." Terrie said trying hard not to cry. "But how on earth did you know what size to get."?

"Have you forgotten already who packed your clothes, Nita and her Mom. They were able to check for sizes then. I told you my Nita was a pretty clever gal. Do you like it?" Jack asked still holding the dress and not exactly knowing what to do with it.

"I love it. Let me try it on. I feel like I've lost so much weight, that maybe it won't fit properly."

"Okay. But we've still got about two hours before we really have to start getting ready. You've plenty of time to try it on."

"I know, but I want to make sure it fits and I really can't wait to see it in the mirror. I'll come back out after I've put it on to get your opinion." She said heading for the bedroom door. Terrie shut the door and took her robe off and laid it on the bed. She took the dress off the hanger and slipped it over her head. She walked into the dressing room to get a look at herself in the mirror. As she walked she smoothed the dress over her figure and couldn't get over how well it fit. She checked out the length—'good deal, just below the knees, exactly where I like my skirts' the long sleeves fit absolutely perfect and 'the bodice of the dress really shows off my breasts' she thought as she ran her hands down the sides and the plunging neckline isn't that plunging. Just enough to truly make the dress sexy. Let's see, should I wear my pearls or diamond necklace with this. This dress is classy; all I need now is my fur stole. I don't remember unpacking it, guess Nita and her Mom didn't find it.' Terrie was thinking when she heard Jack's voice

"Hey have you got that dress on yet, or have you decided you don't like the fit. I thought you were going to let me pass judgment on the dress before you decided against wearing it."

"I'm coming. You've got to realize that I don't have my makeup on, hair combed or shoes on, so don't let those missing things influence your opinion of what the dress really looks like. Just tell me if you like it or not." Terrie said as she slowly walked out of the bedroom, barefooted.

At first Jack was speechless. All he managed was a very low sexy whistle. He had seen Nita absolutely looking like a knockout, but he wasn't too sure that he had ever seen anything quite like what walked out of that bedroom. She was incredible in that off white dress and her black hair and clear blue eyes. 'Funny, I don't remember her eyes being so blue' he thought as he stared at her.

"Well, don't just stand there. Say something, please— anything." Terrie was really nervous, she hadn't had that kind of a response since she was in high school and won the Senior Class Queen Title. Now she wasn't sure whether that look she saw on Jacks face was good, bad or indifferent.

"I'm sorry Terrie, it's just I don't exactly know what to" Jack was literally saved by the bell. Telephone bell, that is, it started ringing. He saw Terrie jump and he signaled to her to keep quiet. He really wasn't too worried, because the only ones with this number were Nita, Clem and the two agents in San Francisco.

"Hello"

"Jack"

"Yeah, who's this?"

"This is Mac. Marty and I were just wondering if you two had made it and if our date was still on for tonight."

"Hi Mac. Yes, of course, we made it and yes we are still on for tonight. Is eight o'clock still okay with the two of you? Fine, see you then." Jack hung up the telephone and turned and looked at Terrie.

"Mac and Marty are the people we're meeting at the wharf tonight and the ones who set this apartment up for us. They were checking to see if we had made it—I forgot to call and let them know. Guess I'll get chastised for that—more than likely from Clem." Jack kind of said half to himself and half just into space. As he stood staring at Terrie he almost wished he was single. ' How come Clem saw her first? Hey Buddy, watch it you're married.' He chastised himself.

"The dress really is you Terrie. I just hope you like it as much as it looks good on you." Jack was trying to recoup from the site of her. The only thing he could think of right at this very minute was "WOW". No wonder Clem chose that dress. He always did choose the right thing for Jan to wear. Wonder if Clem ever plans on telling her that he chose the dress himself.

Terrie was watching Jack and now she was more embarrassed than he was.

"If you don't mind I think I'll go and change and look for something else to wear tonight. I really don't want to put anyone on the spot with this dress. Obviously, this dress is not me. Can you send it back to Nita and have her return it? She can say it was the wrong size, can't she." Terrie started towards the door when Jacks voice stopped her.

"Don't. I mean, I'm sorry, when I saw you I was seeing Nita and I didn't mean to upset you. Since you've never seen my wife, you don't know that she has black hair, just like you, just about the same length and I could just imagine what a knockout she'd be in that dress. I guess it just took me back. The dress looks very nice on you please wear it tonight."

"All right Jack, if that's the way you feel and you don't believe that it's too—ah—er—revealing or sexy." Terrie said as she started again towards the bedroom to take it off.

"Well, no, honest Terrie it looks great on you. Maybe we'll have to take your picture in it and send it to Clem and of course

Nita, so they can see how great it looks." Whew, I didn't think I get out of that one quite so easily, but why did I tell her Nita had black hair, when she's a blond. Oh well, that can be cleared up later. 'If Clem ever found out that I almost blew that and she was ready to send the dress back he'd have killed me. On the other hand so would have Nita. That is the first time I've seen someone that I considered more beautiful, or at least as pretty as my wife. I've got to watch myself. I don't know what happened, but I've got to admit, seeing her standing there in that dress, well she was gorgeous. I best be careful the way I describe her to Clem or he'll be on the next plane our here and that could blow everything wide open.'

'If Jack had that kind of reaction when he saw me in this dress' Terrie was thinking as she was taking it off 'I wonder what kind of reaction I would have received from Clem. Probably none at all. I don't know if he even knows what I really look like' she thought as she put her robe on and went back to the kitchen.

"Now, I'll finish that cup of coffee I poured awhile ago."

"Before I forget, I checked on the champagne in the refrigerator" Jack said as he turned and looked at Terrie, he saw a look of surprise on her face. "It should be just about right to have a glass when we get back from dinner. I hope that is all right with you."

"Of course, it's all right. I'm really not much of a champagne drinker anyway. It will probably be nice to sit and relax, with our feet up and toast whatever. Who knows if it isn't too chilly outside maybe we could sit on the patio for a little bit too."

"You know you were just teasing, about me not knowing what kind of a 'coffee freak' you are, but I really don't know a whole lot about you. Just the small amount that Clem told Nita and me. Maybe" Jack checked his watch, "Yes, we still have enough time, we should go sit in the living room and at least give a thumb nail sketch of what our likes and dislikes are in the way of food, at least, so we'll be prepared for tonight."

"Sounds like a sound idea to me. You lead and I'll follow" Terrie said laughing and heading into the living room.

"Let's see," She said as she curled up on the couch, being sure to tuck her feet up under her and pull her robe over her feet. She had done that since she was a little girl. She had no use for short robes; they had to be floor length so she could cover her feet when she sat down.

"Shall I go first" She asked Jack

"Be my guest" Jack said as he sat his cup on the end table and pushed the chair back into a more comfortable position.

"Well, I like coffee, black with my meal. I love shrimp cocktail, I like a half-inch to an inch steak, preferably sirloin or T-bone, medium rare. I usually have baked potato, butter only and a salad with ranch, house or Italian dressing when I have steak. I don't eat a whole lot and I don't always finish my meal, especially if I'm nervous or upset about something. I'll just pick and then request a doggy bag to take it home and warm up in the microwave. I don't like attention drawn to that fact either. I occasionally like a before dinner glass of red wine, preferably Lambrusco and I don't really care for white wine, that's why I don't drink much champagne. I do like a good burgundy or zinfandel tho. I rarely eat desserts, but I do like cherry pie, chocolate cake or fruit if the situation calls for dessert." Terrie took a deep breath and reached for her coffee. "Is there anything else I can brief you on—oh before I forget, I prefer the man, in this case, you, place my order with the waiter. A lot of men don't do that and to me that is part of being a 'good date'. I'm really not a bitch, it's just I like to be treated like a lady and for the last few years—well, I don't believe I have been—treated like a lady"

"I think you've pretty well covered things, for tonight, at least. Tomorrow we'll talk more about you and your likes and dislikes. You truly are a remarkable lady and I'd like to find out more about you. It would make my job a whole lot easier, you know." Jack said thinking about Clem and how he'd asked him to find out all he really could about this fantastic lady.

"Now, let's see about me." Jack said as he finished his coffee and set the cup back on the table. "I like my coffee black, with two spoons, level if you please, of sugar. No artificial sweeteners of any kind. Like you, I like my steaks medium rare, red wine, champagne, blue cheese on my salad and an occasional after dinner drink. I rarely eat fish, but if I'm at someone's house as their guest I won't refuse it. I like desserts if they are homemade, which I understand you make a pretty mean pecan pie. I hope you'll make me one sometime. I also like baked potatoes with my steak, with butter and sour cream on it. I guess that about does it for me, at least regarding tonight." Looking at his watch Jack said they should start getting ready.

Terrie agreed, "At least I don't have to take a shower." Giggled as she headed to her bedroom. She pulled out the hot rollers, plugged them in and got ready to roll her hair. 'How long has it been since I've had to get dressed up or even wanted to roll my hair or put make up on. Let's see the last time and the first time in a long time was to go to the Mart. Del never liked me in make up or for me to fuss over my hair or for that matter to put a dress on, he preferred me in blue jeans.' When the rollers were hot, Terrie started rolling her hair. She had a time at first getting the rollers in right so that they'd stay. 'It's been so long. Damn, that hurt' she said as she burnt her finger trying to fix the roller. 'One more time and then you're going into a pony tail and won't that look snazzy with the new dress.' Finally hair in rollers she started putting on her makeup. Eyebrows, whoops foundation first, lipstick, blush. Standing back she looked at her job and decided she had just the right amount of makeup. Now for the dress, hose first, then the hair. Smoothing the dress out she looked at herself in the mirror. 'Hmm wonder what Del would think if he saw me now. Tough buddy, you blew it.' Taking her hair out of the rollers, she started brushing it. Between brushing and combing she finally got the look she wanted of natural, not curly, waves, softness around the face. 'Now for the hair spray, I sure don't want this look going away in the San Francisco wind.' Shoes, where did she put those black sling heels, closet, nope, under the bed, that's where I've always hidden them. Sure enough close to the head of the bed, under the bed she found them. Slipping them on she again returned to the bathroom for a last look. 'Don't look to bad, even if I do say so myself. Whoops, I almost forgot my pearls and earrings. Now that's better now let's go see what the other 'half' says.' Terrie had heard Jack moving around, in the shower, his bedroom and she thought she just heard him heading for the living room. She stepped into the hallway and then into the living room where Jack was standing looking out the sliding glass doors.

"Ahem" Terrie cleared her throat, hoping she wouldn't have to say anything else to get Jack to turn around

"WOW" Is all that came out of Jack's mouth when he turned around and saw Terrie standing there.

"I take it you approve" Terrie said laughing

"Yes Ma'am" Jack said as he started for the kitchen. He was afraid to say too much. He thought she was beautiful with the dress on, but now, with the complete package, whew. "Close your eyes"

"What? Not again."

"Yes, just once more."

"OK, they're tight"

She heard footsteps, a door open and close, which she thought sounded like the refrigerator, but wasn't sure, then she heard Jack

"OK open your eyes."

Terrie did and again she was in total shock and disbelief. There before her eyes Jack was holding a beautiful pink rose corsage.

"This is strictly from Clem" Jack said, "He wanted you to have a corsage for your dress tonite. They were delivered while you were asleep. May I pin it on you?"

"Yes, please. It is absolutely beautiful and how typical of Clem," Thinking of her first rose from him.

"There is only one thing missing now."

"What's that? Everything looks pretty perfect, as do you sir." Terrie said as she finally got a good look at Jack in his black suit, powder blue shirt and white tie. "In fact, if you weren't married I'd ask you for a date." She chuckled

"Well, like I've told you many times today, my Nita thinks of every detail. We're supposed to be married; therefore you should be wearing a wedding ring. Clem remembered you no longer were wearing any rings, so here's a band for you to wear." He took her hand and slipped it on her ring finger. He hoped she wouldn't ask where it came from or how he got the right size. She didn't

"Man this must have set the bureau back a small fortune. Or was it confiscated somewhere along the way?" Terrie asked as she stared down at the most beautiful diamond band she'd ever seen.

"Don't worry. It didn't cost me anything and as long as it fits who cares."

"It's a perfect fit."

"Shall we go Mrs. Carrolle? Our public awaits." He said offering her his arm as they went out the door.

---

"Ooooh I ate too much" Terrie said holding her stomach. She and Jack had gotten back from San Francisco and dinner with his associate's changed their clothes and were sitting on the patio enjoying a glass of champagne. "I really do like your friends, they were fun to be with. I haven't gone out like that for so long I had almost forgotten how much fun you could have and Fisherman's Wharf was gorgeous. Do you suppose that we could go up there again sometime before we have to leave this area?"

"Sure I don't see why not we're close enough. I am so glad that you enjoyed yourself. We can't lose sight of the reason we are here tho'. You aren't out of the woods yet. Hopefully things will change, but until that time we still have to be careful. Tomorrow— the phone ringing interrupted Jack's words. Terry got a worried look on her face and Jack just motioned for her to be quiet, as usual.

"Hey Clem how are you and how are things going?" Jack said into the phone loud enough for Terrie to hear.

"I need to talk to you officially, but I want to talk to Terrie, so put her on first then I'll have her give me back to you."

"OK, I'll put her on. Hold on. Terrie, it's Clem and he'd like to talk to you."

"Hi Clem. How are you?" Terrie said into the receiver, hoping beyond all hope that the excitement of talking to him and how nervous she was didn't go through the telephone.

"I'm doing fine Terrie. More important how are you? Are you doing OK? Do you need anything, anything at all."

"I don't know of a thing that I need, but I do want to thank you for the corsage of pink roses you sent and ask that you convey my thanks to Nita for the beautiful dress. I'm not really sure how I looked to others, but I felt like a million dollars. I wore my pearls and earrings with it. Jack said I looked OK." Didn't really want to tell him Jack's true reaction. That's guy stuff. Terrie was thinking. "How are things going out your way? Any news on when I'll move and or to where?"

"Things are going slow, but they are moving along. I don't have an answer for you tonight on exactly when you'll be moved, but I am working on that and if it happens the way I'm planning, well, I think you'll be very pleased. No I'm not talking about you're being able to go home, at least not for a while. Oh, I did hire a couple, cleared by us, to live and run your farm while you're gone. The income from the farm will go into a bank account in a different name so that it can't be traced by anyone, even Del. I've warned the people about him, should he come snooping around and they know what to say. I'm doing all I can to protect you and of course your property while you're away."

"Clem, there is not enough thanks in this world to explain how I feel about you—er—ah I mean towards you and of course Nita, Jack and the bureau. Jack said he'd take a picture of me dressed like I was tonight and send it to you so you can see 'how good' I looked. Of course, it really belongs to Nita, but he said we'd send it to you and you could give it to Nita."

"That sounds great. I'll look forward to seeing, receiving it, and of course I'll share it with Nita. She's an OK gal. I think the world of those two."

"I can see why. I'm hoping to meet Nita someday."

"You will. It's great to talk to you our love to you, now may I speak to Jack for a few minutes?"

"My love to you—er—both and I'll put Jack back on the phone. Take care."

"Yeah Clem, what's going on?"

"We've run into a slight problem. It seems as tho' somehow the 'boys' got wind that Terrie's out west. Right now they've got 2 men going to Denver to look for her, so for pete's sake be careful. I'll alert you if I find out they're going farther west, or what they're up to, in the meantime kind of stay close to the apartment. Have you found anything out about Terrie?"

"I know she likes to be treated like a lady and prefers the man place her order when they eat in a restaurant. She likes her coffee black and seems to have some kind of, what was it she said, 'coffee freak'. In other words she does love her coffee. Oh yes, she prefers that it's fresh ground and her brand is Kona coffee from Hawaii. When I find out more I'll let you know. It's supposed to rain tomorrow so I'm going to suggest that we stay close in and discuss what we like and what are goals are. Should find stuff out for you then."

"Hey, I forgot to ask your opinion of Terrie in her dress. Was she as beautiful as I had said she'd be or what?"

"Clem, she was beautiful and I heard her tell you that I was taking a picture of her to send to you two, well I did take it up at the wharf tonight, but she doesn't know it. I'll get it developed and send to you. Let me know what's going on."

"I'll keep you advised when I hear something. I'll call again in a couple of days or so. Keep my girl safe." Clem said as he hung up the phone

"Boy, that was a long winded conversation. I thought I was going to have to drink this whole bottle by myself, but as you can see I did pour you some more. Share and share alike, or some such silly nonsense." Terry said as Jack came back out to the patio, handing him his glass. Terrie felt almost giddy, like some schoolgirl with a crush on her teacher. "It was great hearing from Clem. Is everything all right with him? I mean he said things were progressing. Was there anything else that he didn't want to worry me with?"

"No, just wanted to know when I was going to get my paperwork done on the other case I was working on before you came into my life. Nothing important. But as I was saying when I was rudely interrupted with his phone call. They say it is going to rain tomorrow. Why don't we just plan on staying close in and maybe relaxing in the living room and getting to know each other."?

"Sounds great to me. I guess I'm a little more tired than I realized, but what with every thing that's happened in the last 24-36 hours I guess that's understandable. Besides this champagne is starting to take effect and I'm about ready to fall asleep just sitting here. If you don't mind I think I'll go to bed."

"No, I don't mind in the least. I've got some of that paperwork to work on before I can go to bed. Good night Terrie, have a good sleep and I'll see you in the morning."

"Good night Jack." Terrie said as she stood and picked up the bottle and her glass "and Jack thanks a lot—for everything."

———

Terrie woke up and looked at her watch—10 A.M. 'Good heavens, when was the last time I slept past 6 o'clock in the morning—several years anyway' she thought. Terrie got out of bed, went in the bathroom, washed her face, and brushed her teeth returning to the bedroom to put on a pair of jeans and a sweatshirt. Having dressed she headed towards the kitchen.

"Good morning" She said to Jack as she walked towards the coffeepot.

"Good morning. Did you have a good night sleep?"

"Yes, as a matter of fact I did." She said pouring herself a cup of coffee and sitting down at the kitchen table, where she'd found Jack sitting. "I was just thinking I don't know when the last time was that I slept past 6 o'clock in the morning. Not even Saturday or Sunday's did I have the luxury of staying in bed past 6 o'clock."?

"You best watch that coffee. I made it the way I like it and some people don't like it quite so strong. Besides, it's been sitting in the pot for a couple of hours now."

"If it's too strong," she said as she took a sip "I'll get up and put some water, warm, in the cup, as I'm doing now. Are you sure it's only sat a couple of hours? You must like you're coffee spoon to be able to stand alone."

"How's about some breakfast. I cook up a mean bowl of Cheerios."

"Not right now thanks. But I'm the one who should be asking you if you'd like breakfast. Rather if I'd gotten up on time, I should be the one asking." Terrie laughed with a twinkle in her eye.

"Oh, that's OK I had breakfast earlier this morning. I had some calls to make; after all I am still a workingman, the reports to finish and my morning constitutional walk to take. It started to rain, really sprinkle on my way back from my walk. Anyway, when I got back I fixed myself a bowl of Cheerios, toast and a glass of juice."

"Good heavens, what time did you get up this morning?"

"Six" Jack said and laughed remembering what she'd just said about six o'clock

"Why didn't you wake me up? I would've fixed your breakfast for you while you were working on the reports and then we could have gone for a walk together."

"I'm sure you would have and the next time I'll see if I can get you up for a walk with me that early in the morning. Today, I just felt you needed your sleep. I did call Nita and passed on your thanks for everything and I also talked to Clem again and he said maybe he'd call you later this evening. That was if you didn't mind, his calling, I mean. I told him I thought we'd be home. We didn't have any special plans for dancing or the opera that I was aware."

"You are so bad. Where did you come up with the dancing etc.?"

"Just wanted to add some humor to this whole thing. That's all right isn't it?"

"Yeah, it's just Terrie's words just seem to trail off.

'Wonder what she's thinking about. It's sure starting to feel, rather sound like Nita was right—these two do care about each other, but their afraid to because of everything that's happening. Oh well, hopefully in the future they'll get together'

"If you don't mind, Terrie I think I'll go take a shower and get out of this sweat suit. Nita hates it when I run and then don't shower and change out of this 'stinky thing' she calls it."

"No, go right ahead. I see you bought a paper, so I'll just pour me some more coffee, take the paper and go curl up on the couch and read."

"OK, see you in a few."

————

"Boy do I feel better. Funny what a shower can do for you, isn't it." Jack said as he walked into the living room rubbing his hair with a towel. "Are you ready to start discussing your future?"

"Sure. Shall we sit in here or do you want to go back to the kitchen table?"

"It's more comfortable in here."

"OK." Terrie said as she laid the paper down and turned toward Jack, curling her feet up under her.

Jack went back into the bathroom putting his towel on the rack, stopped in his bedroom to pick up his briefcase and returned to the living room sitting down in the overstuffed chair.

"Have you read today's paper?" she asked as Jack came back into the living room.

"Yeah, at least most of it."

"Did you read the article about the San Francisco Hotel that reported that they had had a man leave or disappear with out paying his bill?"

"Yes, but it doesn't mean anything to me. At least not that I know of. Does it mean something to you?"

"I'm not sure. It could just be a coincidence, but his name is the same as one of Jay Ryan's business associates that I talked to several times. I also know that Mr. Deco came to San Francisco from Florida and the Bahamas when things got too hot for him in those places. I also know that when he moved out here he traveled a lot to China, primarily Hong Kong. I believe, he bought items that were then shipped back to the U.S. and Jay helped distribute them. I never knew for sure whether he, rather they, were bringing drugs into the states or not. I do know whatever it was or contained it brought them more money than just baubles would have brought. The word around the office at the time was that he was a supplier and the money was laundered through one of Jay's companies. Oh well, it's probably just a coincidence and I'm just paranoid believing that it could be the same man. I am surprised though that there are two Art Deco's that's such an unusual name. Now what do you have to tell me about where I'm going, etc."

"Terrie, I really am sorry that our agents took you with such a grain of salt when we talked to you the first time. You really are a walking encyclopedia about Jay Ryan and his activities. Maybe this isn't anything and maybe it is—but with everything else you've told us I think I'll call Mac and have he and Marty check this out. Why didn't you tell Clem about this before, or did you and he just forgot to mention it."

"No. I didn't tell Clem about it before because quite frankly I'd forgotten all about Mr. Deco. That's the way I am sometimes. Unless something triggers something else in my mind, I forget about it. Some of the things that happened, and there was so much I usually only think about what I'm being asked."

"Well, coincidence or not I think I'll call Mac and have them start checking on it. Who knows maybe this tangled weave will pull more things out." Jack said as he got up to call the operatives.

"Well that takes care of that. Mac is going to check into that tid bit of information and see what he comes up with. Now shall we get started."

————

"I didn't realize that there was or would be so much involved in planning my protection. You really do go to some lengths to protect your witnesses don't you." Terrie said, as she stretched and stood up. It had been almost three hours that Jack had sat and literally drawn her picture after picture of what the near future had in store for her.

"Yes, we do try to protect our witnesses, but like I told you, you have become a special project for us, so we're going with a little more in depth protection. Hey, it's stopped raining. Let's take a walk and get some lunch. You look like you could use some especially since you didn't eat any breakfast."

"I am hungry, but why go out when there's food here to eat?"

"Well, we've been holed up, so to speak for three hours, you haven't been out and besides I saw a real neat Chinese restaurant on my walk this morning that I'm wanting to try. You do like Chinese don't you?"

"I love Chinese food. I haven't had any since I was a florist in Florida and flew out here to meet with some growers. Let me change my shirt, I don't want to go out in this sweat shirt." Terrie said as she got up off the couch again and started towards the bedroom to change.

# CHAPTER 4

"Hey Lonnie, it's me Archie. The boss wants that I should call ya when we get settled. So here I am."

"Hello Archie. Glad you made it safe and sound. Is Morici there with you?"

"Yeah, he's here, ya wants that I should get him?"

"Yes, please" Lonnie said into the phone. He had never liked Archie, his crude ways, vulgar language; he didn't see what his brother saw in him. Morici, now that's different. Even being a cop at one time, he still was a pretty smart guy. Intelligent, manners, my kind of man. True Les had set him up so he'd have to leave the force, but that's OK, that really makes him one of us now.

"Yes, Lonnie. This is Morici. Did you want to talk to me?"

"Yes Morici. Don't let on to Archie what I'm about to tell you. OK?"

"Yeah, sure, I understand. Go on."

"Well, it seems as tho' our little chickadee flew the coup and went to a place just outside of Salt Lake. I'm trying to get the details a little clearer. I'll call you back in a couple of days, so don't stray too far away from the telephone."

"Hey, no problem. We can handle that."

"What's he saying" Archie kept asking and Morici kept signaling just a minute. Finally Morici said, "'Just a minute Archie let me get all the facts and then I'll tell you."

Lonnie told Morici he appreciated the cover up like that. "I knew you could be trusted and would understand what I was saying. Take care and I'll be back in touch."

"OK Lonnie will talk in a few days."

"Lonnie says that we should hit all of the little stores and gift shops up here tomorrow. He says that Terrie loves to go into the little shops. He said maybe we'd see her in one of them."

"Is that all he said?"

"Yes, why?"

"Well, he sure talked along time for just saying that."

"Oh, he was talking about having problems with some of his help. Guess he just needed someone to listen to him bitch." Morici said laughing. "Come on, let's unpack and then we'll go explore the restaurants and bars. Who knows maybe she'll even be in one of those. After all she's got to eat."

---

"Well, that was some of the best Chinese food that I've eaten since I was here the last time." Terrie said as she licked her lips and took Jack's offered arm.

"I told you I thought this place would have good food. As much as I have to eat out you kinda get to know, just by what the place looks like, what kind of food they're going to have." Uttered Jack as they started back towards the apartment.

The telephone was ringing as Jack was unlocking the door.

"Hold on, keep ringing, I'll be there in a minute." Jack yelled as he tried to catch the phone.

"Hello" he said breathless

"What took you so long?"

"Hey Mac, how you doing? Terrie and I walked down to a neighborhood Chinese restaurant and had a bite to eat."

"I hope it was good, so many of them down where you are aren't. I've got some news. Good or bad you figure it out."

"The food was delicious and what's the news?"

"It seems as tho' your girlfriend hit it right on the money.

Now the police are trying to decide if they want to risk going into the Bay to find Mr. Deco's body. We have learned through an informant that Deco did, in fact, deal in drugs in a mighty big way, at least that's the way our party tells it. Bringing stuff in out of Hong Kong he was pretty sure. We were also told that Deco moved out here 'cause it got too hot for him back east. You can tell your girlfriend and see if she knows anything else. This might just be the break that we've been looking for, now if we can just find out the names in Hong Kong.

I'll keep in touch and let you know if we find anything else out. Chow!"

"Well, that must have been interesting, you didn't say a word after what news, not even good bye.

"Well, that was Mac and it seems as if they've identified the man as 'your' Art Deco. Now the San Francisco P.D. are trying to decide whether they want to go swimming in the bay or not. Is there anything else you can remember about this Deco guy that you didn't mention earlier?"

"Let me think about it for a few minutes. Maybe I can come up with something. If I could think of something to associate it with—let me think." She said as she headed towards the living room to take up residency on the couch, as she had so many times in the last few weeks. She lit a cigarette, leaned her head back against the couch and looked up at the ceiling.

Jack had followed Terrie into the living room and was sitting quietly in the chair next to the couch waiting for her to say something. He respected the fact that she was thinking and he didn't want to break whatever spell she was into.

"Finally Terrie spoke. "I remember, but I think I may have told Clem. Art wrote a book that he was extremely proud of, to the extent, that he brought into the office enough books for everyone. The subject was drugs and the dealing in them and how easy it was to get them and distribute them. Why the government didn't arrest him then with the book I never understood, but I guess that comes under freedom of speech now, doesn't it? Funny tho' I thought he was killed a few years back." She said looking at Jack.

"Yes, Terrie. They'd have a heckuva time trying to prove that he was talking, rather telling first hand how to do it. That's what makes our job so difficult. I've seen it happen so many times. We think we've an iron glad case, only for the judge either to throw it out of court or just 'smack' the hands of the guilty and let them go. That's why Clem is so adamant that we nail this case against Les and all of them thoroughly. We don't want them getting their hands smacked and turned back on the streets. I hope you can understand that."

"I do understand Jack, it's just reliving all that has happened, well, I just hope and pray it's not for nothing. I really don't want to spend the rest of my life walking alone."

"Nor do we want that for you Terrie. That's why we have to be so accurate and air tight with everything regarding this case. There may be times that you'll be ready to shoot me for asking the same questions over and over again. I just have to make sure that we've got every little tidbit of information and we're not leaving anything out. What made you think that this Deco guy was killed a few years back?"

"Well, Jay came in one morning early at the office and when I asked him what he was doing in so early he claimed to have things to do. Then he said that Art Deco; at least that's who I thought he said, was dead. When I asked him if he wanted me to send flowers, he just laughed and said 'I don't think they can deliver them to San Francisco Bay.' I don't know Jack, so much has happened in such a short span of time that that conversation could have taken place just last week.

---

"How many more of these damn stores do we have to go into?" Archie asked Morici as they were leaving the 5th store that they'd been into.

"I think that's enough for today. We'll head back to the lodge and rest for a while and then think about dinner. I don't know about you, but that sandwich I had a while ago didn't do too much for me. I think we should have a nice steak dinner in the lodge's restaurant. It sure smelled good when we went by it on our way out. How's that sound to you?" Morici knew that Archie was tired of traipsing in and out of stores and he hated the cold weather, but Morici told Lonnie that he'd pretend they were looking for Terrie, at least until he called.

"That sounds damn good. I can get out of these heavy clothes and the cold. What do people enjoy about being out where you have to wear so damn many clothes that you can hardly move. They really think they're having a good time, do they? That steak sounds good too. I haven't had a good steak for so long I'm not sure what it tastes like. A couple of brews to go along with it wouldn't hurt either."

"I just wish we'd seen Terrie. It'd make this job a lot easier, 'cause then we could go back to Atlanta. According to the weather man they're having a real mild January."

"It figures. Mild in Atlanta and I'm up here freezing my balls off."

Morici winced at Archie's mouth. He just couldn't understand Les's attitude regarding Archie. It was as if Les owed him something. 'Guess I'll try to find out what it is. Maybe if he gets a few beers in him, he'll talk openly. All I can do is try. Can't appear too nosy tho' don't need him telling Les I was asking questions. That might cause some problems.'

The two men braced the wind towards the lodge. It seemed to the two of them that the wind had really picked up since they'd left a few hours earlier.

"Brrrrr. Man am I glad to get back here in the room. Turn the heat up will ya Morici."

"It's registering 80 degrees in here Arch. How much warmer do you need it?" Morici did not like a hot apartment and this was too hot for him. 'I'll wait until he's asleep and then I'll turn the thermostat down a few degrees 72 should do it. By morning he'll be used to it, maybe. If not then I can claim innocence and shove it back to 80.'

"It just doesn't seem too warm in here. Maybe if I get out of some of these clothes and relax I'll feel better." Archie said as he started taking off layers of winter clothes.

"How about me walking down to the little coffee shop, here in the lodge and getting a couple cups of coffee and maybe a piece of pie or rolls or something."

"Sure Morici that sounds good, even if I don't really care much for pies and all. While you're gone I'll take a nice hot shower, maybe that'll help warm me up too."

Morici took the room key, said he'd be back shortly and closed the door. Down in the lobby he spotted a telephone. 'Just what I need and no one will be the wiser.' He thought as he headed for it.

"Two large coffee's and two pieces of your apple pie to go please." Morici asked for from the pretty waitress. 'I'll bet she goes to school around here.' He thought as he watched the waitress box the pie and put lids on the cups.

"I put extra sugar, cream and stirrers in the bag. I also gave you extra forks, sometimes these things tend to break." She said as she handed Morici the bags over the top of the counter.

"Hey, thanks a lot. I appreciate that, don't like to eat my pie with my fingers if I can help it."

"Archie, I'm back." Morici said as he slammed the door.

"Be out in a minute." Archie opened the bathroom door, walked out with a towel around his waist and steam rolling out with him. "Now that's what I call a shower. Man the water was hot and it felt so good."

"Your coffee and pie are there on the table. I didn't know whether you liked apple or not, but that's what I got. Hope it's OK. Cream and sugar and the stirrers are right there with it."

"Hey, this looks like the pie my Mom used to make. Hell it's the only kind of pie I like." Taking a bite of the pie he says, "This is almost as good as my Mom's too. Thanks Morici this hits the spot. Next time you can leave the cream and sugar there, I don't use either one. Just like it hot and black."

"Good. I'll remember that 'cause that's the way I like my coffee. Don't want to mess up that good coffee taste." He said as he took another sip and finished his pie. Damn that was good pie, now if they're meals are as good as this pie, I'll feel like I'm in seventh heaven."

Just about that time the phone rang. Since Morici was the closes one to it he answer it. Wondering who had this number. Lonnie said a couple of days.

"Hello" he answered

"Morici, is that you?"

"Yeah. Who's this?"

"It's Lonnie. Plans have changed. You two are to leave tomorrow on a noon flight to Salt Lake. You can pick your tickets up at the ticket counter; they'll be in your name. You'll be staying at a lodge in a small burg called Huntsville. It's just outside of Ogden, which is just north of Salt Lake. You take the road out of Salt Lake towards Ogden and you'll see the road signs that'll take you to Huntsville. The name of the place is Huntsville Lodge. I've got your reservation confirmation numbers for both the car; it's at Economy, and the one for the Lodge. Have you got a pencil and paper?"

"Hold on and I'll get some."

"Who's on the phone?"

"It's Lonnie. I'll tell you all about it when I hang up."

"OK Lonnie shoot."

"For the car it's 41E78294320 and for the lodge it's HL1983. I'll wire you more money after you call me from the lodge when you get there. I'll also give you the low down on our subject at that time. Be careful, there appears to be a storm heading your way."

"OK. We'll leave here tomorrow morning. I'll call you when we get there." Morici said and hung up.

"Get where? Ya mean we're leavin here so soon? Please tell me we're going home."

"Huntsville, Utah, we're catching a plane out of Denver at noon tomorrow and no we're not going home, at least not just yet."

"Damn, more cold weather. Will I ever see the warm out doors again?" Archie said with a woeful moan.

"Quit worrying about it and get dressed. It is now 7 and I'm starving."

"Hey, where did the time go? It was just about 3 when we got back here."

"It's steak time." Morici said getting impatient with Archie

"OK, OK I'll be out in a minute." Archie said as he grabbed clean clothes and headed towards the bathroom.

---

"I think that's enough for now." Jack said as he looked at Terrie. 'She really was getting tired of all of this. He had to watch his step so that she didn't shut down and not be able to remember anything.' "I'll tell you what. It's 4 o'clock, lets see if "Murder She Wrote" is on. That's one show I really enjoy. It's what I call a no brainer. You can watch the acting and know almost from the start who did what to whom, but it doesn't make any difference 'cause that actress is so beautiful who cares." Jack said getting up to turn TV on.

"I agree with you. I tried never to miss it when I was home. It's some kind of entertainment." Terrie said as she stood and headed for the kitchen. "How's about splitting a Pepsi with me? I'm not thirsty enough for a whole one."

"Sounds good to me. You might bring the pretzels back in with you too. Like to munch while I watch her show."

"Won't spoil your appetite will it?"

"Nope. But since you brought up dinner, what are we having?"

"Something very simple tonight. Grilled steaks, baked potatoes and a salad. How does that sound to you?"

"Sounds great. I'm really not that hungry, so maybe you could plan on dinner around 8ish." Jack grinned. He said that to Nita a lot and she always came back with some smart remark.

"Hey, I'm not some short order cook. But I'll see what I can do." Terry quipped from the kitchen.

"Man you sound just like Nita. She always had some kind of smart remark to make when I said that to her." He said grinning reaching up taking his drink and pretzels from her.

"Hush, here comes Jessica." Terrie said laughing

———

"Archie, will you hurry the hell up. We're going to be late for our flight." Morici said with impatience. 'It takes that man forever.' He thought looking out the window. "Oh great!" he said out loud

"What's the matter Morici?" Archie asked as he put his shaving kit inside of his suitcase.

"Nothing, other than the fact it looks like we got a dusting of snow last night."

"Boy will I ever be glad to get back down south. Where'd you say we were going?"

"We're headed to Salt Lake and a little burg called Huntsville. Lonnie says it's just outside of Ogden, which is just north of Salt Lake. Come on let's go. I don't exactly relish driving on slick roads. We've only got about an hour and a half to get there, turn in our car and get our tickets."

"Hell, Morici, it's only about a forty five minute drive from here. We should have plenty of time."

Morici had already put his suitcases in the car and was waiting for Archie to finish packing his stuff. For someone that knows nothing about traveling or winter, he's brought enough crap to live in the Arctic for a year.

"Arch, how come you brought all this stuff."?

"I don't like to wear the same thing twice, unless it's been washed, and I didn't know when we'd get to a laundromat, of if they even had things like that out here." He said closing and locking his suitcases. "OK, I'm ready. Let's go"

Morici checked around the room to make sure they hadn't left anything, closed and locked the door.

"Here are the car keys. Go on and put your stuff in it and I'll meet you out front. I'll check us out."

"OK. I'll pick you up right out front, but if it's OK with you, I'll let you drive to the airport. These mountains and snow driving don't mix with me."

'God, what a sheltered life he must have led. I don't know anyplace back east, except maybe Florida, where you don't have to drive snow covered streets in the winter time.' Morici thought as he headed for the lobby. 'At least it's a bright sun shiny day. Just so we get out of here before a storm really hits and leaves us stranded.' He thought as he headed for the car.

———

"Well, at least we got here, in spite of the slippery roads, with a few minutes to spare." Morici said as they headed towards the terminal to pick up their tickets.

"Yeah, Morici, that was some kind of drivin' you did. I know I couldn't have gotten down that mountain like you did. I'd been slippin' and sliddin' all over the place."

"May I help you gentlemen?" the ticket agent asked

"Yes ma'am, my name is Morici and we were to pick up tickets for Salt Lake."

"Yes, Mr. Morici I see your reservation. I'll get them for you, how many bags will you be checking through?"

"Three for Mr. Archie and two for me." Morici replied

"There you are sir, your baggage claims are stapled inside here" she said pointing to them "and here are your boarding passes." She said handing Morici the folders. "Have a good flight and thank you for flying Continental."

---

"Well, just settle back Arch, have a drink and enjoy this short flight to Salt Lake." Morici said as he looked out the window. 'Boy, I sure don't like the looks of that sky. Those clouds reek of snow. Sure hope the pilot gets this baby out of here shortly. I know they're going to have a blizzard. Like in the spring when you can smell the rain, but it isn't raining yet, well, I can smell the snow. Not a good sign.' He thought.

Finally the plane started taxiing down the runway. Once they were airborne Morici started relaxing. Archie had already ordered two drinks, so he wasn't going to be a problem. The flight wasn't long only about an hour or so, but if Arch hadn't had a drink he was a miserable flyer. 'Well,' Morici thought 'wonder what we're going to find in Utah. Lonnie seemed a little disturbed about the information, like he really wasn't sure she was there, but he knew she wasn't in Denver, so he had to do something. Wonder where he's getting his information. Doubt that it's from Doug, they've kept him pretty much under raps since the Atlanta thing. That was so stupid, why would he use a house phone. Nothing is that urgent that you can't wait until you can get to an outside phone. Especially a pay phone—they can't be bugged.'

# CHAPTER 5

"Terrie, why don't you and I have some coffee in the living room" Jack said as he pushed himself away from the dinner table.

"Sounds good to me. You go on in, I'll straighten up the kitchen and bring a fresh pot in, how's that."

"I'll help" Jack volunteered "Are you ready to plunge into some really heavy discussions?"

"Yeah, I guess so." Terrie answered with a sign and under her breath said 'I guess this peace and quiet and not thinking about things couldn't last forever.'

"What'd you say?" Jack asked

"Oh, nothing. Just muttering to myself, as per usual." She finished wiping the table, stove and refrigerator. She always cleaned exceptionally when she was worried, upset, nervous or scared. This time she was all of them. She made a fresh pot of coffee and stood staring at the coffee dripping. "What more do they want out of me? What else can I tell them? Well, maybe lots more. I really think I told Chris and Clem all they needed to get these guys behind bars, but—. Guess I have to play pete and repete, so they know that I'm telling the truth. They remind me of a man I knew a long time ago, he had to dot the i's and cross his t's, so to speak. Spending all this money to keep me safe, well that's what they get for not listening to me the first time. When will this nightmare ever end—words that would haunt Terrie for sometime to come.

"The coffee is brewing. Why don't you go on into the living room and I'll bring it in when it's finished. And Jack, thanks for helping with the dishes."

"That's OK. I enjoy helping out when I can."

While Terrie was waiting for the coffee to finish brewing Jack went to his bedroom and got his attaché' case and took it into the living room where he began setting papers, notebooks and his tape recorder up on the end table and coffee table. The last thing he wanted was to break Terrie's trend of thought once she started talking. Checking everything over once again to make sure he had everything.

"Here, I'll take that, you sit down and I'll pour. That's the least I can do after that fantastic dinner you fixed. Clem bragged about that Thanksgiving dinner and I told him" Jack started to laugh "One meal a good cook doesn't make, but now I'll have to tell him you really are a good cook." Jack was sure that this menial talk sounded like bull shit, and maybe it was, but she was a good cook and besides he and Clem had talked about her spirits and self confidence were both gone. Anything Jack could do to bring them back would be great. One of the things they had decided on was the discussion that Jack was about to have with Terrie, followed by a telephone call, by accident of course, from Clem, maybe that would help where everything else failed.

Jack poured the coffee and handed Terrie hers, taking a sip of his he sat down in the chair, placed his cup back on the tray and reached for the tape recorder.

"Well now, young lady, this is called getting down to brass tacks." Jack said as he reached for the tape recorder. "Seriously Terrie, we've been here since January, it's now the 28th of March and we've had very few discussions about why or how we, you, got to this point. Now seems to be the time to try and sort through some of the stuff in your head. OK?" Jack finished and reached for a cigarette and his coffee. Jack was trying to quit cigarettes, in fact, this was the first one he'd had since arriving in California, but he was too apprehensive for just his pipe—got to have something stronger right now, he reasoned with himself.

"I didn't know you smoked, Jack. Well, other than the pipe I've seen you light a few times. I love a pipe. Clem smokes one too, is that an agents prerequisite?" Terrie laughed and took another sip of her coffee.

"I'm trying to quit, but I just felt like lighting one for a change and no smoking a pipe isn't a prerequisite." Jack said laughing.

"OK Jack, where do we begin, ah start?"

"Well—let's see—would it be easier for you if I asked questions, or would you like to just start talking?" Jack poured some more coffee being careful not to spill any this time; it seems he had a habit of spilling it every time he poured. He was sure that she would say questions, but after being with her these couple of months he also knew that she would eventually go out on her own and tell 'the story'.

"Questions" Terrie answered. She was fidgeting with her lighter, turning it over and over in her hand. She was getting very nervous and her stomach was starting to do flip-flops. This used to happen a lot when she thought or talked about Jay and the past. 'It'd sure be easier if Clem were doing the questioning, he knows so much of this I wouldn't have to keep repeating everything. I know they have to have someone other than Clem ask these questions to be sure my stories jive.'

"OK. We know about the bank, we checked out the guy who died in San Francisco and you were right on target—he was murdered and we now have that investigation going on, much to the chagrin of the San Francisco police. Now do you know if Jay did any laundering of money?" Jack and Clem had worked out a list of questions for Jack to start with, kind of like a fishing expedition. Jack really had no knowledge of what or how much Terrie knew. Clem never shared that with him, however, even Jack realized that this lady sitting here must know a lot or at least someone thinks she does, or the 'boys' wouldn't be trying to get rid of her. Jack watched Terrie drinking her coffee. Two full months plus they'd lived here as man and wife and he'd learned not to push Terrie into telling him what all she might know about Jay's business dealings. Jack knew that what with the information that Clem had, he had to get as much of her knowledge out of her as he could if they were ever going to get these guys to trial. Oh he'd heard that they had a couple of surprise witnesses, but Clem said he didn't want to jeopardize their lives again if he could keep from it. 'Wonder who they are' Jack also couldn't get over the fact of how adamant Clem was about 'hanging' these guys. What were Clem's words 'worse than the scum of the earth' Terrie's voice startled Jack

"I guess now's as good a time as any what's the first question?" Terrie said pouring both she and Jack some more coffee. 'Wonder if he's going to ruin the tape again' she thought as she remembered their last attempt at this.

"OK. Let's set up the tape recorder. Hopefully I won't miss anything this time." Jack laughed nervously. He'd goofed during their previous session and lost 45 minutes of her story because he forgot to turn the tape over. He'd been so fascinated with her accounting that he just forgot the tape recorder was running.

Terrie had been relatively quiet since dinner when Jack told her about the conversation with Clem as to whether the two of them, she and Jack had discussed anything more about what she knew. She knew it was not a question of how much more she should tell Jack, but where she should start this time and if she could keep her thoughts in order and not jump around like she did before. Her kids had always teased her about a three-hour lecture that if she hadn't steered off course a few times would've only taken about 30 minutes. Seriously she thought, I hope Jack keeps me at least close on the right track this time plus remembers to turn the tape over.

"Well" Jack said as he rewound the tape "Let's check it out" Finding that the sound was acceptable Jack looked at her and said "It's OK shall we go for it?"

"Question" Terrie replied

"How did the money finders get into Jay?"

"Well, Les and 'the boys', brought in the money finders, at least that's what Jay called them. All of this was very subtle at first and yet very fast. Just a matter of a few months and they had their hooks into Jay and of course his businesses." Terrie stopped put her cigarette out and reached for her coffee, turning the cup slowly in her hands, staring down in to the cup like it was a crystal ball. "You see Jay had run the gamut to the hilt of playing entrepreneur, jetting all over the world, buying companies that were in financial trouble, starting up more companies of his own, like the last one he started with Vince Carnelli. That one was buying oil in one country, getting it out into international waters and selling it to other countries. That one I ran until the bankruptcy boys came and shut us down. Jay was spending the mother companies money like there was no tomorrow, like it would always be there time and again I'd go slamming into his office and tell him he couldn't go on spending money and he had to face reality and he'd just look at me, smile and say 'I know, face reality, but now I need the papers on the coal mine in Kentucky, for instance. That stupid coal mine. He was told more than once that that mine was coaled out and that it should be closed, but he believed, in spite of the report my brother gave him, that he should keep it going. His attorneys told him he could still get his workers to produce more coal out of it. Because of all his spending of company money it was going out faster than we could make it." Terrie stood up, motioned for Jack to turn the machine off. "I've got to go to the restroom and I didn't want that tidbit known by everyone," she said laughing.

While she was gone Jack went to the kitchen and made another pot of coffee. At least we then have a choice of drinks. I like a little variety in my liquids.

"Fresh coffee is brewing." Jack told her as she again sat on the couch and brought her feet up underneath her. 'Hmm that reminds me of a security blanket. It's like she feels safer or protected in someway.'

"Sounds good. Now where was I?" she asked as Jack ran the tape backwards a short bit, and started it up again, so she could hear what she had said.

"Thanks. Anyway some of his 'side' (she made quotation marks with her fingers) companies were brokers, for instance he'd buy something say from a seller in some foreign country, bring it to this country to resell. Yes that sounds legit, but in essence what he was doing was bringing drugs in 'legally' stashed in whatever he'd just bought. He was slick, you could never prove that, about the drugs I mean, but that's what I found out much later in my employ. But that's getting off the track. The name 'money finders' came from Jay that's what he called them. He said they were to find him money, so they were the 'money finders'. Anyway, Jay's major company, like I said was feeling the financial crunch. The accountants were able to 'sell' some of the contracts to legitimate moneylenders, but those sources finally began to run out. Everybody, banks, lending institutions, even the ones with high interest rates, ran out of money for him. They flat out were tired of his bullshit, pardon the expression, but it was the truth. I had a bonding company, for instance, that was willing to bond me and help me out financially if I would run the company for one year, providing Jay would stay out of the business for one year. Oh he could draw his salary, but he had to stay out of the building and business. Do you think he'd do it? NO. He was extremely chauvinistic and under no circumstances was a female going to run his company. After he found that out, he sold his mother's bearer bonds and closed out his kid's trust funds. He even had gotten a hold of some German war bonds and tried to sell them. I never heard whether he did or not. All avenues were closed to him. No place was left. I remember one time when I went into his office and he was crying, I closed the office door and went to a chair across the desk from him and sat down."

Terrie was staring out the sliding glass doors and all of a sudden she was back in Jay's office.

*After sitting quietly for a few minutes across the desk from Jay Terrie broke the silence. "Is there anything we can do to save the company?" she asked Jay*

*Terrie had run or had a hand in the running of most of Jay's companies and she too saw the handwriting on the wall. She too was frustrated. She'd had several meetings with the accountants, but it always came back to stopping Jay and his spending.*

*Jay, startled, looked up as tho' he wasn't aware that anyone else was in the room. Looking at Terrie he managed one of his ever-cunning smiles, opened his desk draw, took out a deck of cards and started playing solitaire. This was something he had done for as long as she could remember. If he had an unsolveable problem or was waiting for what he called a money call solitaire.*

*"Do you know" Jay said as he laid out the cards "I haven't won this game for a long time—I'm due!*

*"Jay, you can't rely on the winning of a solitaire game for solving the problems at hand. She really was still upset that he wouldn't step aside and let her run the company*

*"I'm not. It's helping to clear my mind. Go get Les Rudicio on the phone for me. I don't care where he is or what kind of a meeting he's in, get him now! If anybody can find me money, he can."*

*Terrie got up from the chair and went back to her office. She knew trying to talk Jay out of contacting Les was fruitless. She'd been warned a long time ago that Les was bad news. Jay had gotten mixed up with him a long time ago and from all Terrie could learn Les was Mafia and the Feds had been trying to nail him for something or other. She and Candy had had many discussions about this man and a man named Vince, from Philadelphia. She hopefully thought that these men were totally out of Jay's life, but obviously not when he just instructed her to find Les.*

*"Guess what Candy" Terrie said as she slammed her shorthand notebook down on her desk and dropped down in her chair."*

*"What's up?" Candy asked as she slid her chair back away from the phone console and looked in at Terrie*

*"Jay just told me to find Les. Can you believe that? Honest to God Candy, I'm scared. What's next? We don't need his kind around here" Terrie rushed on as she started looking through the phone files.*

*"Shit" Candy whispered as she got up from her chair and walked into Terrie's office. "What are you going to do?"*

*"What can I do—Try and find Les" Terrie answered shrugging her shoulders and looking at Candy in disgust. Terrie picked up the old phone file and pulled Les' card out.*

*"Well, shit, wouldn't you know it, it's still in this old phone file. I*

*would've thought that this stuff would've been thrown away long before
I came here; especially Les' number, if he was as bad as everyone says."*

*"No, when Judy was fired by Jay's wife, Sharon, the things were
taken out and off of her desk and put in a box just like you found them.
According to Sharon, Jay was not to have another secretary and he
didn't until you proved yourself to Sharon." Candy said*

*"Lucky me. But I wasn't hired initially to be Jay's secretary, as you
remember. What the hell did Sharon have to do with things? Just rheto-
ric, you don't even have to answer that. Guess I best start trying to find
Les" Terrie said as she reached for the telephone.*

"Then that's when Les and Rudy and the rest of the boys
came into the picture as a permanent/temporary fixture?" Jack asked
bringing Terrie back to his time and place.

"Huh! Sorry about that Jack. I guess I was back at Ryan's for a
while. Let me see, you ask is that when Les and all came into the
picture, well basically yes. Quite frankly everyone was so intertwined
that now I wonder how I managed to keep everyone straight, and
realize how powerful each of these people were without a script.
I'm not sure I did realize until we had to move." Her thoughts
drifting away again.

"Stay with me Terrie, don't drift away again." Jack said nudging
her. "Would you like some coffee or take a break right about now."
He thoughtfully asked.

"No, I'm fine. I will take some more coffee tho," she said as she
lit another cigarette. "Anyway, one example of Les was he told Jay
that he had a Supreme Court Judge on his payroll and that this
man had a money lending business down south and he knew that
this guy could get Jay all of the money he needed. Of course, there
were just a couple of strings, pay Les's salary as long as he was
associated with the company and of course pay a large fee to the
judge's company to borrow the money. Well, of course the mother
company paid and paid. We paid for everyone's salary that Les
wanted to bring in and of course the company collateral was never
good or large enough to loan Jay or the company any money."

"Let me stop you for a minute. I'm having a little bit of a problem understanding how Les's involvement, like you just described, caused Jay or anyone else to loose their business."

"I know it sounds confusing how any one man or a few men could cost people their businesses. Let me see if I can simplify this before I go on." Terrie stopped and thought a minute, like she was getting her thoughts or words in order. "These men find company or companies that are destitute for money. They go in, promising the moon, draw large company salaries, after all you can't expect them to 'work' for free, and bottom line, as soon as all of the money is gone out of the company, and I do mean ALL, and the company is going bankrupt—they disappear—saying they're sorry things didn't work out. Now do you kind of understand?"

"Yes, I think I'm getting a picture of the scam now."

"Well, one of the ways, that they pulled this off, was to convince Jay that his one company was the perfect company to launder drug money. That laundering became so bad that my brother quit his top-paying job as the accountant for that company, left the state and took up a totally different profession just to hide his identity, in order to protect himself. As his life was threatened too. See what I meant when I said everything was so entwined. It's hard to try and discuss the Mafia, the money finders and not include the drug deals." Terrie said as she stood up and stretched then walked to the sliding glass doors. Turning around looking at Jack she slowly walked back to the couch and sat down.

"Yah know, I really believed that Jay was a smart business man. I never believed that he was stupid. I'd known him since high school. I really thought he was a smart business man." She said emphasizing the words thought and smart. "That is not until I was threatened. It was about a year before everything went to hell— a man, Kyle Waters, by name, came to the front of my desk one night. I was working late for Jay and was trying to finish what I was typing. I looked up and saw him standing there and asked him what I could do for him. He looked down at me and said something to the effect that what I was doing for Jay was not to be discussed with anyone, either here in the company or at home with my family. It was strictly confidential. I told him I realized that and he said, and I'll never forget the look on his face, don't forget it. We know where you live, what your kids look like and where they go to school. We do have ways of silencing you. Then I started really wondering and trying to make 2 and 2 add up to 4. Then I started realizing how stupid I was to stay there working, but of course if you've never been put in that kind of a position you don't or couldn't understand why anybody would continue working at a place like that. That was part of Del's problem— Why didn't I quit. I couldn't tell him or anybody about the threat. I knew if I quit, they'd carry it out for fear I would talk. Look what's happened to me now. They are carrying out their threats to some extent. The only problem is they can't find me, thanks to all of you, and they don't know where my kids are. Both have graduated from school, one is in the air force and the other one is married. It was as if I was functioning daily, but wasn't really aware of what I knew or what was going on around me. It really sounds strange telling about it now, but after Kyle said that to me. I was no longer afraid for just my self, but my kids, my husband and my brother. This was a very strange kind of fear. Actually I guess it was more like what I've heard people say about an 'out of body' experience. It really wasn't until just this past year, talking to Chris about his Uncle Jay, that I truly, honest to God, began to realize what really had been happening and who the players were. I know this sounds crazy, but it's the truth." Terrie said, as she leaned over, and picked up her coffee cup staring down into the bottom of an empty cup. Putting the cup down she reached over and poured some coffee for her and added some to Jack's cup.

"Would you like to stop for awhile?"

"No, not right now. Not while I've got my thoughts going, let's see where was I—Oh yes, I was explaining how I just existed. I was too frightened to quit and I guess I was just too nosy to want to know what could happen next. I guess you could blame my nose on this whole mess. Well, after Kyle told me that I finished the report I was doing for all of them. Basically the report was how this group of men: Les, Kyle, Matt, Nick, Jay and a couple others were going to take the employees pension money and really out and out steal it and buy some kind of foreign bonds. I'm not sure what all, but bottom line they were stealing our money. Shortly after I did that report something happened with or to one of the contacts here in California, and I don't remember what, but that whole plan fell through. Shortly after that the bank deal came along and they really didn't need the money. Or so they figured anyway. You know about the bank scam, but from then until March or April of 86 things are kind of fuzzy. If you or anyone could ask me questions about that time, specific ones, that is, maybe I could remember things. To sit here and try to remember—it's just a mess of things.

"In other words you remember kind of like word association?" Jack said. Stopping to put another new tape into the machine.

"Yes, that's kind of like it. Del used to say I had a mind like a steel trap. If you want to know something don't press me—just ask and give me a couple of minutes or so and I probably could even tell you what you were wearing at the time." Terrie laughed as she opened another pack of cigarettes, lighting one and watching the smoke drift towards the ceiling. "I'm not quite that good, but—

Jack laughed. "Well, at least you haven't lost your sense of humor" He was glad she'd finally found something to laugh about. He'd sat for the last 3, almost 4 hours and watched the tears roll down her cheeks. The chain smoking was just as bad. Her nerves were shot.

"Hey it's almost 10 o'clock. Why don't we walk down to that little ice cream parlor and get a sundae or a shake or something. I think I saw their sign when I was walking this morning and they're open until 11 on week nights and midnight Friday and Saturday." Jack couldn't understand why Clem hadn't called. That was all planned. Something's coming down I can feel it. "Well what'd you say? Shall we stroll?" Jack said as he stood up and offered her his arm.

"Give me a minute to wash my face off and I'll be right with you." Terrie was both physically and mentally exhausted. Only she knew she'd only scratched the surface of the information Jack wanted and needed. The same information that she'd given Chris and Clem. 'I just hope that I can see this all the way through and give them enough to put all those men away.'

"They have the best ice cream. I'm glad you suggested it." Terrie said as Jack unlocked the front door. "How come, every time we go out when we get back here the phones ringing." She said as Jack hurried towards the phone.

"Hello"

"Don't let Terrie know it's me." Clem said into the phone. "I'll call her tomorrow after I get things sorted out."

"Sure Mac. What else is knew?"

Terrie, finding out it was Mac went into her bedroom, to get ready for bed. When she came out Jack was putting water on for hot tea.

"Thought after that ice cream, maybe you'd be interested in a cup of hot tea. That sounded better to me than coffee at this time of night." Jack found himself stammering. He couldn't let on to Terrie that it was Clem, she'd been hurt that he didn't want to talk to her. 'Since I said Mac, now I have to come up with something he wanted, that we hadn't covered yet—dinner date for later in the week. That sounds good and I can pass it off, to some pressing business, if they can't go. I can always reach them tomorrow morning and set it up.'

"Sounds good. I'm still a little chilled from the ice cream." Terrie said as she sat down at the kitchen table. She had gone in and put on her flannel nightgown, robe and fuzzy slippers. "Did Mac have any more news about Mr. Deco?"

"No. He was calling to see if we wanted to have dinner again, later this week. I told him I'd get back with him after I talked to you." Jack lied. He hated having to lie to Terrie, but after what Clem had said he didn't want to scare her by telling her the truth. That would come out in the next day or two.

Ladies and Gentlemen, may I have your attention. The pilot just notified us that we are on our final approach to Salt Lake City International. As you can see the pilot has turned on the No Smoking Sign and also the Fasten Seat Belt signs. Please extinguish all cigarettes, put your seats in the upright position and make sure your seat belts on fastened. Thank you for flying with us today.

"OK, Morici, here we are in the great city of Salt Lake." Archie said as they disembarked the plane. "Where do we go from here?"

"First we have to get our luggage and then pick up a car. Then we'll head towards Ogden and watch for the Huntsville exit."

The two men headed for the luggage belt, soon the luggage was coming and eventually they both got their suitcases.

Finding the rental agency Morici said to the agent "I'm Morici and I have a car to pick up."

"Yes sir. Do you have your confirmation number."?

"Yes, hold on I know it's here somewhere." He said as he started going through his pockets. 'Why didn't I put it with my wallet. I knew I was going to need it.' He thought as he pulled all kinds of paper out of his pockets. Finally, the last paper he found it.

"Here it is 41E78294320. Sorry it took me so long to find it. I normally don't hide things like that on myself." Morici said trying to apologize and act like he rented cars all the time.

"That's OK sir. May I see your driver's license please."?

"Sure" he said as he shoved his open wallet towards her.

Finishing up with the paperwork, she turned it around towards Morici and asked him to sign and initial it where she had marked.

"You'll go right outside here and as you are facing the curb our shuttle will be the one on your left. It will take you over to the parking lot where you can pick up your car." She said handing him his copies of the paperwork and the car keys.

"Thanks. Have a good day." He said as he motioned Archie to pick up his suitcases and headed out the door.

"Well, this ain't a bad car that Lonnie got us. Is it?" Archie said as he climbed into the front seat of the jeep.

"Naw, this is a pretty decent piece of equipment, especially driving here in the mountains." Morici said as he checked things out and started the jeep.

"How far we gotta go?"

"Well, according to the information I just got from the rental agent, we go about 15 miles north on US 15. He said there should be a pretty big sign on our right, just before the road we turn onto. He said we'd go about a mile or two on that road, turn left and our Lodge will be on our left about a quarter of a mile. He said he knew the owners and they were really nice people and it was one of the nicer, cleaner places out in that area. It's across from some lake."

"All I can say is I hope it's warm inside of it. I'm still cold. I don't think I'll thaw out til I get back to Atlanta."

"Oh, I forgot to tell you, when Lonnie called the other night he said they got a couple inches of snow there in Chattanooga and Atlanta got more than that. Guess it's cold just about everywhere." Morici couldn't resist rubbing it in. Archie was such a wimp, especially growing up in upstate New York. 'Guess they never got snow in upstate New York. Shit, they get almost as much snow as they get out here.'

"That's OK. It'll start warming up when 'they' know I'm coming home." Archie countered

"Hey, Morici, what you thinkin bout. You almost missed our turn."

"Not near as close as it was with you when you almost missed the road to the airport in Georgia. Besides that there were no cars beside or in back of me, so I didn't almost hit anyone or cause an accident. Like you did. Man you almost creamed that Mercedes."

"Yeah, OK, he shoulda been watchin where he was goin." Archie snapped

'No sense in trying to talk to this man, he'd argue with the devil himself rather than admit he'd been wrong. Besides I've got to watch myself in the way I talk about breaking the law don't want them thinking I'm not one of them.'

"This looks like our Lodge coming up here on the left." Morici slowed the jeep down and turned left into a beautiful half moon drive way. Pulling under the archway he stopped turned the motor off and told Arch "Just stay here and I'll go check in and get our room key. No sense in both of us going in right now."

"Suits me." Archie replied.

"Good afternoon sir. May I help you?" the reservationist ask

"Yes, ma'am. Name's Morici and I have reservations. My confirmation number is HL1983."

"Yes, Mr. Morici, I have your reservation right here. You are in suite 198. Here is a map. We are here; go all the way around the building, your suite is the 3rd one from the end. You have a beautiful view of Snow basin. That's one of our most popular mountains to ski. There is coffee in your suite, but if you find that you could use more, please call the desk and I'll see to it that you get more. Have a great visit with us." She said as she handed him the key. "Would you like 2 keys sir? I see that there are two of you."

"Yes ma'am. Two keys would be great." Morici picked up the keys, saluted her with them and headed towards the jeep. 'Thank heavens they've a restaurant here on the property, I'm starved.'

"We're around back on the first floor. Said we'll have a great view of their mountain called snow basin. Who knows, maybe I'll try it out while were here, since I didn't get to go when we were in Denver."

"Be my guest. I'll stay in the room and watch TV."

"Guess I better call Lonnie" Morici said as he finished unpacking his suitcases "Told him I'd let him know as soon as we got here. Check and see if they've learned anything else about our 'friend'.

"Hey, Lonnie, it's Morici. We're here at the Lodge. Got here a few minutes ago. Anything new on your end. Any ideas where we can start looking?"

"Glad to hear from you. I trust you didn't have any trouble getting the plane, car or room."

"Naw, I just gave them the confirmation number and it was a cinch."

"Well, I do have a few tidbits about our friend. According to my sources, she's been seen at the Genealogy building in Salt Lake

City, some kind of theater that they have telling the story of the Mormons, shopping in Ogden and oh yes, you might want to check out the monastery that is located someplace near you. She could be staying with them. I can't find out where she is staying, but the monastery, might be a good place for her to hide."

"OK, we'll start checking these places out first thing tomorrow morning. Does she like to ski? Thought I might try out some of the lifts around here, if she does."

"That sounds like a great idea. I heard that she's very accomplished at skiing. Let me know if you find anything out."

"I'll try and call you in a couple of days. That'll give us time to go to Salt Lake City and look around, maybe have time to go to the monastery too." Morici liked Lonnie, couldn't understand how, except for his brother, he got mixed up with the mob. He's had lots of schooling. 'I understand he went to some of the finest schools, including that fancy law school back east.'

"OK Morici I'll wait for your call, unless I get some kind of information before then."

"Sounds good to me." Morici said as he hung up the phone.

"Well, whatta he say?"

"He's given me some ideas where we can start looking and he included the ski lifts also."

"Like I said leave me out of that ski stuff. I'll soosh, or whatever they call it right here in this room watching TV."

"We'll get up tomorrow morning and go back to Salt Lake and start looking there. Lonnie OK'd that, so that means this afternoon and evening are ours. What would you like to do?"

"Me? I'd just soon stay right here and snooze, or watch TV."

"Think I'll run into Ogden and look around. Maybe I'll find some new ski gloves. Couldn't find any decent ones in my closet to bring and didn't see any in Denver I liked."

"OK. You do that and I'll snooze. Don't forget your key. I might be asleep."

# CHAPTER 6

"You know" Terrie said to Jack, as she poured herself a cup of coffee. "You have all of this stuff on tape, all of our conversations, when you remembered to turn the tape over" She laughed remembering the night that they'd talked almost 2 hours before he remembered to turn the tape over. "But did Clem tell you that he has a lot of paperwork, some even in Jay's handwriting, that I gave him when Chris brought him to my house in Georgia?"

They had worked quite late the night before and Terrie had slept later than usual. Jack had already had his morning walk, breakfast and a shower before Terrie got up.

"He did mention something to that effect to me, but didn't say how much or if it was stuff that we can use in court."

"Well, I'm not sure what can and can't be used, but he's got a lot of it. It was paperwork that I either already had at home or I managed to get out of the office before we were shut down by the Bankruptcy courts. Some of it involved our pension money, some of it involved the mine out in Idaho or Nevada, where ever it was and some of it involved letters that were written either too or from Rudy or some of the other men, like Les."

"Well, I know Clem's gone over them with a fine tooth comb, so if they can be used, he's already got them filed. Terrie, how much time do you think it would take for us to pack up and move?"

"Are you telling me that the time has come 'to move on' so to speak?"

"No, I was just wondering, how long it would take for you to pack up all of your suitcases with your stuff and the stuff you've bought since we've been here. How much notice would you need?" "Well, if I didn't have to due anything, but pack, probably I could do it in an hour or less. If I wanted to clean the apartment, or had dishes to get done, stuff like that it would probably take maybe a day. Have you heard anything from Clem?" "Well, as a matter of fact I have. We don't want to scare or alarm you, but it seems as tho' the mob has sent some 'boys' out looking for you and right now they are either in or headed to Salt Lake City." "Why on earth would they go to Salt Lake?" "It seems as tho' somebody told them you were there once and maybe you'd go back. Someplace in or near Ogden, you've been too and loved. They also heard you have relatives out there. Do you?" "Oh my god, yes. I have a nephew in a little place called Huntsville and my son, daughter-in-law and grandchildren live in a small town west of Salt Lake City. Surely they wouldn't go after them. Would they?" "We don't know. We really don't think so; our informant told Clem that he didn't hear any names, but just to check those areas out. Therefore, we have to be on the alert to move quickly if Clem finds out that they're getting too close. And no you would not be expected to clean, due dishes, nothing, but pack and head out the door. Mac and Marty would take care of everything else." "I can't say that I'm not getting scared, again, because I am. However, you, Clem, Mac and Marty have gone above and beyond what I believe your duties as agents are, to protect me. Therefore I know I'm relatively safe. You all wouldn't go this far to let something happen to me now. I'll tell you what I can do. I can get my suitcases out and pack what I know I won't need for a while. Then I won't have quite so much packing to do when the time comes." "That sounds great. Clem said you were one heckuva a lady and I truly believe him. Not many women could go through everything you've gone through and still be level headed and have a sense of humor. Don't forget we're going to dinner with Mac and Marty Thursday night. That night is OK with you isn't it?"

Terrie laughed, "I'll have to check my calendar to make sure I don't have anything else planned. Of course Thursday is OK. You better call them and tell them we accept, that is unless you'd like for me to make the call."

"No, I'll call them. You go on in and start packing, or take a shower, whatever it is you do first thing in the morning and I'll call Mac. Then maybe we'll hit the tape for awhile, if you're up to it."

"Sure, anything I can do to get this whole mess over with, I'm up to. I think I will take a shower and get some idea as to what all I can start packing. See you in a bit." Terrie said as she headed to her bedroom.

"Whew. I thought sure I was going to get stuck with her calling Marty." Jack was thinking as he was dialing Mac's number.

"Hey Mac, how are you?"

"Jack, this is a surprise. Didn't think we'd hear from you for a while. What can I do for you?"

"Go out to dinner with us Thursday night and act like you called and ask us to go with you two."

"Sure, no problem. What's happening?"

"Well, Clem called and didn't want Terrie to know it was him, so I told her it was you asking if we wanted to go to dinner one night this week and that I'd ask her and she suggested Thursday night."

"That sounds good. Maybe we'll go to Chinatown and have some really good Chinese, instead of that make believe that you two have been eating down there. Seriously what did Clem have to say?"

"It seems as tho' they've sent two men out this way to find Terrie. Right now they're either in Salt Lake City or heading there. Clem is working like Hell to try and find the right spot to move her to, but hasn't found anything yet. He did have a lead on a place that might be perfect, but that's all he'd say about it. Just said he'd keep in touch."

"Sounds like they've got someone very versed on our activities in their organization. Oh, well, where there's a will, there's a way and knowing Clem, he'll find it. Tell me something?"

"Sure what's that?"

"Marty and I were wondering if there is or was something going on between Clem and Terrie and that's why he's so in to this case?"

"Not yet. There very well could be somewhere along the way. Your right, Clem has not taken an interest in a case involving a female, like this since his wife was killed. Nita and I both are hoping, but we'll just have to wait and see. They really would be good for each other, if they're ever given a chance to explore the possibilities. I just heard the water shut off, so I guess I best hang up. I don't want Terrie hearing me talk about she and Clem. See you Thursday evening. Same time and place?"

"Sure I'll tell Marty. See you then and good luck."

———

"Terrie, why don't you make us a pot of coffee and bring it to the living room. You're not ready to go to bed are you?" Jack asked as he unlocked their front door.

"No I'm not. That was a great evening and delicious food, but I could stand a cup of coffee. Maybe I'll even cut some of the cake I made yesterday. Chinese food doesn't stay with me too long, then I'm hungry again. You go on in the living room and I'll bring it in when I'm done."

"Sounds good to me. Especially that cake! I know I've told you this before, but I have to say it again. Clem said you were a great cook and everyday you prove it to me more. Guess I'll keep the cake a secret, even from Nita. Wouldn't want to make her jealous." Jack laughed as he headed for the living room.

Terrie brought two pieces of cake, the coffee carafe and two cups and saucers in on the tray. She poured Jack's coffee and handed it to him, before pouring hers and sitting down.

"Terrie I've put this off as long as I can. Mac asked me tonight if I'd said anything to you and well, er, I said I'd put it off, but that I was going to tell you tonight—

"Oh for Pete's sake Jack spit it out. What are you trying to tell me, that you've been putting it off?" Terrie interrupted Jack

"Well, there's a polygraph team coming down to give you the 'lie detector test' and I've been putting off telling you. I didn't want to upset you, but Mac was right I had to tell you. I'm sorry." In telling her, he had used his 'official sounding voice' what ever that was and he knew he'd sounded harsh. Oh god I didn't mean to hurt her anymore than she's already been hurt. He had tried— even when he questioned her to be relaxed and not 'official' sounding. He knew she'd be shocked at the mention of a lie detector test, but it was routine and they had to cover all of their bases before Clem and the rest of 'the boys' took this mess to court.

"Don't be Jack. I guess in the back of my mind I knew that this would come someday. When will this take place?"

"I'm not sure, but probably before the end of the week. Just as soon as we can make sure that everything will be done on the QT. We don't intend on anyone getting wind of your being in California. Unfortunately the only ones that can run this 'special' test are located in D.C., so they have to get things arranged so as not to alert 'the bad guys' in this case." Jack was really uneasy about this, but Clem was handling everything so he knew nothing would happen. "Terrie, I know this is going to upset you, but I want you to know that this particular test is relatively new and that's why we need these specialists. Besides it's routine to do a test. That way when this gets to court we can say that everything we did was done by the book, so to speak."

Terrie just sat and stared at Jack. Oh she knew this day would eventually come, but she'd tried putting all of this mess out of her mind these last few months. She really didn't want to think about what she had done. She had sat her coffee cup down to keep from spilling it when Jack told her. Now she leaned over picked up the cup turning it oh so slightly in her hands staring into it expecting to see what—she had no idea. All of a sudden she could hear Del's voice screaming at her, just like he did in Georgia—'why are you making over that boy. What's he to us? Why are you telling him everything? Why couldn't you just keep your mouth shut and deny knowing Jay? He doesn't need to know, besides you're trusting that he's who—Terrie hurriedly blinked her eyes and took a sip of cold coffee. As she stood to pour herself some more coffee Jack said "Terrie what's the matter? You look like you've just seen a ghost" Clem had warned Jack that something like this might happen out of nothing more than fear and a reminder of what she'd been through, but Clem also said she's a tough lady and she'll make it.

"I was just thinking" Terrie said kind of dreamily "If only I'd kept my mouth shut, denied knowing Jay to Chris, none of this would be happening and everything would be the same as it was before I talked to Chris. How many times have I thought about what I did to Chris, my family, my children. Will I ever get to see or hear from them again? Deny, Deny, Deny" Terrie said angrily "What a small four letter word. Why couldn't I just abide by it? Maybe I wouldn't have caused so much grief for everyone, maybe even more than that Chris would still be alive." Terrie started to cry as she did every time she thought of Chris since being told he'd been killed. 'I killed Chris just as tho' I'd pulled the trigger.' "Oh, your people would have gone on with your investigation, but without me, and maybe it would have taken you longer, but you would have nailed them eventually. Hell Jack I'm not afraid of that test. I know everything that I've told you, Clem and Chris is the truth, it's just that the thought of that test has reminded me as to everything that has happened and how you and I got here. Not a very pretty thought now is it?"

"I'm sorry Terrie, but Clem and I decided it was best to do it here, before we move you again, than wait and maybe call more attention to you, us than is needed."

"I know Jack, you are right. It's just now that I know about it

I'll just worry until it's over. Not so much as to what I say, the questions that they'll ask, but just this whole damn thing. Maybe I should have kept my mouth shut."

"No Terrie, don't ever feel that way. You will be helping us put away some very bad people for hopefully a very long time. And maybe, just maybe that will ease some of the pain that you're feeling for everyone, including Chris and yourself. Just maybe after all of this is over you will be able to piece your life back together." Jack wasn't exactly sure when that day would be, if ever, but he felt he had to say something to try and build her spirits up.

# CHAPTER 7

"OK, Morici. We've been in every store in Salt Lake City and damn near every town around here. What do we do now? You've been on the slopes, ski runs, ice skating places and we still haven't found her, or anyone who seems to know her. When do you plan on calling Lonnie and tellin' him that we've run out of places to look?" Arch was asking. He was tired of the cold, tired of walking, but most of all, tired of Morici. He really was a pain. He had to look in every nook and cranny he could find looking for Terrie. Archie knew how important it was to find her, but he felt Morici was stallin'. The only thing was he couldn't think of a reason for him to stall. He had been watching Morici's face the whole time he'd been complaining and he could almost hear wheels turning in Morici's head. "Well—when are you callin' him?"

"I'm calling him in about an hour. I want to give the restaurant a chance to slow down a little bit. We don't need to be interrupting him when he's busy. It's almost 8 o'clock in Chattanooga, so I thought I'd wait 'til about 10 then I'll give him a jingle and report on what all we've been doing this past week. Sure don't want for him to come up with some place to look that I haven't thought of first."

"Hell" Archie interrupted "There ain't no place else for you to look unless it's in a snowdrift someplace that we haven't heard about."

"I know" Morici replied chuckling to himself "I just want to prove that you and I have looked every place that a person can think of short of the woman's john. Why don't we go get a bite to eat and then I'll call him when we get back"

"Now you're talking. How 'bout that steak house we tried the other night. I liked all the food you get there and not real expensive either."

"Besides" Morici answered "It's not, but a block down the street, so you wouldn't be out in the cold very long." Morici knew how Arch hated the cold, so it was a game with him to see how long he could keep him in the cold before he really started bitchin'. This was the kind of game Morici really enjoyed. 'He'll rue the day that he met me' Morici thought to himself as he shut and locked the room door behind them.

———

"Now that was some kind of steak dinner. Sure wish we had one of these steak houses down in Atlanta. I'd eat there all the time. Don't think I'd even cook, just eat there." Archie was going on as they walked back to the motel.

"Arch, there is one in Atlanta, but it's closer to Marietta and I doubt that you'd drive all the way up there to eat steak at a buffet house every night." Morici said.

"Are you kidding? Is there really one of these steak houses up there?"

"Yes, Archie, it's called Rian's Steak Buffet. I've eaten there a couple of times. I don't think the food is as good as it is in this buffet, but there is one with all the trimmings. Like I said it's closer to Marietta than to Atlanta, but I found it one night when I was looking for a place to live. When we get back there remind me and I'll take you there some night."

"Gee, Morici, that'd be swell. I'll remind you, that's for sure."

They arrived at their motel room door and as Morici unlocked it the phone was ringing. They both rushed to answer it, and Archie got it first. Morici knew who it was so he went into the bath alcove and started a pot of fresh coffee. He didn't much care for some of the fancy tasting coffee that they served out here.

"It's Lonnie, Morici, he wants to talk to you." Arch said handing Morici the phone.

"Hi Lonnie. No I'm not busy. We just got back from eating and I made a pot of coffee. I was going to call you when we got back. You just called first. I didn't want to bother you during the busy time at the restaurant."

"I should have realized that you would be that considerate, but I was getting a little worried. I haven't heard from you boys for almost a week and well, my brothers called a couple of times and he's wondering what you've found."

"Sorry Lonnie. I didn't mean to worry you or get you into trouble with Les, but you said check everything out and that's what we've been doing. We've checked every store, theatre, and telephone company from Ogden to Salt Lake and back again. We've checked the Monastery, the Mormon Church, their theatre and their geneol, er family place where you can look up your family history." Morici was never to sure how to pronounce that word.

"We've found nothing, nada, nein. No one out here seems to know her, including the light, water and phone companies."

"Oh, Jesus, you didn't tell them why you were looking for her?" Lonnie interrupted

"Hey Lonnie, I was a cop once I know how to do things without suspicion."

"I'm sorry Morici, guess I forgot who I was talking to, guess I'm starting to sound like my brother. Go on with what you were saying."

"Well, like I was saying the only place we didn't look was in a snowdrift. She just isn't here. Do you have any other suggestions? Have you heard anything at all from our contact?"

"No, I've nothing to report. I'm calling Les in a little bit. I'll give him this report and get back to you first thing tomorrow morning. Have a good night and wait for my call tomorrow morning. OK."

"Sure Lonnie. We'll stay right by the phone until you call. Tell Les we said Hi and to stay warm. It's freezing out here." Morici hung up the phone and looked at Arch, laying on the bed, drinking coffee and reading the paper, just as if the phone call was of a personal nature and of no interest whatsoever to him.

"Well, it appears we have to stay in tomorrow morning until Lonnie calls, so how about I go down to that bakery we saw and buy some kind of donuts or breakfast rolls."

"That sounds good to me, just as long as I don't have to go out in the cold with you." Arch answered reaching for the remote. "Should be a ballgame on tonight. Want a watch it?"

"Sure. You turn it on and I'll be back in a few with something good to eat." Morici knew that would get him. Arch did love to eat. Morici knew exactly how long it would take him to get to the bakery and back, so he decided he best run down, that would give him a few minutes for a phone call, get the rolls or donuts and get back without raising any suspicion with Archie about how long it took him.

"Well" Morici said as he opened the door to the motel room

"Shut the damn door" Archie interrupted

"Sorry about that." Morici said as he shut the door "I got a couple of jelly filled donuts, a couple of yeast, 2 sugar twists for breakfast and 2 iced cinnamon rolls for us to have after while along with some coffee. Thought that sounded kind of good. What do you think? Sound OK to you?" Morici said as he put the box and bag down on the table.

Their room had 2 queen size beds, 1 double dresser, a TV, a clock radio, coffee pot with extra coffee packets, a real nice table with 2 chairs and a nightstand between the two beds. It wasn't a top of the line motel room, but it wasn't cheap either. Morici thought his room in Germany was more luxurious, but Archie loved it he thought it was the greatest. He'd never stayed in a motel like this one before. He did like traveling with Morici. He found that with him everything was done first class, cars, airlines, meals and the motel rooms.

"That sounds good. I could probably eat one of them now, but I'll wait a little while. Oh, I couldn't find a ballgame, so I've got this mystery movie on something about Orient Express—oh well, it's pretty good with this foreign Belgium playing a detective. Hope you like mysteries, 'cause I'd like to finish watching this, it's pretty good. This detective thinks—"

"Yeah, I've seen it. It's a mystery by Agatha Christie. I used to read her books, she writes pretty good. By all means leave it on. The murder just happened from the looks of it." Morici said as he got a cup of coffee and sat down at the table.

"Yeah." Archie said sipping his coffee and trying not to spill it. He normally lay down to watch TV, but he'd learned traveling with Morici not to lay down, but to put pillows against the headboard and lean back against them "that way when you're drinking or eating something you won't spill it or drop it on the covers." Morici had told him in Denver after he spilled his coffee and had to sleep with wet covers.

———

"Good morning Morici did I waken you?"

"Heck no, Archie and I were just having donuts and coffee and reading the paper waiting for your call. Did you hear anything about our friend?"

"Well, yes and no. By that I mean, it seems as if our friend is not in Salt Lake, but out in San Francisco. At least somewhere in that area, we're not sure exactly if she's in San Francisco or in one of the little towns outside of there. You know like Oakland, maybe even down as far as Monterey. Right now what we would like the two of you to do is go to San Francisco and meet with some men that we have out there. After you've filled them in on all you know, along with giving them the picture that you have of her, you two can fly home, back to Atlanta."

"Gosh Lonnie, that sounds swell. How soon will we be leaving?"

"I will try and get you out of there tomorrow morning. I'll call you as soon as I have everything tied up. Just hang loose and wait for my call. Let's see, it should be around 10 your time, so I'll try and call you by noon. That way you can go to lunch and then pack. Anyway I'll call you as soon as I have everything set up."

"OK Lonnie. We'll wait for your call."

"Well, what's that all about?" Archie said pouring another cup of coffee and plopping on his bed.

"It seems as though our 'friend' has been spotted in the San Francisco area. Lonnie is making arrangements for us to fly there, meet with some of their associates, give them what we know along with her picture, then we can fly back to Atlanta."

"Whoopee when's that going to be? Our flying back to Atlanta I mean."

"Just as soon as we turn everything over to the other people in San Francisco. I'd say we should be home by the weekend. We have to stay here in the room until Lonnie calls us back with all of the particulars."

"Hell, I'm going to start packing then. It can't be too soon for me." Archie said as he grabbed for his suitcase.

"While you're doing that I think I'll take a shower. Then I can pack and maybe Lonnie will call with the news of when and where." Morici said as he headed for the bathroom.

Just as Morici turned the water on in the shower the phone rang. Archie answered it\

"Gee boss. We didn't think youse'd be callin' so soon. Morici's takin' a shower. Do you wish I should have him call ya back?"

"Yes, Archie, please have Morici call me back here at the restaurant." Lonnie could not tolerate Archie. Couldn't understand his brothers attitude with him and certainly didn't have a faith in discussing 'company' business with him.

Archie finished packing most of his things, poured a cup of coffee and sat down to watch television until Morici came out of the shower. He figured he would take his shower while Morici was on the phone with Lonnie. He really didn't like or trust Lonnie, but he was the boss's brother so he knew he had to be nice and polite to him.

"Well, Morici, it's 'bout time ya got outta the shower."

"I wasn't in there that long. Did Lonnie call?"

"Yeah"

"Well, what did he say? Did he give you the information about when we fly out of here?"

"Naw. He said that you should call him at the restaurant."

"OK. I'll give him a call."

"I'll go take my shower. I'm just about packed. Just my stuff in the bathroom and the clothes I've got on."

Morici picked up the phone and proceeded to dial Lonnie's restaurant.

"May I speak to Lonnie please. This is Morici and he's expecting my call."

"Hey, Morici thanks for calling back so quick. I've got your information, do you have pen and paper?"

"Yes sir. I'm ready anytime you are."

"OK. You fly out of Salt Lake at 4 this afternoon on Continental Flight 2856. You'll land at 3 San Francisco time. Go to the Mirabar Restaurant there in the terminal. Oh, do you happen to have a red necktie?"

"As a matter of fact I do. I just bought it here in Salt Lake."

"Good. Wear that. When you get to the Mirabar sit at a table as close to the entrance as you can and make sure your tie is visible. Two men will approach you and comment on your tie asking where you bought it. Then when you acknowledge that you bought it in Salt Lake they will introduce themselves. Their names are Tony and Lou. When you are sure they are who they are, I'll leave it up to you and your 'police' instincts, give them her picture and tell them what all you know. You then will catch Delta flight 1067 to Atlanta. You can pick your tickets up anytime, after you get to the airport. It leaves San Francisco at 9 PM, California time and gets you into Atlanta around 4 or 5 AM, Atlanta time. When you get there go home I take it you've got wheels there. Get some sleep then call me here at the restaurant when you get up. Have you got all of that?"

"Yes sir. I'll call you sometime tomorrow. Will you be at the restaurant all day?"

"Yes. I'm expecting several deliveries and unfortunately I can't trust anybody around here to check them in—you wouldn't consider coming to work for me, would you. I'm just kidding I know you enjoy working for my brother and I wouldn't want to steal you away from him. I'll talk to you tomorrow. Good luck."

"Thanks Lonnie. Who knows maybe I'll take you up on that

offer one of these days if I get tired of traveling." The two men hung up just as Archie came out of the bathroom.

"Well, when we leaving?"

"We have to be at the airport in about 4 hours." Morici said as he started throwing things into his suitcase making sure to keep his sweater and winter coat out.

"How come you're keeping winter clothes out to put on?" Archie asked as he sat on the bed watching Morici pack.

"Well, it is cold here, cold in San Francisco and we leave there at 9 tonight getting into Atlanta around 4 or 5 tomorrow morning, so it'll be cold there. I have no intention of catching cold this late in the game." Morici replied. 'Man he really is stupid. You have to explain every little thing to him. I'll be glad when this trip is over.'

"Think I'll run down to the drugstore and get some smokes. You want to go with me?"

"Naw. If I want anything I'll look for it at the airport."

"Would you like to go get a bite to eat before we head to the airport or do you want to eat there?"

"I'd rather eat there. Makes me know how much closer to home I am."

"OK. I won't be that long. On my way back I'll stop in the office and tell them we're checking out. I don't think we'll get charged for another day. If I remember right check out time is noon and we should be out of here by then. See you in a few."

"OK. I'll be right here." Archie laughed

# CHAPTER 8

"Terrie" Jack called at her bedroom door. "Are you awake?" Getting no answer Jack knocked and called again. This time if he didn't get an answer he was going in. The news Clem had just given him was bad, bad, bad. Come on Terrie wake up.

Finally Jack heard a very quiet

"Come in"

Jack opened the door and went inside. Terrie was sitting on the edge of her bed and Jack could tell he had awakened her.

"Sorry, Terrie, but you've got to wake up. Clem called and we've got a lot to get done in the next, hopefully, 2 days." Neither one of them were exactly sure just how many days they did have. Clem had gotten a phone call that the 2 men would be heading their way within the next day or so. He said he'd call back with more exact information as soon as he heard, and that he was to sign papers for a house where Terrie would be moved today. "Sure hope Terrie can keep her word on packing in a day and then be able to just sit and wait." Clem had said to Jack just before he'd hung up.

"Give me a few minutes to get dressed then I'll be out to get some coffee, then you can tell me what's happened." Terrie said as she reached for her robe.

"I'll pour your coffee so that it'll be cool enough to drink when you come out."

Jack laughed as he shut her door. He knew from being with her these last 5 months that she hated hot coffee. She didn't like cold coffee either. It had to be just cool enough to drink. That was perfect coffee for her. The phone was ringing as Jack went to the kitchen to pour Terrie's coffee. After answering the phone he poured Terrie's coffee wondering how she was going to take what Clem had just said.

"Here I am. Now what's happened that I have to be bright and cheery eyed so early in the morning?" Terrie said as she took a sip of her coffee and sat down opposite Jack at the kitchen table.

"Clem just called back. Well, let me start at the beginning. While you were still asleep, Clem called and said we'd have to be ready to leave within the next day or two and that he'd call me back when he had something more concrete. Well, like I said he just called back. It seems as tho' we have to be ready to leave here and be at the airport by 3 to make a 3:30 flight to Salt Lake, then on to another airport, but Clem didn't say which one. He just said our tickets would be waiting for us at the Salt Lake ticket counter of Continental Airlines. He also said he'd be quite busy today as he was going to sign some papers for a house he was renting or buying for you, but there again he didn't say which he was doing. Just that he was signing papers today. He then will make, or has already got into operation the moving of some, if not all of your things from Georgia to this new place."

Terrie was speechless. She knew this time would be forth coming and she'd been warned that she might not have a lot of time, but this was a tad much and frightening.

"What has brought all of this about so quickly?" She asked as she poured some more coffee for the two of them.

"Well, it seems as tho' Clem had received a phone call that 2 of Les's men would be heading here within the next day or two, but he just got another urgent call that they would be in San Francisco this afternoon. Therefore we have to move quickly. I hope you can do it." Jack finished. Looking at her he was sure she could do it, but he could also tell that she was frightened.

"Guess I best get finished packing. I'm just glad that I had a heads up a couple of days ago. I've got a lot of stuff already packed, so it shouldn't take me more than an hour or so. Is that time enough?"

"We don't have to be at the airport until 3. We're special, I guess you could say, 'cause we just have to walk in, show ID and go to the plane. Just make sure your wallet is handy to show your ID. I'm just about finished packing, so I can check around and make sure we haven't left anything laying around out here." He said as he waved his arm around encompassing the apartment. "I have to call Marty and let them know, so they can make arrangements to get this apartment closed up and emptied of things by next week. We don't want to let the manager know that we're gone. He can just think we're leaving next week. That should give us a week's head start." 'Why did I have to say a week's head start and scare her more? Oh well, I did it and that's it.'

"Do I have time to finish my coffee?" Terrie said trying to sound light hearted.

"It's only 10, so we have plenty of time." Jack said as he poured more coffee. "Like I said before, I'm almost through packing and I've had my shower, so I'll recheck everything out here and you can take your shower, finish packing and check your rooms. Just be sure to leave warm clothes out to wear on the plane. This maybe May, but since Clem didn't say where we were going it's still cold in some parts of this country."

Terrie looked at Jack and said, "You're right. I hadn't thought about that. It's still cool here early in the morning and late in the evening, but some parts are still just as chilly as it is here. OK, I'm going in to take my shower and finish packing. Be back shortly." Terrie finished as she headed towards her bedroom. Taking her shower Terrie stood under the hot water a little longer than she normally did thinking about what was happening. 'I knew this day would come sooner or later. I knew I couldn't stay here forever, but I had hoped it would be later than sooner. What's to become of me? How long will I have to hide? Will I ever get to see my kids and grandchildren again? Well, missy standing here under the water isn't getting you packed so you best get busy.' She admonished herself. Shutting and locking her suitcases she looked around the room, checked her closet and then went into the bathroom. 'Chee, where did I get all this stuff.'? There hung her bathrobe and nightgown. Going back into the bedroom with these articles and opening her suitcase she looked around and decided not to shut and lock this one until she was sure she had everything in there. After rechecking everything she went out to the kitchen where Jack was talking on the telephone. Not wanting to eavesdrop she went into the living room. There on the coffee table was the card that had come with the flowers Clem had sent her so long ago. 'Why hadn't I thrown that away' she thought as she picked it up and headed for her bedroom and suitcase. When she came back out Jack was off the phone and was fixing soda for the two of them.

"I know it's rather early for soda, but thought maybe you'd rather have something cold to drink after all the work you've done." Jack said turning and smiling at her. Man for someone 'hit with the pack we've got to leave' she's really got it all together. She really is a trooper. 'I just wonder what's going on in that pretty little head of hers.'

"That's exactly what I need. Thanks. What will I do without you looking after me?" Terrie knew this subject had never been brought up, but she knew once she left the San Francisco area she'd probably be on her own with no body guard—just a lady who walks alone.

"You'll do fine. I have all the confidence in the world in you. Maybe you'll have time to write that book that you've talked about. Maybe you'll get that afghan completed that you started. Who knows? One thing I do know you'll make it." Jack and Clem both had that kind of confidence in her. They knew with all she'd been through, that this was just a small stumbling block that she'd cross with no trouble.

"Well, you maybe right. I have been known as being bullheaded. I don't like someone to back me up against a wall, cause I come out fighting. I've done it a dozen or so times, but I am getting tired of doing that. I just wish this was all over with. I can't say I wish it'd never happened, cause it did. Now I just have to learn to live with it and get on with my life as best as I can. After all I am a survivor."

Jack looked at her still amazed at how well she handled all of this. 'I don't know of very many women that would handle this like a trooper like Terrie has' he thought to himself.

"Would you like a bite to eat before we head out to the airport, or would you rather eat there or on the plane?" Jack asked her

"I'm too nervous to eat right now. The airport doesn't sound too appealing and I'm sure we won't get anything on the plane except peanuts and drinks. Can we just kind of roll with it? Maybe I'll be hungry on our way."

"Sure that sounds good to me. I called Marty and she said they'd take care of the apartment next week and for us just to leave the keys on the kitchen table. They have a set just for this reason. They'll come down and get cleaners in here and then they'll tell the manager that they don't need the apartment any longer. She'll give him some kind of an excuse. Well, it's 1" Jack said looking at his watch. "Why don't we get our things in the car and head north towards the airport. It's an hour's drive and if we get a bite to eat that gives us an hour before we have to boad the plane. Seriously I heard that they have a pretty nice restaurant at the airport called the Mirabar. Maybe we could give it a try?" Jack knew how upset, scared she was, but he also knew that she had to get something to eat, at least before they left Salt Lake. The San Francisco airport sounded better to him, but he really didn't want to push her. He truly had no idea where they were going. All he knew was that Clem would meet them at an airport when they got there. He said that there itinerary would be waiting for them when they picked up tickets in Salt Lake. 'I agree with Terrie. I'll be glad when this is all over.'

"I don't know where I got all this stuff. When we arrived here 5 months ago I had 2 suitcases, if my memory serves me correctly. Now I have five. What on earth did I buy?" Terrie was laughing as she brought out her last suitcase from the apartment for Jack to put into the car.

"I hope this is everything, cause I don't think I can pack one more thing."

"Oh, I've still got my carryon and my large purse, but that's all that will be checked through." She laughed as she climbed into the car.

"I guess you've left checking everything out in the apartment to me?" He chided as he headed towards the door.

"As a matter of fact." She called out the window. "I checked everything out, including the locking of the sliding glass doors. I even picked up the vase that we left on the porch and packed it in my carryon, but you go on and check everything out if it will make you feel better." She laughed. 'Men she thought, they got me into all of this trouble, but it's men that are helping me get out of it also. Guess they aren't all bad.'

# CHAPTER 9

"Ladies and Gentlemen the Captain has turned on the No Smoking and Fasten Your Seatbelt signs. We are on our final approach to San Francisco International Airport and will be landing shortly. We ask that you maintain your seats until the airplane comes to a complete stop. On behalf of Continental Airlines, the Captain and all the crew we want to thank you for flying with us today and hope you have a pleasant stay while here in San Francisco."

"Hallelujah!!" Archie said, "That means in just a few hours we will be on a plane back to Atlanta. It can't be too soon for me."

"I have to agree with you there Archie. I'm looking forward to getting home myself. I'm tired of living out of a suitcase. At least in Germany I was in the same place for more than a few days or weeks. This kind of traveling gets on your nerves after awhile."

"When does our plane leave?"

"It's supposed to leave at 9 tonight. When we get off we have to get our luggage and then go to the Mirabar Restaurant and meet Tony and Lou. Hopefully that won't take too long then we can relax, shop or have a few drinks and think about going home."

"What all are we supposed to tell these two?"

Morici sat and looked at Archie for a couple of minutes before he answered him. Morici had learned it didn't make any difference how many times you told Archie something he didn't remember it for more than 10 minutes. That's why Morici hated telling him anything until the last minute.

"OK. I'll go over it one more time. I have Terrie's picture and her description, so I will do most of the talking. If after I'm through you think of something I missed then you can chime in or if they ask something that I don't know about this situation and you do I expect you to say something."

"That sounds fair enough. I'm not much of a talker anyway. Do you know what these two look like?"

"Yeah, kind of, Lonnie gave me a description and a couple of questions to ask. Then he said he'd leave it to my old police instincts to know if they were who they said they were."

"That's good enough for me. Man, Lonnie really does trust you, doesn't he." Archie said as he stood, moved into the aisle and reached for his carryon."

"Yeah. I guess he does. I kind of like him too." Morici said as he followed suit.

"I'll tell you one thing." Archie said as they started down the aisle

"What's that?" Morici asked, leaning forward slightly so he could here him

"I'm sure glad we had that wind at our ass so we got in early. Now we can have a quiet drink before we have to meet those two guys."

"We didn't need to get in early to have that drink. We're meeting them in a restaurant that I'm sure serves drinks." What a jerk, wonder why Les keeps him around, unless it's because he's Les' gopher. 'I wouldn't have had him on my squad for more than probably two hours before I'd have gotten rid of him. If there's one thing I can't abide it's someone who's stupid and shows it.'

———

"Do you suppose we could eat at that restaurant that we ate at when we first got here?" Terrie asked Jack

"I don't see why not. We have enough time." Jack turned and smiled at Terrie. Trying to watch traffic but pleased with her question. She'd been plenty quiet since they left the apartment.

"I just thought it would be nice to stop and kind of say goodbye. You know where it is?"

"Checking the time, I would say we should be getting quite close to it, yes, there it is." Jack said slowing down, making sure nothing was coming up on his right side, crossed the lane and went down the off ramp.

"Man that was a close call. Sure glad I didn't ask any later." Terrie laughed.

"I'm glad too. I'm also glad traffic is as light as it is I'd never made this ramp other wise."

———

"That was good. Thanks for stopping now I think I'm ready for anything and I can at least make it to supper. Speaking of supper, wonder where we'll be at that time?"

"Well, according to what Clem told me on the phone, the soonest we'll know that answer is after we land at Salt Lake. We're to go to our office in the airport and pick up our tickets and our itinerary. Then we'll at least have an idea as to where we're going." At least I hope, Jack thought. Clem was awfully vague when he spoke to him this morning. Sure wish I knew what was going on. The least he could've done is tell me he knows I wouldn't say anything to Terrie. If and when I finally see him, maybe, just maybe he'll explain why he didn't tell me everything. "Well, it looks like we'll get this car returned and into the airport right at 3 PM. Guess we couldn't have timed that any better if we'd tried."

"I'd still like to know where we're going, but I'm sure Clem has his reasons for leaving us hanging. Precaution I guess you'd call it. What do we do with our luggage when we get to the gate? With us not having tickets how can they get tagged to get sent on to—wherever?"

"Guess we'll find that out when we return our car." Jack said as he pulled into the return car parking lot. I just wish I knew how that was going to be handled.

As Jack was helping Terrie out of the car he heard someone ask if he needed help with his luggage.

"Yeah, we could—good heavens Mac how did you know—would you like to fill Terrie and me as to what the hell is going on."

"Well, it seems as tho' you two don't have tickets and you need to ship your luggage on to your destination, there about anyway. That's where I come in—shipping your luggage on a different plane to your last destination, or there about, like I said. I, as the bus driver, will take you to your terminal where you will go to the first ticket counter you come to. Give your names, show your ID, take your tickets and head to the correct terminal as directed by the counter girl. Once the plane takes off the chief stewardess will bring an envelope to you. Your instructions will be in there, along with tickets and some money."

"Good lord, this sounds like something out of a Mission Impossible show. Cloak and dagger or something." Terrie said as she climbed into the bus.

"Terrie, we've gotten you this far safe we're not for about to loose you now." Mac said as he finished loading their suitcases and closed the bus door. "We're glad you got here when you did. You were to board at 3:30, but those plans have changed and you're to board as soon as you pick up your tickets. So the word is hustle. Do not stop, do not pass go." Mac said laughing. "Seriously you are pressed for time, as the plane is waiting for the two of you to board, so don't dilly dally. Hope to see you again sometime Terrie. It's been our pleasure meeting you. You truly are some kind of lady. Marty sends her best."

"It's been nice knowing you two. Please tell Marty that I hope we'll see each other again someday under better circumstances." Terrie said as she was helped off the bus and waited for Jack to disembark.

"This way my lady" Jack said as he headed towards the door. They got their tickets and were told to go to gate 12A to board their flight.

"Should we run or just walk fast? Oh I forgot 'do not pass go' so I guess that means, don't run, but walk fast." Terrie said as they headed up the stairs towards the terminals.

"Like he said, don't let any grass grow under our feet. However, my legs are longer than yours, so I guess I'll let you lead the speed in which we travel across the concourse to the terminal and our plane."

———

"Hello Morici" The man stood up extending his hand as Morici and Archie entered the Mirabar.

"Tony?" Morici said as he shook the mans hand sizing him up and remembering the description Lonnie had given him.

"At your service. Sit down Lou and I have already ordered our drinks. We got here a little early so we could assure ourselves that we had a concourse table."

My, Morici thought. Now I have to tend with someone almost as intelligent as Lonnie. What a difference. Archie sat with his back to the concourse and Morici sat across from him facing the traffic.

"Would you two gentlemen like to have something to drink?" She asked after sitting Tony and Lou's drinks on the table.

"Yes, I'll have a Bud in the bottle" Archie said

"I would like, ah do you have Lambrusco?" Morici asked, smiling at the waitress

"Yes, sir. Would you like a glass or carafe? We do have the small bottles of Lambrusco that holds maybe one and a half glasses of wine if that would be more to your liking.

"Yes, that sounds good. Bring me one of the little bottles and a glass please."

"We can talk shop, after she brings our drinks back and we know we won't be bothered for a few minutes. Right now we can act like good buddies." Morici knew the routine from years on the police force. Small talk, act like buddies that haven't seen each other for a long time. Then when it's 'clear' get down to business.

"Sounds good to me" Tony replied

"Well, what do you think of the Giants? Do you think they stand a chance this year?" Morici said

"But of course, who else stands a chance at the Pennant?" Tony came back

"Do you need anything else right now Gentlemen?" The waitress asked as she sat Archie's beer and Morici's wine down on the table.

"No. Not right now. Thank you. We'll call you when we get ready to order dinner." Tony said as he handed her a bill to pay for the drinks.

"Now what have you got" Tony looked at Morici and asks

"Here's her picture. I wrote a description of her, hair color, eyes, height and approximate weight on the back." Morici said handing the picture to Tony. While Tony looked at Terrie's picture and read the back, Morici was watching the people go by. All of a sudden he started chocking and reached for his wine, spilling the bottle all over the table.

"Jesus, Morici, look what you did. What's the matter with you?"

"Just clumsy I guess. Waitress" Morici called as he tried to compose himself. 'At least they didn't have a chance to look around and see what I just saw scooting through the concourse.' He thought to himself. "I'm sorry," he said as the waitress walked up "It appears I've made an awful mess with my clumsiness."

"No problem Sir. I'll have this cleaned up in no time." Looking down at the table she saw the picture "I hope it didn't ruin your picture" she said as she reached for it.

Tony quickly picked it up and carefully dabbed at the back of it and said

"No problem. It's a picture of my sister whom I haven't seen for a few years and my friend just gave it to me. It's fine. It didn't even get wet. Please just clean up the mess as soon as you can."

"Yes sir and I'll bring back another bottle of your wine sir."

"Thank you. I'd appreciate it and this time I think I'll let you pour my first glass. Then maybe I won't spill it."

As soon as the waitress left the table Morici said "Now where were we before I pulled that stupid stunt. Oh yes, Archie and I have chased all over Denver, Salt Lake and surrounding area, then Lonnie said they got a phone call that she was either out here in San Francisco or was headed this way. That's why he sent us out here to meet with you and fill you in on what we know about her, which isn't much I'm afraid."

"Do you know what kind of work she used to do? Something that would give us a possible direction to start in, you know, office, secretary?" Tony asked looking at the picture that Morici had given him.

"She's not a bad lookin' babe now is she?" Lou remarked after looking at her picture.

"No, for her age she's pretty. One thing, outside of the obvious, of being Jay's secretary, I understand she was in some kind of flower business at one time."

"How do you know that Morici" Archie asked "I don't remember the boss mentioning that."

"When I talked to that girl in Germany she told me that. That's why I went to so many flower places while I was there. I figured if she liked that kind of work, she might go back into it figuring that no one would know that about her."

"That stands to reason." Tony said "And out in this area it does give us some places to start looking. We've got some of the best growers and suppliers in the industry out in this area. Besides I've got some friends in that business. I can start by checking some of those out tomorrow morning."

"Would you gentlemen like to order dinner now?" The waitress asks as she sat Morici's wine bottle down after pouring some in his glass.

"Yeah, why not. I'm hungry." Archie said

"Hell, you're always hungry. Tell me one time that you haven't been." Morici chided him

"Ah Morici just order and get off my back"

Everybody laughed and each man ordered steak, baked potatoes and a salad.

"Typical meal for men I guess" Morici laughed after the waitress left the table.

"Yeah" Tony said, "I don't know many men who eat vegetables anyway. When do you two leave?"

"Our plane leaves at 9 tonight and thank heavens we're going home. It's been 5 months since we've been in Atlanta. Seems like a lifetime. We're both tired of living out of suitcases."

"Man. I don't think I could do that. Live out of a suitcase, I mean" Lou said

It was like Tony and Morici had both told the other two men Lou and Archie, not to speak unless spoken to, as that was really the most Lou had said since they all sat down at the table.

'Funny' Morici thought, 'both Tony and I must feel the same way about Lou and Archie. They're both stupid. Man I'll be glad to be rid of him for awhile.'

"What's happening next, what job are you going to be doing when you get back there?" Tony asked Morici

"Lonnie didn't say. I'm just to call him after I get up in the morning. He's kind of running things while the boss is out of the country. I guess you could say."

"Here you are gentlemen. Hope you enjoy your meal. If you need anything just give me a holler."

"Sure thanks" Morici said as he picked up his glass of wine. "I feel like a toast. To a brighter tomorrow"

"Amen. I think we'll all second that," Tony said

Lou and Archie were too busy digging in to their food to acknowledge any thing else.

# CHAPTER 10

"Whew. That was a little close for comfort." Jack said as he and Terrie settled into their seats.

"What's that Jack"

Not wanting to scare her by telling her who he thought he saw he just said

"Almost missing this plane. Clem would have had a fit. Wonder which one of the stewardess will be giving me an envelope?" Jack said looking around the airplane

"Don't you think she'll maybe wait until we're airborne and maybe she's passing out drinks or something before she'll blatantly had you an envelope for everybody else to see. I don't think she could cover that very good, but handing you or me a napkin with the envelope underneath it, well, that just makes good sense to me."

"When all of this is over would you like to join the force? We could sure use someone like you. You seem to be ahead of me by one step almost all of the time."

"I'll give it some thought. You all need a woman's intuition to tell you when you're wrong." Terrie said with a giggle, settling back in her seat.

———

Clem walked in the door and looked at Jeb Stewart and sighed. "Well, that takes care of the house. I just finished signing the papers, took a two-year lease on it. I've got the keys, but something I thought of coming back here, how do I get Jack, Terrie and me up there without arousing suspicion."

Jeb Stewart, like Jack had been his partner almost from the beginning of his career with the FBI. The three men had gone through a lot together both in the field and in their personal lives. Clem trusted Jeb and Jack with his life. They were more than just friends the three of them were like brothers.

"Isn't that like putting the cart before the horse, in a matter of speaking. When are they due to land in Minneapolis, by the way?"

"Well, let me see. They left San Francisco yesterday at approximately 3:15 got into Salt Lake City around 6 and I'd given them instructions to go to a motel right there and catch an 9 am flight to Minneapolis, so let's see that should take about 4 hours with the time change, so they'll be landing in Minneapolis around 1 pm. Besides you can't sit there and tell me I didn't have to push to get all of this done when we found out that the 'boys' were going to San Francisco. We sure as Hell couldn't have left Jack & Terrie there to be discovered. Could we?"

"No. I know we couldn't, but it would've been nice if we'd had a little more warning. That's all I'm saying."

"Hey, we got the call as soon as our friend knew. Couldn't ask for anything better. Now you tell me how I'm getting all of us up there. Me from here and those two from Minneapolis without any thing looking suspicious to catch some bodies eye."

"Well, you could rent a car and drive to Minneapolis, pick them up at the airport and drive the rest of the way."

"Yah, I could, except, if I'm being watched I'd have to go around red robins barn, so to speak to get to Minneapolis and I sure has Hell don't have that kind of time."

Clem sat down at his desk and started tapping his pencil on his desk pad. This was a bad habit he had when he was thinking, worried or couldn't put his finger on something that seemed all wrong.

"Damn, will you quit tapping that pencil. You're making a nervous wreck out of me."

"I'm sorry. You know how I am."

"Yes, I do and it still irritates me every time you do it. Wait a minute. Didn't we have an Indian on the payroll, at one time, that lived up in that area, who was a hot-shot pilot?"

"Now that you mention it we did. What was his name? I remember it wasn't Indian sounding, if I remember correctly he flew for the Marines in Korea. Put a call through to Washington, let's see if we can find out his name and where abouts, in a short very short period of time. It is now 8 am and if I have the time figured right I have about 4 hours to get all of this coordinated."

"Gee, Clem you don't want much do you!" Jeb said as he reached for the phone.

It only took Jeb about fifteen minutes to get the right man, who not only remembered their Indian "friend", but had flown with him in Korea. Within minutes of speaking with him a fax came over and gave them all the information they needed on him. He still lived up in Northern Minnesota, still flew and to the best of the records still had at least 2 seaplanes. One even had wheels, so he could take off from land and still land on water.

"Hot damn. Here's everything we need" Jeb said handing Clem the fax.

"Good. Now let me see if he's home. What's his name—oh here it is Steve. I knew it didn't sound Indian." Clem said as he reached for the phone.

"Is this Steve Cosloski?" Clem asked

"Yes it is. Who's calling?"

"Steve this is Clem, Clem Brown with the Federal Bureau of Investigation."

"Yes sir. What can I do for you?"

"I understand you still have your airplanes."

"Yes sir. I have two."

"Is one of them equipped to take off from land and land on water."?

"Yes sir it is." Steve was wondering what was going on and he wasn't really sure if he was talking to the FBI or not.

"Would you or could you meet me at Chicago O'Hare and then fly me where I want to go?"

"Ah, Mr. Brown, Clem. You kind of caught me at an awkward time. Could I call you back in say about 30 minutes?"

"Sure, if you have to I'd appreciate it. I'm kind of on a tight schedule, but I'll stand by."

"Thanks. Give me your telephone number and I'll get back to you shortly."

Clem gave him his office number and then sat and waited for him to call back.

When Steve hung up the phone he called a friend of his with the FBI in Washington to check this Clem Brown out. After getting the information he needed he picked up the phone and dialed Clem's office.

"FBI, Kansas bureau. Clem Brown speaking. May I help you?"

"Clem, this is Steve. Now what do you need and I'll see how I can work it out."

"Well, it's like this. We have a young lady that we are keeping in hiding for reasons I don't want to go into on the telephone. If you could meet me at O'Hare in say about 2 hours, with the plane that takes off from land and lands on water I'll explain everything to you then."

"Ah, are we going to discuss finances then or now?"

"Then. I'll go into all the details. You will, however, be well compensated for your plane and your time."

"OK. I trust you. I'll meet you at Hanger 22 in about two hours. That's pretty secluded. I mean out of the publics eye and I know the guy that owns it."

"That sounds good. I'll meet you there." Clem said as he hung up and looked at Jeb. "Well, now. If I'm going to meet him in three hours I guess I better go pack a bag. Call the airport for me and charter me a plane to Chicago O'Hare. Call me at the apartment and give me the details. I should be home in about twenty minutes."

"OK Clem. Just be careful. This whole thing is getting more dangerous by the minute. It sure isn't one of our normal type cases is it?" Jeb said as he watched Clem. 'What's with this guy. I haven't seen him this worried since his wife and kids died.'

"You know I'll be as careful as I can. I have to take every precaution possible to get Terrie up to that house without anyone knowing where she is living. I'll be gone a couple of days. I should be back in the office by next Monday. Cover for me will you."

"Sure I will. Don't I always when you're hot on something. Just be careful. The Bureau can't afford to loose the likes of you." Jeb said half heartedly as he watched Clem walk out the door and he picked up the phone to call the charter service.

———

"Hi Steve." Clem said as he held out his hand. "I'm Clement Brown. Clem to my friends."

"How soon do we leave and where are we going?" Steve asked as he sized Clem up. He'd heard some pretty impressive things from his friend about this man. His friend referred to Clem as a one-man army, set out to destroy the Mafia. 'Well, Clem, that's one helluva program you've set up for your self. I'm not sure you or anyone else can accomplish that, but we'll see.'

"Has your friend got a place where we could have some coffee and talk in private here at the hanger?"

"Sure. Follow me."

Clem followed Steve inside the hanger and down a hallway to the 'coffee room'.

"We can sit here. No one will bother us. Not many people around right now anyway. His mechanics are all busy, so they won't be here for about another hour." Steve said as he looked at his watch. "Now what's the program?"

"I've, er, we've, the Bureau, that is, have this young lady that will be testifying against the Mafia and we've got to keep her safe. I had her with another agent out in California and found out the 'boys' have sent some men out there to look for her. I've rented a house, or cabin, on a lake up in your neck of the woods. Right now she and the agent are winging their way to Minneapolis. I need to pick them up there and fly them on up to this lake. They should land in Minneapolis in around one o'clock. Can you do it? There will be all their luggage plus my bag."

"Sounds like a piece of cake. Do you have a private hanger in Minneapolis where they can go to get out of site of people?"

"Oh shit. That's the one thing I forgot about. Do you know anyone up there you could trust?"

"Sure, I've got an old service buddy. I can contact him, but how are your people going to know about it?"

"You contact your buddy and I can use your plane radio to contact their pilot to get a message to them. That'll work won't it."? Clem said. Mad at himself for not thinking this whole thing through and covering that part of it.

"Let me call him and then we'll go out to my plane and you can work it out with your people."

"Thanks" 'How could I miss something like that? Did I expect them just to know by osmoses or some thing?'

"OK. That's taken care of, let's get up in the air and your can contact your people."

---

"I had no idea you had such influential friends" Clem said to Steve as he stood watching the ambulance back up to the plane and watched as someone was lowered onto a gurney with a man along side of it.

"Well, I told you I served with this guy in Korea. I didn't say and you didn't ask what kind of a hanger he had." Steve said as they waited for the ambulance that was coming towards them. Steve's friend was a medic in service plus a chopper pilot. When he got out of the service he started the one kind of thing he was most familiar with a helicopter/airplane ambulance service. In these parts he was considered the best pilot around.

"Well, this is one kind of a cover that I never considered. I'll have to put this in my 'little black book' in the event that we'll need something like this again sometime. In fact, it could be within the next year or two." Clem said as he and Steve walked towards the ambulance as it backed into the hanger.

"Well, this is the shortest ride I've given someone, but the most fun." Hap said as he got out of the front seat of the ambulance and headed towards its back doors. "I haven't made money this easy since we were in that poker game on Guam." He said as he winked at Steve.

"We don't need to discuss that thing right now." Steve said laughing as he walked over with Clem to meet the lady on the stretcher and the gentleman with her.

"Man this was one close call." Clem said as he stuck out his hand to shake Jack's.

"A little too close for comfort if you ask me." Jack said as he shook Clem's hand.

Terrie got up off the gurney, looked at Clem and didn't know whether to shake his hand, give him a kiss or a hug. She opted for the latter. Looking up at Clem she said, "You really are a sight for sore eyes. How've you been? And now were are we or am I going?"

"You're looking pretty good yourself, Terrie." Clem said as he looked down at her. "No worse for wear. Guess Jack did his job keeping you safe."

"Yeah, he did, but I'm sure he's glad he's about through with me. I'm sure he'd like to go home to that beautiful wife of his. Almost six months is long enough to be separated from your loved one, don't you think?"

"Yep. And I intend on rectifying that in about a week. By the way Jack I've got a letter for you from Nina." Clem said as he reached into his pocket and brought out a fairly thick envelope.

"Thanks Clem. Do I have time to read it privately before we take off?"

"Sure. We'll go down to the coffee room. You can catch up to us there."

———

"About how long of a ride is this?" Terrie asked as they all got aboard the plane in the hanger.

"About 2 and a half hours, if the wind and weather stays with me." Steve answered her as he climbed into the cockpit and prepared to move the plane out onto the runway.

"In that case, do you suppose there's a blanket around I could use and maybe a pillow. I'd like to sleep for awhile." Terrie asked as she looked around the plane. It was a bigger plane than she thought a seaplane would be, but still not as big as a passenger plane. This plane looked like it could handle eight or nine passengers easily.

"There are blankets and pillows in the back, under one of the seats." Steve yelled as he revived the motors.

"Thanks." Clem said as he went back and got a blanket and pillow for Terrie. After making sure she was covered he moved towards the front of the plane where Jack was sitting.

"Didn't she get any sleep last night?" Clem quietly asked Jack.

"She hasn't been sleeping very well at all lately. It's as if she knew this was going to take place and she was scared. Imagine how scared been if she'd known that our friend was sitting in the airport restaurant."

"You didn't tell her who you saw?" Clem asked

"No. I figured she was scared enough, even tho' she tried not to show it, and I didn't need to add to it, by telling her who I saw. It wouldn't have meant anything to her anyway, unless I told her everything and you and I agreed not to, therefore what she doesn't know, doesn't need to hurt her. Right?" Jack said studying Clem. Narrowed eyebrows always told that Clem was extremely worried about something. And they were very narrowed right now. "What's worrying you Clem?"

"I'm just hoping that nothing has leaked out about this part of her move, at least not yet. I'd like to get her settled in, introduce her to some key people and all first."

"Where is this place we're going to and are you sure she'll be safe?"

"I've scoured all around the country, including Canada, where we've got others, but I decided that wasn't the place to put her.

This place has been checked out thoroughly and I know she's going to be safe and protected there."

"How can you be so sure?"

"This place, rather the camp that's across the lake from where she'll be living, has the secret service all over the place in September, October and May every year."

"Why is that?"

"This is the camp where the President goes fishing and hunting. Thus the secret service. I've already explained the situation to them and they've assured me that I couldn't have found a safer place than Pike Lake, the Lawry's Island and of course Northwoods Lodge owned by the Fitzgerald's. The Lodge is where the secret service stays and all, along with the President. It seems as tho' several big wheels in Washington and here in this state have had these people checked out thoroughly."

"Well, I sure as Hell hope she likes the backwoods, wild animals—they do have wild animals there don't they?"

"Sure. They have black bear, timber wolves, fox, deer, moose everything. Especially in the summer when the animals swim from island to island."

"Even the bear?"

"Yeah. It seems as tho' they are terrific swimmers. I've also been told to tell Terrie how to discard her trash. Like not leaving food, bags, fish scales and guts, well just about everything outside the house. This is a whole new way of living and yet not that different from living in Georgia. Besides why wouldn't she like this kind of life? Look where she lived in Georgia way out in the country with fields of cotton and peanuts for her neighbors. This can't be that different. Can it?"

"Well. All I can say is I hope you're right. After all she has spent the last almost six months in a pretty good size city, not far from malls, makeup and all the things ladies like."

"In that case. Keep your fingers crossed that I did the right thing in leasing this place. I really wasn't worried until you just said all those things." Clem was now more worried than ever. He hadn't taken in to consideration that she just might not like this backwoods life style. "Oh Hell, it's too late now to worry about it. It's over and done with and she'll just have to accept it." He wasn't near as angry as that statement sounded, just scared that she wouldn't like it. He thought he knew her fairly well, but maybe not as well as he thought, or would like to—'I'll know soon enough he thought.'

"How close are we getting to landing?" Clem asked Steve. He'd walked up to the cockpit to check out the scenery and thought things were starting to look familiar. He'd flown over the area once or twice before deciding on checking things out.

"Well, that's the reservation down there on the left, so after I bank this sucker a little bit, I'll be approaching the lake and landing. I'm sure glad you chose these people to dock up with. They are extraordinary people. I've known them since I was a kid. Way back when they were good to my tribe during an altercation. It'll be good to see them again. This is the first chance I've had to fly up here for about five years." Steve said as he started his approach.

"Guess I better go wake Terrie"

"Oh, I see Jack already woke you up." Clem said as Terrie walked towards him.

"Yeah, I heard what Steve said about landing so I decided I best go wake her."

"Where are we?" Terrie asked as she looked out the window

"Getting close to your home. At least for the next maybe two years, or at least until this thing gets settled." Clem told her scared to pieces that she wasn't going to like it. 'Please dear God see to it that Terrie likes this place and arrangements.'

"Wait a minute." Terrie said as Steve landed and moved ever so slowly towards the dock. "Don't tell me. Is this Northwood's Lodge we're pulling into?"

"Well, yes, it is. Do you know this place?" Clem said with a startled look on his face.

Even Jack couldn't hide his surprise at how she recognized this place.

"Know it! I grew up here. Well, kind of anyway. My Mom and

Dad honeymooned here when there was just a dorm here. No lodge to speak of, no house and of course no cabins. They brought Bud and I fishing here the rest of our lives. Well, with me until I got married. Bud still comes up here every year. And every year he calls and tells me he's coming up and looking through their picture albums and every thing and he knows how jealous I am. Gosh it'll be good to see Tom and his wife Iris. Come to think of it, Rickey their son is running the place now with his wife Laura. At least that's what I kind of remember Bud told me. Is this where I'll be living?"

"Well, not exactly. You'll be living on that island over there." Clem said pointing to an island out a ways from the land.

"Oh, that's Lawry's. I use to swim from this pier to Lawry's Island when I was a kid." Terrie's heart was skipping a beat so fast that she thought it was going to jump out of her skin. She was finally coming home. At least to her this was home and Bud didn't have anything up on her now. "Do you suppose that I'll be able to visit with Bud when he comes up later on this summer?"

"Let's get you settled. Then we'll sit and discuss what we feel like you can and can't due while you're here. I can tell you this much these people have been checked out by our people and they are extremely trustworthy. So you will be able to come here and visit. We know that only people that have been coming here for years are allowed in here. From that stand point of view we really are grateful."

"Well, we're here, so I guess everyone can unload." Steve said as he acknowledged Dave tying up the plane.

"Steve, we can't thank you enough for all you've done for us. As I told you, you will be well compensated for this trip." Clem said as he stepped down on the pier turning around to help Terrie disembark. "Watch your step, I don't need you falling and hurting yourself.

As Terrie took Clem's hand you gave Steve a look of recognition. "Wait a minute, aren't you the one that used to bring you're plane in here and take people for rides."

"Yes I am." Steve answered looking at her like do I know you?
"Now I remember. You flew in Korea and if I remember Mom
telling me correctly, you helped catch some foreigners that were
up to no good. You had the reputation that you could land on a
dime and give nine cents back as change." Terrie said laughing

"Yep, that's me. I'm the guilty party. Wait a minute. I heard
what you were telling Clem about your Mom and Dad. Your Bob
and Vivian Wilson's daughter aren't you?" Steve said scratching his
head and laughing.

"Yes sir, I sure am. It definitely proves that it is a small world.
I haven't seen you since I was about eighteen."

"Well, I must say you've grown into a beautiful lady" Steve
said wondering why they brought her here and why the secrecy.
He knew enough about the Feds not to ask questions, so he didn't.

"Thank you Steve. You're just as good looking as I remember
you from years ago."

"Hey, wait a minute it wasn't *that* long ago. Long enough, but
I'm not over the hill yet." Steve remarked laughing.

"If you two don't mind could we finish unpacking this plane
and get on with getting you settled." Clem said as he climbed
back into the plane to retrieve the luggage.

"Yeah, sure. You all finish up. You don't need my help. I'm
going up to visit with Tom and Iris, Dave. Will you keep your eye
on my baby till I get back."

Dave nodded and Steve continued, "Thanks everybody and
thanks Dave I'll see you in awhile. The plane isn't going to bother
anybody is it?" He said looking at Dave.

"Oh no sir. We knew you were coming in, so I've taken care of
moving the boats of the people that aren't out either onto the
other side of the pier or put them back out at their mooring. You're
fine. Not to worry." Dave said. He was the 'boat boy'. At least
that's what every body called him. In fact there wasn't much he
didn't do around here. He was considered one of the best employees
that Tom and Iris had had in a long time.

"I'm thirsty. Can we go up to the Lodge, please? I would like to check it out and see if there's been any changes since I was here last." Terrie asked almost in a pleading voice.

"Sure in fact you go on ahead. Jack and I can finish getting your luggage and then we'll be up. I have some things to work out with them. Besides we're having dinner in the Lodge before we go out to the island." Clem let out a sigh of relief as he turned and looked at Jack. "What's the silly look all about?" he asked Jack.

"Well, if I didn't know any better I'd say you were a tad jealous of her and Steve when they realized they had known each other years ago." Jack said as he climbed back into the plane. "I'll hand the stuff out to you and you can sit it on the pier." Grinning at Clem as he said it.

"Why would I be jealous" Clem said as he reached for a suitcase. "Besides, that was years ago." Clem had to admit to himself that he had a tinge of jealousy hit him, but he didn't want Jack or anyone else to know.

Terrie walked slowly up to the Lodge taking in as much as she could. 'Every thing looks the same. It's just as if time stood still. The lodge building stood as stately as ever, with it's slanted roof over the solarium. Never could understand why they called the glass enclosed porch that, but they did. Its' still painted yellow with the white trim. There's the 'big house'. Never figured that one out either, but every body, including the Fitzgerald's called it that. Oh, the flowers are a little different, but that's about all that's changed. Wonder if they've built anymore cabins since I was here last. I see what Bud was telling me about Cabin 2 being moved down off the hill. Wonder if they still use the icehouse for icing the fish. Wonder if Tom still cuts the ice for everyone around the lake like he used to do.' All kinds of thoughts were running through Terrie's head as she reached for the screen door. 'Oh the drums are gone and so is the player piano. Guess they got rid of them when Tom, Sr. passed away. Lots of fond memories with those things remembering how Senior played and others sang. He was quite a drummer. Guess that's one of the things that has changed.' She thought as she walked into the dining room. Standing

there looking around she saw things definitely had not changed in
here. There's the bass my uncle caught hanging as proudly as ever,
and there's Lucifer. Mom had told me that she had found a ceramic
white seagull and had given it to Tom and Iris after Lucifer died.'
Lucifer had been the pet seagull of the camp. Everyone knew that
when they cleaned their fish at the fish house they put the skin,
head and guts in the covered garbage can. These then would be
taken out to a special small raft and dumped for Lucifer. Lucifer
would not allow any other birds around to feed. That was his and
only his. 'He was funny' Terrie thought as she stared at his likeness
on the fireplace mantel. He would sit on an incline by the cleaning
table, while people were cleaning their fish. He'd just sit and watch,
knowing that that would soon be his dinner. He never tried to
peck or hurt anybody, just sit and watch. Guess he just wanted to
make sure that they didn't cheat him out of anything.' After staring
at Lucifer, she looked down and saw the big bear rug lying in front
of the fireplace. 'Wonder if that's the same one that always lay
there. That things got to be close to 50 years old by now. Well
maybe not that old,' she thought, 'but at least it's still there.'

   "Well, are things still the same or have there been changes?"
Clem said as he walked up behind Terrie as she stood in the dining
room.

   "Things are still the same as they were when I came up here
last. Oh sure, there are subtle changes, but all in all everything
seems to be like time stood still. It's beautiful," Terrie said with
tears streaming down her checks. All of a sudden, for her, looking
around the past came flowing. All of the fun times, all the times
that she'd been yelled at or bawled out for doing something she
shouldn't do, like cutting through the woods, taking the boat to
town at the age of ten. Sure as a kid she got mad when people,
Tom, Jr., her Dad, friends bawled her out and told her how
dangerous the things she'd done were, but right now, all she could
see, hear and think about were the fish she caught, the friends
she'd made, her Mom and Dad. Her whole childhood went spinning
past her.

"I wouldn't change any of my past up here for anything in the world. I always called this place home. I felt nearer to God here, than anyplace else on earth that I've traveled or lived, even Georgia." Terrie had turned and was looking at Clem when all of this had poured out of her mouth. "Thank you for choosing this place, no matter the reason. I know I'm safe here and I'm home. I'll go in the kitchen and tell everyone Hi and then we can do what ever you have planned for me. That is if it's OK with you."

"By all means go in and tell everyone Hello. We will see them later as we're coming back here for dinner. As soon as you're through with your Hello's come back down to the dock and we'll go over to the island. I want to check things out with the lights and all before it gets dark." Clem said looking at her and how truly happy she finally seemed. 'What luck finding this place. Was it luck, I wonder, everybody says that luck has nothing to do with things. It's fate. What ever that means. Oh well, I'm just glad that she finally feels as if she were at home and finally feels safe. Clem thought as he headed down the hill to the dock.'

Arriving back down at the dock Terrie was disappointed seeing that Steve's plane was gone. 'I'd hoped to tell him goodbye. Oh well, maybe I'll see him again sometime.'

"Man, this is some kind of a whopsie doodle boat. What's it called? Is it mine?" Terrie asked as she climbed in and put on her life preserver.

"To answer your last question first yes, it is yours. This is a bass boat. It's brand new and has top of the line everything on it, depth finder to find the 'big ones', twin 30 horse engines, trolling motor and it even has a ship to shore radio. That's just in case something happens you'll be able to call Fitzgerald's for help."

"What kind of 'something' are you talking about?"

"Well, lets say that you run out of gas out on the lake, you'll be able to call into Northwood's and Dave or Tom will answer you and bring you out gas." Clem said not wanting her to be scared of something else. He'd searched all over to get this boat and have it top of the line in case of any kind of an emergency. Of course it didn't hurt that this was the exact boat he'd always wanted. He had laughed at himself, as had Jeb when he went into the office and announced that he'd found the perfect fishing boat for Terrie. Jeb had teased him, 'kind of putting the cart before the horse aren't you'. Clem was positive that he'd find someplace on Pike Lake to put her, he neither knew how or why this was a necessity, why this particular lake, all of this was unknown to him, but when he bought the boat he knew it would happen. Boy am I ever optimistic. He just knew it had to happen.

"Well here we are, home sweet home, at least for awhile." Clem said as he steered the boat into the boathouse.

"Mmmm" Terrie said as she climbed out of the boat onto the short pier. "It appears that I'll have some wood repair work to do" as she looked down at some of the broken boards. "Sure don't want to fall on any broken planks."

# CHAPTER 11

"Well, guys I guess it's about time Lou and I left and got to work trying to find this lady" Tony looked at his watch and said besides, it's about time you two started towards your gate. Didn't you say it leaves at 9?"

"Yes. You're right, come on Archie let's pay the check and get out of here. We sure don't want to miss this flight. Home has been a long time coming." Morici said as he stood and shook Tony's hand. "I hope you two have better luck than we did trying to find her. Hell, I was even in Germany chasing after her."

They paid their checks and headed towards the gate just as the ticket taker (that's what Archie called them) announced their flight over the PA system.

"Man" Archie said as they settled into their seats. "This has been a long trip and I'll sure be glad to get home. I don't see how ya did it—I mean Germany and all."

"I agree with you this has been along uneventful trip. I too will be glad to be home. Germany was a breeze 'cause I got to see a different country, their customs and it was totally different from here in the states. I'd like to go back sometime."

"Maybe you'll get to, who knows, maybe that broad'll show up again over there and Les will send you back to try and find her."

"Nah, I don't think that will happen. I tend to agree with Lonnie, she's here someplace. Think I'll try to get a little sleep. I've got to call Lonnie as soon as I get up in the morning and I sure don't want to sleep too late." 'Little do you know Archie how little everyone knows.' Morici thought as he closed his eyes. He really didn't want to sleep, but he was tired trying to keep up with Archie. Besides he wanted to think about things. Like want was coming next. He had a lot to think about. Like the reservations that ended up in Vancouver, British Columbia.

———————

"Good morning Lonnie. This is Morici." He said into the telephone.

"Good morning Morici. Did you have a good flight back to Atlanta?"

"Yes sir we did. In fact I slept most of the way and from the way Archie was acting and sounding when we got off the plane, he drank most of the way home. Of course, he was tired too. Have you got anything for me?"

"Well, first off how did things go in California? Did you meet up with Tony and Lou?"

"Oh yes sir. They both seemed quite capable of handling the situation out there. Of course Tony did most of the talking and asked all the right questions, but I guessed that Lou is a lot like Archie, the muscle."

"You pegged it just right. Like you said Lou is the muscle. I spoke to my brother last night and advised him as to what had happened so far and your coming back to Atlanta and he said to tell you that he'll call you at the office tonight about 9 o'clock. He figures most everyone will be gone by then."

"Ok. I'll get a hold of Archie and have him meet me down there about 8:30. That should give us enough time to get into the backroom and settled before he calls."

"Ah, I'm not sure he wants Archie there. At least he didn't say anything to me about him being there. He only said he'd call you."

"Hmm, wonder what that's all about." Morici said 'wonder in deed.'

"I think it's just that he trusts your judgment and knowledge and would rather discuss things without Archie chiming in his two cents worth. If you get my drift."

"Yes sir. I think I'm catching it. I won't say anything to Arch. I'll just tell him I did talk to you, but that we had a couple days off to kind of catch up on our rest. That'll pacify him."

"Sounds good to me. Ah, Morici"

"Yes sir"

"Would you mind calling me when you get through talking to my brother tonight."

"No sir. I'd be glad to as soon as I hang up."

"No. Go on home after your conversation with him and then call me—ah, from your place."

"OK. I'll talk to you tonight around 11ish?"

"That sounds like a winner. Talk to you later. And Morici thanks for all the help."

"Sure thing." Morici said as he hung up the phone. 'That's interesting, why does he want me to call him from here instead of the office? Wonder what he has in mind. Not double-crossing his brother, I'm sure. Oh well, guess I'll find out tonight.'

"Good morning Archie. It's almost 11:30 I hope you are awake." Morici said into the phone.

"Yeah just barely. I haven't even had my coffee yet. Man that flight was murder on me. I feel awful."

"How about I come over and we go have some breakfast. That'll make you feel better."

"Did you talk to Lonnie this morning?"

"Sure did. In fact he said the boss said to give us a couple of days off before we have to go to the shop. Guess they want us to thaw out a bit. Whatever the reason, I'm glad to have a couple days off. How 'bout you?"

"That's the best news I've heard besides being told that we was comin' home. Sure come on over. I'll take my shower and be standing out front."

"That sounds great see you in about 30 minutes." Morici hung up the phone and started thinking 'what the Hell do I have to talk to him about. Nothing. Oh well, that's part of the game.'

Morici picked Archie up after breakfast he took him grocery shopping. After all they'd been gone almost 6 months so both of them had a lot of shopping to do. Morici decided since they were on the far north side of Atlanta he'd go on up to the buffet steakhouse that he'd told Archie about. As he suspected Archie was thrilled with it and ate heartedly.

"Gee, Morici I'm sure glad I gotta friend like you. You seem to know all the right places. Thanks a lot for taking me with you." Archie said as he got out of the car.

"I'll help you get your stuff into the house. You've got enough for an army. What all did you buy?" Morici said as he picked some of the bags of groceries.

"Oh, just the norm. Of course, I had to get my snacks 'cause the ones I had got stale on me. Then my beer, coffee and oh you know, toilet paper. Just that kind of stuff."

"Yeah, I guess I can't say too much about yours. I've got a lot myself." Morici said as he took the last sack into the house. "Well, I'll see you later. If you need anything give me a call."

"OK Morici and thanks again."

Morici spent the next few hours cleaning his place. He had a lot of food to throw away. Nobody thought they'd be gone that long. After cleaning and putting the food away he checked the clock 6pm. 'Time enough to watch the news, take a shower and then head for the office. Can't be late for that call. Wonder what he wants with me instead of talking to his right hand. Oh well, no sense in worrying about it. I'll find out soon enough.'

"Good evening Morici. I want to say a job well done ah out west, I mean" Les said as Morici answered the phone

"Good evening Mr. Rudicio. And thank you. I'm just sorry we had to leave it up to someone else, at least for now. How are you this fine evening?"

"I'm doing fine. I hope this finds you well rested after your trek out west."

"Yes sir. I'm rested and ready to do whatever needs to be done."

"Right now, Tony and Henri are doing everything that has to be done. In order to keep the electronics firm going I mean. They are very good at that. Mr. Waters seems to be very pleased with their knowledge of everything and how well they can get everything for him that he needs at a moments notice."

Morici knew what Les was saying. 'I'm cautious for fear some how these phones are taped. Read between the lines.' Morici was very good at that and he knew that Kyle must still be feeding the guns to whoever needed them in exchange for oil from Ali.

"That's good to hear. Being away as long as we were we haven't had time to catch up on the business. Speaking of which—did you have a special reason for me coming in this late?" He knew he shouldn't ask, but this place was creepy with the electronics in the front and the back full of all kinds of things, from guns to knapsacks, and he was wanting to get out of there.

"As a matter of fact I did. Lonnie is having some trouble with his deposits and all and I was wondering if you could go to Chattanooga and work with him for a while. Check things out and see where the problem is, if you know what I mean."

"Yes sir I get your drift. What ah cover would I use with his employees?"

"Well, how about security. That way you could be there when they count the money and you could take it to the bank. Then I know it's deposited right away. What do you think?"

"Hey that sounds great. Just as long as I don't have to deal with the books. You know that wasn't a prerequisite at my other job." Morici said and laughed.

"No. Just oversee the money counting and deposit. Then lend Lonnie a hand with any other problems he's got. He seems to like you and of course he trusts you. Guess you two kind of hit it off OK."

"Yes sir we did. I like him too he's a good kid. I'll go up and see what I can do.

Will he be expecting me?" Morici knew Lonnie had asked him to call him when he got home from this call, but he didn't want things too obvious.

"I'm going to call him when we hang up. You might give him a call tomorrow and see when he'd like for you to come up."

"OK I'll do that."

"One more thing. Don't be too obvious, right at first, in insisting on counting the money. You might just have to stand by for a couple nights. Can you handle that?"

"Yes Mr. Rudicio I can handle that. I understand what you're saying." 'He was saying that he didn't trust his brother. He thought he was skimming—what off the top? Or was there something else. Guess I'll find out in a couple of days.' Morici thought as he left the office, made his way through to the front of the building and told the security guard good night. 'Wonder if he's an ex-cop too? Who cares? Come to think of it I might someday.'

"Hey Lonnie, how you doing?" Morici said into the phone. "Told you I'd call after I spoke to your brother, but he said he was going to call you, so I thought I'd wait until closer to closing time. Just in case he had trouble trying to get through."

"That's OK Morici. He called about a half hour ago. Didn't talk too long, but said you'd be willing to come up and help me out with security and all."

"Sure Lonnie. I don't have a problem with that. It's kind of up my alley, so to speak. When would you like for me to come up? And should I get an apartment or will I be there that long?" Morici knew that he'd be there for a while. Les didn't come out and say so, but he was pretty sure Les meant for him to be there more than just a day or two and he wasn't too sure exactly what Les had told his baby brother. 'Don't want to give too much away.'

"Well, why don't you come up say tomorrow morning and I'll take you around the city and maybe we can find you a place to stay, at least for awhile. Then you can go back to Atlanta and move some of your things up here and then start on Wednesday. Friday gets pretty hectic around here, so I'd like for you to be kind of settled in here before then. With my employees and all I mean. I'll discuss everything with you when you get here tomorrow morning OK."

"Sure Lonnie. That sounds good to me. See you in the morning." 'Wow, I'm beginning to feel like this stuff is getting a little bit too hairy even for me. Wonder why Les doesn't trust his brother. What's he skimming that he shouldn't be, business is either lousy or awfully good. Oh, well, no sense in worrying about it anymore tonight. I'll find out sooner or later.'

# CHAPTER 12

"Well, Terrie, I guess it's about time for us to say goodbye. We've been here a week, checked everything out both here and in town and we can't find anything that will cause you any problems. I feel pretty good about leaving you here all alone." Clem was trying to reassure Terrie that everything was fine even tho' he wasn't too sure himself. He and Jack had taken every precaution they could think of in securing the island, making sure she knew how to handle the boat and checked out all the towns' people. The funny thing was that most of the old timers remembered Terrie from her childhood and were glad that she had bought the old Lawry place. The week they had been there she not only showed she knew how to run the boat, but she also out fished both of them.

"Guess I haven't lost my touch here on the lake." She chided them one day when she brought in two northern and two bass and the guys had only caught some pan fish. "Nothing wrong with pan fish" she said "Besides all you have to do with them is clean them, then fry them. Of course, you have to know how to clean and scale them and have the tools to do it with, which you were nice enough to supply me. Besides with what you caught yesterday it'll make a pretty good supper tonight. As far as the northerns and bass I'll clean and fillet them and put them in the freezer." Terrie had fished this lake since she was a kid and even tho' she hadn't been up here for a good spell the lake was still the same. 'Oh this year, the lakes a little lower than normal and a few more rice paddies showed up, but the rocks were more prevalent than she remembered them. At least they stood above the water now where she could see them.' She thought as she picked up their catch of pan fish and headed outside to the cleaning table.

---

"Man, that was some kind of meal. I don't know when the last time was that I've eaten so much fish and loved every bite of it." Clem said as he pushed himself away from the dinner table. "You totally out did yourself Terrie." He exclaimed

"Actually I didn't do that much. A few potatoes, some coleslaw, homemade cornbread and the fish you two caught. Oh, I forgot I baked a cherry pie for dessert." Terrie said grinning. She loved to cook especially when the people she was cooking for loved to eat.

"You baked a what?" Jack asked

"Cherry Pie. If I remember correctly you told me, shortly after we got to California, that cherry was your favorite pie."

"She doesn't forget a thing does she Clem."

"Nope. But I vote that Jack and I do the dishes, afterwards we can sit out on the porch and watch the sunset and eat the pie. How does that sound?"

"I don't know I think I should be the one to clean up the kitchen." Terrie said

"Sorry, but you're out voted" Clem said as he walked over to her chair, gently pulling on it. "You go out on the porch and when we're done we'll bring coffee out to you."

"No. When you finish I'll come in and make the coffee and cut the pie while you two sit on the porch. I've had Jack's coffee and I'm really not in the mood for stand-alone spoon coffee tonight. Just teasing you Jack. Your coffee isn't that bad. It's just something I want to do." She said laughing while she was teasing Jack. After almost six months of sharing the cooking with Jack she knew he made a pretty decent cup of coffee. Turning to look at Clem she said "Jack's coffee has been the subject of teasing every since he made the first pot the morning after we settled in California. That morning he let me sleep in. He made coffee at 5 a.m. and then he went jogging. I didn't get up until around 9 or 10 so you can imagine just how strong that coffee was after sitting on the warmer for that length of time. Every since then, I've teased him about his stand alone spoon coffee."

"Ok. We'll split hairs." Jack said We'll clean the kitchen, I'll start the coffee and I promise I won't make it strong then you can come in, cut the pie and by then the coffee should be done and you can bring it out to Clem and I on the porch. Does that suit you better?" Jack said as he started laughing.

Clem was feeling kind of jealous. He could tell that Jack and Terrie had really had a good time those months they were alone together.

"Oh alright, you two. I'll be waiting on the porch." She said as she headed towards the porch. She loved this place. How many times when she was a kid up here did she swim from Northwood to this island, she swam with a brother and sister that were up here at the same time. It was about a half a mile one-way and to 12 and 14 year olds that wasn't far at all. Besides, if my memory serves me correctly their Dad followed us in a boat. That, he said, was just in case one of us got into trouble and had to get out of the water he'd be there to help us. Sitting here looking out through the tall 'jack pines' and birch trees I can see Northwood's dock. 'How many times did Bob, Jr. yell at me don't tear the bark off those trees you'll kill them. He then told me that the Indians used to use the bigger around birch trees to build canoes. I never understood why my peeling the bark would kill the trees, but Bob, Jr. said it would so I had to listen.'

Even though Jack and Clem had been there a week with Terrie there were certain things that they had not discussed. Like how often could she visit over at the Lodge? Could she go visit her brother when he was up here. What were her boundaries for coming and going? What was she supposed to do in the wintertime? Small things like that. 'Hopefully these will be things that we'll discuss tonight' she thought as she heard the two men coming towards the porch.

"Well, are you two through playing in the kitchen?" she said kind of laughing to herself. She knew, after six months that Jack was well versed in the kitchen, but she didn't know about Clem.

"Yes, your royal majesty" Jack said as he handed her a towel "The coffee is cooking so now you can go slice the pie and bring it and the coffee to us as we sit staring at the water."

"You are such a nut case." Terrie said as she took the towel from him and returned to the kitchen.

"It seems as though you two really hit it off in California, didn't you?" Clem said to Jack as Terrie left the porch.

"Yes Clem, we did. She's everything and more than you said she was. Now I see why you care about her. She will make a great wife." Jack said watching Clem's reactions.

"Wife? Who said anything about me marrying her? I just feel sorry for her and all she's been through. She hasn't had a decent break for how long. First she works for a jerk that gets involved with 'the boys', uproots from her home and flees to another state, leaving her friends and family and then they find her and her jerk water husband up and leaves her, then she's almost killed. Who wouldn't feel sorry for her."? Clem said in a fit. He didn't want anyone, including Jack to know how he really felt about her. How could he bring something like that up? 'Yes, someday,' Clem had thought to himself, 'maybe, I will ask her to marry me, but that's no bodies business but mine.' "What on earth made you possibly think I would be interested in marrying her?" He asked Jack.

"Oh I don't know. Maybe the way you two look at each other, or maybe it's the way you've gone about protecting her, sometimes at your own expense. The way you worry about her. More than most cases we've been involved with. But hey, that's your business. Nina and I won't say or do anything, but I just want you to know we do approve." Jack knew he had to tell Clem like it was. He and Nina both recognized how much Clem cared about Terrie. Why should he hide it, except for the fact that he was FBI first and a man second. Nothing or no one would get in the middle of his doing a job.

"Well, I do—," Clem was interrupted by Terrie asking someone to open the screen door for her.

"That pie was absolutely delicious. You know Jack the way to a man's heart is through his stomach and this young lady sure has found the way to do it, hasn't she." Clem said as he set his empty plate down.

"I told you that that Thanksgiving dinner was only a tempting treat. She truly is a marvelous cook and the nice part about it is she loves to cook." Jack said as he picked up Clem's plate and headed towards the kitchen.

"Guess we have some things to discuss before we leave here tomorrow, don't we?" Clem said as he took a sip of his coffee and looked at Terrie.

"Guess we do. There are a lot of things that I still don't know about. I really do appreciate all that you and Jack have done for me this past week. I couldn't have gotten that garden in by myself, fixed the fireplace, repaired the dock, cleaned off the other end of the island and fixed the roof over the boat house. Sure I could have done most of it in time, but you two got it done in just a few days. The only thing I have to do now is to remember to water the garden. It's going to be great having vegetables to put into the freezer. Which reminds me, have I thanked you for bringing a lot of my things up from the house? It helps to have things of my own around me to work with. It gives me a comforting feeling. Maybe I can settle down and not worry about the outside world for a while. I'm sorry, I forgot we were going to discuss things after you two are gone."

"That's OK Terrie." Clem said "I was waiting for Jack to get out here before we began talking and making lists for you."

"OK, dishes are done and a new pot of coffee is started. Have I missed anything?" Jack said as he sat down on the porch swing. "I've always loved porch swings. Glad you two sat in the chairs. I've got the swing all to myself."

"You've not missed a thing and you're most welcome to the swing. I'll have plenty of time to use it after your gone." Terrie said. The porch was a wrap around on three sides of the house. It had rattan chairs and table plus the swing on one end, right outside the front door. The rest of the porch was glass enclosed with a door leading to it from the dining room. The room could be heated with a small two-burner wood-burning stove that was in one corner of the room. The backside of the house, kitchen side, looked out over the lake on the northeast side of the island. It had a backdoor and steps leading out to the clearing where her garden was now. The view was gorgeous from any place in the house. Terrie knew she would be happy here. She was worried that she would get lonesome during the winter months, but Clem had seen to it that all of her yarn, material, patterns, books and sewing machine had been brought up, so she knew she could spend a lot of time doing what she loved and that was crocheting and sewing. She also could use a lot of things off the island to make flower wreaths and decorations. Who knows, maybe I'll even get new curtains and linens made for the bedroom. Heaven knows I've enough material to make almost anything I want to, crocheting, yes they had brought all of her yarn, so she could make all kinds of afghans, sweaters maybe even gloves if she put her mind to it. The house had four bedrooms, dining room, living room, country kitchen and two bathrooms all on one floor. It was truly rustic. The outside was built out of native logs and the inside was rough sawn cedar. 'If I had a horse I'd really be happy. Kind of stupid, tho' cause I don't have enough island to have one, besides all of the wild animals it probably wouldn't live.'

"I'm sorry Clem did you say something to me?" Terrie said as she poured herself some more coffee and offered some to Jack and Clem. She knew one of them had said something, but she'd been in her own world and hadn't heard him.

"I was just saying that we had to get started talking about the do's and don'ts that we feel you should follow while we're gone." He didn't want to be too hard on her because he knew she'd get lonesome during the winter months, but there were some precautions that had to be taken.

"Well, let me get a notepad, so I can keep the list handy until I get used to everything." Terrie said as she stood and headed for the house. "Oh, let me take the carafe and I'll fill it with the fresh coffee while I'm inside." She said as she reached for it the same time Clem was picking it up to hand it to her. Their hands touched and she felt a chill go up her spine. 'Hmm, guess I best bring a sweater back out here with me. It's getting chilly.'

"Terrie will you please bring me my tape recorder" Jack asked

"Sure, where is it."?

"Laying on the dining room table."

"OK. Be back in a few."

Jack looked at Clem, "You look worried. What's wrong? Don't you think Terrie's going to be safe up here?" Jack knew Clem so well and he could tell when something was wrong and this time the feeling was extremely strong.

"No, I'm really not worried. I know Terrie will be safe up here. No one should even think of looking up here, especially with an informer on the inside, letting us know what's going on. I just don't like leaving her alone in the middle of the lake."

"But, she's not really alone. She's got the short wave radio, walkie talkie to the Fitzgerald's, the boat with a radio—why do you say she's alone?"

"Let's face it—sure she's used to being alone, but she's had you around for the last six months and knowing you, you didn't leave her alone too often. I'm just worried about her being alone in the winter and who's going to cut her wood for her fireplace, oh hell, I don't know what I'm saying." Clem said. He knew his mumbling was getting him into all kinds of trouble. It was showing his vulnerable side and he was starting to sound like he truly cared about Terrie and he didn't. At least he didn't want anyone to know he cared.

"OK. Here's a fresh carafe of coffee and another pot brewing. I figure we'll be sitting here for awhile and will need it." Terrie said as she slammed the door behind her. One tape recorder for you and I also brought my tape recorder along with a notepad." She said as she handed Jack his recorder.

"Now if you two are through with your tête-à-tête we can get started." Clem said irritated.

Jack and Terrie looked at each other, shook their heads and sat down.

"OK Clem we're ready" Terrie said as she finished pouring each of them a cup of fresh coffee and picked up her pen and turned her tape recorder on.

"OK. Let's see what kind of a list of Do's and Don'ts I've come up with. For right now—there won't be a lot of don'ts. The don'ts really start in September. That's when most of the traveler's have headed back home, the lodge starts closing and you will be alone. When that time comes I want you to remember, if something happens that you don't think is right, if you see strangers either on the lake or in town, you're to call me eh, the office on the short wave radio. I'll be here in a flash. I mean I'll have Steve up here ASAP. I know he's trustworthy and a damn good pilot. Besides that, you know him and he's a lot closer here than I am, eh the Bureau. I really don't have a lot to tell you except just be careful and use your head. I know Bud comes up for 3 or 4 weeks and I see no reason why you can't go to Fitzgerald's when he's here or he can come out here. We've checked out everyone that is coming up here this summer, so if you get too lonesome go visit with the Fitzgerald's and their guests. I really don't have a lot to tell you except just be careful and use your head. I do have one thing and I know you're not going to especially like it, but—

"What, what is it?" Terrie interrupted. It sounded like he was stuttering or something and this was hard enough, them leaving, she didn't need him dragging things out.

"I want you to make a list. Put a pad and pen on the kitchen table, or on your night stand next to the bed. Every time you think or remember names, places, companies or incidences write them down. Even if you think you've already told one or both of us. I know you're tired of all of this and you truly believe that you've told us everything, a thousand times, but there's a possibility that there's some little thing that you haven't told us for whatever reason you've not thought of it or remembered it. Up here, all alone, you just might have a thought cross your mind that you thought you told us, but just maybe you didn't. No matter how large or small. That way we can compare that list to what we already have and make sure we do have everything we need to get those scum bums off the streets. Do you think you can do that for me Terrie?"

"Sure, no problem." Terrie answered him. 'What could there possibly be that I've forgotten to tell them? Oh, well, I'll humor them.'

"During the winter we will have Steve bring you mail and any supplies you might need. Do you have any questions? Ahh Jack do you have anything to add to what I've just said?"

"I don't have anything that I can think of right now." Jack said looking at Clem. Man he really does care for her. Why can't they both see how they feel? Not the right time or place I guess. Wait till I get back and tell Nina. She'll just look at me and say 'I told you so.' With that silly smurk that she's gets when she's right and I'm wrong.

"Terrie what about you. Do you have any questions?" Clem asked turning towards her. "Coffee?" he asked as he lifted the carafe.

"Yes, please. Coffee, I mean. No I can't think of any questions right now. If after the two of you leave, am I at liberty to call on the short wave or go to Fitzgerald's to talk to you. I mean to ask questions?" Terrie felt like she was blushing, but she sure hoped not. She didn't want anyone to know how she was feeling.

Clem poured coffee all around and then said, "Sure." He was afraid to look at her directly for fear she'd be able to see in his eyes how he really felt. Speaking of the Fitzgerald's after we finish this, why don't we go over and have a drink with them. They're such nice people I'd like to at least say good-bye."

"That sounds like a great idea. If you two don't have to leave until day after tomorrow why don't we make arrangements to have dinner in the lodge tomorrow night."

"What and miss your good cooking" Jack said laughing

"I think Terrie's right. A meal in the Lodge tomorrow night sounds like a great way for a send off." Clem replied. "I'll call Steve and tell him to come up day after tomorrow instead of tomorrow," He said as he stood and headed into the house.

"You know Clem better than I do Jack, but is it my imagination or is he unusually edgy tonight?" Terrie asked quietly.

"Oh, I don't know that he's unusually edgy. I think he's just worried about you being up here alone."

———

Terrie awoke to the sound of propellers. 'Oh good heavens, I've over slept.' She thought as she jumped out of bed and dressed. Rounding the corner into the kitchen she saw Clem on the porch, drinking a cup of coffee and staring out over the lake. She didn't see Jack. After pouring herself a cup of coffee she strolled onto the porch.

"Good morning. I guess I over slept. Where's Jack?" she said as she walked up next to Clem.

"Good morning. He went down to the dock to help Steve tie off the plane."

"I'm so sorry that I slept through my alarm. I was going to have a big going away breakfast for the two of you." Terrie hated it that she had overslept. She so wanted to give Clem something to remember her by. She had it all planned; at least last night she'd planned it out in her head, bacon, eggs, homemade biscuits and pancakes.

"No problem Terrie" Clem said as he turned and looked at her. God she's beautiful, even first thing in the morning. Jeans, flannel shirt and a ribbon tying her beautiful hair back. She really is at home here. I'm so glad I found this place, she should be safe here. I'm really going to miss her, but with the short wave radio and Fitzgerald's, as long as I call from a pay phone I'll be able to talk to her. "Here comes Jack and Steve now" he said looking down at her.

"Good morning folks. How are you two this fine beautiful morning?" Steve said as he came up the steps to the porch.

"We're fine Steve. Would you like a cup of coffee?" Terrie asked

"Sure"

"What about you Jack, you ready for a cup?" Terrie asked as she started towards the kitchen.

"Sure. I'll come help you."

"No need for that. I'll just bring the carafe and cups out here. Then you all can fix your coffee the way you like it." Terrie went into the kitchen and arranged the carafe, cups, sugar, creamer and some napkins on the tray.

"Well guys" Steve said as he set his coffee cup down on the tray and stood up "I guess we best be taking off if you two want to get back to civilization anytime soon."

"We've got our suitcases already down on the dock, so I guess we're as ready as we're going to be." Clem said as he stood and looked at Terrie. "Guess this is it. Just remember if you need anything, anything at all just give me, us a call."

"I know Clem, I truly do appreciate all you have done for me. You, Jack, Nina and now Steve. What can I say, but I hope this is over soon. Not that I want to leave here" she said as she looked around at her new home "But just this whole nightmare."

"We know Terrie" Jack said as he stood and put his arm around her shoulders. "Walk down to the dock with us"

"Of course. I couldn't stay here in the house and let you fly off into the wild blue yonder. I've got to give you the final wave." Terrie said putting her arm around Jack's waist.

"Let's get rolling" Clem said as he headed towards the door not wanting to look at Terrie or Jack for that matter, walking with their arms around each other. 'That should be me, not Jack' he thought.

Jack leaned down and kissed Terrie on the cheek. "Take care of yourself Terrie. Let us hear from you now and then. You know through the radio or you can call us from the Fitzgerald's."

"Thanks Jack. Please tell Nina that I said Thank you so much for lending me her husband. I couldn't have gotten through these last 6 or so months if it hadn't been for you." Terrie watched Jack and Steve climb aboard the plane. Turning around she saw Clem walking towards the rope ties walking towards him she said "None of this would have been possible without you and your caring, Clem. What do I do now?" She carefully laid her hand on his arm and felt the chill go up her spine. She'd felt that before, when she had touched his hand when she was pouring their coffee. 'What's with this'?

Clem looked down at her, leaned down and kissed her on the cheek, putting his hands on her shoulders. "You'll be alright and safe up here. This will be over in a short while now and then you can live again. I promise. Remember I promised I'd take care of you and protect you and I mean to carry out that promise. If anything important takes place down South I'll personally come and tell you. How's that?"

"Can I count on that?" she said holding back the tears and trying to get her heart to quit pounding.

"You can count on that sister" Clem said, trying to sound like Humphrey Bogart.

"Come on Clem. Get that rope untied so we can take off." Steve yelled

"I'm coming." Clem said wanting to stay and see them off and knowing that his job wasn't done until he put those 'scum bums' in prison where he knew then that Terrie would be safe.

"Take care you guys and Steve you can come visit anytime."

"I'll see what I can do." he yelled over the drone of the planes engines.

Terrie stood there watching as they took off over the water. Waving until she couldn't see them anymore with tears streaming down her face. 'Well, here I am again. Guess you could say; I'm the Lady Who Walks Alone, but for how long? Who knows? The guys that are in that plane.' She turned and walked back towards the house feeling all alone and yet in away was glad she was alone. Now she could try to return to some kind of normal being. Here on the lake she truly felt at home. 'Hey, wake up broad you've got a lot of work to due around here.'

# CHAPTER 13

"Hey Lonnie" Morici yelled sticking his head in the front door. This guy, that looked like a bouncer, was trying to keep him from coming in, but Morici told him that the boss was expecting him and he best let him in.

Lonnie looked up from the table where he was sitting with a lot of people around him and yelled at Morici "It's about time you got here. What's kept you?"

"Sorry I'm late, but you know what the traffic's like out on 75 plus there was this real bad accident that tied up traffic for about a half hour." Morici knew he was expected at 10:30 and here it was almost 11:30, but he'd not been in a real big hurry to get here. Besides there had been an accident so he hadn't lied. Morici crossed the room and stood next to Lonnie.

"This is Morici. He's a friend and needed a job, so he's going to be with us for a while. He's going to be working with me in the back, so he's not a waiter, bartender or gopher, so don't anybody be getting a funny ideas about him replacing someone. OK" Lonnie said as he stood and introduced Morici to his restaurant staff.

Everyone started introducing themselves and Morici started laughing.

"Hey, don't expect me to remember all your names, not here at first, but I will try, at least in the next week to know all of you. It's nice to be here and I'm sure we'll all get along great."

The 'bouncer' was standing off to one side and he wasn't sure whether he liked this guy or not. 'Who sent him and why was he here?' He'd find out soon enough. He didn't like people being brung in like this. 'Wish I knew how to get hold of the boss. Then I'd find some things out.' He thought as he walked towards the kitchen.

"Well, Morici let's you and me take a ride." He turned towards the group standing there and said "We'll be back in a little bit, so I expect to see the work done when we get back. OK?" Lonnie looked around at his employees

"Sure, Lonnie, we'll have everything done by the time you get back." One of the waitresses said. Everyone in that room knew what Lonnie meant and they also knew everything better be done. No loafing. Lonnie was a fair boss, but he also could be real tough and was known for firing someone, for what most of them thought was unfair, but they knew better than to cross him.

"OK, Lonnie, now do you want to tell me what's going on?" Morici said as they got into the car.

"We've got plenty of time for that. First we've got to find you a place to live." Lonnie said as he headed towards the south end of town.

After about 2 hours the two men settled on an apartment on the south side of town. It really wasn't much, one bedroom, small living room, dining room and a kitchen just large enough to put a small table big enough for two people.

"Well, now that that's done, let's go get you some food to put into these cabinets and refrigerator." Lonnie said as they headed back to the car.

"Lonnie, I really appreciate all of this, but I still don't understand why I'm here. What am I supposed to do while I'm here. Is there someone in your restaurant that's stealing?" Morici was asking as they headed towards the grocery.

"Morici" Lonnie interrupted "For right now you'll be helping me in the office and helping George, the bouncer, the one that wasn't going to let you in, count the money at the close of the night. I don't want him thinking I don't trust him, so you'll just be there observing, like you're just learning part of the business."

Lonnie kind of hesitated, looked at Morici and then continued, "as time goes on you and I will have some long talks. But right now is not the time."

"OK, Lonnie. Whatever you want I'll take care of it." Morici said. 'Man, this whole business is starting to smell. Les doesn't trust Lonnie, for some reason, Lonnie doesn't trust someone in his restaurant wonder how long it's going to take me to find out what the hells going on. Who's side will I wind up on? Guess I'll know eventually.'

--------

Morici had been with Lonnie for about two months and so far saw nothing going on out of the way. George counted the money every night correctly, the bartenders, waitresses and all checked out every night correctly. So far Morici had found nothing wrong. He hadn't heard from Les, and Lonnie wasn't talking either. 'Am I being setup' Morici thought. 'Guess I'll make a few phone calls when I get to the apartment tonight. Maybe I can find out something from them. Wonder what Archie might know. Guess he'll be one of my phone calls. This not knowing anything is driving me crazy.'

"Hey Archie. How you doing?" 'Not that I really give a shit, but I've got to find something out and you're the only sucker I know that'll spill the beans to me.'

"Morici. Man am I glad to hear from you. Where are you? I was told that Lonnie needed you to run some big operation up there in Chattanooga. Is that what you're doing?"

"Well, I am in Chattanooga, working with Lonnie, but there's no big operation going on. I guess Les just didn't have anything for me right now, so he sent me up here for Lonnie to keep his eye on me."

"That's not the way it's being told down here. One of the guys talked to Les the other day and when he hung up he said Les had heard some tales about Lonnie not depositing all the monies coming into the place, so he sent you up there to check things out and see who was skimmin'. He said he also heard Lonnie was running a straight up operation instead of running the money through the bank."

'Oh' Morici thought 'now I know what's going on. I'll figure something out to get Les off Lonnie's back. What I'm not sure right now, but I'll come up with something and thanks Archie I knew you'd spill.'

"Oh, well I haven't seen anything out of the way. Lonnie may be putting the money in the deposit he makes. That way no one up here would be the wiser, if you know what I mean. As far as 'straight' up I don't think you could call Lonnie's place that. He still has dealings with some of the guys, 'cause I see them come in and go to the back. I don't follow 'cause I haven't been asked yet. Since I've only been here a couple months I guess their sizing me up to make sure I'm really what Les says I am, a good cop gone bad. When they're sure then maybe they'll include me in their talks."

"Yeah. Youse probably right. How's it going otherwise? Did you find a nice place up there?"

"It's going alright. My apartment isn't as nice as the one in Atlanta, but it's OK. Well listen Arch I guess we better hang up just in case Lonnie's trying to get hold of me. He knows I don't have any friends up here, so I don't like to stay on the phone, if you get my drift."

"Yeah, sure I do Morici and hey give me a call again sometime soon. I really miss talking to you. We've been through a lot together ya know."

"I'll keep in touch," Morici said as he hung up the phone. 'One more phone call then I can get some sleep.'

# CHAPTER 14

'Damn, if I have to mop this floor one more time I'm going to scream.' Terrie thought as she again started mopping her kitchen floor. 'Look at the time 2 o'clock and Bud is due between now and 3 PM according to the Fitzgerald's. I wanted this damn cake in his cabin when he arrived.' Terrie had baked her brother his favorite cake, German Chocolate with Carmel Icing, but she'd spent the whole morning practically mopping the floor. First she spilled her coffee, then part of the cake batter and this time she'd turned the icing pan upside down on the floor. 'That's what I get for trying to hurry. Maybe I should have bought the icing instead of trying to make it.' She wanted something special for him. This was the first time she'd seen her brother in over a year. He was 11 years her junior, but they'd always been extremely close and for Terrie not to have seen or talked to him for this length of time was really hard on her. She wanted to share all of her experiences with him. Tell him what all had happened since Chris found him in Tennessee plus she wanted to find out how the family was, especially her kids. He was her way of keeping track of the kids since she'd had to flee the state, after all no one had been looking for him like they were her. So much had happened she wanted to tell him everything plus find out everything. 'Why don't you just go out on the porch, sit down, have a soda and a cigarette and try to calm yourself. Then come back in and make the icing and be careful this time.' She thought to herself. 'Good idea' and out on the porch she went. Here it was July already. She'd been here since May or was it April, she couldn't remember everyday just was like any other day and they all ran in together.

Terrie finished the cake put clean shorts and tank top on and headed with her cake towards the boat. For some reason she had an anxious feeling. She'd had it all day, but couldn't shake it. 'Oh well, can't figure anything ominous is going to happen' she thought as she climbed into the boat and put the cake down on the seat next to her, started the boat and headed towards Northern Woods.

----

"Hi Terrie" Tom called to her as she glided into the dock. "Bud hasn't gotten in yet, but you might want to stop at the Lodge before you go up to Bud's. I think a phone call came in for you just a few minutes ago." Tom said as he leaned down for the rope to tie off Terrie's boat.

"Have you got any idea who called" Terrie asked as she climbed out of the boat and reached for the cake.

"Afraid not, but it might have been Jack or Clem. One of the gals will know. Go on up and I'll take care of this." Tom said as he reached for the cake.

"Thanks, but no thanks" Terrie said laughing as she carefully carried the cake up towards the Lodge.

"Hey everybody. Tom said someone up here had a message for me." Terrie said as she walked towards the kitchen.

"Hi Terrie" Iris said turning around from the sink, where she was peeling potatoes for dinner. "There is a message for you from Clem in on my desk. He said it wasn't urgent, but he'd appreciate a phone call as soon as possible."

"Thanks Iris. I'll go in and call him." Terrie had a calling card, so she picked up the telephone number and headed for the pay phone that was located in the solarium, right inside the side door.

"Hey someone down there called Northern Wood." Terrie said into the telephone. This was a code that they'd decided on before

Clem and Jack had left. No names were to be used, just the Lodge name.

"Yes, just a moment and I'll transfer you right away." Jeb said into the phone.

"Hey beautiful, how are you doing?" Clem asked

"I'm doing great. Mopped my kitchen floor three times today." She said into the phone as her heart started pounding.

"Why on earth would you mop that kitchen three times?" Clem said laughing. He knew she was a neat freak, but not that much.

"It's called coffee, cake batter and icing." Terrie said laughing into the phone. It really sounded ridiculous now that she was telling someone about it. "Guess you should have been here to understand."

"Wish I had been." Clem said quickly following with "We had a near scare a couple days ago."

"Oh, what happened?"

"I'll tell you in a minute. First how are you coming with that list I asked you to make?"

"Well, I've written a few things down. One item comes to mind that I'm not sure whether I've ever mentioned it or not."

"What's that?" Clem interrupted her. He was really anxious about the list. He wanted to make sure that they had everything. Things were getting close and he wanted to nail everything, all at once. He didn't want to say anything to Terrie about how close he believed they were 'cause he didn't want to get her hopes up, but one more loose end and they'd have everything. They'd even gotten their indictments on 'all the layers', but there again he didn't want her to know yet. When it's all over, then I'll fly up and tell her, but not until then. Right now it appears that she won't have to appear in court. Sure hope that stands. "I'm sorry Terrie what were you saying, I wanted to write it down and missed some of it, so would you please start over, slowly."

"Sure. I said, there was a time when I was going on vacation in Florida and Jay asked me if I'd do him a favor. He said I could stay in Florida about two weeks, and I was only going for 4 days, at his expense. He'd give me the money before we left, if I'd agree to do him this one favor. I asked him what it was and he replied that he wanted me to check out a marina on the East Coast and two on the West Coast and also a title company. I would meet a Pauline Costa and her boss at the first marina; they were the owners (silent partners, I think is what he called them) in this title company. Well, I met with them and they introduced me to the owners of the first marina, but Pauline got me to one side and told me I really didn't want to purchase that marina, as they were under investigation of drug running. They then took me across the state to check out two other marina's, one was really too small, the other one was under the RICO act, so Pauline said I sure didn't want to invest in that company. I told her that I really couldn't make any decisions until I talked to Jay, but I took lots of pictures of all three marinas. Then we went to her title company. I inspected the books, interviewed the girls that worked there and spoke to Jay on the phone about it. He asked me to have Pauline fly up to our business where he could talk to her at some lengths."

"Wow, why did he want to buy the marina's and the title company, did he say?"

"Later he told me that there was a foreign country that wanted to buy, especially the bigger marina on the West Coast, dredge it out deep enough where they could bring in large ocean vessels. I found out later that the marina on the East Coast was one of the places that his 97.5 would send the dingy in with drugs. Why you people didn't find that out and nail Jay then I don't know oh yes, he also wanted the title company for his money laundering."

"Just another time that we let something slip through our fingers. Is there anything else? Did they buy the marina or the title company?"

"No they didn't buy any of the places they sent me to check out. Pauline and I became good friends after that and I stayed with her a lot of times when I went to Florida, but I guess time, money and whatever was running out for Jay and the rest of the boys."

"Do you know what has happened to Pauline and/or her company? And are they or were they legit at the time you knew them?"

"I haven't talked to Pauline for at least 3 years and yes they were very legit. They were just getting caught up with Jay's BS if you know what I mean."

"Yes, I think I do."

"OK, now what about this scare you mentioned?"

"Well, I didn't want to alarm you, so I waited until it was all over to make this call. It seems as though' some men showed up in town wanting to be flown to an island in Lake Kabetogama, just north of you."

"Yes, I know where it is." Terrie interrupted

"Well, it seems as if Steve was at Johnson's when they inquired and so Steve stepped up and asked who they were looking for claiming to know just about everybody up there that owned or lived in that area. They said Connie Whitfield. Since Steve didn't recognize that name he asked them if they could wait until the next day as he was the only one in the area that could fly them up there, but that he had a fishing party to take in the opposite direction right then. Anyway, he talked them into waiting til the next morning. He went home and called us and gave us that name. Immediately we told him who that was and he said no problem he'd get rid of the men, but instead I sent Jeb up and guess what they were two of Les' boys from Atlanta. It wasn't the two that had been following you that we ascertained, but it was two from Atlanta. Right now we have them in custody and their attorney is trying to get them out. I think we have a pretty good charge against them, so they won't be going anywhere, for a little while any way. Boy we are really lucky to have Steve on our side. He seems to smell trouble without even knowing it. Now besides mopping the kitchen floor three times today how are you doing?"

"I'm doing just fine. Bud is due in with in the next half hour or so. That's why I baked a cake. The garden is doing great, that is as long as I can keep the deer out of it. The green beans are coming along quite well, so hopefully I'll be able to start putting some of them in the freezer soon. I bought some apples last week and made and froze some applesauce. Oh yes, I made new curtains, bedspread and pillow shams for my bedroom and new curtains for the glass-enclosed porch. They are heavier than the ones that were hanging there and I thought that would be good for winter. Oh yes, I went into town oh about a month or so ago and bought some light blue paint and painted my bedroom also."

"Well, it sounds like you've been a busy bee." Clem said wishing he were there with her. "I guess we've talked long enough for now, so I'll let you go. Tell everyone I said Hello will you."

"Sure will and how's Jack and Nina?"

"They're doing great. Jack, of course, is busy in the office and elsewhere with me, but otherwise they are both OK. They did say to tell you Hi when I talked to you."

"Please give them my love and I guess I'll talk to you again, soon."

"Of course. I'll call you if there are any changes also. See you Terrie." Clem said as he hung up the phone. He sat with his hand on the receiver for a few minutes before turning to Jack and telling him Hi from Terrie.

"I thought that was who you were talking too. Did she sound upset when you told her about the two men that were picked up in town?" Jack asked as he strolled over to Clem's office.

"No. She just took it in stride, as we knew she would. She really is something else." Clem started to laugh, "You know what she did today. She mopped that kitchen floor three times, it seems as tho' Bud is coming in today and she wanted to bake him a cake and she spilled coffee, cake batter and some kind of icing causing her to mop three times. What a nut case."

"Yes she is" Jack stated, 'but you love her and we all know it. I sure wish this case were closed so you could go to her and make your feelings known. How did you make it while she and I were in California together? Nina said you called her almost daily. Talk about a nut case.'

"Come on Jack," Clem said giving Jack a kind of disgusted look "We've got to get to work. Let's see if we can check out the restaurant in Chattanooga. For certain peoples sake I sure hope that business is legit." Clem said as he handed Jack his coat and the two of them walked out of the office.

Terrie sat for a few minutes staring at the phone, 'what was it Clem had just told her, that 2 men had been picked up in town and they were there looking for her. Well, I'm safe for now with those two men in jail.' She thought as she stood and headed out the door. Just as she started up the hill towards Cabin 6 she saw Rickey and Dave in the golf cart.

"Hey, what's ya carrying?" Dave yelled

"A homemade cake for Bud."

"Well, come on hop on the back and will take you up there. He's in the Lodge, so it will give you time to put it on his table before he gets to the cabin." Rickey said

"Hey, thanks I could use a lift. These hills aren't as small as they used to be."

Terrie replied as she stepped across the railroad ties and headed across the lawn to the driveway.

"How are you doing out there on the island? We haven't seen a lot of you like we thought we would." Rickey said as Terrie climbed into the back of the golf cart.

"Well, I've been kind of busy. I've made new curtains for most of the windows in the house and some heavy duty drapes for the glass-enclosed porch. I also made a new bedspread for my bedroom and of course I've been tending to my garden. What's left of it when the deer get through eating I mean." Terrie said kind of laughing. She knew she would have the deer to contend with, but she really didn't expect them quite so early in the planting.

"Well, we had a pretty early winter last year and I guess the deer are extremely hungry and of course winter lasted longer than usual." Dave said steering the golf cart down the hill next to Cabin 10, Bud's cabin. "I don't dare park this thing too close to the road or Bud will run over it when he comes in with the car and boat. He's come close to it a couple of times before."

"Can't say that I blame you." Terrie said laughing as she started up the steps to the screened porch of the cabin.

"Here comes your brother now and hey he's got WJ with him" Rickey said as Bud backed the boat up towards the house. "Thought you weren't coming up this year," He said to WJ as he shook his hand.

"Well, I wasn't, but Dad told me on the sly that Aunt Terrie was possibly going to be here and I wanted to see her and make sure she's alright." WJ said as he headed towards the steps.

"WJ I didn't know you were coming." Terrie said as she hugged her nephew and started to cry. He'd been called by his initials WJ every since he was born. He was named for their Dad and Uncle, but the initials suited him more for some reason.

"I came to see you Aunt Terrie. Are you OK? I mean, most of us have been so worried about you. What's with the tears?" WJ said as he backed away from his aunt.

"Oh god I'm so glad to see family again. These are tears of joy. Where's that ugly father of yours?" Terrie and Bud always teased each other. They were 10 ½ years apart, Terrie being the older, but they were closer than most brothers and sisters that Terrie had ever known.

"Hey uglier than I am. I'm standing right behind you." Bud said as Terrie turned around. He put his arms around her and held her for the longest time. They hadn't seen each other for over a year and he had really been worried about her. Oh yes, Clem, the FBI guy had called and said she was fine, but that's all he would say. Bud knew that the feds were 'taking' care of her and keeping her safe, but it was different being able to see her and knowing she was OK.

"What's with the tears?" Bud like their father didn't believe in crying, but he too was ready to cry he was so glad to see her.

"Hell, you're just like Daddy and WJ. I have a right to shed tears when the two favorite men in my life just show up and I haven't seen them for a whole year."

"Well, I guess I can give you that. You gonna help us unload the boat so Dave can put it in the water or you gonna stand here and sob."

"Oh, shut up let's go get the boat unloaded." Terrie said putting her arm around her brother's waist and heading towards the door.

"It's about time you two decided to do some work around here." WJ said laughing as he carried a box into the cabin.

"Do you want to ride down to the launch and help Dave and Rickey put the boat in the water?" Bud asked Terrie

Before she could answer WJ said, "Why don't you and Aunt Terrie stay here and start unpacking and I'll go with the guys and then bring the car back."

"That sounds like a good idea." Bud said as he handed him the boat keys.

"What would you like for me to do?" Terrie asked her brother as they went into the cabin.

"Nothing. You just sit down and start telling me everything that's been going on and who's this guy Clem? What's this?" Bud said as he finally saw the cake sitting on the table.

"Well, I've missed your birthday two years in a row now and I just couldn't let you come up here without baking you your favorite cake, German Chocolate with homemade Carmel icing. At least it shows I've missed you." Terrie really didn't want him to know just how much she had missed seeing and talking to her brother. "Besides, I haven't baked a cake in a long time, so I thought this was as good a time as ever. I can use you as a guinea pig. If you get sick then I know not to bake cakes anymore." Terrie was teasing again and Bud knew it. His sister was an excellent cook.

"OK. I'll make a pot of coffee, but we won't cut the cake until WJ gets back and we'll let him eat the first piece then if he doesn't get sick I know it's safe for me to eat." Bud said laughing heading towards the coffee pot.

"Hope you brought decent water to make coffee with. This iron water will kill you." Terrie said as she reached for coffee cups. She knew her brother always brought some, but he also used what was furnished in the cabin. This was the family trait. Every since their Mom and Dad had first come up here they brought their own towels, washcloths, soap, toilet paper etc. That way the Fitzgerald's didn't have to worry about keeping their cabins furnished.

The coffee was done, WJ was back with the car and the cake was cut.

"Now Sis can you tell us what all's been going on—where you've been, how long you'll be here and how close are they to 'hanging' those guys. What happened to Chris, Jay's nephew? I heard that he was killed."

"Slow down Bud I'll do my best to answer your questions. It may take me the better part of your three weeks though. I can answer one of your questions real quick. Clem did tell me that Chris was shot and killed in cold blood. For some reason I want to say that cop, that's been chasing me all over the world did him in, but I don't know for sure. So much has happened and if it wasn't for Clem your sister would be dead."

"Wait a minute" Bud interrupted "Who or what cop?"

"Well, his name, as I understand it is Morici, and Clem said he's a good cop gone bad. And the 'boys' have had him chasing after me all over the world. Georgia, Germany even California. I had a scare when I was in California. I found out he and some other guy went to Utah looking for me and my kids. Fortunately they didn't find either one of us."

"OK. So who is this Clem? He called me one day and said that our mutual lady friend was doing fine and we'd talk later and I haven't heard a word since."

"Clem is the reason I am alive and living safely up here. He's been absolutely super. He and his associate Jack. Jack was with me posing as my husband out in California. But enough about me for right now. Tell me about the rest of the family. Have you talked to my kids lately? How are my grandkids? I miss them so much, but I have to keep them out of any of this. I don't want them hurt. I hope they all understand."

"They do understand Sis. They are like the rest of us anxious for all of this mess to be over so they can have their Mom, Grandma and Aunt Terrie back." Bud said as he started unpacking the groceries and putting them away. "Laura said that you'd arranged for us to have dinner in the lodge tonight. How come?"

"I just thought it might be easier than either one of us stopping to try and cook something. Besides we can discuss stuff in the lodge, as they are well aware of what's going on and have been keeping their eye on me. Thank heavens we have such good friends. Did anybody tell you Steve flew us up here."

"Steve did? How did he get involved in this?"

"Well, to make a long story short. Clem found out about him through Bureau records, hired him to fly some highly confidential people up here, that was me, and he agreed. When I first saw him in Minneapolis, where he picked Clem, Jack and me up, I wasn't too sure if it was really Steve. I wasn't really introduced to him. I had no idea where I was being moved. I still didn't know, but if this was the man I thought it was, meaning Steve, then I knew it was a lake, probably up North. Imagine my surprise when he pulled up to this dock."

"I can imagine. After all these years. What on earth possessed them to choose this lake and that island?"

"I don't really know, but boy was I glad. I've really felt like I was home, if you know what I mean. I do have one question to ask of you?"

"What's that?" Bud said looking up from the floor where he was sitting putting canned goods away.

"Would it be OK with the two of you if I'd spend tonight here, instead of going back to my place? Ah, I just thought it might be easier than my going home after midnight." Terrie was so scared that Bud would say No not tonight that she felt she had ants running around inside of her.

"Of course it's OK. Besides the Bass Tournament starts tomorrow and I'm sure you want in on that."

"What's that?"

"Well, every year the same four couples, WJ and I make up

one of the 'couples', plus one of the sons are here at the same time and we have a bass tournament. It costs $5.00 per person and at the end of a week we have a bash in the bar and Rickey and Laura fix up finger food of some kind and we give out trophies. First prize is cash and host for the next year's tournament. Then second prize gets some goofy trophy then there's the biggest yarn (liars story) that one gets a mounted cloth bass for a year and then there's the smallest fish and they get the booby prize. It's loads of fun. I don't think anyone takes it totally serious, but they're a good group of people."

"Oh you betcha I'd love to be in on that. I've had plenty of time to check out all of their hiding places. I will skunk you, you know that don't you?" Terrie started laughing. She hadn't laughed this much since Clem and Jack left. They always made her laugh. She was just warm inside knowing that her brother was finally here. It wasn't that she was afraid, but after what Clem had just told her about the two men, she knew that now she truly had protection and she again felt safe.

"I'll tell you what. Let's let WJ go to sleep and you and I can go down to the dock and see who all's here." Bud said as he nodded towards WJ lying on the couch.

"Sounds good to me. OK if I take my coffee cup with me?"

"Of course. Where I go my cup goes too."

"Hey, whatever happened to that girl you were so crazy about. Is she still around?" Terrie asked as they headed towards the lodge.

"Yes, but we'll go into that later on. That is if it's OK with you?"

"Why wouldn't it be? Let's face it little bro' we've a lot to talk about and catch up on over the next three weeks. Did you by any chance bring any pictures with you?"

"Yeah. I'll get them out one of these days and give them to you. I want to go over to your place too. According to Rickey and Laura you've really been working hard over there fixing the place up."

"In the beginning I had help what with Jack and Clem both

being here for a couple of weeks. They even dug the ground and helped me plant a garden. They fixed the dock and roof on the house and a few other things that I could've done myself, but it is nice knowing these things are done and I don't have to worry about them."

"I know you came over by boat so what's it like?" Bud said as they walked around the lodge.

"Well, you'll see it soon enough. I think I can proudly say it's much better than your bass boat and it's totally outfitted. When Clem bought it he said he thought of what kind he wanted and bought it. Boy I'll tell you this much, this whole mess better get over soon, it's costing the government a buddle to keep me in hiding. Evidently they feel it's worth it. Funny, if they'd just listened to me in the beginning none of this would've been necessary." She said as she moved her arm around surrounding everything in site.

"No, it might not have been necessary, but you might have lost out with a change of identity and then none of us would ever have you back." Bud had thought about that a lot lately and he didn't even like the thoughts of it let alone saying it out loud. To never be able to see, talk or hear from Terrie ever again was a whole helluva lot more than he wanted to consider. Oh, he teased her all the time, but he really did love his sister and was proud of her. 'She's got more guts than I think I'd ever have.' He thought as they started down the wide dirt steps to the dock.

"Well, it looks like Tim and Tiny are in I saw their van and there's Lucy and Allen's boat, so they must be in and I'm sure Shel's here someplace too. Shel is the son of Lucy and Allen. He's got a truck and normally pulls the boat up for his Mom and Dad. Jake and Kathie will be in later on today. They always stop at one of the gambling casinos on their way up. WJ and I had breakfast with them down at Superior this morning and they said they were going to the casinos and grocery shopping then they'd be in camp. Hey Allen how was the trip?" Bud said as he hit the bottom step and stepped onto the dock.

"We had a terrific trip. No problems and believe it or not no traffic to speak of either." Allen said as he looked up from his boat "Allen, I'd like for you to meet my sister Terrie." Bud said as Terrie stepped up next to him. "She bought Lawry's Island."

"Terrific maybe we can have a big picnic out on her island while we're all here." Allen said

"Sure, I'd love it. It would give me a chance to show off what all I've done out there."

"Here comes Tim and Tiny. Where's Lucy and Shel?" Bud asked

"You might try looking behind you Buddy boy." Shel said as he walked up behind Bud

"There you are. Sure didn't think you'd miss the bass tournament."

"Where's WJ didn't he come up this year?"

"Asleep where else. Hey Tim. Hi Tiny. Lucy it's great to see you again. Since all of you are down here let me introduce my sister Terrie. She bought Lawry's Island"

"Great" Tiny said laughing "Suppose she'll let us have a picnic out there for a change."

"Oh, I already told ah, it is Allen isn't it?"

"Yes Terrie. You have to forgive my sister. She's having her senior citizen moments and she isn't even a senior citizen yet." Bud said laughing

"Keep it up and you'll go swimming." She laughed

"Hey, who's fancy boat?" Shel had walked down towards the end of the pier and was staring at Terrie's boat.

"It's mine" Terrie said starting towards it. She didn't want to brag, but she was proud of it and she knew, looking around, it was the best and fastest boat tied up to the dock. Of course it had to be, just in case anything happened she would be able to out run anybody else, or get a hold of Fitzgerald's in a moments notice.

"Man Bud your sister must have gotten all the money in your family. What do you do for a living?" Tim said as he strolled with everybody else down to the end where Shel was standing.

Trying not to be rude Terrie ignored the question pretending it must be rhetorical. Bud, however, took advantage of the question and said that she was a professional gambler.

"Bud, I wish you wouldn't say those things. People might take you serious." Terrie said half embarrassed by her brother's remarks and yet glad he said something

"Anyway, despite the fact that it looks like she's got an advantage over all of us, Terrie would like to be in the bass tournament that is if it's OK with you guys." Bud said laughing and pretending he didn't hear his sister's remark. He really didn't know how to explain her and her money and he was kind of uncomfortable, but worried at the same time. He knew she was really hiding, but that no one, outside of the Fitzgerald's were to know that. He assumed that the feds had checked this whole crowd out before she was even allowed to come over here.

"Sure, we'll take her money. We can skunk her just as good as we can skunk you" Lucy said

"Good now that that's settled. I wish Jake and Kathie would get here so the 'meeting' could come to order." Shel said

Bud had explained to Terrie earlier that Shel had won the tournament last year and therefore headed up this years tournament, but Kathie was the secretary every year and nothing could get started without her.

"They'll be here shortly" Bud said "Well, look who's coming down the hill, sleeping jesus himself. You sure didn't sleep very long son."

"Naw. I didn't I'll sleep better tonight if I don't sleep now. Hey everybody how's things goin'?" WJ said as he walked up next to his Aunt Terrie and put his arm around her shoulder.

"Aunt Terrie, is *that* your boat?" WJ asked pointing at the last boat

"Yep, sure is. Wanta take a spin?"

"Wow, come on Dad let's go"

"OK, we'll be back in a few. See you later. What time's the meeting Shel?" Bud called over his shoulder.

"Thought we'd have it around 5 o'clock. Jake and Kathie should be here by then."

"OK. We'll be there with bells on." Bud said as they climbed into Terrie's boat.

---

"I'm sorry I went to sleep on you last night," Bud said to Terrie the next morning at breakfast.

"No problem. I'm just surprised you stayed awake as long as you did. I knew you were tired. After I help clean up the kitchen I'm going home, change my clothes and see if I can beat my favorite brother at fishing."

"You don't have to clean the kitchen," Bud said as he set their plates in the sink. "That's WJ's job. I do the cooking and he does the cleaning."

"Man, with the mess you made just cooking bacon and eggs I feel sorry for him having to clean up after you cook a meal." Terrie said laughing and pouring another cup of coffee.

"Oh, it's not too bad Aunt Terrie. Normally Dad goes fishing early like this and I've got the cabin to myself with peace and quiet."

"You're not going fishing?"

"Naw. Dad goes out for about an hour and then he calls me on the radio and asks if I'm ready to go and if I am then he comes in and gets me. I don't have to beat the waters to win the contest. Besides I won it year before last and I don't want to win it too often."

"Come on Sis I'll walk you down to your boat." Bud said pouring himself a cup of coffee and heading towards the door.

"OK. I'll see you later WJ"

"You go on out to the island and I'll be out in a few minutes. I do want to fish, but right now I want to talk to you without anyone else around. Is there enough room in the boat house to put my boat in there behind yours?" Bud said as they reached the dock.

"Sure. In fact you can pull it in beside mine. I'll meet you at the house." Terrie said as she climbed into her boat. "Remind me to give you your coffee cup back when you come out. See ya!"

"OK. Now start talking" Bud said as he walked into Terrie's house.

"I've got coffee brewing, so let me show you around first. I know it's been a long time since you've been in the house."

"Yeah, about 6 years. Every since the Lawry kids had to sell it."

Terrie took Bud around, even outside to her garden. "Clem and Jack dug the garden for me while they were here."

"It looks great. You've done a beautiful job. I don't know when I've seen this place look this pretty." Bud said as he walked through the house and garden. 'Man she's done a lot around here. Once again Bud thought how proud of her he was. She'd been through so much and yet she still had the knack of making a house a home. 'I'm sure her heart hasn't been into this too much either.' "OK let's go have that coffee and you can start telling me all that's been going on. Starting with who is this Clem and how serious are you about him."

"Well," said Terrie as she poured them coffee and sat down at the kitchen table. "Like I've said before if it wasn't for Clem I could be dead. We, some agents sent to Georgia to protect me, were going into the Flower Mart in Atlanta when all Hell broke loose, shooting, men yelling and somebody grabbing me trying to take me out the front door, when someone else grabbed me and threw me into the back seat of a car. That someone was Clem. I didn't know where I was being taken, but I did trust Clem. Anyway we went to the airport where I was put on a plane with this man named Jack. Clem told me I could trust him and that he would be at my side for a while. We wound up in California, Sunnyvale as a matter of fact. Jack was posing as my husband and there were two agents out there that set everything up for us and kept our backside, so to speak covered. Then word came that we were moving again and that's when I was moved up here."

"Do you know if you are really safe up here?" Bud was more frightened for his sister than he'd ever been before.

"Well, I knew that they'd checked everyone out before I was brought here and then all guests for all of the lodges were checked out through and including September. They figured only the locals would be left by then. I do know that Clem called yesterday, before you got here and told me of a close call that we had and thank heavens for Steve he was able to get the two men picked up by Clem's office."

"What happened?"

"Well, according to Clem two men came into town asking for someone to fly them to Kabetogama. They had a friend that lived on an island up there that they wanted to go visit and they understood the only way to get to her place was by plane. Well, Steve overheard the conversation and asked who they were looking for and they said Connie Whitfield."

"Oh, my god Terrie that was you."

"Yeah, I know, but Steve didn't. He did, for some reason smell a rat and asked if they could wait until the next day as he had a commitment for that day, but he could fly them up the next day and they agreed. He got on the phone to Clem right away and Clem took it from there."

"How come he called this Clem?"

"Because he knew everyone up there that lived on the islands and he'd never heard of this Connie, so he called the one person he knew that might be interested and that was Clem."

"Thank god for Steve"

"In more ways that one." Terrie said "Anyway Clem said they had them in custody, and that their attorney was trying to get them out, but he said they had enough against them that he wouldn't get them out for awhile and then it would be too late. What ever he meant by that I'm not sure."

"Do you have any idea how much longer this is going on or when it's going to court or if you have to appear?"

"Nope. I just sit here and wait. They did clear it for me to be with you and your friends so I know I'm here for awhile."

"If this lasts through the winter what are you going to do up here by yourself?"

"Hibernate! Seriously, I have enough wood to keep me warm and if I need anything from town Rickey or Tom said they'd take care of me. I'm really not too worried. At least I don't feel like a vagabond now. Before I had guards and felt like I was always on the move, but at least this is a home."

"Then you really don't know what all's going on with the case."

"Nope. You probably know more than I do. I don't even take a paper. Oh, I've got a dish so I get the news on TV, but that's so depressing that I hardly watch TV anymore. Besides which I'm too busy right here. Once in awhile I'll turn it on in the evening while I'm crocheting or needle pointing, but that's about all."

"Guess I better go out to the boat and call WJ and see if he's ready to go fishing. He's only got this week up here and then I take him to Minneapolis to catch a flight back home."

"OK you do that and I'll change my clothes and go fishing myself. When I catch a bass I bring it in to Fitzgerald's and let some one in the contest measure, weigh or whatever?"

"Yeah."

"OK I'll see you after while. I don't know how long I'll fish today, but I'll see what I can do."

"OK I'll see you after while." Bud said as the two of them walked down to his boat.

Terrie walked back up the path towards the house thinking of her conversation with Bud. 'He's right I really am in the dark' she thought. 'Sure wish Clem had said something more about what was going on right now and where everything stood.'

---

"Well, Mr. Brown how do you feel about things now?"

"Pretty good. Of all dumb things to use a coffin. Did they think we wouldn't catch on! I guess it's time to move on, get things rolling." Clem was sitting in the director's office and they had been going over some of the things that had happened within the last week "I'd say we're ready to go to court."

"My thoughts exactly" the director said "Get your team and witnesses ready. Are you going to use the girl?"

"Not if I can keep from it. I believe with the surprise witnesses that we have now we will be able to keep her name out of it. At least I hope so. She's been through enough and I'd like to see her be able to see her kids and grandkids again. Maybe not by Christmas, but this time next year anyway."

"Well, start getting things ready. You know it will take us a good six months to get this thing into court and then how long will it go on after we get everybody to court. By the way do you plan on trying them all at the same time?"

"Yes sir. If we can't try them all at one time then the element of surprise will go out the window and we certainly don't need that to happen. If that happens somebody will get off and there's no way I'm going to let one of these sob's walk."

"Like I said get the ball rolling and I'll talk to you later. If you need my help give me a call." With that statement the director went back to paperwork on his desk and Clem knew he had been dismissed.

"Hey Bud did you hear about your sister?" Allen yelled as Bud and WJ pulled into the dock.

"No did something happen to her?" Bud was afraid to ask not knowing what the answer would be.

"Nothing happened to her, but according to Tim and Tiny she brought in one whale of a large bass. It looks like your sister's going to win this contest I don't see how anybody can bring in one any bigger. I guess Tiny asked her if she was going to keep it and have it mounted and she said no and released it after Tim took her picture with it. The whole camp is talking about it. Looks like your sister went and skunked all of us."

"Well, I don't know about that. We still have two days left before the end of the contest and I think WJ and I will go out tonight and see if we can't bring in something bigger. How much did you say it weighed?"

"Didn't was waiting for you to ask me. 7 lbs 2 oz's how's that for a bass. Tim and Tiny said it was gorgeous."

"Where's my sister now? Did she go home?"

"I didn't talk to her. Ask Tim or Tiny here they come down the hill now."

"Hey Bud, what till you see the picture I took of your sister's fish. Man that thing was beautiful. Allen told you she put it back didn't he?" Tim said as he walked onto the dock.

"Yeah. Do you know whether Terrie was going home or back fishing?"

"She said something about fixing a 'crow pie'. Whatever that means."

"She just thinks I'll eat crow." Bud said laughing as he started up the hill towards his cabin. 'Maybe I can raise her on my radio, if I can, then I'll have her meet me and we'll go to town for lunch.'

"Bud to Miss Crow are you about?"

"This is Miss Crow Bud, what's ya need."

"Meet me at the house and I'll treat you to lunch."

"Be there in 2 minutes I'm down by the blind."

The blind was an island, owned by a young man in town, and he built duck blinds for the hunters to use. It was too small for a house, so he used it for duck blinds. Terrie went down there a lot just to sit on the island and get away from everything. She found that was an ideal place to meditate and she'd been doing a lot of that lately.

"Man you must have flown." Bud said when Terrie pulled in next to his boat at her boathouse.

"Nah. This boat just moves out." Terrie said as she climbed into his boat. "Did you hear about the bass I caught?"

"Yes. Allen and Tim told me about it. Guess you'll win the bass contest, which means, no matter what happens in your life over the next year, you have to be here to host the party. That is unless someone brings in a bigger one, which I doubt. Since you released it I've got a card up in the cabin of a guy that can duplicate your fish from a picture. Why don't you have Tim send you a copy and have it duplicated? It's bigger than what Uncle Bob has in on the wall of the lodge.

"Guess I might do that. That was a tough fight though' and I caught it on, of all things, a worm."

"A worm" Bud questioned

"Yeah. I was really just pan fishing over by the blinds when the silly thing hit. I'd been bottom fishing and decided to just cast into the weeds along shore. I hadn't anymore than cast into the weeds when I hooked it. I really thought I was just caught in the weeds, but low and behold he broke water and I nearly fell out of the boat I was so surprised. It took me about 10 minutes to get it into the boat. Then I had a devil of a time getting the hook out of him so I wouldn't kill him. Thank god for live wells."

Terrie got out of the boat and tied the bow to the dock while Bud secured the back end of the boat.

Walking into the café Terrie saw Alicia. Alicia was Iris's niece and years ago had been one of the cabin girls that Terrie ran around with when her family came up to the lake.

"Hey Alicia how are you? What are you doing? I haven't seen you in years."

"Hi Terrie. I'm doing just fine and I deliver the mail around these parts. I heard you were back and bought Lawry's Island. Iris said you'd be in the Lodge for dinner Friday, so I'll probably see you then. I still go out and help them when they have a crowd coming in for dinner."

"It's great seeing you and I guess we'll see you Friday night." Terrie said as she walked over to the booth where Bud was seated.

"One of the reasons why I brought you here for lunch" Bud started

"May I take your order." The waitress asked

"We'll both have the Pork Tenderloin sandwich." Bud answered "No fries and two large Pepsi's."

"Well, little brother, you still remember what I like to eat anyway."

"I just know that we both always ordered those sandwiches

when we came in before. Anyway getting back to what I was saying—Allen, Tim, Shel and I are going up to Canada to visit some castle they have up there and I wanted to ask you if you wanted to go. WJ said he didn't want to go and none of the other gals wanted to go."

"Oh, so I'm last choice." Terrie laughed "I'd love to go and I'm sure I don't have to clear it with Clem since he OK'd all the guests at Northwood's."

"Well, I'm sure you don't have to clear it. I checked the pilot out that will be taking us and it's none other than Steve."

"Then I know I can go. He'll take care to make sure nothing happens to me."

"That's what I figured."

"When is this taking place?"

"Well, the party is Saturday night, so we've reservations for Monday. We tried to get Steve for Sunday, but he's busy, so Monday is the day."

"What time."

"Can I get you anything else?" the waitress interrupted

"No, I think we're fine." Bud looked up and smiled at the waitress. "Just the check." Turning back to Terrie he continued "Steve is due in at 9am. That isn't too early for you is it?" Bud laughed. He knew his sister was up way before that, but he was on vacation and he didn't have his second cup of coffee until about 9.

"Well, I do tend to sleep late, but I'm sure I can manage 9, which actually for me will have to be closer to 8:30, so Dave can get my boat anchored over on one of the drums out of Steve's way."

"What time is the party Saturday night? Is it in the Lodge, bar or Shel's cabin?"

"It's at the Lodge. We normally meet in the bar around 9 for a few drinks and then move to the dining room shortly thereafter for the prizes. You may as well stay with WJ and me Saturday night. So when you come across just tell Dave to move your boat out to one of the drums and you don't have to worry about going back across the lake late."

"That's a good idea. I'll also have to remember to bring a change of clothes. Would you like for me to bring anything in the way of something for dinner?"

"No. I'll either fry chicken or we'll have pork chops."

"I'm sure glad Mom made sure you knew how to cook. Otherwise you and WJ would be eating in the café for three weeks or starving to death. Which reminds me when would you two like to come over for dinner?"

"Maybe we'll make it Sunday, depending on what the weathers like. That is if that day is OK with you."

"Sure it is. What day should we have the picnic at my place?"

"We'll decide that Saturday night when all of us are together."

———

"Well, Sis I guess you're the big winner, but after the tale you told me on how you caught that baby I wonder if you shouldn't have gotten the tall tale prize instead." Bud was saying laughing after Terrie was awarded first place.

"Oh shoot you're just jealous 'cause you're sister beat you."

Everybody started laughing. They knew how much the two of them teased each other. They didn't quite understand why Bud was as protective of her as he'd been this past week, but they all decided two things; one it was none of their business and two maybe it was because they hadn't seen each other for so long. This little item of protectiveness had been the main topic of discussion, especially when the wives were down at the dock.

Sunday came and went with nothing much happening. Bud and WJ went over to the island for lunch, which they had out on the porch. The weather had finally broken and it was a beautiful day. Not a cloud in the sky and no rain forecast for all of the next week.

When Bud and WJ left for the mainland Sunday, Terrie set out to get some much needed cleaning done around the place. She hadn't really touched the house since Bud had come into camp.

Monday morning Terrie got up at 7 o'clock and hurried about having breakfast and getting ready to go over to Northwood. She was really anxious to see Steve and see if he'd heard anything from Clem. This not hearing from him was literally driving Terrie crazy. It wasn't that she expected to hear from him all the time; she knew he was busy and had other things on his mind, besides her. It was just—she missed him. 'Sure I talked to him last Saturday, but that was over a week ago.' She thought as she pulled into the dock.

"Good morning Dave. How are you this fine beautiful morning." Terrie said cheerfully. "I'll be going up with Steve and the others, so you can tie my boat out on one of your drums."

"Ok, thanks Terrie. I'll do that right now. Most of the other boats are still tied up, so it's only your boat that I would have to worry about. Guess the guys are all going with you and the women will go shopping." Dave said as he hopped into his boat to take Terrie's boat out to moor.

"Good morning everybody" Terrie said as she strolled into the kitchen

"Good morning Terrie." Iris and Laura answered "Where are you off to so early in the morning?" Iris asked

"The guys minus WJ are headed to Canada to go visit that Castle that they've got up there. May I have a cup of coffee, please? The last cup I had was the only one I've had and that was at 7 o'clock this morning. I know Bud is hardly stirring, so he won't have coffee yet."

"Sure, help yourself. You know where the cups are. Who's the pilot?"

"Steve. Thank heavens. I don't think I'd go if it were anybody else."

"Smart move" Laura said

"I'll bring your cup back on our way back to the dock." Terrie said as she headed out the kitchen door.

"What do we tell Clem, if he should happen to call?" Iris asked following Terrie out the door.

"Tell him I'm out flying with Steve and to either leave a phone number or call back late this afternoon"

"OK. See you later and have a good time."

"You wouldn't believe it. I wouldn't have if I hadn't seen it with my own eyes."

Terrie was saying to Tom as she sat at the bar in the lodge. "This place was huge. It must have had three maybe four floors in some parts. It has what I call turrets at each end and in the center with a bridge from the center one down to one of the other floors on one side and it's all made out of logs. It looks out over Rainy River, and it truly is worth people going to see."

"I think part of your problem and happiness, right now is it's the first time you've been away from here since you were brought up here and you probably would have loved an old outhouse if it was away from here." Tom laughed and poured Terrie another glass of wine. "Speaking of which, you did have a phone call from Clem, he said he'd call you around 8 tonight. I told him I'd make sure you were here."

"Thanks Tom and your probably right about my happiness, but that Castle really was a sight to behold." Terrie didn't mind having another glass of wine, after all she and Bud had decided that she'd spend the night with he and WJ, so she wouldn't be driving the boat home tonight. Terrie was sitting in the bar waiting for Bud to come up from the dock. She'd said her goodbyes to Steve and climbed the hill to the lodge while the guys stayed down there to talk to Steve. She knew better than to stay around when the guys wanted to talk, she, Steve and Bud didn't need anybody thinking there was something between she and Steve.

"There you are." Bud said as he walked into the bar. "I went up to the cabin, but WJ said he hadn't seen you, so I figured you were here. Come on and I'll cook us some dinner. The gang is coming in here tonight and we can come back ready to party."

"OK. See you later Tom. Keep my wine chilled." Terrie yelled over her shoulder as she went down the steps.

Terrie and Bud went to his cabin where he fixed a great supper of pork chops, mashed potatoes and peas. Terrie wasn't crazy about the peas, but she ate them anyway. She preferred the early June peas that were fairly small, but dinner was delicious anyway.

The fun part of eating with Bud and WJ was that they always challenged Terrie to a came of Skip-o. This was a card came that Terrie and Bud's Mom had taught them the last time they were all together here at the lake and it rained all day. Terrie won a lot of times, but when Bud won she always accused him of cheating. They knew no one cheated, but the teasing was always done in fun. Besides this game always passed the time quickly. They even played it down at the lodge at night. That was always fun. They either played Skip-o or dominoes and, of course, it was a good excuse to sit at the lodge and drink.

Bud and Terrie walked into the bar at 9 o'clock and they had already started playing liars poker. That was a fun game they had taught Terrie last week. She still didn't understand how to play, but she put her quarter in and sat down. A cigar box is passed around with 5 dice inside, the box is shaken and the person doing the shaking opens the box and tells the person next to him or her that they have 3 twos. The box is then handed very carefully to that person and it is up to them to either challenge the person that handed them the box or accept what they said and shake the box themselves and tell the next person that they have, for instance, 3 threes and so it goes until there is only one winner. Depending on how many are playing the pot normally is no more than a couple of dollars and every bodies had a ball trying to figure out if the preceding person is lying about their dice or telling the truth—thus liar's poker.

Clem didn't call that night; like he had told Tom he would, but Terrie was having so much fun she didn't even remember it until she was in bed.

Bud and Terrie had a fun time the rest of their two weeks together, whether it was fishing, having the picnic on Terrie's island or going places like the castle, Kettle Falls or the old open pit iron ore mine.

"Well Sis, I hate to go, but you know how it is work beckons me and I'm not sure the hotel will continue much longer without my supervision." Bud really did hate to go, but he knew his sister would be well taken care of and protected by the Fitzgerald's.

"I know" Terrie said as she put her arms around Bud's neck "I don't want to see you go either, but next year will be here before we know it and maybe by then all of this mess will be over with. Surely it can't last much longer. Have a safe trip and if anything happens, good or bad you will be the first to know. Tell my kids that you talked to me and that I'm fine and I love them."

"Will do" Bud said as he and WJ climbed into their car and headed home. "See ya next year."

The rest of the summer was uneventful. In fact Terrie didn't go back to the Fitzgerald's unless they called her to come over for messages or dinner occasionally. She knew they all would have plenty of time to visit after the hunters left in September. She spent most of her time putting up her vegetables in her freezer, crocheting or needlepointing. Sometimes time passed quickly and other times she sat on her porch wondering just what she was doing up here instead of picking pecans off her trees or going out and picking bunches of peanuts for boiled peanuts. She reminisced a lot, which she knew was not good for her, but all this waiting and not hearing anything from Clem she had a lot of time on her hands.

# CHAPTER 15

One evening, early in November, she heard a plane going over. It sounded like it was going to land, but she knew no one, especially Steve, was supposed to be coming. If anyone like that was coming someone would have contacted her and let her know so she wouldn't be frightened. 'That plane is going to land' she thought. Starting to get scared she didn't know whether to go down to the dock or hide in the house. Her curiosity got the better of her so she put on her parka and headed for the dock. 'Sure hope who ever's flying that plane has ski's on it. The winter had come early that year and the lake was already frozen. When she arrived down on her dock she saw the smiling face of Steve through the cockpit window. She grabbed the line that he threw at her and tied the plane up. She was taken aback when a female first alighted from the plane. Almost frightened, not knowing who this person was and yet knowing Steve wouldn't bring trouble to her, she headed towards the lady to introduce herself, but stopped short when she saw first Jack and then Clem get out of the plane. She literally threw herself into Jack and Clem. "What on earth." Terrie was so excited all she could do was stutter.

"Come on, Terrie spit it out. What are you trying to say? Surprised to see us?" Jack was standing there with his arm around her laughing. "This was Nina's idea that Clem, well all of us come up and spend some time with you and maybe have an early Thanksgiving Dinner. Sure hope the house is cleaned up." He chided. Jack knew, from California that Terrie always kept a clean house. "Do you suppose we could get our gear and go inside where it's warm." Jack was doing all the talking. Clem could only stand and stare at this beautiful face peeking out of the parka hood. "Oh hell, where are my manners. Left out in California I guess. Come on let's go up to the house and then we can catch our breaths." Terrie said as she took Steve by the arm and headed towards the house. She so much wanted to take Clem's, but was too nervous to do that and didn't want him to be able to feel her nervousness.

"Steve you're going to stay for awhile aren't you. I haven't seen you since this summer." Terrie was saying after everyone was settled on the side porch.

"No. I have to get back. Can't be gone too long or people will start wondering how long it does take to fly to Duluth. Come on guys I'll help you bring everything up and then I've got to take off." Steve said as he headed out the door.

Clem and Jack went back down to the dock with Steve and Nina stayed in the house with Terrie.

"Clem thought it would be nice if we all got together for like Thanksgiving to let you know we still care and think about you often. Me, personally I was tickled to think I'd finally get to meet this courageous lady. I feel like I know you, after all I've packed your clothes, cleaned your home and lent you my husband, so I really feel like we're bosom buddies." Nina said

"I know" Terrie said "One of the last things I said to Jack was that I hoped I'd get to meet you sometime. Please sit down and I'll pour us a cup of coffee. You do drink coffee don't you? I'm sure Jack mentioned it, but I'm not sure of anything right now, other than the fact I'm thrilled to see all of you."

"Yes, I'd love a cup. The guys will probably want one too. From what I've seen of your home it's beautiful. It was so pretty flying in over it. All nestled down in the trees with the snow all around it's quite a site."

"Thank you. I was able to see it this summer. Steve flew me, my brother and 3 other men up to Canada for the day and when we came back he flew low over the island so I could see it from the air. I was very pleased with what I saw. I am so lucky and happy that Clem or whomever chose this place. I don't know if you were told, but I grew up on this lake, knew the people that owned this island, so I really feel like I'm home."

"Do you ever miss your place in Georgia?" Nina interceded

"Oh once in a while, but then I go outside and look around and love this place maybe even more. At least this place doesn't carry the sadness that the other house does."

"Will you ever go back to the old house?"

"Oh I don't know. Clem told me one time that they had real nice people living there. Maybe they'd like it enough to buy it and then maybe I could buy this place. Who knows?"

The men came slamming in the front door yelling Help!

"Guess we should go see what their problem is, hadn't we?" Terrie said as she stood and headed towards the living room.

"Sure. Why not. They are typical men and they always need help," Nina said as she started after Terrie.

"Where would you like for us to put this stuff?" Jack said as he stood there grinning from ear to ear.

"I told you, men, they can't figure anything out. Jack you two have been here before. You both know which bedroom is mine, so go pick a bedroom and put your stuff in there." Terrie was laughing. 'Sometimes men are so helpless and other times— well you can't tell them that they're needed they tend to get the big head.' She really was so glad to see them she didn't know what to do and she was nervous too. 'What if Clem just brought Nina and Jack up for moral support so he could tell her she had to go back and face all those men in the courtroom or better yet, they were all free to do whatever they pleased and she'd have to change her total identity.'

"Terrie stop your day dreaming and tell me where to put all these boxes?" Clem stood there with his arms loaded with boxes. All sizes and shapes.

"What on earth have you got in those boxes? If you don't tell me what's in them, I won't know where to tell you to put them.

Oh, just put them over there on the floor." She said as she pointed towards the corner of the living room

"Thank you." Clem said as Jack came in with more stuff

"Good heavens what did you bring up here 'Fort Knox'?"

"Pretty near" Nina answered "If it wasn't Jack saying you needed something it was Clem going shopping. Let's you and me go back to the kitchen and let them fend for themselves. From what I've seen so far they aren't quite finished unloading poor Steve's plane. He too asked them if they'd brought you a whole new house." Nina laughed and headed back to the kitchen.

---

"Well, Terrie" Nina was saying, "Now I know why my husband came home bragging about your cooking. That was some kind of a feast you put on just now for us."

"Thanks Nina, but I'm afraid it wasn't much after all I wasn't expecting guests to 'drop' in. If I'd known you were coming I'd a baked a cake." Terrie replied laughing.

"I told you she was a good cook," Clem said getting up to get the coffee pot "More coffee anyone?"

They all answered, "Yes" and handed Clem their cups.

"Why don't we go out on the side porch? We can watch the sunset. It really is beautiful this time of year what with the snow on the ground and I believe there's supposed to be a full moon out tonight. By the way did Fitzgerald's know you all were coming up?"

"No they didn't. Guess tomorrow we better go over and introduce Nina and let them know it's us."

"Maybe they've talked to Steve." Terrie said. "How about I make a fresh pot of coffee. I'll get it started and you all can go sit out on the porch. I'll bring the carafe out with it when it's done and maybe I can find some cookies to go along with it."

"I'll stay in here and help Terrie clean up the kitchen. You and Clem go rest on the porch, but don't steal all the good seats." Nina said as she stood and started cleaning off the table.

"You don't have to do that, Nina, you are a guest in my home. Guests are just supposed to relax and not work."

"Gee, I'm sorry" Nina said acting hurt, "I thought we were family and families always work."

"You are family. "Terrie said emphasizing the word family. The dish soap is under the sink." Terrie said laughing as she reached for the coffee pot. "Seriously I'll wash and you can dry. How's that."

"That's great. Go on shoo," Nina said to Jack and Clem. "Us women vant to be alone." She continued in her best vamping voice. "You are a nut." Terrie said laughing. "Jack told me that you had a great sense of humor now I believe him."

———————

"You were right Terrie, the sun setting was beautiful, but the full moon over the lake with the snow and ice and all is spectacular." Clem said, "I don't know when the last time was that I witnessed such a phenomenon."

"It is beautiful, but it is now 10 o'clock and past my bedtime." Jack was saying, "Besides which I've had a beautiful dinner, coffee, dessert and great conversation, but I am ready for bed. Come on Nina; let's hit the sack. See you two in the morning."

"Good night Jack, night Nina. I'm really glad you're here. See you in the morning."

"I guess I best be going to bed too. It's been a long day and I'm exhausted." Clem said. Feeling a little embarrassed being left alone with Terrie. Oh, it wasn't that he didn't want to be left alone with her, but he just felt a little self-conscious. "I'm sure that Jack and Nina went to bed thinking that I maybe would talk about your case and tell you where we are etc., but I'm sorry Terrie, I'm really too tired to try and discuss it tonight. Anyway, I wouldn't tell you something that they, at least Jack, didn't already know. So if you don't mind I'll call it a night and talk to you later about the case."

"I don't mind at all, Clem, I'm a little tired myself. After all I've had quite an afternoon and evening. One that I certainly didn't expect. Good night Clem. I'll see you in the morning. You should have enough blankets on your bed, if not there are some in your bedroom closet." Terrie said as she stood and headed for the kitchen with the tray of cups and the carafe.

Terrie crawled into bed after straightening up the kitchen and getting the coffee ready for morning. 'I guess I'm still in a state of shock. What a nice surprise. I'm glad that Jack and Nina came up too, I'm not sure I want to be alone with Clem. At least not right now.' She thought as she drifted off to sleep.

Terrie was awakened the next morning by the smell of bacon sizzling in the kitchen. At first she thought 'what the heck, who's in my kitchen' then she remembered and decided she better get dressed and get out there as a good hostess would do.

"Good morning" Terrie said as she walked into the kitchen "I'm sorry I overslept."

"You didn't over sleep, Clem and I are early risers, as you know. Nina's still in bed. Clem and I have already walked the island. Oh yes, we saw you had the boat radio up here hooked up so we called Fitzgerald's and let them know we were here and would be coming to visit sometime in the next week or so." Jack said as he continued to tend to the bacon. "We're having bacon, eggs and toast. Would you care to join us?"

"You know I'm not much of a breakfast eater, Jack, but I'd love to join you."

"Good. When I finish the bacon I'll add another egg to the pot. Add another toast Clem." Jack said trying to sound like a short order cook.

Terrie walked over to the coffee and poured herself a cup before she sat down at the table. "I trust you two had a good nights sleep?"

"Probably the best I've had in months." Clem answered as he finished buttering a slice of toast laying it on a plate with the others he'd buttered.

"Is there any chance that I could get one of you two to tell me what's going on? I mean with this case of mine?" She said as she took a sip of coffee. "Sorry I spoiled your making coffee this morning Jack." Jack turned around and made a face at Terrie and she started laughing. "At least my spoon wouldn't stand alone in this cup." Since the first pot of coffee that Terrie had tasted of Jacks out in California she'd teased him about the spoons standing alone. This certainly was no different. If Clem hadn't been standing near by and knowing Nina was in bed she'd sworn they were still in California.

"After breakfast to answer your question." Clem answered sharply. He was having a real hard time with Terrie and Jack teasing each other. 'They aren't still in California. Why don't they knock that shit off? Careful ole boy your fangs are showing.' He thought. "What I meant was, Jack and I talked about it while we were walking and since Nina knows a lot of this anyway, we'd sit out on your beautiful glass enclosed porch build a fire in the little fireplace and sit and talk. That is if it's OK with you."

"That's great. I'm just curious and a little bit hopeful that this will all be over soon and I will be able to start living a normal life. What ever that is."

"Let's just enjoy a nice breakfast and small talk and then we'll get serious later." Jack said putting the plate of bacon and eggs on the table.

"Are you leaving anything for Nina?" Terrie asked as the guys devoured the bacon and eggs.

"She only has toast and coffee for breakfast. She really isn't much of an eater this early in the morning." Jack acknowledged

"Well, you know I wasn't much of one either out in California, but after being here for awhile I've gotten quite an appetite. Guess that's all this fresh air."

"Good morning. Am I too late for coffee?" Nina said as she strolled into the kitchen.

"Heavens No." Terrie answered, "Sit down and I'll pour you a cup."

"Good morning Honey." Jack said as he walked up and gave her a kiss on the cheek.

"Did you have a good nights sleep? I hope you had enough blankets. I told Clem before he went to bed where there was extra blankets for his bed, but you two had already gone in when I remembered I didn't tell you."

"We were plenty warm. Thanks Terrie. I might get another blanket to put on for tonight tho' just in case Jack decides to hog all the covers." Nina said laughing

"Well, if you need them there's some in the closet in your bedroom. I tried to make sure each bedroom had extra blankets in the closet just in case. Not that I thought I'd have any visitors, especially in the winter, but I put them there anyway."

"Smart thinking. I keep all of our blankets in a hall closet then forget to tell our guests where they can find them, or even forget to offer the blankets to them. I can't tell you how many times Clem alone has told me he froze during the night. Now he's learned to stop at the hall closet and pick one up on his way to bed." Nina started laughing again thinking about the morning Clem came out with all kinds of winter clothes on saying he'd had to put them on during the night just to get warm.

"What is this pick on Clem day?" He said as he finished fixing Nina a piece of toast.

"Thanks sweetie. I do admire a man that spoils his wife. Just because you aren't my husband spoiling me I appreciate it anyway." Nina said winking at Jack.

---

"Well, I built a small fire in the porch fireplace, so we can go out there and enjoy some coffee." Clem said as he came back into the kitchen.

"You all go on out with your cups and I'll pour the coffee into the carafe and bring it out. Should I start another pot or how does a change to hot chocolate sound?" Terrie said as she went for the carafe.

"Hey, have you got whipped cream or marshmallows?" Clem asked

"I've got both. Go on I'll fix hot chocolate and bring the mugs out to you all." 'Can't get over the fact he even likes his hot chocolate like I do.' Terrie was thinking as she started the water. Terrie made her hot chocolate with Carnation Hot Chocolate mix then added enough dried cream to cover the chocolate, then poured the hot water in almost to the top of the mug, leaving enough room for a big glob of whipped cream. Everyone had always told her she made the best in town. This morning she made it in the carafe, instead of individual mugs and took the whipped cream on the tray with the mugs.

At the last moment she put a few large marshmallows in a bowl on the tray. Maybe the others don't like whipped cream.

"Here you go. I brought both whipped cream and marshmallows, just in case one of you would rather have the marshmallows. Of course if we don't put them in our hot chocolate we can always cook them over the fire in the fireplace. I love toasted marshmallows."

"Me too. I remember as a boy scout that was one of the highlights of having the bonfire—toasted marshmallows. Yummy yum that does sound good." Clem said as he poured his hot chocolate and put whipped cream in it. "Now this is what I call the drink of the day. Good friends, good conversation and a beautiful view." After taking a sip of his hot chocolate he said "and excellently made hot chocolate."

"Thank you kind sir." Terrie said laughing. "I have been told I make the best in town, oops I guess it will have to be the best on the island."

"Since you're the only one making the hot chocolate around here. I guess you could brag it is the best on the island." Jack said laughing.

"Can we now get down to the nitty gritty?" Terrie asked fixing herself another cup of hot chocolate.

"Well, Terrie" Clem started "We don't want to get your hopes up, but we are slowly getting the men arrested and off the streets. I hope you realize that it takes a while to get this mess on the court dockets. We figure six months to get it all into the courtroom and then probably three months of court time. Right now we are looking at maybe this mess being over by May, next year at the earliest."

Terrie looked rather downtrodden

"Don't be so dejected. Time will go by very quickly. I was just talking to the Director the other day and he was very pleased with the progress. I will tell you now what I told him then. I do not want to haul you into court if I can keep from it." Clem was trying to build up her confidence, but he wasn't sure it was working.

"Don't be disheartened Terrie. All of this legal mumbo jumbo does take time, but Clem is and has been doing an excellent job and you're information that you've given us has been fantastic. By the way Clem told me about that Pauline woman in Florida and I contacted her. It seems as though her business partner, boyfriend; boss whatever you want to call him did two things. One he moved out of town without anyone knowing about his move or where he'd gone, with a large sum of company money and I guess when Pauline finally found him, she found his wife and was told that he'd died a couple months earlier and she knew nothing about the business or money being stolen. In essence she told Pauline to take a long walk on a short pier. Guess it's just as well that 'your' company/boss didn't get involved with them."

"Well, I feel sorry for Pauline. I know she invested some twenty-five or so thousand dollars with that company. She must be out all of it. Knowing what Del did to me—well I do feel sorry for her. Sure hope she finds some happiness and money some where."

"I wouldn't feel too sorry for her. It seems as though she found and married some really nice guy, a deputy sheriff, I think she said and he carves wood with a chain saw. She seemed to be quite happy and glad all that nightmare of hers was behind her. She did ask if I knew you and if you were all right. I told her yes, I knew you and yes you were all right, but that that was all the information I could give her. She said thank you and hung up. So if she was telling me the truth, about the sheriff, then she's quite safe."

"Well, I'm glad to hear that. She is really a nice lady that a man used. Does that sound familiar? It sure does to me. Have you heard anything about Del, Jim, where he might be or what he's doing?" Terrie really hoped that they either knew nothing about him or that he was dead. She didn't wish him ill will, but she sure didn't want him coming back into her life again.

"I guess I may as well tell you about that 'darling' soon to be ex of yours." Clem started

Terrie interrupted "What do you mean soon to be ex?"

"Well, I may have over stepped my bounds, but I didn't think you wanted to be married to a jail bird, so I instituted divorce proceedings on your behalf. It should be final by the end of this month." Clem sure hoped he did what she wanted. Maybe he did over step his bounds, but he was about to find out. Quite frankly, no paperwork had been done yet, but the judge told him two weeks tops from the time the paperwork was handed to him until the finality of the divorce. He almost held his breath, as did Jack and Nina. Both of them knew what Clem had done and was doing and why.

"Jail Bird. Get that divorce over with. I sure don't want that hanging around my neck. Good riddance to bad rubbish I say. But how is he a jailbird? What on earth is he guilty?" Terrie was having a hard time believing what was just told to her. Del, Jim a jailbird. That was almost funny she really couldn't imagine him of all people being in jail.

"We, rather, I hate to tell you this." Clem stammered, "He was connected with the drug end of Jay's business. He was one of their runners and collectors, if you know what I mean. That's one of the reasons why they always knew where you were. We're surprised the mob didn't kill him when he left you that last time. Before they made him come back to you, but that last time, no matter what they threatened, I understand even threatened to break one of his wrists if he didn't go back to you and he still told them no. He'd had enough. They let him go. Totally unbelievable, but our sources told us and they are most reliable and that's how we were able to find him. So he will be part of the group that I'm preparing papers on."

"Good lord. I lived with that man all those years and I wasn't aware of his drug usage let alone his contact with them. I guess I should have known, and maybe I did, but just didn't want to admit it to myself. Yes, you are doing the right thing. Get me that divorce and while you're at it could you by any chance get my maiden name back for me at the same time?"

"I'm not sure, but I'll try." Clem said letting out a small breath. "Like I said earlier, just hang in there a little while longer. Maybe the next time you see me, ah, us I, we'll tell you it's all over."

"That can't come too soon. Could you like leave now and come back next month?" Terrie said half giggling and half snickering.

"What, what are you talking about." Clem said looking rather puzzled. Sometimes this woman drives me crazy with her double talk.

"Well," Terrie said dragging the word out as long as she thought necessary to get her point across "You said the next time I saw you or you three, maybe you'd tell me it was all over, so-o-o."

"You are some kind of a nut case. You know what I mean. I told you maybe by May."

"Does that mean that's when I'll see you again?" Terrie knew the answer, but she didn't like it. She really secretly didn't want him to leave her ever again, but

"Guess that's exactly what I mean. Hell Terrie, once I get this thing into court I don't dare leave until it's all over. I don't want to come up here with my head between my legs and tell you I lost." That was the one thing he was sure of—he would win this case and get all these scum bums put away.

"Oh Clem. I didn't mean to upset you. I guess I was just wishing out loud. I know you can't leave. I just truly appreciate the three of you taking the time to come up here now."

"Come on Clem get your coat on and let's go find that tree." Jack said as he shoved his chair back and stood up. You want me to stoke this fire before we leave?"

"No Jack, that's not necessary I'll do it in a little bit. But what tree are you two going out looking for?"

"We're going to find you a Christmas tree. Nina said she sent all of your decorations up here when she and her Mom packed up the stuff to send up. So, we will not let you sit up here, all alone with out your decorations."

"Well, just be careful. I know the lake is frozen, but there are some wild animals moving around."

"Yes, we're well aware of that we saw some this morning when we were out walking." Clem said as he came back out on the porch with his parka on. "Let's go. I've got the ax."

"Oh good heavens, are these two safe letting them go out with an ax?" Terrie said to Nina, laughing.

"I'm not too sure, but all we can do is pray they come back in one piece." Nina answered.

"All right you two. We'll show you how good we are. Wait until you see the tree we bring back."

When the two of them left Nina and Terrie straightened up the kitchen and Terrie was telling Nina what all she had made and all the decorating she had done in the house. She also explained the things that the guys had done before they left her back in June.

"How about showing me some of the things that you've been telling me about. It sounds like you are quite handy around the home."

"Sure, come on and we'll start in my bedroom. Of course I already showed you the drapes I made for the enclosed porch." Terrie hung up the kitchen towel and the two women headed towards Terrie's bedroom.

"Oh, my goodness" Nina exclaimed, "You made these drapes and this quilted bedspread?"

"Yes. Thank heavens you sent all of my materials and sewing machine. Except for the three weeks that my brother was up here, over at Fitzgerald's I've had plenty of time to make things. I'll show you the afghan's that I've crocheted. There in the hall closet."

The two women went down the hall passed the bedroom that Jack and Nina were staying in to the hall closet. Terrie opened the door and pulled one of the afghan's off the shelf.

"This one took me about a month to do, but that's because I was making other stuff along the way. That's the trouble with me, I start something then I think of something else I want to do, so I put that item on the back burner and start something else. I'm lucky to get anything completed."

"How many of these things have you made? I wish I could do this," Nina said rubbing her hand across the afghan. "But I'm all thumbs. Heck I even kill silk plants."

"Now that's rather difficult to do" Terrie laughed and reached for another one of her afghan's. "This one is queen size and I made it because I love blue. I wasn't too sure how it would come out using two different shades of blue with white in the middle, but after I got it done, well, I'm really proud of it. Because of its size this took me a little longer. I normally crochet at night when I'm sitting watching TV."

"Oh god, this thing is outstanding. If I'd send you the yarn could you possibly make us one of these? I'd gladly pay you for it."

"I'd be more than happy to make you one, but I won't take any money for it. You pick out your yarn, have Jack or Clem send it up to me and I'll get it done as soon as I can."

"Oh, there wouldn't be any rush on it. I'd just love to have one just like this one just to lay across the bottom of our bed. It is so elegant."

"OK you send the yarn and I'll make it." Terrie said quietly thinking to herself, 'don't need the yarn, I'll just wrap this up and send it home with you as a Christmas present. Shit, if I do that what will I give Clem. Hmm maybe, he'd like the brown tweed colored one that I made. I'll wrap it also. What's he going to do return it, I don't think so." "I do have something in the spare bedroom, ah, the bedroom Clem's in that I would like to give you right now. It isn't much, but I made it and it's kind of neat. You just put it on your refrigerator." Terrie walked into 'Clem's' bedroom opened a drawer and pulled out what she called her teacup.

"How pretty and the poem is special too. Thank you very much. I will take it home and put it on the refrigerator." 'Then when I look at it I will remember the one lady that I've met that is strong and courageous.' Nina thought

"I guess I should go get the Christmas stuff down before the guys get back. I don't want them thinking we've been sleeping the whole time they were gone."

"I'll come help you. Where are you going to put the tree?"

"Well, I could put it on the side porch, but I think I'll rearrange the living room furniture and put it in there. I don't want it too close to the fireplace though. Let's go get the boxes and take them to the living room, then I'll decide where I want the tree."

Terrie and Nina climbed the hidden staircase to her attic and pulled and pushed the boxes down the stairs until they had all thirteen boxes at the base of the stairs.

"Boy, I didn't remember packing all this stuff" Nina said panting "That's a lot of hard work." She said as the last box was taken into the living room. "Sounds like we didn't get this done too soon. It sounds like the guys coming now."

"Ok, the tree hunters are back. We need a bucket of water to set this tree in until you get the decorations down and decide were you want the tree."

"Well, Mr. Smarty" Nina said to her husband "The decorations are already in the living room and Terrie and I were just getting ready to rearrange the furniture." She loved to tease her husband. Between the four of them enough teasing went on that an outsider would have thought even Clem and Terrie were married. 'Sure wish the two of them would make it known to the other one how much they did care about each other' She had said this to Jack just shortly after they arrived and he told her 'just give them time and let Clem get this case over with. This is the most important case that he's ever worked on and he's bound and determined to win it. If he doesn't I don't know what he'll do.' She'd answered with 'if he loses he'll come get Terrie and retire into the north woods where no one could ever find them.'

"If you men will help me I'll try to decide where I want the tree and then we can arrange the furniture accordingly. I know I don't want it too near the fireplace."

"Why don't you put it over here at the window. I'm sure you won't have a whole lot of people that will see it, but it would be a pretty site from outside." Clem said after surveying the room.

"That's a great idea and only that table will have to be moved. Smart thinking hon. er Clem." Terrie could feel her face turning red from that near miss. Why can't this all be over, so I can find out if Clem feels the same way about me that I feel about him. 'Careful, Bud warned you, be careful that you really do care and that it's not just misled feelings because of the way he's been with you.'

"There, now all we have to do is find your tree stand and we're in business." Clem said as he returned from Terrie's bedroom where she'd had him take the table.

"I know where that is," Nina said as she headed towards one of the boxes.

"Terrie, why don't you go fix us some lunch and while you're doing that Jack and I can put the tree up and put the lights on it. That is if we can find the lights."

Once again Nina went and unpacked the lights.

"That's a good idea. It's just that after the lights are on I have three very special ornaments I must put on myself and then you men can decorate the rest of the tree while I have Nina help me decorate the rest of the house."

"Three special ornaments? What do they look like so we'll know them and can lay them to one side when we find them." Clem said as he was straightening the light strands out.

"They are solid. One is a large blue ball there's one small blue ball and an identical one to the small blue one that is green. The large blue ball was on my Dad's first Christmas tree, the small green one on my Mother's first Christmas tree and the small blue one, was given to my folks, by a couple that lived next door to us when I was born, after it had been on their first Christmas tree when they got married, for my first Christmas tree. They had been married fifty years when they gave it to Mom and Dad for my tree."

"Now I see why they are so special. I'll be very careful when I'm unpacking the ornaments." Jack said as he started opening boxes.

"Wait a minute." Nina said, "I remember those balls, Mom and I talked about them and how old they must be. Let me think a minute, maybe I can remember what box they're in." Looking around she headed towards one of the large plastic boxes. Opening the lid she exclaimed, "Here they are. I thought I'd remember where we packed them if I thought about it for a minute."

———

"The tree is beautiful," Terrie said as she stood looking at the job that the men had done. She could feel the tears rolling down her face. She didn't want anyone to see them, so she headed for the kitchen. "Why don't one of you build a fire in the fireplace while I'm gone."

"Where you going?" Clem asked

"To the kitchen. I've got a special bottle that I've been saving for a special evening and I can't think of a more special time. I'll be right back."

"What is it?" Clem asked. Stopping Terrie in her tracks

"It's a German wine that they serve at the top of the mountains in the winter time. The skiers love it and it's called Gluhwein. It is served warm. Not hot and definitely not cold. Not even room temperature. It is simply warmed and served in little glass mugs."

"Would you like some help?" He asked. Hoping she'd say yes and knowing full well that she'd say no.

"If you'd like to sure." Terrie said and then continued on into the kitchen.

"Well, maybe we're, rather they're finally getting some place." Jack said as he lit the tree and sat down next to Nina.

"I hope so, but I'm not sure. Oh I know how they feel about each other. Terrie talked to me a little bit today, but I don't think either one is really ready to commit. At least not right now, with this whole thing hanging over their heads. Besides Clem has to keep his mind on this trial if he wants to win and he can't think about her and what she's doing."

"I don't see why not. For crying out loud he thinks about her all the time now. What difference would it make?"

"We'll just see." Nina said settling back against Jack's arm that was across the back of the couch.

"Terrie, there are things that I would like to say to you" Clem was saying as he helped her in the kitchen "but I don't believe this is the time. If you know what I mean." He looked at her hoping that she knew how he felt, but he wasn't sure.

Terrie looked at Clem and thought she was going to melt. She had read something in between his words, but then again she wasn't sure.

"Yes Clem." Terrie said holding her breath for fear he'd see how he truly affected her.

"It isn't that I don't want you to know how I feel about you, I think you do, but I've got to concentrate on putting these s.o.b's behind bars for life." 'Well there I've said it without really saying it'

Terrie's heart skipped a beat, maybe two or three. Finally she could open her mouth "Yes Clem I do know what you're not saying and I agree with you. You must concentrate on that trial. All I can do is pray it's over quickly."

Clem leaned down and kissed her on the cheek. 'That will have to do for now. Maybe I'll give her a proper kiss before we leave.' He thought as he looked down at her. 'How much I would like to hold her in my arms and never let her go. This place is perfect. If we ever can get together, I think I'll buy this place outright and we will live here. I don't think she wants to go back to Georgia. Her kids and grandkids could come up for the summer'

"Hey, Mr. Day Dreamer, would you like to help me here for a minute please."

"I'm sorry Terrie. I was just watching you and guess I got hypnotized."

"Yeah, right. I seem to have that effect on every man I come in contact with. Would you please carry the tray with the wine and cups into the living room? I'll bring the cookies." "Sure" Clem said picking the tray up carefully and headed towards the living room.

"Wow, that wine makes those cups really pretty especially with the tree lights and candles and all." Jack was saying. He and Nina had decided to light the candles while the other two were gone. 'Maybe if we give them a romantic setting they'll get the idea.' Jack said.

'Oh you are such a terrible romantic' Nina had teased

"The living room really does look beautiful with the lights turned out and the tree lights on and candle light. Thank you all very much. I thought I wouldn't have a Thanksgiving and here you all are and I knew I wouldn't have a Christmas tree and here it is. You all have made this very special for me. How can I ever thank you?"

"By making a fantastic Thanksgiving dinner like you did once before." Clem was saying. "Here sit beside me" patting the floor next to the fireplace. "That way we can enjoy the tree lights and have the warmth of the fire at our backs. How much more romantic can it be than that"

"You hit the nail on the head." Jack said raising his cup "In fact I want to make a toast. To the four of us. May we always be happy and friends as we are right now."

"Here, here" The others said as they touched their cups with each other.

"May I make one?" Terrie asked

"By all means, lady of the house." Clem said laughing. This wine was delicious and he felt like it might be going to his head, or was it the company he was with that was making him feel this way.

"To the nicest sweetest three some that I've ever known. I hope one day we can, maybe be a four some." 'Why did I say that'? Terrie thought. 'Now my face is turning red.'

"I'll drink to that," Nina said. "Is there any more of this delicious stuff?"

"Yep, sure is and I'll pour" Clem said reaching for the carafe that Terrie had poured the wine into after she warmed it.

"I wonder if anyone has thought about the fact that we've been here almost a week and that means we've only a few days left—9 to be exact." Jack was saying moving his cup back and forth as if he was directing an orchestra.

"Did you have to ruin such a beautiful evening with your words of wisdom?" Clem snapped

"Oh come on Clem. Jack was just bringing us back to reality. He didn't mean anything more than that." Terrie said as she put her hand on Clem's knee.

"I know it. It's just I'd rather not think about that and yet he's right. Hey, why don't we snowshoe across to Fitzgerald's tomorrow? Say maybe around noon."

"An excellent idea. We'll call them tomorrow and make sure they're going to be home." Jack said as he stood up. "Come on my lovely wife we are headed for bed. Good night you two. See you in the morning. Don't forget to snuff out the candles and turn the tree lights out before you go to bed."

"Yes Mother" Terrie said with slight sarcasm in her voice. "Good night. Don't forget if you need more blankets they're on your closet shelf." Terrie stood up and reached for the wine tray.

"May I help you?" Clem asked handing her the tray

"Sure. I'm just going to take this stuff to the kitchen. I'll wash them tomorrow morning."

"Nah, I'll wash them and you can dry. It won't take us but a few minutes and then we don't have to get up to a dirty kitchen tomorrow."

"Ok you win." She said laughing and heading towards the kitchen. "Let's turn the lights off and snuff the candles before going to the kitchen then we won't forget them."

"You go to the kitchen and turn a light on and I'll take care of this stuff."

"OK. Meet you in the kitchen" Terrie said as she picked up the cookie tray too and went into the kitchen.

"You know Terrie this could become a pretty nice habit." Clem was saying as he washed the cups.

"I know. I hope I didn't take too much for granted with my toast tonight."

"No. But it's like I said I have to keep my mind set on this trial. Oh, I'm not saying I don't think about you because I do. But, I need a clear head so I can win this thing."

"I understand." Terrie said as she put the dried cups away. "Looks like the dishes are all done."

"Do you mind if I walk you to your door. I am a perfect gentleman when I want to be." He snickered

"That would be lovely kind sir. After all a girl never knows what maybe lurking around these parts." Terrie chuckled

Clem walked Terrie to her room with his arm around her shoulder. "Here you are kind maiden. Safely at your door." Clem leaned down and kissed her on the cheek. "See always a gentleman. See you in the morning sweet thing."

"Yes you are. Good night hon." Terrie said as she closed her bedroom door behind her. Lying there on her bed were the two afghans she was to wrap. 'Guess I better wrap those before I go to bed so I don't forget them.' She thought as she opened her closet door and pulled a long box out from the floor. 'There that does it' she thought as she eyed her work. 'I'll take them out and put them under the tree tomorrow morning.

That way I won't forget to give them to them before they go home.' Satisfied with the way the packages looked she put them on the stool by her dressing table and went to bed.

'Good heavens! I just went to sleep how could it possibly be time to get up' Terrie thought when she was awakened by her alarm. Rolling over she checked the clock and sure enough it was 6:30. 'Rise and shine and go fix breakfast'.

"Good heavens Jack isn't there any time that I can get up before you do?" Terrie asked as she entered the kitchen.

"Nope. I've already been around the island. It's cold out, but it really is pretty. Sit down and I'll pour you a cup of coffee. What time did you and Clem finally go to bed? He's normally up by now and I haven't heard him stirring at all."

"We did up the dishes, so we weren't more than 30 minutes behind you two. I'm not too sure what the wine did to him, but I know I had to take two Advil before coming out here this morning. I only hope I didn't embarrass myself or anyone else last night"

"That wine was delicious and no you didn't embarrass anybody. We'll have to do that again sometime. Maybe after all of this mess is over and we really have something to celebrate."

"That sounds like a really good idea. But I'll have to fly to Orlando and go to Epcot to buy the wine in the German area. That bottle, Nina or some body was kind enough to pack and have shipped up here. That bottle came from Germany and it was the only bottle I had."

"Well, maybe we'll just have to try a different kind next time."

"Pour me another cup of coffee would you please. I've got something I have to do and I may as well do it right now before I forget it."

"Sure, no problem, I am but a mere slave for the beautiful princess." Jack said waving his hand and bowing. "Her wish is my command."

"You nut. I'll be back in a minute." Terrie wanted to get the two packages out under the tree before any one else got up. She knew they would be the only packages, so she wanted to try and kind of hide them behind the tree. The only thing was when she got into the living room there were a lot of packages under the tree, so she just placed hers as close to the back of the tree as she could. 'Where on earth did all of these packages come from? They weren't here last night.'

"The weirdest thing" She was saying as she entered the kitchen "I went in to check on the tree for water and there's all kinds of packages under it. I know Santa wasn't here. I would have heard his reindeer."

"Oh, well, since Nina and I won't have much of a Christmas together because of this damn trial, it's being held down South. We didn't think you'd mind if we brought our presents up here and shared our Christmas with the two of you." Jack said with a silly grin on his face.

"How sweet. I'm glad you thought of that. Now it really is special."

"Have you thought about what you will need from the store for Thanksgiving Dinner?"

"I'm glad you mentioned that I've got to get the bird out of the freezer so it can start to thaw." She said as she got up and pulled the bird out of the freezer. "I gave a list to the Fitzgerald's the other day when we went over there. Laura said she and Rickey would be going in to town before Thanksgiving and they'd pick the things up for me. It's just some fresh vegetables and salad stuff things I forgot to pick up when we were in town."

"The Fitzgerald's have really been good friends to you, haven't they?"

"Oh yes the best. I don't know how I'll ever repay them for all they've been doing for me."

"Knowing you, you'll find away."

"Good morning! Guess I kind of slept in this morning." Clem said as he strolled slowly into the kitchen.

"Good morning. How's your head?" Terrie asked as she got up to pour him a cup of coffee.

"Well thanks to aspirin it's not too bad. Have you got any tomato juice? I think I'd rather have that right now instead of coffee."

"Sure. I keep a bottle of it in the refrigerator. That's my favorite juice. It seems as tho' when I lived in Florida I tried to drink all of the orange juice that came off the trees and now I have trouble even drinking a small glass of the stuff. Guess I put too much acid in my system. One glass of tomato juice coming up." 'How 'bout that he even likes tomato juice.' Terrie was thinking as she poured his juice and sat it in front of him. 'The more I find out about him, the more I find out all the things we have in common.'

"I see the bird is thawing." Clem said motioning towards the counter top.

"Yes, if Jack hadn't mentioned it I would have forgotten to

take it out and then we'd had frozen bird for our Thanksgiving
Dinner, or at least no dressing. I would have had to cook the bird
all day tomorrow and Sunday to get the thing done. I don't know
why I bought such a large bird, there's no way I could have eaten
a 20 lb bird all by myself."

"Guess you knew you'd have company."

"If I was that physic I'd know the outcome of this trial and
when it would be over. No, I don't think I even thought that."

---

"Well," Clem said as he pushed himself back away from the
table. "That was an excellent dinner."

"Did you save any room for pie?" Nina said as she stood to
start clearing the table.

"Oh, I couldn't eat another thing right now." He said as he
reached for another olive.

"You certainly know how to put on a feast Terrie. I couldn't
have cooked all of this and still be happy and rested like you appear.
What's your secret?" Nina said as she took the potatoes and gravy
over to the sink counter.

"Just the love of cooking, I guess." Terrie answered as she picked
up the empty bowls that had housed the green beans and pickled
beets. The beets had come out of her garden so she was especially
proud of the way they came out. "I love to cook as long as I have
someone who loves to eat. I just don't like to cook for someone that
picks at their food or says 'I don't like that'."

"I don't blame you. Did you pickle the beets yourself? I notice
there's not a store bought jar that they came out of they were
delicious. I've never had hardboiled eggs in pickled beets before.
How did you come up with that idea?" Nina really did envy Terrie.
With everything she had and was still going through she cooked,
baked, gardened, decorated—what couldn't she do? 'Like Jack had
told her Terrie was a very special lady.

"That's an old family recipe. My Mom never made fresh

pickled beets without putting hardboiled eggs in them and I've just followed suit. My Mom was a fantastic cook, strictly down home type, nothing fancy with all the seasonings and all, but just good family style. She also loved to make big dinners. She loved to entertain and I guess I'm just a chip off the ole block."

"Well, if I may interrupt this conversation" Jack said "Why don't you two lovely ladies take a cup of coffee and go sit out on the porch and Clem and I'll do K.P."

"That sounds like a great idea. Besides maybe helping clean the kitchen I'll be able to work off some of these calories and be ready for a piece of that Pecan Pie."

The two women laughed at that thought. "We'll definitely take you two men up on that offer, however, the two of you keep your fingers out of the pies." Nina said as she refilled her coffee cup and headed towards the porch.

"Don't put the meat and stuff away right now. I like to pick at the bird and besides, after awhile we may want to start snacking. Maybe you can just find the storage containers and transfer stuff to them so you can wash the dishes, but just don't put the stuff in the frig."

"We can do that." The two men echoed

"Dishes are done and put away. The foods on the counter top ready to be picked at or plates to be made for dinner. I'm about ready for a piece of your 'famous' Pecan Pie." Jack said as he walked through the door.

"Right now?" Terrie laughed not believing that they could be hungry already.

"Nah. I can wait a little while." Jack said, "I thought maybe, if it was alright with you people, maybe we could have a little Christmas this evening sitting around the tree."

"That sounds like a great idea." Clem said, "I was trying to figure out just when we could do it. Time is getting short. We leave day after tomorrow."

"So soon?" Terrie inquired

"Yes, unfortunately we have to be in Atlanta on Thursday, so that doesn't give us much time to get everything ready to take

with us. We told Steve to be here early Tuesday morning, so that
we could be back home by about 3 o'clock. Then we have to pack,
of course Jack has Nina, but I have to pack my business suits myself."

"Oh, you poor thing" Nina said, "If you were married you
wouldn't have to do that yourself." She said winking at Terrie.

"That comes later." Clem said glancing over at Terrie. "Anyway,
we've a lot to do before we get on that plane Thursday morning. I
don't want to forget a damn thing so I guess I'll burn the midnight
oil for a couple of nights."

"Getting back to tonight. There's not much Christmas, but
we thought, Nina and I thought that tonight was a good night
since technically the Christmas season officially starts this evening."

"OK tonight it is. For now let's go for a walk around the island.
That should walk some of the calories off of you." Terrie said
laughing. As if any of them needed to walk off calories. None of
them were over weight. Slim and trim is the way Jack had described
Nina one evening. Jack and Clem both had good builds and
appeared to have taken really good care of themselves.

"Can we make it a short walk? I'd really rather sit here and
have pie." Clem said.

"No way lazy. Once around the island isn't going to hurt and
besides maybe you'll work up an appetite. It didn't look like you
had much of one at dinner." Nina laughed as she went in to get
her parka.

"What a wise one she is." Clem said as he followed the rest of
them into the house.

"If the truth hurts—oh well." Terrie said as she put her gloves
on.

———

"Whew! That was fun, but it sure does build you an appetite.
If I'd been hit with one more snowball, I swear one of you men
were going in the drink, even if it is frozen over. Hey, while we
were out did you notice the icehouses out on the lake. Several men

have been ice fishing. I forgot to mention it earlier, but I've had a good time watching them. I don't know how they do it. Go out there and sit all day long in those little shanties. I'd freeze my you know what off."

"And I thought you were an outdoors gal." Jack said teasing Terrie as they all took their parkas off.

"Oh, I am that, but I don't need to go sit on that cold ice trying to catch fish, that if they're smart enough, are laying on the bottom of this lake. I figure if I can't catch enough fish in the summer to put in the freezer for the winter then I don't need to eat fish in the winter." Terrie said as she went to the porch and started to build a fire in the fireplace.

"Why don't you let me finish building that fire and you go in and fix some of your famous hot chocolate and cut that pie." Clem said as he walked up behind her

"That's the best offer I've received today." She said laughing heading towards the kitchen.

"Hmmmm. That undoubtedly was the best Pecan Pie I've ever eaten." Jack said as he finished his third piece.

"You shouldn't need anything more to eat until tomorrow morning after what you just put away." Nina laughed as she carried his plate back into the kitchen. "You really are a pig. Do you know that?"

"Well, even pigs get fed well." Jack yelled sarcastically. Tapping his stomach. "Guess it's time for a nap." He said as yet drank the last of his hot chocolate.

"Now that's a great idea," Clem said

The men went into the living room to take a nap and Nina and Terrie made some more hot chocolate and went back out on the porch to talk.

"You know Terrie, Jack and I don't know when the last time was that we saw Clem as content as he's been up here. You know he does care a great deal about you."

"Nina, I care about him also and I'm glad he's content and happy. Ah, how do I say this so that you will under stand? My brother asked me if I cared about Clem as a man, or was it just everything he was doing for me. That's my question about Clem. Does he care about me, as someone that someday he'd like to be married too, or does he just feel sorry for me and all that I've been through?"

"Jack and I have known Clem for a long time. Way before his family was killed. We've seen him on lots of cases, some involving females. But we've never seen him take such an interest in a case or worked so hard to make sure that he's crossed his T's and dotted his eyes. Believe me when I say he feels sorry for you, in a way, he respects you tremendously and he truly cares about you and Jack and I believe once this whole thing is over he will ask you to marry him."

Terrie was relieved and yet all of a sudden she was scared. 'What if he did ask her to marry him—would she?' She knew her brother was right, what she was feeling for Clem was it strictly gratitude for the way he's protected her. Only she could answer that question and right now she didn't want to even think about it. She knew she did care for him and she did miss him when he wasn't around, but like Bud said 'Why?'

"Well the naps are over and we're starved." Jack said coming out on to the porch. "Clem is building a fire in the fireplace in the living room, so after we eat we can go in the living room and have a nice cozy fire. You two look so serious what have you been talking about."

"Just girl talk. Come on Terrie let's fix these guys a plate of food before they starve to death. Poor babies they've been asleep for about an hour and to them they think they've been asleep all night." Nina walked into the kitchen still mumbling about the guys wanting to eat again.

"Well, the leftovers were just as delicious as the first go around." Jack said as he stood and started cleaning off the table. "We can go into the living room, have Christmas and then have some more pie. There is some left isn't there?"

"Yes Jack, there is both Pumpkin and Pecan left. Nina and I didn't want to spoil dessert for you and eat the rest while you were asleep." Terrie chuckled winking at Nina.

"Well, come on let's get to Christmas. Leave the dishes go until after the pie and Clem and I'll do them."

"Would you like coffee in there now or would you rather wait until you had your pie?" Terrie asked as they all started to leave the kitchen.

"Let's wait until we have our pie." Clem said as he started towards the living room. "Jack can't wait that long to see what Santa left him." He said laughing.

"Speaking of Santa Claus who wants to play him and give the gifts out?" Jack said as he sat down on the couch.

"Obviously you don't want to or you would have sat on the floor" Terrie said "Besides it's my house, and since I doubt that there's anything under the tree for me I'll play Santa. That is if it's OK with the rest of you." She said as she sat down on the floor.

"Be our guest. Start handing them out."

Terrie picked up the first package and it was for Clem, she handed it to him and said, "Open it."

"No, not until everyone has one to open."

"But then you don't get to see what someone got you."

"Oh all right. This is from Jack and Nina." He said as he slowly, carefully and methodically opened the package.

"Oh for cryin' out loud Clem would you please hurry up and open that thing. We will not be saving paper this year." Terrie said laughing.

He finally got it unwrapped and it was a beautiful light blue sweater. "Hey guys this is really beautiful. I don't have a light blue one either."

"We know, that's why we got it. You haven't worn light blue for years and it's about time you started wearing it again." Nina said as she kind of held her breath and touched Jack's hand. They both knew that light blue was Clem's wife's favorite color for him, but that was in the past and it was time he forgot that and got on with the rest of his life.

"I don't know why you haven't been wearing it. It is a gorgeous color and if you don't want it I'll wear it. How's that?" Terrie said laughing as she reached for another package. This one was for her from Jack and Nina. "This is no fair. I didn't know we would be having Christmas together so I didn't have time to properly shop."

"Who cares just open the damn box and don't take as long as he did." Jack said

Terrie opened the box, looked down at it and almost cried.

"Well, let's see it what is it?" Clem was saying

"A light blue sweater just like yours. Thank you, you two. All I want to know was this done deliberately or by accident."

"Deliberately!!" Jack said laughing

"The next gift is for Jack. I guess I may as well hand Nina this one and the two of them can open them at the same time."

"Hey, that means I don't get the lime light like you two did." Jack said pouting

"Oh you poor mistreated baby. Open yours I'll wait. Men, they are such big babies." Nina laughed teasing her husband once again.

While they were opening their gifts, which were from Clem, Clem slipped behind Terrie and handed her one, quietly and whispered in her ear for her to open that one. She shook her head No, but he insisted. When she opened the lid of the box, it had a letter or note on top of the cotton. She looked at Clem quizzically and he nodded for her to open the letter. It was very short. It just read please wear this and think of me. When Terrie removed the cotton she saw the most beautiful pearl and diamond necklace she'd ever seen in her life. She tried to pick it up out of the box, but her hands were shaking so badly she kept dropping it.

"Oh for pete's sake Clem help the poor girl out." Nina was saying

It wasn't until then that Terrie realized that they, Jack and Nina, weren't opening their gifts, they had been silently watching her open her gift from Clem.

"Clem this is the most beautiful thing I've ever seen. It must have cost you a fortune."

"No, just a few cracker jack box tops."

"Oh will you please be serious for at least 2 minutes." Terrie said leaning over and kissing him on the cheek. "Would you please fasten it around my neck for me." Turning her back to Clem, so he could easily fasten it for her.

"Did you two ever open your gifts?"

"No, we were too busy watching you."

"Well-l-l I'm not opening anything now. So let's see what you got."

Jack opened his box and it was from Nina and was a new white shirt with a beautiful blue tie that had white stripes in it.

"I guess my wife is trying to tell me I need to dress for this trial." Jack grinned

"You damn sure better. We've got a lot at stake and we best be presentable."

"What's in your box Nina. It's awfully large. Maybe it's a new blender." Clem said chuckling. "She's been complaining about needing a new blender."

Nina unwrapped the box, opened it and there was another wrapped box inside, she pulled that one out unwrapped it, opened it and there was still another smaller box wrapped inside of that box. "How many of these phony things do I have to unwrap?" She turned and asked Jack

"Just open the damn box and quit complaining."

Nina unwrapped that box and inside was a small ring size box. She gasped and you could tell she was afraid to open it.

"Come on, come on open it. What's in it?" Clem said leaning forward to get a better look inside the box.

Nina opened the ring box and just sat and stared. Then the tears started coming down the side of her face. "It's the most beautiful ring I've ever seen." She stammered lifting it out of the box. "Here Honey, put it on my finger." She said as she handed the ring to Jack and held out her left hand.

As Jack placed the ring on her finger he leaned over and kissed her. "When we got married I didn't have enough money to buy her an engagement ring. Now she has one. I love you sweetie."

Even Terrie had tears in her eyes. He was such a gruff man, but so sensitive too. "Just a big old pussy cat is all you are." Terrie said as she reached for another present.

"I need help on this one Clem would you please pick it up and hand it to ah, oh, it's to both Jack and Nina. It's kind of heavy."

"Ok, Clem what'd you buy?" Jack said as he took the package in his hands almost dropping it.

"Don't drop it you big klutz. It might be breakable." Clem said Nina unwrapped the box and there was her new blender. "Thanks Clem. You're right I have been complaining that I needed a new blender." Reading the outside of the box she exclaimed, "Wow it does everything, but the dishes. Thanks again. This is great."

Terrie stood up and walked around to the side of the tree picking up one of the packages she started towards Jack and Nina. "I told you that this was kind of unfair 'cause I didn't have a chance to really shop, but Merry Christmas you two anyway." After handing them their gift she went back over to the same spot at the side of the tree and picked the other one up and handed it to Clem.

Nina and Jack opened their gift while Clem sat and watched. When Nina saw what it was she couldn't believe her eyes. "Oh my god Terrie, are you sure you want us to have this?"

"Absolutely. It isn't much, but please with my love." Turning to Clem she said "Well, aren't you going to open yours?"

"I'm so got. I didn't expect or want anything from you."

"Tough buddy, you've got it. Of course if you don't like it I'll take it back." Terrie kind of laughed hoping beyond all hope that he really would like it.

"Good heavens Terrie did you make this?" Clem asked as he held the brown tweed crocheted afghan up.

"She sure did, just like this one she gave us. I asked her when she had the time to do this kind of stuff and she said while she watched TV. Can you believe that?"

"This is beautiful. Thank you." Clem said as he leaned over and kissed her on the cheek.

"Hey Clem isn't something missing around here?"

"You're right. Where'd you put it?"

"I thought I put it right there on the front of the tree." Jack said as he got up and started towards the tree.

"Are you two looking for the envelope?" Nina asked

"Yeah. Do you know where it went?" Clem asked

"Yes, it fell off the tree, so if you'd look more towards the back of the tree on this side, you'll find it. I picked it up off the floor and put it where I thought the wind and all wouldn't drop it again." Nina said

"Terrie, this gift is from the three of us. We know you can use it, but we didn't know what else to get you. Sure hope you like it." Clem said as he handed Terrie a large manila envelope.

Terrie took the envelope and opened it. Inside were instructions and a warranty for a snow mobile. "What? Where is it and how on earth did you get it here. Or is this some kind of a joke?"

"It's no joke Terrie. We brought it up in Steve's plane. That's what took us so long unloading everything. Right now it's down in the boat house." Clem said

"Lets go see it. Does it have lights and all? Maybe I'll take it for a spin."

"Terrie look outside. It is now very dark. We will take you down tomorrow morning to see it and then we'll take turns riding on it with you. That is if that's OK with you." Clem said as he stood up. "Now I'm ready for coffee and pie. Anybody want to join me in the kitchen?"

"Sounds great to me. Come on Terrie. You can read all the instructions later."

"I can't believe you all bought me a snow mobile. Thank you so very much. Now I won't have to always use my snow skis to get to Fitzgerald's and maybe I'll be able to go to town on my own. This is super." Terrie couldn't get over them buying her such an expensive gift. "What wonderful, considerate, kind friends you three are. I love you all." Terrie stopped short realizing what she'd said. 'Guess that would be called an o-o-oops.' She thought.

"Well, Terrie, these two weeks have passed far too quickly, but Steve will be here around 6 tomorrow morning. No late night for us tonight plus we have to get our stuff packed." Clem was saying as they walked back up to the house. "Today was a blast and you handle that snow mobile like a pro, so I guess we don't have to worry about you wrecking the thing. Just please be careful. I don't want to come back up here next year and you're all crippled up by some stupid accident."

"I'll be careful. You just be careful. Those men that you're dealing with aren't pikers when it comes to putting people away."

"We've got most of them put away, at least until the trial begins and then they'll be gone for a long time, so you don't have to worry."

"Would you like some help packing honey?" Jack asked Nina as they went in the front door.

"Nope, you just go out in the kitchen and have Terrie make up a big pot of her hot chocolate. It won't take me too long to finish packing. I really hate leaving this place. It is so beautiful and peaceful even in this cold. I hope we'll come back in the spring or summer, after this trial is over. Who knows, maybe when you retire we can move up here."

"Would you seriously like to move up here? Even before I retire I could probably be transferred to maybe a desk job down in Virginia."

"Let's get you two through this trial and then maybe we'll talk about it. I really do understand why Terrie loves this place so much. I even love the quaint town."

"Ok, you go finish packing and I'll keep Terrie company in the kitchen." Jack said as he headed towards the kitchen and Nina started towards their bedroom.

The rest of the day was comprised of them getting things packed and into the living room, next to the front door.

"You certainly aren't taking home near as much stuff as you arrived with." Terrie laughed looking at the suitcases. "I could have sworn you even had more suitcases when you came up than your leaving with."

"No more suitcases. Just more room in them once the Christmas was taken out of them." Nina laughed. "We also came with a lot of boxes, but there again it was stuff that we either ate, brought up to you, or was Christmas."

"I really hate to see you all leave. This last two weeks has been great. I guess I'll go back to crocheting or painting to keep from being let down too much when you leave."

"Just remember one thing," Clem said putting his hand on Terrie's shoulder "We will be back!" Trying hard to sound like Arnold with his accent.

"Does that mean that you and Jack will come back in May, June or whenever it is that this things over?" She turned to Nina and asked

"Oh, I sure hope so. I told Jack we *will* be discussing our moving up here. I can see why you love this place so much."

"That would be terrific, but I guess I will have to see if I can buy this place. How much do you think the government would ask for it?" Terrie turned and asked Clem

"Oh I doubt that they'd ask a whole lot. Hopefully not any more than it cost them in the beginning." He answered her. 'Hopefully I'll be able to pick it up for a song. Maybe part of my severance pay' he thought. 'I'm really glad I found this place. Even Jack and Nina are happy here. Of course, what's not to love about it.'

———

"I hate good-byes, so I'll just say adios and I'll see you in the funny papers." Jack was saying as the four of them headed towards Steve and the plane.

"If you're trying to be funny, you're not. But I do understand I don't like good-byes either." Terrie said as she got to the pier and set one of the suitcases down. "Are you sure you've got everything? What about the blender?" Turning to look at Nina.

"Yes, the blender is packed and if I've forgotten anything else I'll get it our next trip up here. Hang in there Terrie it'll all be over soon now. I'll send you letters addressed to the Fitzgerald's inside the brown manila envelope. Take care and we'll see you soon." Nina kissed Terrie on the check and climbed into the airplane.

"See you soon, short stuff. Don't take any wooden nickels and we'll see you in the Spring." Jack said as he leaned down and kissed her on the cheek.

Clem was the last one to climb aboard. "Be careful, start watching the news, take care of yourself and I'll see you in the spring." He said as he too kissed her on the check.

Terrie stood and waved as long as she could see the plane. Then she started what seemed to be a very long walk back up to the house.

# CHAPTER 16

Spring came rather early the next year. Even the Fitzgerald's had been surprised at its earliness. They said normally with an early hard winter like they had had last year, Spring didn't start until mid-May, but this year the lake started to thaw the latter part of April. The weather was really weird Laura had commented when she and Terrie went to town. Terrie had made it through the winter without too many problems. She even managed to drag the Christmas tree over to one of the vacant islands on the back of her snowmobile. Tom had called that morning and said he was sending Dave over to pick up her boat and take it back to their place for a good going over, before he started on the Fitzgerald's boats and motors.

"Is this going to be inconvenient for you Terrie?" Tom had asked when he'd called.

"No, that's fine. I have plenty of groceries. I went to town with Laura yesterday, so I'm well stocked. Come on out and get the boat."

"Dave will probably have it a couple of days. If you need anything, anything at all before he gets it back to you, you will give us a call."

"Sure. Like I said I shouldn't need it. Tom thanks for everything."

"No problem. Watch for Dave so you can give him the keys."

"Will do." Terrie hung up the phone and looked out the window. It looked like Dave walking down to the dock right then.

She went to her jewelry case and took out the boat keys. Slipping on a windbreaker she headed for the dock.

"Hello Miss Terrie. Did you have a good winter?"

"Yes, as a matter of fact. It wasn't a bad winter at all. At least not nearly as bad as I had thought it would be last summer."

"Good. I'll try to get your boat done today, but if I don't I'll get it to you tomorrow morning as early as I can."

"Thanks Dave, but like I told Tom there's no hurry. I've already been to town for what groceries and supplies I needed so I won't be going back for a few more days."

"It looks like it's going to be a great summer what with Spring coming so early. Sure hope fishing is better than it was last year." Dave said as he lowered the boat from its winter storage, into the water. "Heard that your brother might be coming up here in a couple of weeks. Guess he wants to check on you."

"No, if he's coming he's coming to try and catch the 'big' one before anyone else does." Terrie laughed as Dave backed her boat out and tied his onto the back.

Terrie went back into the house and decided to make some ice tea. 'It must be at least 75 outside.' She thought as she headed to the kitchen. 'That is warm for up here even in July.' 'Well wonder how the case is coming along. I've gotten very little news about it up here.' A blurb once in a while from the Duluth station, she found she learned more, if you could call it that, from the Canadian station than she did Virginia or Duluth. All she knew was the trial was coming to an end and something about surprise witnesses. 'Wonder who that could be especially since I'm sitting up here. Oh well, guess Clem and Jack will tell me when they get here. At least I hope they're still coming. I haven't heard a word, even from Nina since let's see when was her last letter—oh yes, now I remember the end of February. She was telling me about the flowers Jack had sent her from Atlanta for Valentine's Day, lucky woman I didn't get any flowers. Even *she* didn't say anything about the trial. Guess out of site out of mind is the truth where I'm concerned.' Terrie put the water on for the tea, got the pitcher out of the cabinet, the teabags and sugar.

She took her glass of ice tea out to the porch. She had the windows raised and the lake breeze and the smell of the water were welcome odors to her. 'Good clean, fresh country air' that's what I like about Minnesota.' She thought drinking her tea. She closed her eyes for just a moment, but when she opened them again it was sometime around 2pm she could tell by the placement of the sun. 'Good heavens I've managed to sleep this day away.' Then she heard a knock at her door. Who on earth. She wasn't expecting anyone. She was almost afraid to open the door when she did there stood Bud with a grin all over his face.

"Come on Sis let's go to town and get a bite to eat. I haven't eaten yet, have you?"

Terrie just stood there with her mouth hanging open. Finally she managed to put her arms around her brother's neck and hug him. Pushing back away from him she said, "Where on earth did you come from? How did you get here? I didn't hear a motor. Dave was over earlier and mentioned he'd heard you might be coming up, but I didn't think this soon. Come in, come in. I've got ice tea come sit a spell we can go to lunch later." She said pushing him into the kitchen. "What on earth brought you up here so early?"

"To answer your first question, I came over in your boat. I was sitting in the lodge when Tom called you. Next I was on the phone with Rickey the other night and he said that spring had come early and the lake was thawed out and fishing might be pretty good, so here I am. How have you been Sis? Have you been listening to the trial?"

"I don 't get very much news about the south, no matter what it involves. Once in awhile I've heard things from the Canadian channel. Why anything good coming down?"

"Well, since it involved Jay and the company, they've carried quite a bit of it on the Tennessee stations. When I left home it sounded like it might be getting close to the end. I'll tell you this much, that friend of yours, Clem, well, he presented some kind of a case. I don't want to go into the details I've heard about, at least not now, but what a helluva man. Maybe I was wrong, maybe you should marry him." Bud just looked at his sister. He knew her pretty well and from what she hadn't said last summer, he was pretty sure that was in the back of her mind. "You want to pour me some more tea, please, this is pretty good. Almost as good as what Mom made. Mind if I wander thru' the house. I'd like to see what you've done this winter."

"Be my guest. Are you going to stay here or over at Fitzgerald's?"

"I'd kind like to stay over here for a couple of days so we can get caught up on things. That is if it's Ok with you."

"Of course it's Ok you silly thing." Terrie said pushing her brother into the hallway. "How many others do you see here? It isn't like I don't have the room. Come this summer I might be crowded, but not now." She finished teasing him.

"Wow Sis you've really worked hard around here the place looks great."

"Thank you kind sir."

"Hey when I drove in the boat house I saw a snow mobile. Who bought you that? It isn't a cheap one either, I checked it out."

"I know it's not a cheap one. My friends, Clem, Jack and Jack's wife Nina."

"Jack that's the one you lived with in California, isn't he?"

"Yep. The three of them came up about 3 weeks before Thanksgiving and stayed until the Sunday before Thanksgiving. They helped me put up a Christmas tree. In fact the two guys went out and chopped down a tree and brought it back to the house. The house was really pretty and I wasn't nearly as lonesome as I thought I would be."

"This Clem guy sounds pretty nice. Maybe I'll get to meet him someday."

"Maybe sooner than you think. He, Jack and Nina are coming up shortly after the trial is over. You'll at least get to meet them in July when you come back. From the way they all sounded they intend to spend a good percentage of the summer up here. You'll like them. They're really super nice, decent people."

"Well, let's go eat. Sorry you have to drive my boat. Where's yours?"

"I didn't bring it with me this time. Normally if I come between now and the first of June I bring the boat up and leave it, but this time I didn't. I'll bring it up in July when I come back. Come on let's go eat. I'm starving."

"Where's your stuff? I don't see it here in the boat and it wasn't on the porch." Terrie said as she climbed into her boat next to her brother.

"It's still in the car at the lodge. I figured we could stop there on our way back from town."

"Ok. Tom said this kind of weather is highly unusual for up here. Winter set in extra early the lake was frozen by oh, I'd say mid to late October. I know it was solid, solid when Steve flew the guys up here. I don't care about the reasoning as to why it's warm now I just love it. Now I can open my windows and get the fresh smell of the lake and the lake breeze."

———

"As always the sandwich's were delicious. There isn't anybody else that can make the old fashion pork tenderloin sandwich's like those people can." Terrie said as she and Bud headed across the parking lot towards the grocery.

"Your right. The drive-in back home is long gone. A lot of things are gone that we enjoyed as kids." Bud said as he opened the grocery store door. "What are you going to get in here?"

"Well, I thought I'd get some bitter sweet chocolate and some white Karo syrup and make some fudge. I haven't had any for awhile and I thought it sounded good."

"Your right. I haven't had any for well; let me see, since the last time I was down at you place in Georgia. What's that a year or two ago? While we're here in town I want to go down to the General Store and get my fishing license also."

"Yeah, something like that." Terrie said as she looked for the Karo.

"Don't forget to stop by Fitzgerald's on our way back. They

will let you leave your car parked there won't they?" Terrie said as Bud started the boat.

"Oh sure. Besides I'll probably stay there a night or two before I leave anyway. Rickey said something about running down to the gambling casino one night."

"I'll be glad when all of this mess is over, so I can go down there. I understand they're supposed to build one someplace on the back or north side of this lake. I just don't know when or where exactly."

"That'll be nice. Then you can just take your boat and go drink and gamble."

"You know I don't drink, so that won't bother me. I would like to go gamble though'. I miss that. Certain machines are relaxing for me, especially when I start hitting on them. Oh well I guess that'll come in time."

"Don't push it Sis, you're so close. Take your time on everything. It'll all come out in the wash, so to speak."

"You can stay here, I'm just going to run up and get my bag. I'll be right back." Bud said as they pulled into Northwood's dock.

"Don't forget your fishing rods. Maybe we can get some fishing in while you're out at the house."

"Will do." Bud yelled as he ran up the steps to his car.

"Were you surprised when Bud brought your boat back?" Dave asked Terrie. He had come down on the dock from the boathouse when he heard them coming in.

"Boy was I ever. I'm sure glad he's here though. It's nice to have company again."

"I'm sure it is you've been out there a long time without any visitors."

"Yes, but I've come in here through the winter, so it hasn't been too bad. Not nearly as bad as I thought it was going to be. I must admit though, I am tired of being the lady that walks alone."

"I imagine. You aren't the hermit type. At least not what I observed over here last summer. Well, here comes your brother. Have a good one and hope to see you again soon." Dave said as he helped Bud stow his gear and shoved us away from the dock.

"I saw Rickey and he said to tell you Hi and not to become a stranger since the weather's broken." Bud said as he steered the boat towards Terrie's island.

"Oh, I won't. I was over there quite a bit this winter on my snowmobile. I didn't venture too far on it for fear something might happen and I couldn't get word to anyone. I was afraid I might get hurt and freeze to death, so I stayed pretty close to home."

Bud and Terrie sat and talked a lot while he was at her place. She showed him pictures of the 'group' while they were up and he seemed to like the looks of Clem. She showed him the necklace that Clem had given her for Christmas and the sweater that Nina and Jack had given her.

———

"Well, Sis. I guess I better go over and stay with Rickey and Laura for a couple days and then head back home. It's been great being here with you and I am very impressed with what you've done around here. Don't take any wooden nickels while I'm gone." Bud was saying as he finished packing his bag and picked up his rods. "You don't mind taking me back to Northwood's do you?"

"Heavens no. I wish you didn't have to leave here so soon, but you should visit with them for a couple of days too. Come on bring your stuff and let's get going." Terrie said as she headed out the door.

"I'm not going up to the lodge with you. I'll just say adios here and head back home. Be careful driving home 'little brother."

"I will Sis and I'll see you in July."

"Tell my kids and all I said thanks for the pictures and I love them." She said as she steered away from the dock. Bud had brought all kinds of pictures, letters and drawings from her kids and grandkids. 'Damn how I miss them, but one day soon, very soon I'll have all of them up here. Then we can be a family again. Hopefully I won't be the lady who walks alone much longer.'

# CHAPTER 17

Clem walked out of the courthouse feeling very smug.

"Hey guy. Great work in there."

This was the response he was getting from everybody. Granted without the witnesses and Terries information he'd never have been able to get this to court, but he sure did feel good about everything.

"Well, Mr. Brown." The Director said as he stepped out of the courthouse and saw Clem standing on the steps. "That was a job well done. I wasn't really sure you could pull everything off without your 'star' witness, but you had told me that you didn't want to use her unless you absolutely had too. I do have one suggestion, that is if you'll take it."

"What is that Sir?" Clem not really wanting to hear the suggestion. He was afraid that it was the same one as always—when can we expect you to move to headquarters and come out of the field. He just wasn't ready for that right yet. 'Oh well I've heard it before so I may as well listen to it again and this time maybe I'll surprise him and myself.'

"Why don't you take a month or so off? Maybe go do a little fishing. I know you've got the time coming."

"Why I" Clem stammered. He certainly didn't expect to hear that out of the director.

"Well, you think about it" the director interrupted

"Then when you get back maybe we can talk some sense into you and get you to come to headquarters and out of the field. You deserve a position with us. You've certainly earned it after all of these years."

"Thank you Sir. I just might take you up on that leave. I could sure do with some fishing. Get away for a while—hmmm it does sound like a good idea. Thanks again. I'll talk to you later about it."

When Jack came out of the courtroom and started towards Clem, Clem was whistling.

"Hey buddy, what makes you so happy, other than the fact that you must feel pretty proud of yourself after the beautiful case you put on over the last 3 months."

"I'll tell you later. I'm starved let's go get something to eat. I feel as if I haven't eaten anything at all in these last 3 months."

Clem and Jack walked down the street towards the restaurant. They'd eaten here often since the trial had begun. The food wasn't the Waldorf, but they had quick service and the waitresses were real friendly. They made a point of remembering what it was you drank, besides water, and normally what you liked to eat. Besides the atmosphere was great and the food was good. They walked in and were seated almost immediately. Their waitress they had had several times before.

"You two want your regular coffee?" She smiled as she sat the water on the table and handed them menus. "Are you ready to order or do you need a few minutes? As many times as you two have been in here, you should have the menu memorized."

"Yes we'll take our regular coffee, but give us a few minutes on the menu." Jack said as he looked at Clem.

Clem nodded and stuck his nose in the menu. "We might know the menu by heart, but I still don't know what I want. With this thing finally behind me I'm more nervous than I was the first day."

"You've been running on adrenaline you'll calm down once we get away from here and head home. I do have to say you did a helluva job in that courtroom. When you had the prosecutor bring that one witness in I damn near fell out of my chair. Man you kept that one, as well as a couple others, even away from me. How come you didn't tell me about them? I'm supposed to be your partner."

"That's called the 'art of surprise' I couldn't afford for anyone to know, with the exception of the prosecutor, when I handed him their name. You might say he was 'slightly' upset with me and screamed from time to time when we were setting all of that up, about how could he build a case without knowing names. I told him it was my way or I was backing out and he'd have nothing. Fortunately for me the director backed me and told him to do it my way and we'd have them all behind bars at the end. Thank god the director trusted me totally on this one. As you know he hasn't always, but he did this one and even he didn't know the 'surprise' witnesses. Most everything regarding the witnesses I was able to keep secret because of the information that Terrie had supplied us. Man she truly was a walking encyclopedia of knowledge. Like she said one time, she had no idea what so ever what was going on or how much she knew."

"Man, pulling this off, you came out smelling like a damn rose. Not to mention the precedent that you've set."

"I don't give a damn about precedents I just wanted them off the streets and I knew the only way that was going to happen was to do it my way."

"Ok boys, are you ready to order now?" the waitress asked as she filled their cups.

"Yes. I'll have a tuna fish salad on white and could you please make sure that the lettuce and tomato are on the side this time please?" Clem said. This wasn't the first time he'd ordered that sandwich. In fact, he normally ordered it and each and every time they put the tomato and lettuce on the sandwich and he had to take it off.

"You want fries with that?"

"No thanks"

"I'll have the hamburger platter all the way." Jack said

When the waitress left the table Jack said, "Now do you want to explain the whistling when I came out of the courthouse."?

"Well, the director came out and said I should take some time off and go fishing that I'd earned it. He also said when I got back then maybe I'd be willing to sit down and talk to him about taking a desk job at headquarters. I told him I'd think about the vacation. I didn't want him to think I was too anxious. I'd leave today for Minnesota if I had everything packed and the apartment closed."

"Well, what are you going to do about either one, and are you going to invite Nina and I to go to Minnesota with you? I've got quite a bit of vacation time coming and I am thinking about retiring or transferring to a Minnesota desk job if there's one available."

"I didn't know you were thinking along those lines. And of course you and Nina are invited to go to Minnesota with me. I don't think Terrie would ever forgive me if I came up there, after all of this, without the two of you."

"Good now that that's settled. Let's eat lunch and go home. We can discuss the job and Minnesota on the plane and when we get home. I don't think it would take Nina more than a day to get packed for up there. She really did fall in love with that place."

The two men ate their lunch and headed for their hotel. All that was going through his mind, right now, was calling Terrie and telling her they'd be up shortly. That it was all over and he'd tell her everything when he got there.

——————

Terrie's telephone rang and it surprised her. She didn't get any phone calls after 8 o'clock at night. In fact she received no phone calls unless it was the Fitzgerald's so she was a bit concerned when it started ringing. She had an answering machine so she stood looking at it. 'If, whoever it is, wants to talk to me they better leave a message.' That thought no more went through her head until she heard a voice screaming, "it's me honey, Clem, pick up the phone." She grabbed the phone up and yelled "hold on til the answering machine shuts off."

Once the machine did its thing Terrie's first words were "Where are you?"

"I'm at home, but Jack and Nina and I will be up there

sometime this week. I have to get a hold of Steve and I felt it too
late to call him tonight. How've you been? Had any problems?"
    "Is it all over? What happened?" Terrie held her breath. She
knew it had to be over or he wouldn't be calling her directly, but
she was still afraid of his answer.
    "Yes it's all over. We'll tell you all about it when we get there.
I may have a friend of mine fly up next week some time that is if
it's Ok with you. He loves to fish and I was telling him about your
place and he said it sounded fantastic and would it be possible for
him to come up sometime, so I suggested next week, but I'd have
to check with you first."
    "Of course it's Ok. If he's a friend of yours then he's a friend of
mine also. The only thing is he'll have to bunk in there with you
or sleep on the hide a bed in the living room."
    "That's no problem. There's twin beds in my bedroom so he
can bunk with me. I'm going to hang up now, but I'll call you and
let you know exactly when the three of us will arrive. I can definitely
say it will be at least on or before your birthday. See you soon and
Terrie" Clem hesitated
    "Yes?"
    "Nothing I'll tell you when we get there. Stay safe and we'll
see you soon."
    Terrie hugged the telephone after they hung up. 'It's finally
over. I'm calling Bud. No I better wait until Clem gets here before
I make that phone call. Besides he said he gets the news out of
Atlanta, so he probably already knows. I've got to tell somebody or
I'll burst.' Just about then the phone rang again.
    "Terrie, it's Nina pick up the phone"
    Terrie grabbed the phone and blurted out "Hey girl. I'm so
excited I don't know what to do. I just hung up with Clem and he
told me the good news. I can't wait to see you."
    "Hey are you going to give someone else a chance to talk?"
Nina interrupted her.
    "Gosh, I'm sorry Nina, but I'm so ecstatic right now I don't
know what I'm doing. And I just knew if I didn't tell someone I'd

burst. I'm so glad you called. I'll let you talk now. I can't believe it's all over. I started to call my brother, but decided to wait until Clem gets here and I want to talk to my kids" she was gushing

"Terrie"

"Oops, I said you could talk. I'm sorry go ahead."

"Gee thanks. I just wanted to see if there was anything in the way of thread or material that you wanted or needed that I could bring up. Also what kind of clothes should I pack? Terrie you're right. Just wait until we get up there before you start making any phone calls."

"I know. It's just, well you just can't imagine how I feel right now."

"I've an idea. Just find something to keep you busy until we get there. I'm sure you'll do that."

———————

Terrie rose early the next morning and her first thought was to get in her boat and at least go tell Fitzgerald's. Then she remembered she needed some stuff from the grocery so she grabbed her purse and headed for the boat. In town she bought all kinds of cleaning things that she knew she probably didn't need, but she'd use them eventually. She bought a turkey, pecans, piecrusts, hot chocolate mix, powdered cream, all the things she knew Clem liked, at least for one meal. The meal of celebration. After that they can have fish, soup and sandwiches. Standing in line she thought about cookies and fudge. Guess that's the least I can do. Make fudge and some homemade cookies. Finally standing in line she thought 'if I buy one more thing I will have blown my budget for a year.' Not that she was hurting for money, but she didn't like to spend, at least for her own needs, no more than half the rent money from her home in Georgia. That she felt was very smart and frugal. Del always accused her of spending beyond their means, but she knew she didn't. He just believed in taking more than what was his, like when he left her the last time he drained all the accounts and left her with $25.00 saying that should last her a few months. What a jerk and then to be told he was part of Les's operation. Going back in the boat she decided she had too many groceries to stop at North Woods so she would unload her packages and then go across and have a drink with Tom and all of the rest of them. 'Maybe Tom could order me a good bottle of wine for my celebration. I'll ask him when I go over.'

'Good heavens,' Terrie thought as she was putting away her groceries. 'I knew I bought a lot, but why on earth did I buy more chocolate squares and Karo syrup. I just bought that stuff not two weeks ago and there's no way a body could use all of it up making one batch of fudge. Oh well it keeps and I'm sure I'll be making more fudge as time goes along. I'll just put the chocolate in the freezer and the Karo in the pantry. Once she finished putting all her groceries away she went back down to the boat and headed over to Northwood's.

"Good afternoon, Ms Terrie" Dave said as he reached for the bow rope. "Will you be staying very long?"

"Oh probably about an hour or so. Why? Is there a problem with me parking my boat here?" Terrie asked as she climbed out on the dock.

"Oh no ma'am, but that party boat from across the lake is coming here for dinner this evening and I wanted to make sure I had room for him."

"Oh I'll be gone before he gets here. If I remember from last year he normally gets here about an hour before dinner so they can sit in the bar."

"Yes ma'am you do remember. I hate to ask, but have you heard anything about, well you know what I mean."

"Yes Dave, that's why I'm here. Clem called a while ago and he Jack and Nina will be up here sometime next week. It's all over." Those 3 words she almost screamed.

"Oh bless your heart I know how happy you are. You go on up and give the Fitzgerald's the good news. They too will be tickled for you. We've all talked about what a trooper you were. Most of us couldn't have done like you, we'd been in the loony bin by now."

Terrie literally ran up the hill into the lodge. Tom was, as she knew he would be, behind the bar.

"Hey pretty lady what you doing here so early? Want a drink?"

"Of course. Are Iris and Laura in the kitchen?"

"Sure are go on in. I'll have your drink waiting for you."

"I'd rather tell all of you at once, so hold the drink and follow me." She took Tom's had a pulled him towards the kitchen.

"Hey everybody, gather round."

"What on earth. Tom, is she drunk?" Iris turned from peeling potatoes to ask.

"Nope. She hasn't had a drink yet."

"Well, then what's the matter with you. I haven't heard you this excited since, I don't remember when." Iris said walking towards Terrie

"I just wanted all of you to be here together so I could tell you all at once." Terrie was so excited she was stammering all over the place.

"For pete's sake will you spit it out." Laura said

"I'm free. The trial is over and Clem, Nina and Jack will be here sometime next week to fill me in. But it's all over. Can you believe it?"

"Oh Terrie" Iris said hugging her "We're so happy for you. So what's next? Do you plan on staying here or moving somewhere else?"

"Right now I don't know. I do know I don't want to leave here, so I guess I start working on staying here. This is my home now. Funny, I always thought of this as my second home growing up as a kid and now it is my home. Well, gotta go have my drink in the bar and go home. I'll let you ladies get back to your cooking."

"Terrie, good luck and remember to bring your friends over when they get up here."

"Oh I will. For sure." Terrie said hopping back into the bar

"Tell me Tom. Can you order me a bottle of wine from your distributor?"

"Sure, what would you like?"

"Well, you know I love Lambrusco, but that's not fancy enough. Something along that line though. What do they call that a red sweet wine, anyway that's what I want. Can you do it?"

"How soon?"

"By Sunday"

"Well, let me see this is Wednesday and my next delivery comes in Saturday, so sure. I'll find something extra special for you."

"Thanks Tom. I hoped you could. Is it Ok if I pick it up Saturday afternoon?"

"Sure. I'll have it ready for you. If I'm not here Iris or Laura will know where to find it."

She finished the last of her wine. "Guess I best get back across the lake I've a gazillion things to do. See ya." She said as she went bounding out the door and down the front steps.

# CHAPTER 18

Terrie was up early Monday morning listening for the engines of Steve's plane. When Clem called Saturday night he said he'd finally gotten a hold of Steve and the plans were to fly up to the lake on Monday AM, but he wasn't sure how early. She didn't care how early, just that they got there Monday. She'd slept very little Sunday night she was so excited. Tomorrow is her birthday and he'd promised they'd be here at least by her birthday. All of a sudden she heard engines of a plane. She jumped up out of her chair, where she'd been sitting on the porch, and ran out the front door. She just knew that those engines belonged to Steve's plane. They had to and sure enough as soon as she reached the clearing out in front she saw the plane starting to turn to come in for a landing. She ran down to the dock so she'd be there to get the rope to tie the plane up. She was so excited she tripped over a small stump and rolled down the rest of the hill almost falling into the lake catching herself at the side of the dock. 'That damn stump. Maybe the guys will have time to get it out of there this time. I don't need go in the lake. I'd look like a drowned rat when Clem gets off the plane.'

Clem was the first one off the plane; he grabbed Terrie and gave her a big hug and a kiss. Next came Nina who also hugged her and last but certainly not least came Jack. He too grabbed Terrie and gave her a kiss. Steve started helping the guys unload their stuff.

"Good heavens are you here to live." Terrie said laughing. She was so nervous; especially after the kiss from Clem she wasn't too sure what she was saying. "Can I help? Give me a suitcase, something, I'm not helpless I can carry something."

"Somebody hand Terrie a suitcase so she'll get out of everybody's way." Clem said laughing at her as he picked up some of the large boxes and started towards the house.

"Here Terrie I'm sure you can carry this" Jack said as he handed her a small over night case.

"You smart aleck. I can carry more than that. Give me that suitcase." The one she was pointing to was fairly large.

"That's got Nina's stuff in it and it's awful heavy. Are you sure you can handle it?" Jack laughed as he was picking up some of the other boxes that Steve had taken off the plane.

"Steve you will come up and have some coffee, won't you?"

"Maybe one cup, but today's my day to take tourists up, so I'll have to be across the lake in about 30 minutes."

"Well, you don't have to fly over there just kind of drift, so you've plenty of time to come have some coffee and maybe a piece of homemade coffee cake." Terrie said over her shoulder as she started up the hill with the two suitcases.

When she got to the top of the hill Nina was coming out of the house. "What the heck have you got in here anyway, the kitchen sink?"

"Just about, but I didn't want to tell Jack. Just sit it on the porch I'll take it into our bedroom when I get back up here." Nina answered as she headed down the hill.

"What a nut you are." Terrie yelled after her.

"Well, that's the last of the boxes, suitcases and fishing gear." Steve said as he walked into the kitchen. "Where's my coffee and cake that I was offered."

"Right out here on the side porch Steve. Come on out. The rest of your party are putting their things in their rooms. They'll be out in a minute. I told them not to unpack. They can do that later. How was the flight? How have you been? I haven't seen you since last summer when we all went to Canada. By the way thanks again for that ride it was great."

"What ride?" Clem asked as he came through the door from the kitchen.

"This summer Steve flew up and took my brother, some other men and me up to Canada to see some castle. It was neat."

"I'm fine Terrie. The flight up here was uneventful and I've had a terrific winter. Now I'm looking forward to a very busy summer. Your brother coming up again this year?" Steve finally got to answer her.

"Yeah. As a matter of fact he was here about two weeks ago to visit and will be back at the usual time in July."

"Great I look forward to seeing him. We always have a good time together."

"That's great, your brother coming up. I'll finally get to meet him." Clem said as he poured himself another cup of coffee.

"Who you going to meet?" Jack asked as he and Nina came out on the porch.

"Terrie's brother is coming in July."

"Good. We'll all get to meet him. It's about time that we get to meet more of this ladies family."

"What? You mean you all get to stay for a month or so?" Terrie started to say more, but saw the all to familiar look on Jack's face. She saw it quite a bit while they were in California. It meant don't ask any more questions or we'll talk later.

"Yeah, maybe a month we'll just have to wait and see." Clem was answering her.

"Well, ladies and gents I hate to break this up, but unlike some people I've got to get to work. I'll stop by some other time, when I'm not quite so pressed for time." Steve said as he stood up "Thanks for the coffee and cake it was delicious. I'll definitely have to stop by for more of that."

"I'll walk you down to the dock and untie for you." Clem said as he stood and started after Steve. "I'll be right back."

When Clem and Steve got to the dock Clem handed Steve a piece of paper with a name on it. "This man will be calling you either Sunday or Monday. It's Ok to make arrangements for you to bring him up here. The only thing I ask is as soon as you get his phone call and the arrangements are made call me here at Terrie's. If I'm not here just leave a message for me to call you as soon as possible. Do not" Clem said emphasizing the words "give Terrie any information about this call. This man is to be a surprise to her and I don't want it spoiled."

"No problem Clem. I'll call you as soon as I know when we're coming."

"Man the government owes you big time for all you've done for us."

"They already have sent me a pretty decent check. No other award is necessary. I like this little lady. I've known her a long time and her folks were really nice people, so it's been my pleasure to help out."

"Now, what's with this, you're going to be here in July when my brother comes up." Terrie asked Jack as soon as she heard the front door slam. "I recognized that look on your face. What gives?"

"Its not much. Clem and I both have some thinking to do regarding our employment while we're up here. But we both have a little over a month and none of us could think of a better place to be than here with you. So here we are. We'll go in to a lot of stuff and discussions before this time is over. Just don't push Clem. He's had a hard, really hard last 3 months and he really needs to just unwind before he gets into any heavy discussions." Jack was saying as they heard the front door shut.

"Well, now it's just the four of us. Who would like to go fishing?" Clem said as he entered the porch and sat down.

"Why don't you and Jack go and I'll stay here with Nina. I'm sure she'd like some company while she unpacks." Terrie was saying. She'd rather go fishing, but after what Jack had just said decided it was best for the two men to go fishing. "Maybe you could catch supper. That is if you two remember how to fish."

"We will take you up on that." Clem said as he stood up. I've got to change clothes first, but that will only take a minute or two. Grab the fishing gear Jack and I'll meet you down on the dock. Where are the keys to the boat?"

"Wait a minute. I have to change too, so just go change and

I'll meet you back here when you're done." Jack said as he headed to their bedroom to change clothes.

"Do you need my help or can you find your jeans and shirt on your own." Nina asked laughing. "Men, you pack for them and then they can never find anything and you have to go find it for them."

"Never you mind. I'll find my own clothes thank you very much."

After the guys left to go fishing Nina and Terrie sat and talked for a while. Nothing meaningful, just idle talk. Finally Terrie said, "Why don't you go on in and start unpacking and I'll clean up the dishes. When I'm finished I'll come in and help you. Of course, I'll probably just sit in the chair and talk, but I'll call that helping."

"That sounds like a decent idea. I know where everything is in there so it shouldn't take me too long. See you in a few." Nina got up, carried part of the dishes to the kitchen and then went into their bedroom to unpack. 'We haven't told Terrie that we are staying here a couple of months. I hope she doesn't mind, but if Jack and I can find a place to buy we'll go back home and sell out. It's up to Jack whether he goes back to work or retires. Oh well no sense in worrying about it now. Like Jack said we'll discuss it later on when the men have had time to recoup after these last three months. Jack didn't know when Clem was going to ask Terrie to marry him or if he was going to ask her, but oh well Nina quit worrying about it.' She admonished herself as she unpacked. She too had a lot going on in her mind and she too had to learn to take things in stride. This was going to be an entirely different kind of life whichever way Jack chose.

Terrie finished the dishes and walked into the bedroom. "Any thing you need help with?" she said as she sat down in the chair.

"No, not really. I'm almost done. You've made this a comfortable place that it's easy for someone to come in and put clothes away in the dresser or closet. You've allotted a lot of neat things and places in each bedroom. That's nice." Nina said as she hung up the last pair of jeans and closed the closet doors. "I can't stand it any longer.

I've got to ask you Terrie have you thought any more about what you and I talked about. Your answer to Clem if he does ask you to marry him?"

"Yes, I have thought about it and I talked to Bud about it when he was here last month. I don't want to get my hopes up, but in the event that he does ask me, the answer will be yes. The only problem I see, outside of the fact that he hasn't even indicated that he might ask me, is the fact of my divorce. Do you know if it's final?"

"He hasn't said anything, but according to what he said before it should be final. Your answer sure does take a load off my mind, Jack's too, as far as that's concerned. We love Clem as if he was our own brother and we don't want to see him hurt. We know he cares for you tremendously and you two belong together. He's so different since he met you, happy for a change and thinking about his future, not just what case is coming up next. He truly has buried himself in his work. Now let's go to the kitchen and see what you've got for lunch."

———————

The men came back from fishing and they caught just enough for a nice fish fry.

"We'll have these for dinner. That is after I clean them," Terrie said turning to

Nina, "You realize that these men can go out and catch these things, but they don't know how to clean them. Leave it to a woman to do." Picking up the fish she headed towards the lake where she had set up here cleaning area. She knew there wasn't much to cleaning these they were just pan fish, Scale, gut and get ready to fry. 'Big deal.'

"I'm coming with you" Clem said "Maybe I can learn how to clean them and then you ladies won't have anything to complain about."

"You want to bet" Jack said winking at Nina

"Really Terrie" Clem said as Terrie prepared to go about cleaning the fish. "I know how to scale and clean, but I thought I'd come keep you company and maybe we could talk a little bit."

"Ok." Terrie answered afraid of what he wanted to talk about.

"Here I'll help. Do you want to gut or scale?"

"I'll gut you scale. Just keep them out of my hair."

"What would I put fish in your hair?" he laughed

"The scales silly. What would you like to talk about?"

"Well, first I've got your final decree of your divorce in my attaché case. Also that ex of yours got 10-20 for his part in the drugs etc. 2$^{nd}$ I really don't want to go into detail because it shouldn't matter, but I wanted you to know a little bit about my wife. Julie and I were married almost 6 years and had one son Mathew. I was working on a murder case and during that time Julie had taken our boy to one of the water parks and they were both gunned down. I was out of town, working under cover and it took Jack almost 24 hours to locate me. I was devastated more than you or anyone could imagine. I was on leave of absence of about six months trying to find a reason why. Why did this have to happen to me? Not to my family, me. I suffered, my work suffered, but most of all my friends, Nina and Jack suffered. They finally got me help. That, believe it or not was over fifteen years ago. Have I ever looked at a girl, lady, woman since, no not really. Oh sure I'd tease with the guys about this one or that one, but they really meant nothing to me and I couldn't tell you what anyone of them looked like. When I met you, well, I don't know whether it was the build up Chris had given you, the meal we had with you, but there was something there."

Clem took a breath and Terrie said, "You don't have to tell me all of this. It doesn't matter to me, other than the fact I can see how you're hurting." They were done with the fish cleaning, but Clem sat down on one of the large rocks that was right at waters edge.

"I know I don't have to tell you, but I want you to know. You are very important to me and this next month or so we have some serious talking to do, besides about the trial. That's over with and you're free, so you can relax and begin living your life again. I guess I'm fumbling with my words. What I'm trying to say is, I want to be a part of that life. Would you ever consider that?"

"Clem, yes you are fumbling with your words. As a matter of fact I'd say your stuttering also. Is there something you want to say or ask? If so spit it out."

"Would you, ah, consider, ah" Clem was stuttering

"There you go again stuttering. Clem are you asking me if I'd consider letting you be a part of my new life?"

"Yes. This is not the time or place to ask you the real question. But—"

"There you go again. Yes. Does that help you."?

"Oh god it does make things a little easier for me. It's been so long since I wanted to propose to a lady, even date one, "

'There he goes again babbling. Help him out Terrie. Quit making him suffer' she admonished her self. Picking up the pan with the cleaned fish in it Terrie looked down at Clem still sitting on the rock. "Did you just propose to me Clem?" She asked smiling.

"Yeah, I guess I did. I sure didn't do a very good job of it though did I? I promise I'll do better later when I've got a ring in my hand. I don't know that I caught your answer," He said standing up and starting towards her.

"Yes" Terrie said turning and starting back up to the house. Her knees were shaking and she wasn't sure she'd be able to make it back up to the house.

Clem grabbed her by the arm and spun her around almost making her drop the pan of fish. He tilted her head and kissed her. "Yippee sealed with a kiss. We just won't tell them." Nodding towards the house. "They'll know when you have the ring on your finger. Ok."

"Sure. It will just be our secret." 'That won't last long' she thought as she continued up the hill.

"Man, that was the best dinner I've had since—well I guess Thanksgiving."

Jack said as he pushed himself back from the table. "You really out did yourself again Terrie."

"Hey, I didn't do a lot this time. Nina did most of it. She even fried the hush puppies. So let's be giving credit where credit is due. Come on let's take our cups and go out on the side porch and sit in the swings. We've a little while before the mosquitoes come out once they come out its bombard city. They are huge. You two got a small taste of them when you brought me up here, but just wait they get thicker and bigger."

"Isn't there anything that can keep them from biting you?"

"Yeah, but there's only one thing I found, it's a skin and body cream it's better than anything, including the mosquitoes spray for fishermen, that I've found."

"To the porch it is, but don't feed the mosquitoes." Clem said as he headed towards the door.

"Your in an awfully good mood tonight Clem. What's up?" Jack asked as he pushed the door open with his tush.

"Nothing really I just am happy. I guess I'm happy cause everything is finally over." He said winking at Terrie

'Here it comes, I knew it wouldn't be able to keep it secret very long' Terrie thought as she looked at Nina and Jack. She saw the exchange of noddings. They weren't fooled for one minute. 'You may as well tell them.'

"I guess I may as well tell the two of you, but no one else is to know for a while, pretty short while, but a while anyway. We, ah, Terrie and I were talking while we were cleaning the fish and well I ask if I could be a part of her new life and she said yes. I guess that kind of means we are semi-engaged."

"Hallelujah!! It's about damn time, but what is this semi-engaged. Either you is or you ain't?" Jack said beaming from ear to ear.

"Well, we're not engaged until I properly ask her and put the ring on her finger."

"Well what the hell's taking you so long?" Nina asked smiling at Terrie and shaking her head yes.

"When I feel the time is right. It sure wasn't the right time when we were down cleaning tonight's supper. We were both up to our elbows in fish guts and scales."

"Hells fire Terrie don't let him get by with that. Tell him you want the ring now."

"I will not. When Clem feels the time is right—well, I'm not pushing that and I'm quite comfortable with the way it is, for right now."

"Anyway you two should be happy about that. At least I've made some progress and on our first day here. I told both of you coming up here I would take my time and down by the lake the time was right. Anyway, let's just enjoy the rest of the evening."

"Clem, you haven't unpacked yet. Would you like some help?" Terrie inquired

"Not tonight honey. I'm too tired and happy to go tackle something so mundane."

"Man, now listen to him. Using the big impressive words like mundane, instead of his old boring. He's hooked." Jack said as he started laughing

"You know something."

"What Terrie?" Nina turned and asked

"I've laughed more with the three of you, all of us together, since I can't remember when. All I can say is thanks. I love you all for that."

"Like the song says—'That's what friends are for' "Jack answered her

"Oh boy here we go again. What song's next Jack?" Clem said "When he's in a good mood he starts answering questions with lines from songs."

"Ain't no bodies business, but my own."

"On that note, I'm going in for more coffee. Maybe I can even find a homemade cookie or two. Anyone care for any?"

"Bring on those homemade cookies. We can devour them in a hurry." Clem said

"I'll come help you" Nina said as she stood up and headed

towards the door. "Jack and I are so happy and pleased that you said yes. Even more so that he asked already. We figured he'd have to be here at least until Sunday before he got up the nerve.

———

"Those cookies were delicious, but you know something." Clem was saying "The mosquitoes are starting to bite and I'm getting chilled and sleepy. Guess with the full stomach and some nervousness, for what I don't know, over with" he said as he winked at Terrie "I'm ready for bed. For the first time in months I really am relaxed enough to go to bed and sleep. Would any of you mind if I went to bed?"

"No Clem. You go to bed and get a good night's sleep. We'll see you in the morning." Terrie said as he came over and gave her a peck on the cheek. 'Sure different than the one earlier.'

"I think, if you ladies don't mind, I'll hit the sack too. Don't go complaining my dear sweet wife, I'm beat." Jack said winking and kissing her on the cheek.

"I don't mind at all. In fact as soon as I help Terrie get this mess cleaned up I'm going to bed myself."

"Even I'm pretty exhausted." Terrie said picking up the rest of the cups and following everybody into the house.

———

"Good heavens, do you all realize that we've been here almost a week?" Jack was saying as he poured himself another cup of coffee. "Breakfast was delicious as usual Terrie. What a breakfast for Sunday morning. Does that mean we don't get anything else to eat for the rest of the day?"

"Good heavens no. You mean you can't smell what's cooking?"

"Now that you mention it something does smell awfully good. What is it?"

"Well, I was up at 6 this morning finish dressing a turkey. I thought we could have a turkey, all the trimmings and maybe some wine that I had Tom pick up for me. Kind of a celebration type dinner. With all the fishing we've done this week coupled with some of the things that have taken place" She said looking at Clem "I thought it would be kind of nice."

The telephone ringing interrupted Terrie's explanation of the turkey dinner. "Now who on earth could that be?" She said as she got up from the table and went to the living room to answer the phone. Coming back into the room she looked at Clem and said, "It's for you."

"Thanks. I don't know who it could be. I'll be right back." He knew who it was. Only one person had this telephone number. He hadn't even given it to the director. He just told him that he was going to the back woods to go fishing. "Hello" he said into the telephone "That's great what time? Ok I'll meet you down at the dock. This is great timing on his part." Hanging up the phone he walked back to the kitchen. "What time's dinner?"

"Around 3 o'clock. That is if it's Ok with everybody. The bird should come out about 2:30 and I figured by the time it rested and the rest of the food finished cooking, well it should be like I said, around 3 o'clock. Why?" Terrie said looking at Clem with wonderment.

"Well, that was that friend of mine and he'll be here around 2:30 so I wanted to make sure that we'd be here and maybe there'd be some food left for him." 'Man, will you be one surprised lady.' He thought.

"Oh, sure we'll just set another place on the table. Guess we should use the fancier dishes though so we can impress your friend." She said laughing. They all knew there was only one set of dishes in this house.

"What can I do to help with dinner?" Nina asked as she poured more coffee.

"Well, since we're having company I guess we'll have to use a table cloth and for right now the guys can do the dishes while we go look for it."

"How did we get rooked into doing the dishes?" Jack asked Clem

"Beats the hell out of me, but if that's what the gals want I guess we can humor them a little bit." Clem chuckled. He had helped do the dishes all week, so everybody knew that he was pulling someone's leg.

After the girls left the kitchen Jack said, "Do I know this 'friend' of yours? How come you didn't tell me that you'd invited someone else to come share our dream hide-a-way?"

"Yes, you do know him. I have my reasons for telling no one. So don't try to start guessing who it is, just get started on the dishes. Are you washing this time or is it my time?"

"I'll wash, you dry and put away." Jack said rather perturbed with his partner. 'Who on earth could he have invited up here and wouldn't share it with me. We've still got a lot of discussing to do we sure don't need an outsider here.' Jack was thinking. He really was upset with Clem. He knows we've got to decide if either one of us is going back to work, transferring to a desk job up here or retiring. 'If I retire or change jobs I have to look for a place to live and I wanted Clem's input. Damn!' "Sorry Clem what did you say?"

"I said you're slopping water all over the place. I have no intentions of mopping this floor, so cut it out." 'What on earth had gotten into Jack.'

The morning passed quickly what with Clem staying most of the time in his bedroom straightening it up, for his guest, there was very little conversation. Nina and Terrie had busied themselves getting dinner cooking. Terrie said she'd made two pecan pies and they were in the freezer. She'd get them out about 1 o'clock so they could start thawing a little bit and then when the turkey came out of the oven she'd put them in to bake. That way they should be done by the time dinner was over and the dishes done.

"Have you any idea what's going on between Jack and Clem?" Terrie asked Nina

"No. The only thing Jack mumbled was how could he bring someone up here when we have some much to talk about. Right after that he went into town, as you know, and when he came back took a cup of coffee and the paper and went to the porch. Men."

"I agree with you there. Clem on the other hand has been hiding in his room. I had no idea men could pout as badly as these two have done, so far today. I hope this 'friend' of Clem's is good enough to have provoked this tension."

"Me too. Is that a plane I hear? If it is maybe it's Clem's friend." Nina said as she stopped talking and was listening to the plane.

"If that's Clem's friend who's flying him up here?"

"I'll be right back," Clem yelled as he went out the front door.

"Well we at least know it's his friend."

"Was that Clem I heard going out the front door?" Jack asked as he came in off the porch.

"Yes it was. I guess we'll find out in a minute who this mysterious friend is." Terrie said as she dried her hands on the towel. She too was a little perturbed. Of course, she'd said it was Ok for him to be invited, but this dinner was special and she didn't want some stranger here ruining everything.

"Hey everybody how are you" Steve said as he walked into the kitchen.

"Steve, when did you get here? Was that your plane Nina just heard?" Terrie said as she walked over and gave him a hug.

"Yep, that was my plane. I understand and can smell turkey cooking is it Ok if I stay." Terrie knew this wasn't Steve, he was sounding so funny, but she said, "Of course you can stay. There's plenty for every" Terrie stopped talking. She couldn't say a word and she knew tears where rolling down her cheeks. All of a sudden she got her breath and screamed as she literally ran across the kitchen, knocking Steve out of the way. "How, I thought you were, thank god you're not" she just kept rambling but her arms were around the neck of Chris.

"Good god" Jack said, "I never thought of him. I should have realized," he said as he put his arm around Nina. "That my darling wife is Chris, son of Jay and one of the star witnesses in this trial.

Even I thought he was dead, but lo and behold he was a material witness. Now I understand why Clem has acted so funny this week in not wanting to discuss anything. He was putting it off until Chris got here so he too could join in the celebration." He walked across the room to where Clem was standing grinning. "I'm sorry partner. This is a great surprise and you're right for not telling me. I probably would have blabbed."

"I know. That's why I didn't tell you." Clem said grinning and putting his arm around Jack's shoulders. "Why don't we all sit down at the table? We'd probably be more comfortable."

"Clem you certainly owe me an explanation." Terrie said angrily ignoring everyone else and sitting down next to Chris.

"Terrie, honey, I'm sorry, but he and I talked about it and we could not let any one know that he was alive. He was a star witness. And we sure didn't want him killed when we went to the trouble we did."

"Well, where have you been hiding him?" She asked in a hurt sounding voice

"In the cold dismal far north. Alaska to be exact."

"Hey everybody is everything unloaded from my plane so I can leave?" Steve said

"Hell I forgot all about you. Sorry about that Steve." Clem said, "Did you get all your stuff Chris?"

"Yes I've got everything Steve and thanks a lot. I guess I'll see you in about a week."

"Yep, I'll be here. See you everyone."

"Wait a minute. I thought you were staying for dinner?" Terrie said looking up and realizing what was being said.

"Sorry about that Terrie. I'm not staying for dinner that was just a ruse to keep you busy while Clem snuck Chris into the house. I hated to deceive you, but it had to be done. See ya."

"What do you mean a week? Can't you stay any longer than that?" Terrie turned to Chris and asked

"Afraid not Terrie. I've got a practice to get back to. Thank god I have the partner I do. He didn't change a thing the whole time I was gone. He said funeral or no funeral he knew I was still alive and I'd be back. I took this time to come up here and he knew this was important to me, but he also said if I wasn't back in a week he'd ring my neck. Quite frankly I've been 'dead' long enough. So it's back to work for me in a week. But now I can come fishing whenever you invite me."

"Does your Mother know you're alive?"

"Well, Mom's been sick with pneumonia, but my Dad and Sister both know and they promised they'd break it to Mom as soon as she got better. Plus I'm to go out there in a couple of weeks for Sunday dinner."

"I just hope your Mother forgives you."

"Oh Dad and Sis were upset for a few minutes, but they both understood it was necessary. I brought a headline out of the Atlanta paper I thought you'd like to see. I'll go get it."

"Not now Chris, no serious talk, remember." Clem said

"This is just the headline. I think she'd like it" and turning to Terrie Chris said "you won't ask any questions when I show it to you will you."

"No, not if I'm not supposed to I know somebody will eventually tell me everything, but believe it or not, right now I'm not in a hurry to hear about it. Bring on the headlines."

"TaDa" Chris said when he brought out the newspaper headlines FEDS PRODUCE SURPRISE WITNESSES. "How 'bout those headlines. Thanks to Clem every thing worked and it's all over and hopefully things can get back to normal, whatever that is." Chris laughed

"Well, Mr. Celebrity I am impressed." Terrie said when she read the headlines.

"Still a little out of sorts with you for not telling me about Chris, but I'll get over it." She teased as she stood and headed for the oven. "Time for me to get the bird out of the oven before I burn it."

"Would you like some help" Chris asked as he pushed his chair back

"Yeah. This bird is rather heavy. I almost dropped the whole thing this morning trying to get it in the oven, without waking anyone."

"Why don't you men take Chris a walk around the island or something and let Nina and me finish dinner. I've still got rolls to put in the oven and everything else to finish, so scoot."

"Looks like we just got thrown out of the kitchen." Jack laughed, "Come on Chris let's you, Clem and me take a walk. Either one of you want something to drink to carry with us?"

"Do you have something cold to drink?" Chris asked

"Sure do. Ice Tea. Honey would you please get a glass for Chris. My hands are kind of full right now." She said as she was peeling the celery.

"I'll get us all tea to drink. That sounds good." Clem said as he took 3 glasses out of the cabinet. Pouring the tea he said, "Come on guys lets take a walk. I can tell we're not wanted here. At least not for the moment."

"Men. They can be such snits at times. You can't live with them and you can't live without them. What's a woman to do?" Nina said laughing as she went over to check on the potatoes. "What else can I do? Except for the celery you're stuffing the relish tray is ready, the potatoes aren't quite ready for mashing. I've put the tablecloth on and set the table."

"Yep. You're family so I don't feel as though I have to ask you to do things around here anymore. I just figure you see something that needs to be done you'll do it." Terrie said as she checked the pies.

"Looking good. The guys will be pleased with those pies. I just can't make pecan pies, there's always too much gooey stuff in them and Jack won't eat them. He sure brags about yours though." Nina said looking over Terrie's shoulder at the pies. "Maybe sometime you'll give me your secret."

"There's no secret. I just add oodles and gobs of pecans and line the pie dough with pecan halves. That way that gooey stuff you mentioned isn't really there. Just enough is there to hold the pecans in place."

"Ok then when we move you can give me your recipe." Nina said going back to the table to finish setting it.

"What do you mean when you move? I haven't heard anything about that."

"Well, the guys, Clem, mostly I guess, want to wait to discuss that stuff and the trial until after Chris leaves. But between you and me, promise you won't say a word. Not to Chris, Clem nobody."

"I promise. Let's have it."

"Well, the guys are trying to decide whether they want to stay with the bureau or retire. Clem has been offered a position at headquarters and Jack is thinking about transferring to Virginia, Eveleth or Hibbing's bureau. Clem would rather retire and stay right here, on this island with you. Me I'd rather Jack retired. I've lived this life long enough and I want out. If he retires, or even if he does transfer to a desk job up here, we are planning on looking for a place near by, then going back home selling everything, but the bare things I can't do without, sell the house and move lock stock and barrel up here."

"That's terrific, no it's better than that it's wonderful, marvelous etc. etc. etc. What fun for all of us to be near each other. Maybe there's another island near by for sale. You could buy that and during the winter months we could 'walk' on water to each other's house." She laughed "No pun intended"

"Don't forget you promised. You cannot let it slip or I'm dead meat and neither one of those men will ever speak to me again. Jack would claim its grounds for divorce."

"You are kidding aren't you? I mean divorce."

"Of course, but he sure would be mad at me for a while. Hush I think I hear them coming. Don't forget mums the word."

The men walked into the kitchen just as Terrie was shaking her head yes to Nina's sentence.

"Are we having a nervous twitch or did we miss something that called for a yes answer and you didn't want us to know." Clem said looking at both the women.

"It really was neither. I'm busy over here and Nina was saying she'd like a pie recipe of mine and would I give it to her, just as I put a piece of celery in my mouth, thus the nodding of the head. Satisfied?" Terrie laughed and shoved a piece of stuffed celery into his mouth. Where promptly he shook his head. "See that's all you can do."

"I'm finding out it's tough to try and get ahead of my girl." Clem said

"Dinner is just about ready to dish up so why don't you men go wash up or something so we girls can finish." Nina said taking the potatoes off the stove.

"Would you like for me to mash the potatoes? I'd be glad to you know." Clem said as he walked up behind Terrie and put his arms around her waist.

"I think that would be a splendid idea. Thank you sweetheart." Terrie was trying to sound sarcastic, but she wasn't pulling it off too well

"Nina would you dish the green beans up and I'll get the beets out of the fridge. Which one of you men want to carve the turkey, after I get the dressing out of it."

"Let Jack. He can carve a turkey newspaper thin and that's the way I like it." Clem said laughing.

"Well Jack? Here's the knife and fork. It's even electric so all you have to do is guide the knife through the meat."

"Ok you smart alecks give me the knife and fork. This is Jack the carver speaking get me a plate and get outta my way."

"Hold on you can't due anything silly until I get the dressing out of the bird." Terrie was laughing so hard she was almost doubled over.

---

"Man that dinner was delicious. Just as I remembered the first Thanksgiving I had with you down in Georgia. Weren't you there too Clem."

"I sure was. That's when I first met this lady."

"Thanks guys I appreciate the compliment, but I'd like to get out of this kitchen for a while. I feel like this is the only place I've been all day today and I'm sure Nina feels the same way, so if you don't mind, the pies have to cool for about 10-20 minutes before they should be cut, so Nina and I are taking our coffee out to the porch. If anyone would care to join us we'd love the company, if not we're going any way."

"Honey, you and Nina go on out on the porch and the three of us will do the dishes and straighten the kitchen. Yes we will stay out of the pie and no we won't put the bird etc away. Just change into storage containers, no lids and leave on the counter. See everything I've gone through lately I remember what you said Thanksgiving. Go on" he said pushing the two a little bit towards the door.

---

"Well, Chris, you've been here a week. I'm not sure you got much rest, what with everything we've had you doing, but it was different and you did manage to catch a northern. Have you enjoyed yourself, in spite of us?" Clem was asking as they all had breakfast waiting for Steve.

"I've had a ball fishing, gambling, seeing the Indian reservation, going up to Kettle Falls, what an interesting place and that boat ride on those lakes. I've never been on such rough lakes before, visiting with your friends over at Northwood's, but most of all spending the time here with such beautiful people. I am sorry I have to leave, but I'm not one of the lucky ones, at least not yet, I'm too young. I still have to work."

"We're going to miss you Chris, but you are welcome here or anywhere I am anytime you want to come." Terrie said. 'I almost forgot this isn't really my place anymore. It's the governments. Sure hope I don't have to leave here any too soon. Guess Clem will tell me after Chris leaves.' "Do you have everything packed and ready to go?"

"All but the fish."

"I'll take them out of the freezer when I hear Steve's engines and put them in a cooler with some ice. That should hold them until you get home. It won't take you that long to get there." Terrie said

"Speaking of engines" Jack said "I think I hear them now." Getting up and heading towards the front door. "Yes, it's Steve."

"You people go on I'll get the fish and bring them down" Terrie said as she headed towards the freezer.

"I'll stay and help. That way you won't have to carry them down to the lake. That things going to be heavy. I think you gave him enough fish to last all summer and next winter."

"Well, I don't know when he's going to get up here again and I don't want him to forget us." Terrie said putting the last piece of fish into the cooler. She started to pick it up, stopped and just looked at Clem.

"See I told you it'd be too heavy for you to carry," He said picking the cooler up "Come on hon.' let's go see our boy off."

"Good-byes are hard so I just like to say adios or till we meet again," Terrie said to Chris as she kissed him on the cheek. "Don't make a stranger out of yourself and give us a call now and then. Also call us when you get home so that we know you got there alright."

"Yes Mom I will." Chris said as he kissed her on the cheek and shook hands with Clem.

He climbed aboard the plane with Steve and waved as they pulled away from the dock. Terrie stood there until they were out of site. Clem put his arm around her shoulders and said, "Come on honey, the planes out of site."

"I know. It's just after just getting him back I didn't want him to leave. All this time I've blamed myself for his death and now" hitting Clem "I find out he's alive."

"Well, now we're alone maybe it's time to start telling you what all happened in court. Maybe you'll feel better when you know everything."

"First things first. Why don't you make a fresh pot of coffee and you, Nina and Jack go out on the porch. I've a phone call to make then I'll be out there."

"Ok see you in a few" Terrie said as Jack and Nina went to the porch and she made a fresh pot of coffee.

"Now" Clem said as he came out on the porch and poured himself a cup of coffee before sitting down. "We have a dinner date over at Northwood's at 5 o'clock today, which means, it is now a little after 10, that we literally have all day to cuss and discuss the trial and some other things. Which it's the other things that I want to talk about first."

"Ok Clem shoot" Terrie said looking at Jack and Nina and seeing only blank stares.

"Well, first things first" he said as he crossed the porch until he was in front of Terrie where he proceeded to get down on one knee.

Terrie's heart was pounding so hard she knew that Jack and Nina could hear it clear across the porch. She was afraid to even look at one of them. All she could do was stare at Clem.

"Terrie I told you that when I felt the time was right I would propose the proper way, so here I am on one knee asking you if you will marry me and be my wife for the rest of our lives."

Terrie started to cry. She had never had anyone be so sweet or propose in that way with those words before.

"Well?" Clem's hands were clammy and he couldn't stand waiting much longer for her answer. 'What if she says no after all this?'

"Clem did you hear me?" Terrie was asking.

"I'm sorry no I didn't." 'Now I've really blown it.'

"I said yes it would be my honor to marry you."

"Hallelujah. I'm sorry you guys it's such a special moment and Nina and I are so tickled that that just popped out."

With that explanation Clem laughed and leaning over took Terrie's hand and placed the engagement ring on her finger. After placing the ring on her finger he stood up, pulling her up with him and gave her a proper long kiss.

"Man am I glad that that's finally settled. You two would drive a person to drink. Congratulations you two" Jack and Nina both said as Nina kissed Clem and Terrie and Jack kissed Terrie and shook Clem's hand. "Congratulations Terrie, but I should be jealous after all you were my wife before his." He laughed

"Hey, that was in name only" Both Nina and Clem said together. Terrie just stood and laughed at all of them.

"You all are nuts. No wonder I love you all so much" Looking down at her ring she couldn't believe the size of that rock. 'It must be at least 2 to 3 carats.' "May I ask a question of you Clem?" She said looking at Nina and winking

"Sure honey you can ask me anything"

"Whose back did you stick a gun into to get this ring, or was it your payment from the mob." The look on Clem's face was priceless. He didn't know whether to be surprised or pissed.

"What, what do you mean" He finally started saying

"Busted. I have tried every since you three got here, no since Chris got here, to get you for keeping the Chris info away from me. Tee Hee Hee I just did it. I love you sweetie." She said holding up here hand to look at the ring again. "It is truly the most beautiful thing I've ever seen."

"Ok we're even. Now the next thing is living where, retiring or transferring. Since this really does involve all of us we all have to be a part of the decision. First though, Honey, this house, island, boat and all are ours. It has both of our names on the title. The only problem is you have to go into Cook Monday morning and sign the papers. They wouldn't let me sign for you. I don't understand that. It's like they didn't trust an F.B.I. agent."

"Honest injun?"

"Yep"

Terrie got up out of her chair and went over and hugged Clem's neck and gave him a bit kiss. "Now that's news I'm tickled to hear. I was afraid I was going to have to move and none of this, raising her ring finger, would ever take place. Now I am sitting on top of the world. I've got the man I love, two of my most favorite people and my home. Who could ask for anything more."

"Would you?" Nina said laughing "I wouldn't I know a couple of them. I'm going in and make a glass of ice tea, any body else want one?" she asked as she headed into the kitchen.

"Why don't you just put the pitcher, glasses and some cookies on one of the trays and bring it out. That way whoever wants coffee can have it and if they want ice tea they can fix it." Jack said. "Right now I can't make up my mind, so humor me."

"Please don't talk about me while I'm gone."

"Now can we get back to some serious talking please? We've waited two weeks to start these talks and now no one wants to discuss."

"Honey, I don't think it's that. For once now all of us can relax. Now we are family and no one has to worry about opening their mouths in front of somebody. Couple more minutes and Nina will be back and then you can get serious."

"I'm baaaack. You can quit talking about me now."

"Now we need thoughts from the wives, that means you too Terrie, about their feelings of our retiring, moving to different offices or staying in the field.

"I don't feel I should make the decision. I don't know finances or what all being in the field, offices or headquarters means." Terrie said. 'I'm not rich, but because of good investments and the rent from the house in Georgia I can manage, but what about Clem and his finances.'

"Granted you don't know about money, but if Jack and I are contemplating retiring, then you can assume that we must have enough money set aside that we are comfortable with those thoughts." Clem said to Terrie

"Then let Nina air her views first. While she's talking I can think and maybe be able to get into the discussion. After all you have to admit I'm new to the group. Not like some people been there done that type. So I yield the floor to my esteemed colleague Nina." Terrie laughed and bowed to her.

"I don't mind taking the floor. I have been there done that. Jack and I have talked quite a bit about all the aspects, at least since the guys got back from Atlanta. I'm ready to have my man home all the time. If I want to get rid of him for a day I'll send him shopping or tell him to go play golf, or if we're here, go fishing. Jack knows how I feel I want him to stay home. We can afford it, so why go to a desk job that you hate."

"Now Terrie, do you have any input? Please honey, say something."

"Well-l-l-l after listening to Nina and thinking at the same time"

"Oh boy now we're in trouble." Jack interrupted her

"Oh hush Jack I'm not that bad. As I was saying, selfishly I would like to have Clem home, at least till I got tired of him." She laughed winking at Nina "But I would like him around so we could really get to know each other."

"I don't think that's selfish" Nina chimed in

"Thanks. Anyway, I lived with a man for some 5-6 months that wasn't my husband he was somebody else's and I know that wife would have rather he was at home with her instead of a woman she didn't know. That's a trust in a marriage, husband that I've never had the privilege of having. And after being with Jack and Nina and of course you too Clem I would like the chance of building that kind of a relationship and I don't think that it could be done if you were out in the field, as you called it. Also, as I understand it, we are just putting this island in our name, so I sure don't want to move to headquarters. That sounds like a large city, bah humbug. But I'll do whatever my husband wants to do. If he feels like he can retire and we can 'make it', whatever that means on his retirement, then I'm for retirement and enjoying the rest of our lives together. Have I said enough? I would however, like to hear how you men feel." She said timidly, almost afraid of what the answer will be.

"You've said enough that I think my decision has been made for me." Clem said looking and smiling at her.

"I don't want to make your decision for you. That has to be

made by you. I don't ever want you to be able to come back to me and say you're miserable retired and that it's all my fault." Terrie said defensively.

"Don't worry about that honey, I was pretty sure what I was going to do, before you stated your feelings. I just wanted to make good and sure you wouldn't mind having me under foot."

"Well, doesn't anyone care how I feel?" Jack said pityingly.

"Well, no I guess the two women decided for the two of us." Clem laughed

"Well, I just wanted to put my two cents worth"

"Honey, I hate to tell you this, but I'm not sure your thoughts are worth two cents." Nina interrupted Jack.

"Guess I'm the little boy no one wanted to hear from"

"Guess you cried wolf too often." Clem said

"I want to hear" Terrie said, "I lived with you and I know your ideas aren't that great, but the poor little boy should have his chance to speak." She said kindheartedly.

"I guess Terrie's right. I too know what he's like when he doesn't get his own way. His ideas are never that great, but go on Honey, let's hear from you." Nina responded

"Oh hell all of you go to hell. So I'm a spoiled brat with no good ideas huh. Well, my idea is that it's almost noon and I say we somebody should go fix some sandwiches, before I starve to death." Jack started laughing. "Guess this is pick on Jack day. Oh well. Come on wife of mine let's go make sandwiches." Jack got to the door, heading into the kitchen and turned around "Turkey sandwiches OK with you two? By the way, since no one cares, my vote is for retiring and finding us an island just like this one on this lake." Slamming the door behind him, not waiting for an answer.

"Guess we shouldn't have been so hard on him." Terrie said as Jack disappeared

"Oh it's good for him. Keeps him on his toes. Thank you for what you said, about my retiring and all. But I had seriously already decided, that is, if it was Ok with you I was going to retire. This is a strenuous job and I'm not getting any younger, besides I want to have your kids and grandkids come up and spend some time with us. That I'm really looking forward too. I don't have a family, outside of Jack and Nina."

"You three are really close and after what you've told me I can understand. I really like the idea of having them live close to us. It's a shame this island isn't big enough to put two homes on."

"I thought of that too, but when we go to the realtors tomorrow maybe they'll"

"Here's the sandwiches. Nina's bringing the drinks." Jack interrupted "Did we miss anything while we were gone."

"No, Terrie and I were just saying this island isn't big enough to put two homes, but when we go into Cook tomorrow for her to sign the papers for this place, maybe there will be another island near by that's for sale. That's one of the reasons I like this lake, there's no For Sale signs sticking up all over the place."

"Well, it seems as though you men have decided to hang it up and drive us crazy for the rest of our lives." Nina was saying in between bites of her sandwich. "Don't get me wrong that's the best news I've heard for a long time. Guess I'll start thinking of all the things we can get rid of and what all I can pack to bring up here."

"Don't get the cart before the horse," Jack said choking on his drink. "Sorry, it went down the windpipe. Anyway, we have a lot of planning and things to do before next winter. Hopefully Clem will be right and that realtor will have a place for us."

"Well, you know what kind of space I, ah, we have, that's going to take some getting used to, the we, anyway you're more than welcome to bring stuff and store it here. I know you all had planned on staying a month or so, but what's to say, we take a few days and go down to your place, pack some stuff and bring it back."

"Hey that's a marvelous idea. Why didn't I think of that?" Clem said smiling at Terrie. We could have Steve come pick us up

Tuesday and fly back on Friday. I'm sure Fitzgerald's would watch the place while we're gone."

"What's to watch, there's no way you can get here except by boat and there isn't anything here right now worth anything." Terrie said looking around.

"Oh yes there is—you."

"But I'm supposedly going with you three."

"Whoops you're right. I still think we should tell them this evening."

"Don't you think you better see if Steve is available first? Maybe he won't want to haul your stuff in his plane."

"Oh we'd just bring clothes and stuff. The big stuff Jack and I could fly down, rent a truck and drive it back."

"Ok, but please go call Steve before we get too excited." Nina begged.

"Oh all right, come on Jack you can come with me."

"What's the matter you need someone to hold your hand?" He laughed following Clem into the house.

"Have you got a pad and pen I could use?" Nina asked Terrie "Sure, I'll go get it."

After looking at the pad and seeing it was brand new Nina asked, "May I keep this?"

"Sure, I've plenty of them"

"Well, I want to start making a list, as I think of it of things I want to bring up, keep, store until the guys can go back for them and things I'll sell. If that realtor has an island reasonable, as long as it isn't one like the one over on the other side of this island, well I think I'll take my check book with me tomorrow just in case."

"You mean you'd buy it sight unseen?"

"No. I plan on having you take me around the lake after we leave Fitzgerald's so I can check things out. I know Jack's been around a few times, but I haven't."

"Ah I understand. There is an island right behind this one and I think it's about the same size. I know it was for sale at one time, but I'm not sure about now. Anyway, a boat sightseeing trip coming up after dinner. But why wait. Why can't we leave here around 4 and peruse the islands and lake before dinner? Then if we get there early we can go into the bar for a drink and see who the new people are in camp."

"Great idea."

"What's a great idea?" Jack asked as he came through the door

"What did you find out?" Terrie asked

"We're set. Steve will be here Tuesday morning around 8 o'clock. That should put us down home by noon anyway." Clem answered

"Now what's a great idea? Isn't anybody gonna answer me?"

"Should we?" Terrie answered

"Oh come on you guys. Or was it something you don't want Clem or me to know?"

"Guess we better quit teasing him and tell him. We are going to leave here around 4 to go to dinner and take me on a tour of the lake, since I haven't been anywhere, but to Northwood's or town. Then if we get there early we can go into the bar and have a drink and check the newcomers out."

"Sounds like a terrific idea." Clem said

"Honey are you sure you want me to go with you all on Tuesday. I was just thinking that if I stayed home there might be more room in Steve's plane for your stuff.

"It's not stuff thank you very much and yes I want you to go. You can pack up my kitchen for me while I'm packing the rest of the apartment."

"Do you have furniture or anything like that that you're bringing up?"

"I'll have to wait and see when I get back. You figure I was only home about two days when we came up here. I frankly don't remember what all I do have. Basically I guess you would call my place a bachelor pad."

"Don't let him kid you Terrie he's got some really nice things. You will bring your entertainment center won't you along with all your CD's."

"Yeah, that I probably will bring. I'll just have to figure out where we'll put it when I get it here."

"I'll take a tape measure out of my tool box and a pad and I'll take measurements of the things I think you should move up here. How's that!" Terrie suggested

"What if I want to bring something you don't want in the house?"

"Well" winking at Nina "I guess we'll just have to build you a mini house on the other end of the island for you to stick that stuff. Or better yet, we could just buy a shed and put out there and then you could go out there and stare at it every once in awhile."

"You are impossible lady." Clem said after walking over and giving her a kiss on her cheek.

"I know, but you love me anyway." She responded

---

"That soup was delicious, Iris what was it?" Clem asked as he handed Iris his dishes.

"It's like chicken soup with wild rice. But of course my recipe."

"What ever it was it was delicious as was the roast. You'll have to give the recipe to Terrie so she can make it out on the island for us."

"I'd love to. Terrie did I see a ring on that left hand?"

"Yes ma'am."

"Well, tell us. Laura, Tom, Rickey come here quick. I think Terrie has something to tell us."

Instead of saying anything Terrie just held up her left hand.

"Oh my gosh, that thing is beautiful. When's the date?"

"We haven't set a date as yet, but when we do you will be the first to know." Clem said "We are going to go down to our place Tuesday morning and bring some stuff up, so while we're gone could you kind of keep an eye out on the place. I don't mean go to the island or anything, but see if there's any lights on at night—you know."

"Sure, we'd be glad to watch over it. When will you be back?"

"I haven't made arrangements with Steve yet, but probably Friday."

Iris looked at Nina and said, "Does this mean that you two are moving up here too?"

"Yes, it sure does. We fell in love with this lake, so here we hope to move that is if we can find a place to buy. We like to find an island similar to Terrie's."

"I think that island right behind Lawry's is for sale. At least it was. It isn't quite as big as Lawry's, but its still a pretty island. Take a look at it sometime."

"Oh, we did go around it on our way over here today, that one and several others. If the price is right we may buy that one if it's still available. Our problem is we'll have to build a home on it and we guess, Terrie and Clem will have to put us up until it's done."

"Oh, you can stay at one of the motel's in town you don't have to stay with us." Clem teased.

"Why don't you all go into the bar and Tom can fix you something to drink, on the house. In fact give them two drinks. One for the engagement and the other because they're all moving up here and will be our neighbors."

"Sounds like a great idea. Come on folks before it gets too crowded in there." Tom said as he headed towards the bar.

———

"Well, I guess we didn't do too bad. We got a lot more in Steve's plane that I thought we would." Clem was saying as he carried the last of the boxes into the house. "Now all we have to do is figure out where to put everything."

"Well, a lot of Nina and Jack's boxes can go into their bedroom. We can rearrange the furniture and move the bed over against the wall. It might be a little crowded, but until we can get the living room and porch straightened up and move some furniture around it would have to due." Terrie was saying. "At least we could still get through the house without falling over any boxes."

"I feel like we're causing a lot of trouble with our mess." Nina said

"Hogwash. Don't be silly. Why don't you and I go out to the kitchen, sit down at the table with some coffee and think this thing out? Everything can be arranged for comfort. I just have to think about it for a few minutes and then the guys can start rearranging or placing the boxes. I'm pretty good about putting stuff up if I think about it for a few minutes." Terrie was saying as she went to the kitchen to make some coffee.

She knew what it was to try and arrange things, so that everything was in its place, but still usable. She didn't want Jack and Nina to feel like they were crowding things with their boxes. They had questioned coming back where we would put everything. Terrie knew she could find the room if just given the chance.

"Ok." She said after drinking her second cup of coffee and having everyone staring at her. "Clem, the boxes you aren't going to unpack right now, winter clothes, shoes, we'll make sure there's moth balls in them and we'll put them in the attic. As for the few small pieces of furniture you brought, we'll rearrange my bedroom and put them in there since mine is the largest bedroom. A lot of your clothes can hang in my closet and I'll empty some of the drawers in the one dresser and you can put clothes in there. After all you will be moving in there eventually. The stuff that's in that dresser can be moved to the credenza. It's mostly tablecloths and should be closer to the kitchen anyway. That leaves room in your closet and dresser for Jack and Nina to put some clothes away and put boxes up on the shelf. We could, no that won't work, they'd get wet."

"Terrie I really do feel bad about this. We should have thought this out a little better before we started hauling this stuff up here. A lot of this could have stayed down at the house at least until it sells or ours is finished over on the island." Nina was saying.

"Nina quit your worrying. I'm so use to rolling with the tide, so to speak, that these things will work out. I just don't want you to feel as if your imposing because that is a big fat no your not. Granted if Clem and I were already married it would be easier, but that will come in time. First things first and right now that's getting stuffed arranged in here to accommodate all of us. They said your house would be done probably before October and this is June 21$^{st}$, so that's not that far away. Besides you're going to want to start buying stuff for your house and I want you to be able to bring it here. There's no reason to wait until the last minute to do things."

"Didn't I tell you she was a fantastic lady."? Clem said marveling at how she was thinking. "We could go to town and buy a shed and Jack and I could put it up out back. We probably could use one anyway, but for right now it would give them more room for their things. I agree with you about them buying things. No sense in waiting until the last minute when we've got the space" he started to laugh looking around at all the boxes "well, we can make the room."

"You know, you two will have a lot to do in the next few months what with picking out cabinets, faucets and everything else you want, plus selling your house and bringing the rest of your stuff and Clem's up here. Anything I can do to help make it easier for you I'll do. Come to think of it Clem's right. We should go buy a shed. The barge could bring it over."

"Well, I for one want to get this place straightened up so that we'll be able to sit down and talk about the trial. I was there, but I still don't remember everything that happened or why." Jack said pouring more coffee for everyone.

"Ok that's settled. Everyone agrees that where there's a will there will be a way. Since it's late in the day, why don't we go for a boat ride, stop at Fitzgerald's for a drink and let them know we're back relax for awhile, go into town and eat. I guess what I'm saying let's goof off the rest of the day then get up early tomorrow morning and hit it. I bet we could have this place all straightened up by tomorrow evening." Clem said looking around and seeing all the boxes. 'I can't believe we got all this stuff in Steve's plane let alone where we're going to put it here, but I do have confidence in Terrie and she says it'll work. What a gal I'm marrying.'

"Man, that sounds like the best idea yet. We've worked pretty damn hard these last four days; maybe it's time we did play for a few hours. Then maybe, just maybe we'll have a clear head on where all this stuff will go." Jack said waving his arms around just the kitchen and all the boxes piled up. "I'm for going into town first though."

"You know the one thing none of us have thought about." Clem said

"No. What?" Terrie said

"You and I need a car. Jack and Nina will bring theirs up when they bring the truck, but I don't have one 'cause I always had a company car."

"Maybe Fitzgerald's will have an idea on where we could buy one. Guess I'll ask them when we stop there. Also where will we park it and store it for the summer and winter. Man, we've got a lot of things to figure out don't we?" Clem said

"Well, we don't need a car right now, but it would be convenient to have one so we don't have to impose on them when we need to go to Cook." Terrie said as she stood up and started putting the cups into the sink. "I'll wash those when we get back. Let's go to town. What's the matter Nina you haven't said a word?" Terrie said as she turned around and saw Nina just sitting there with her head in her hands.

"I'm just thinking how much we're putting you out. Maybe we should have waited until after the house is built to bring this stuff of ours up."

"Nonsense. Will you quit your worrying? It's not like your someone I can't stand and we don't get along. Everything will be all right you'll see. Now come on let's go to town."

———

"Well, in the last two weeks we've accomplished quite a bit. We have a car, the boxes are all unpacked or stashed; you guys built a nice shed on the back of our island. Now we can just enjoy life until your house is done and then we'll start this moving mess all over again. The only difference is we don't have as far to take it in the boat. Most of your stuff will come by barge. Maybe he could stop someplace along our island and pick up your boxes at the same time. Then we could go by our boat with the rest and help unload the barge." Terrie was saying as the four of them were eating lunch.

"I had no idea that this place would look so nice and all the boxes out of site. I just couldn't imagine. Terrie you truly are a genius I think I'll have you come to our house and help me unpack and arrange. I know what I'd like to do, but I don't know how to do it. You are so talented." Nina said as she finished eating her fish sandwich.

"I don't think I'm that talented, but I'll be more than happy to help you. After you get in and decide what kind of curtains and all you want if you'll pick out the material I'll make them for you."

"Wow. Can I start looking for material now?"

"Good heavens Nina I thought you already had. You've bought enough stuff these last few weeks to—" Jack was saying when Nina interrupted him.

"Oh hush. I haven't bought any material yet. I really have been waiting for the walls and windows to go up before I thought of curtains."

Everybody started laughing. Every time they went down to Virginia to just look at things Nina was buying.

"You know there is one thing that has not been discussed and I think it's about time we start talking about it." Clem said picking his plate up from the table and putting it in the sink.

"What's that?" Terrie asked as she followed suit with the rest of the plates.

"The trial. I know, Jack probably asked you to give me time, but we've been doing so many other things, that I flat forgot what brought all of us together."

"You're right" Jack said, "There are things I'd like to hear about that trial too."

"Weren't you there?" Terrie asked

"Oh I was there. Sitting in that courtroom everyday and occasionally reminding Clem of something that had not been brought up that was on 'your' list, but I still don't know a lot of what happened. Until Chris came up here I didn't know where Clem had stashed him. There were others too." Jack was saying when Clem interrupted him.

"Don't get the cart before the horse Jack. Let's get some cold drinks and go out on the porch. We need to be relaxed. This might take a while."

After they were all on the porch with their drinks Jack said, "Before you start talking Clem I've got to brag on you 'cause I know you won't. Let me tell you if it hadn't been for this man here, the prosecuting attorney would not have won his case. First Clem had to convince him so that he could go convince the judge that all of the men had to be tried at once. Clem felt he couldn't afford to have them tried individually. I didn't understand why, until we were really into the case, in fact, nearing the end when all hell broke loose. But he did convince the prosecutor who in turn convinced the judge. This set a precedent as their attorney said it had never been done before and he felt his men would not have a fair trial, but after the prosecutor talked to the judge the judge overruled the defense attorney. This man needs all kinds of accolades bestowed upon him."

"Oh come on Jack I wasn't that great. It's just that I knew if they weren't all tried at the same time the act of surprise would be wasted and the defense attorney would get them all off, with the exception of which ever was the first to be tried. Besides I knew that it could last up to a year or more and I didn't want that to happen. Most of the time I was just lucky." Clem said as he stood and poured himself some ice tea. "Anyway, the trial finally got under way, under protest from the defense attorney, but there sat all of the men, in a row, just like birds on a fence. Because of all of the publicity this trial had been getting the courtroom was loaded. It was almost standing room only. I was afraid there might be a riot of some kind. I recognized some of the faces of some of the men sitting in the courtroom as men we'd dealt with before."

"May I ask a question?" Terrie interrupted

"Of course Honey, what?"

"Who all was tried?"

"Well, let's see, your ex of course, Archie, Doug. You remember him. He worked for me; well he was a spy in our headquarters. We thought he was when Hugh, Stan and Doug were supposed to be watching over you in Georgia. Anyway Kyle Waters, Ali, Mark and someone you might really be interested in Les Rudicio."

"Les? How on earth? I thought he'd left the country." Terrie said anxiously

"Well he did leave the country, however, he tried to come back into this country in, of all things, a coffin. We were tipped off and picked him up in the airport freight and baggage department. We had him isolated for about a month. We managed to keep even his attorney away from him for awhile, which was no easy feat."

"See, didn't I tell you how great this man was—er is." Jack interrupted

"If you people don't quit interrupting me I'll forget where I was and you'll lose everything." Clem replied, "Now where was I, oh yes, Les and of course his brother Lonnie. He really wasn't guilty of anything except owning a restaurant and allowing his brothers men to work there. Anyway it was the whole group, about 15 were sitting there. We had all the men from the Atlanta operation, Chattanooga and the offices at Ryan Enterprise. We had arrested them all. Some we couldn't really hold because they were just innocent bystanders, just like you'd been, but the rest were sitting there in court. It really was a silly looking sight, even if I do say so myself. They had their regular attorney and maybe three others that are in his office. It really looked like we were going to have a party. It took a week to choose a jury. First thing out of the bag Ali claimed immunity as a foreigner. He eventually was turned over to his Consulate with the understanding of deportation with no appeal. The rest of them along with their attorney's tried every dirty trick in the book to no avail. After one bit of evidence after another, mostly that that you gave us, you know letters, legal documents, the bank papers when Jay said he didn't get any money. Every time the prosecutor would bring something up against whoever was being questioned their attorney would claim here say evidence. However it got to the point where the judge just automatically overruled him. I guess he got tired of our prosecutor taking your paperwork up to him and proving it was not hearsay evidence. After about two months, your ex, Archie, Mark, and a couple others, including Doug were singled out and given the chance to plead guilty to lesser charges than RICO and drug running and the judge sentenced them right then and there, without word from the jury or anybody else, to 10—20 in the federal prison. The attorney really screamed at that, but the judge said he'd had enough and had heard enough to know these men were guilty, as they had been charged. Then their attorney asked and fought saying that the rest of the men should be released or charged right then and there. That this split up of parties was really setting a precedent and the judge just looked at him and said that's my privilege. Basically that only left Les and Kyle. The best part is now coming. Since Les and Kyle were really the culprits that had had Chris murdered."

"Wait a minute," Terrie interrupted "What happened to that cop that I was told killed Chris?"

"I'm coming to that. On the morning of the first day of the first week of the third month I handed the prosecutor a piece of paper with a name on it. He turned white as a sheet, but it was his witness to call. He stood up and called Mr. Morici to the stand. Well, that's when Les stood up ranting and raving and the judge admonished him and told his attorney to keep him quiet or he'd be nailed for contempt and Les would be taken directly out of the courtroom to a jail cell. By this time the judge had just about had all of the attorney's objections and outbursts he could handle. He was not in the mood to listen to Les too. I think that we'd already won our case long before this, but the judge had to go through the motion of listening to everything we had to throw at them. I must say I was pretty proud of myself. I had helped the prosecutor shoot down every objection and complaint that they'd had up to this time.

"Do you realize that it is now almost 6 o'clock and we've been sitting here since lunch time? Why don't we call it a day and pick up with this after breakfast in the morning." Nina said standing up, picking up the tray of empty glasses and heading towards the kitchen.

"I was just getting to the good part, but I think you're right. It has waited this long we can wait one more day." Clem said standing and stretching. "I didn't realize how tired I am. Reliving this is almost as hard as sitting there in the courtroom for 3 months. Tomorrow morning it shall be. Let's go see what we can fix for supper."

Terrie was disappointed. She wanted to hear all of it, but she realized that straight 6-7 hours of sitting and reliving this was hard. Jack was tired also and said as much.

"I think I'll even hit the sack early. I'm bushed. We've accomplished a lot and this is as good a time as any to break and come back fresh tomorrow morning."

# CHAPTER 19

"Ok, now that breakfast is over why don't the three of you take your coffee and go out on the porch. I'll clean up the dishes and bring fresh coffee and munchies out when I get done." Nina was saying "After all Terrie's brother is due up here within the week and I'm sure Terrie would like to spend some time with him and also be able to tell him that it's all over. Right now all she knows is what you've told her so far, and last night we kind of left her hanging."

The three of them took their cups and went to the porch. After getting comfortable Clem started

"Let's see. I left off last night with the prosecuting attorney calling Morici to the stand. Well you can imagine the uproar that defense attorney raised, but the judge just looked at him and once again said 'overruled'.

*Prosecuting Attorney: Please state your name and occupation*
*Answer: Morici, Police Officer*
*Prosecuting Attorney: Can you tell the court what your duties*
*  have been for the last 2-3 years?*
*Answer: Yes sir I worked undercover*
*Prosecuting Attorney: In what capacity did you work under*
*  cover and for whom?*
*Answer: I worked for Mr. Les Rudicio. I was searching for one*
*  Terrie Cooper.*
*Prosecuting Attorney: Where and how hard did you search for*
*  Ms. Cooper?*

*Answer: I was in Germany for between 3-4 months there I hooked up with some of Mr. Rudicio's contacts and finally found a girl that knew her, but that Ms. Cooper was no longer in the area.*

*Prosecuting Attorney: What happened after that?*

*Answer: I was brought back to the states and after a few months two of us were sent to Denver and Salt Lake City and then on to California where we handed the search over to two operatives of Mr. Rudicio's out there.*

*Defense Attorney: Your honor I object*

*Judge: Over ruled. Continue Mr. Prosecutor*

*Prosecuting Attorney: Thank you your honor. Mr. Morici do you have first hand knowledge what either one of these men do or are involved with? Pointing to the two defendants.*

*Answer: Yes*

*Prosecuting Attorney: Would you please explain that answer to the judge and this jury?*

*Answer: I have been in several meetings where drugs, money laundering, and other illegal projects have been instituted. One meeting in particular Mr. Rudicio asked me to accompany Kyle to the warehouse and help him prepare to fly down south, outside of the United States to meet that Ali. Kyle was exchanging guns supplied by Rudicio's company, for oil.*

*Prosecuting Attorney: Do you of your own knowledge know where either the oil or the guns were going?*

*Answer: Yes sir. Every other load of guns went to the Sandinistas and every other one went to the Contra's with the oil coming into this country via Rudicio's Alaskan oil company.*

*Prosecuting Attorney: There is one thing I would like to ask how did you go under cover. Didn't these men know you were a police officer?*

*Answer: Oh, yes sir. But the FBI contacted our office and said they needed the best man our department had to infiltrate the mafia. They selected me and proceeded to set me up, so it would make the newspapers and all what a bad cop I was. Rudicio took the bait and I was in his organization.*

"Good heavens, Clem. What you've just told me is that Morici wasn't a bad cop at all." Terrie said. Trying hard to comprehend all that she'd just heard.

"That's right." Jack said, "You should have been there just to hear that defense attorney and Rudicio talk and try to get the questioning stopped."

"Terrie by the time Morici got off the stand I knew we had won and all of them were going down. However, I still had two more aces up my sleeve, one of which was Chris when they called him."

"Boy, I wish I could have been there as a mouse. I would've loved to see their faces when Chris came out. I mean all this time I thought he was dead, so I know Morici totally convinced them that he was dead." Terrie started laughing "Oh what a site that must have been.

"Well, after Morici and Chris testified to everything I, we still had one more witness to present."

"One more weren't those two enough?"

"No you see, I needed, we needed someone that could corroborate everything that you had given us."

"But Clem, who could that be? I know Candy wouldn't, Bud didn't know a lot, I can't think of anyone else that was close enough to Jay to do that."

"How about Jay himself."

"How could that be he died quite a while ago. Some poison that he used on his orchids."

"That's what we needed everyone to think. Terrie we saved his life and concocted that story. I'm sorry honey, but this was a vital piece of evidence that, along with Chris, had to be top secret."

"If I'm comprehending this, which I'm not sure I am—you are telling me that Jay is really alive." By this time Terrie was having a hard time keeping up with everything and she knew if she stood up for any reason she'd faint.

"Yes, honey, he is alive. Now we have put him under protective custody, changed his identity and no one will ever find him again. He sure did make a good witness though and he corroborated every piece of evidence that you had given us. I know these last 2 or 3 years have been exceptionally hard on you, but I hope you can understand why it was so important for me to keep everything quiet. I didn't ever want you hurt again. No more Lady That Walks Alone. I love you and want us to be able to be a family, with your children and grandchildren. I didn't want your identity to have to be changed and this was the only way I could do it. I hope you will forgive me, but selfishly the only time I wanted you to change your identity was from Cooper to Brown. Can you forgive me?"

"Forgive you I love you and the sooner my name is Brown the happier I'll be. Next year we'll have all the family up here for a reunion. But the first reunion will be with Bud in about a week. You have made me so happy." Terrie said

Printed in the United States
1289300001B/379